The Harvest of Lies

Bian's Tale: Book 1

An Athanate Novel
by
Mark Henwick

Published by *Marque*

Bian's Tale 1 : The Harvest of Lies
ISBN: 978-1-912499-06-9

Published in July 2018 by Marque

Mark Henwick asserts the right to be identified as the author of this work.

Author's notes

Asian names:

Throughout this series, except where specifically stated, I use the Western sequence (First, Middle, Last Name) to depict names, so as to match with the majority of characters in the Athanate books. Most Asian societies would use Last, First, Middle Name.

Saigon:

The geography of Saigon used in this book is reasonably accurate, as is a lot of the history, at a broad brush level. For details about Saigon in the 1890s, I am indebted to Tim Doling who runs the Historic Vietnam site and Facebook group:

http://www.historicvietnam.com/
https://www.facebook.com/groups/865130223501356/about/

Names of places and institutions:

I have used a mixture of genuine and invented names—Opium Regie, Quai d'Orsay are real for example, but the promenade was never designated Quai du Commerce and Quai de la Marine. I have used the accented Western script for some Vietnamese and Chinese names except where the accenting makes the name difficult to read.

Part 1 - Innocence

纯真

Prologue

My name is Bian Hwa Trang.

I do not grieve.
What I was before, I am no longer.
I am at peace with myself.

I am female. I was born in Sai Gon, in Nam Kỳ, about one hundred and thirty years ago. You now call the place of my birth Hô Chí Minh City and the country, Vietnam. I am unsure of the exact date of my birth. I know that I was sold in 1890; that was Dan—Year of the Tiger. I estimate I was about nine at the time; I know I was Mao—Year of the Cat.

I was sold by my parents.

This was an act of the greatest love and sacrifice on their part.
My blessings, such as they are, on them, on their memories, on my brothers, their children and their children's children in that unhappy land.
And on my dear sister.
My love and reverence for them, always and forever.

I am *Athanate*.

That is the word for the people, the language and the culture of which I am now part. The word means *undying*. It means I can say *forever*.

As a child, I heard stories of the *ma cà rông*.
In the West, those stories would have been about the *vampire*.
They are wrong.
I am Athanate; I take blood to sustain me.
I am not a demon. I am not an animated corpse.
I have a soul.

I am more like you than you think.

As to what I was and how I came here … this is my tale.

Chapter 1

"You cheated! You cheated," I shouted, as I leaped up.

"Phew," said my sister, holding the mango even higher and flapping her hand in front of her face. "Don't get any closer. Ma's been washing your hair in buffalo piss."

"Has not! You're lying and you cheated."

"No, I didn't. If it's not your hair, then what's that smell?"

"You stepped in the dung, smelly foot."

That was clever of me. If she'd looked down, I would have grabbed the thick rope of her plaited hair and used it to help me jump up.

She didn't look down. I hated her. I hated her even more than I hated the fat little man who'd chased us out of the orchard. He had plenty of fruit. Why did he have so much? He couldn't eat it all.

Without Nhung, I would never have been able to escape over the wall. But I was the one who had climbed the tree, who'd plucked the big, juicy fruit. I wanted my half. She'd told me I could have half and she wasn't giving it to me. She was going to eat it all, I knew she was. She was horrible to me, even though she'd taken me out for a walk.

"I hate you," I said, and my lip trembled.

"Never say that, little sister." Before I could stop her, she swept me into her arms and hoisted me on her hip as if I were a baby and not nine years old.

I struggled, but not much. She gave me the fruit, and we shared it on the way home.

"Never say you hate me," she whispered, burying her face in my hair. "Whatever happens. Promise me."

"It doesn't smell bad? My hair?"

She shook her head.

"Why are you crying? Is it because I said that bad thing?"

"No, Bian. It's nothing, just dust in my eyes."

"I love you really, Nhung."

"I know. And I love you, too. Now, you're too old to be carried like this and I'm too tired. You must walk; we're nearly there."

She put me down and, as evening fell, we walked together into the sprawling village where we lived.

Nhung had known another world—one outside of my imagining at that time—but I had been born on a sampan, a small wooden boat, in a floating village. I accepted the stink, the noise and the crowding of shelters as simply the way things were.

Of course, I knew people lived in big houses; some of those houses were even made of stone. And those people ate every day, sometimes three times a day. I knew Sai Gon, which I thought the biggest city in the whole world, and I'd seen the stone houses. But the people in the stone houses were now as distant to me as the dragons in the stories my mother told me at night. I'd never talked to anyone who lived in a stone house, and for all I knew then, they too had long forked tongues and teeth like knives.

This was my world. Little Ap Long—on no map, reached only by paths. Or by river, of course.

We passed huts made from screens of woven palm-leaf braced between bamboo struts. These flimsy structures were real to me; the stone houses of Sai Gon had all the substance of dreams. Real homes smelled of palm oil and wood fires and sweat and shit, not perfumes and spices. They were rough and light, with dirt floors and straw matting, not smooth and heavy, with tiles and silks.

As we got closer, my friend Minh passed the other way with his mother, carrying pots to fill with water. He jumped one of the smelly puddles and came up to me, puffed up with the importance of news.

He put his pots down. "You have an aunty come to visit," he said in a low voice, fingers twisting around each other.

"An aunty?" I looked up at Nhung. She untied her hair and let it fall across her face.

"Minh, take the pots. Come away. Now." His mother called him back.

She didn't like to speak to my parents, but she had been kind to me and Nhung before.

Maybe her husband was smoking opium again. Minh told me that always put her in a bad mood, when he wasted what little money they had.

"We can go to the rice field together tomorrow," Minh called out as he was dragged away.

I didn't want to think of working in the rice field, so I just waved.

A visitor. So exciting and mysterious. We had never had one in Ap Long that I could remember.

"We have an aunty?" I asked Nhung again, but she just shook her head without looking at me and took my hand.

"Whatever happens," she whispered as we walked on.

And so we arrived home, hand in hand, with the sweet taste of stolen fruit still on my lips, on the day the world I'd known began to come apart.

∞ ∞ ∞ ∞ ∞

I didn't like Aunty Kim. She smelled of old joss sticks and piss, but I was polite. I knew she must be very important because we had fish with the rice at dinner. Only the bits of catfish left over, for sure, but tasty all the same.

We children sat on the floor on one side of our home and our parents sat with Aunty Kim on the other, as if that separated us. My eldest brother, Lanh, could have reached out and touched them. I sat between Tuan, my younger brother, and Nhung.

A small lamp in the middle of the floor was the only light, but it was bright enough for me to see Aunty Kim's face clearly, and she didn't look like my parents.

Aunty or Uncle can be used for anyone really; I called Minh's mother Aunty. But we'd never had an aunty visitor before. Even if I didn't like her, she was so exciting. She had a piece of silk, real silk, like they had in Sai Gon. It smelled of flowers, and she kept dabbing it against her face. Maybe she didn't like to feel sweaty.

That was silly, though. Everyone sweated. When I had complained once that I was hot, my mother had told me that to breathe is to sweat. I said that to everyone until they got tired of it. Maybe a bit longer than that.

"She's very thin," Aunty Kim said, as if there was any other way to be. She spoke in French, like the people in Sai Gon, and I didn't understand all of what she said. I was certain I understood the words, but they didn't make sense. She could only be talking about Nhung or me, and we were just like everyone else we knew.

Well, there was the fat man who guarded the orchard. But who would want to be like him?

"She speaks well, and she works hard," said my father. Aunty Kim must be very grand, because he was stern tonight. He hadn't laughed once.

"Her French is good," said my mother. "And she can barter with the market sellers in Cantonese, Han and Tamil, even Trade—"

"She hasn't worked in a house before," interrupted Aunty Kim, making it sound like that was more important.

"She learns quickly, and she is honest, and strong," said my mother.

It was as if they were bartering. I couldn't understand why, and Aunty Kim started using words I didn't know. But it had to be Nhung they were talking about, because my sister was all of the things that my parents claimed, and beautiful too, even if she was hiding behind her hair tonight.

With the meal in my belly and the words over my head, I was sleepy. I leaned against Nhung and she put her arm around me and squeezed. Too tightly, but it didn't matter. It was nice.

"And the child ..." I heard Aunty Kim say, as I fell asleep. "It might make it easier for them. It might be a chance for her to learn. But that would be a cost, not a fee."

My head came to rest in Nhung's lap, and I didn't hear the reply, or any more of the talk.

I didn't meet Minh to work in the fields the next day. I never saw him again.

Chapter 2

I woke in the night and I knew that I was on the Mother of Waters.

I knew her sounds and smells; I knew the creaking, the gentle swaying and drifting in her arms. My earliest memories were of helping my father catch fish, and sleeping on the sampan as we made our way back. That was all before Bác Thảo had heard of my father. Before men came asking for him and we had to escape from Khánh Hôi to distant Ap Long, where we were safe. Where we could be farm workers, invisible amongst the tide of country people seeking work closer to the city.

Bác Thảo had ears in the water. My father said that when he thought I wasn't listening. I looked many times and never saw any ears in the water. The fish would just eat them anyway. But I knew I was supposed to keep away from the river and the people on it, and I did, mostly.

And yet here I was, in a sampan again, with the old smell of fish guts and sweat. What had happened?

I reached out to Nhung for comfort and reassurance, but it was my mother next to me.

"Shh, my baby. Not a sound, Bian." She hugged me tightly to her, and rocked me along with the Mother of Waters. A little spray must have come through the weave of the cover because her cheeks were damp.

Everything was all right if she was here.

It was all a mystery and exciting, but not so exciting to me that I couldn't sleep. I could always ask Nhung tomorrow why we were on the river. She'd tell me.

There was no Nhung the next day, and no answers.

We came up the Sai Gon River, past Khánh Hôi and into Arroyo Chinois with the fishermen and rice sellers. Sampans covered the face of the creek there, every day. As we had needed to many times before, we walked from boat to boat to reach the quay. But today, we greeted no one. My family slunk away from the docks like dogs, our straw hats pressed down over our faces.

The whole family except for Nhung, who I couldn't see, not even in any of the other boats.

"Don't look around," hissed my mother. "Keep your eyes down."

Everyone seemed scared, and that scared me.

I was frightened by what I didn't understand. I wasn't scared of Bác Thảo. He was a monster that came for bad children. I hadn't been bad, had I?

But then I remembered the mango yesterday. It hadn't been ours. That was bad. Had Bác Thảo found out about that? Did he have ears in the orchard as well? Had he taken Nhung?

"Where's Nhung?" I asked my mother.

"Hush, Bian," was all she replied.

"Are we going to work?"

"Not today. Hush."

"Then where are we going?"

"Be quiet! No more questions."

I was sad that no one would talk to me, but we were walking through Sai Gon, and maybe I would see a dragon today. Lanh had told me they danced in the city streets sometimes, but I was never sure when he was teasing me.

It was so noisy, I put my hands over my ears.

We passed through the market. People flowed like an impatient river between the stalls and the shops. Great-wheeled bullock carts forced the torrent to divide and added the squeal of their wooden axles to the clamor.

I was swept along, Lanh's hand gripping my shoulder.

It wasn't like Ap Long, where we knew everyone and we might stop to talk. Here, everyone was talking and none of them to us. No one seemed to even see us. I was scared that if I fell, they'd just walk over me.

It seemed to go on forever. Even where there were no shops, there were buildings being built. Dust billowed around us.

My parents made us hurry, and we came to a quiet road lined by funny buildings with no windows. They had little arches that went nowhere and walls in the shape of a half moon, all guarded by statues of strange-looking animals.

"What are they?" I whispered to Lanh.

"The houses of the dead," he replied. "Don't look at them, or they'll follow you home."

That was silly. Everyone knew only hungry ghosts that hadn't received proper attention from their families went walking.

Still, I looked straight ahead.

And where was home now? I didn't dare ask my parents yet.

About noon, we were back surrounded by people. The streets here were narrow and the buildings all short. This was Cholon, Lanh said. I could feel my parents weren't so worried any more, but still no one would tell me anything.

We stopped at a house, a real stone house.

It was a single room, so big you could fit four families in it, maybe more. Inside, there were only some old Chinese men and a lot of sacks of spices which made me sneeze.

The front was open to the street, but it was cool and dark at the back. We sat there on straw mats while my father talked to the old men. I saw him hand some piasters to the men. One of them brought us tea and tiny chipped cups.

He spoke nicely to my mother and she smiled.

"Such a fine son. Strong," he said and clapped Lanh on the shoulder. Lanh called him uncle and thanked him for the tea.

The old man lived in a stone house, but his tongue and his teeth seemed quite normal, not like a dragon at all. Despite that disappointment, I thought I liked him.

My parents went out, leaving us to wait.

Tuan and Lanh argued about what we were doing here and when Nhung would join us. I opened a sack and sniffed some spice which burned my nose and made my eyes water. The old men laughed and closed the sacks.

One of them taught us a board game, Xiangqi. I watched Tuan and Lanh play. It was nice not to work, but Lanh was worried and trying not to show it.

I fell asleep in the afternoon.

It was evening when my parents returned. I jumped up, expecting Nhung to be with them, but she wasn't.

They brought food—noodles and fish soup, and pork as well. Pork! We sat at the back of a stone house in Cholon and feasted like the Emperor.

Yes, it would be nice to live here and eat like this every day, so long as we were all here.

My parents didn't seem to enjoy the food as much as we did.

When we had finished, we sat quietly and waited. In Ap Long, we spoke while we ate, and afterwards too. Here, we knew things had changed. I was worried, but it wasn't so scary as long as my mother and father were with us. They wouldn't let anything bad happen.

"Father," Lanh said eventually, "where is Nhung?"

My father looked around. The old men were sitting outside, in the street, playing mahjong by the light of a smelly, hissing lamp.

"My children," he said quietly. His voice caught, and suddenly I was very frightened, for no reason I could name. "My children, a bad thing has happened. It is my fault and it isn't." He stopped and my mother put a hand over his.

"Bian Hwa," he said, "do you remember when we had to leave Khánh Hôi to go to Ap Long?"

"Yes, we left because Bác Thảo was looking for us and he has ears in the water."

"Hush, Bian, do not say that name." My mother glanced out into the street. "Say … say the tall man."

"The tall man," said my father, "is very bad. He found us in Khánh Hôi and he found us in Ap Long, and he will find us again unless we move far away." He stopped and blinked. "And that is very, very difficult. To go, we need money—money for papers and food. Money for travel."

I didn't understand anything about papers and money. And to travel, you just walked, or rode in a sampan.

"Will Nhung be there waiting for us?" I asked.

My mother bowed her head.

"No," said my father. "There are too many bandits in the countryside. Travel would be dangerous for her … and for you. You must both stay."

My mother began weeping.

"It's my fault," I said. I'd been the one who wanted the mango. Nhung would never have done that on her own. I'd wanted it so badly, and she'd wanted to make me happy. Now she was being punished. I couldn't let them punish her.

"No, Bian Hwa, it is not your fault. The tall man and the government are not your fault. They are everybody's fault."

I didn't understand anything.

He paused and tried again. "We cannot stay here, and we cannot take you with us." He saw my face. "Until it is safe to come back," he said quickly.

"We must not lie," said my mother, wiping her eyes fiercely. "This day of all days. Nhung will work in Sai Gon as a maid. She will be safe." She moved closer to me. "Bian, you are too young to work as a maid and too young for the journey up the country." She paused; she looked so sad and angry at the same time. "Much more than that, we want you to be happy, and free of the tall man. We want you to be truly free. Free of the curse of bad luck that has followed us. Free of our shame." She put a hand softly on my arm. "And to escape that, you must go further than any of us, my daughter. Far, far away."

"Mother, how—" Lanh started.

"Look around us, Lanh," my father interrupted. "Where are we?"

"The Cholon district of Sai Gon, in Nam Kỳ," he replied proudly.

"No! Our leaders are exiled; our rulers are French. We are not supposed to even leave this place unless they give us permission. Forget Nam Kỳ, all of you. Forget the puppet Emperor. That world is gone. This is Saigon, in Cochinchina, part of the French empire."

I was scared that they were angry. I didn't understand what they were arguing about.

"Then we should join the Black Flags and fight the French." Lanh spoke to his friends like this when he thought I wasn't listening, but he'd never spoken to our parents this way.

"No, Lanh." My father shook his head sorrowfully. "It is too late for that. The Black Flag Army is gone. The bandits that use the name are nothing but an irritation to the French, and they will be swept aside soon. No. It is time for a different path."

Lanh was still angry but kept his face blank as he lowered his eyes dutifully.

"Bian, listen." My mother pulled me against her. "We are happy for you. You will be safe. You will wear pretty clothes and eat good food. In time, you will go far away and learn so many things. You will have a good life, free of the tall man. Don't you want that?"

I cried. I didn't want to go far away and learn things. I wanted to go home and I didn't know where that was anymore.

"But how?" said Lanh.

"We knew the tall man was getting closer, and that gave us just enough time to prepare. We've made an agreement with a good Frenchman and his wife," replied my mother. "An important man in the government. They are a rich family with no children. They want to adopt a girl before they go back to France."

"Bian," she hugged me again, tears shining on her cheeks, "you will have a new mother and father, and you will live well in a big stone house and see so many beautiful things. You will be happy, won't you?"

Chapter 3

My name is Bian Hwa Trang. Bian Hwa Trang.

Bian means secret; Trang means honored. You cannot be both secret and honored. Between them, they crush the fragile flower, Hwa. Maybe this was what made my name so ill-omened.

My father had been honored. I knew it even then, like I knew the tales of dragons. He had been an important man, my father, the youngest mandarin in the service of the Emperor. I didn't know what these words meant when I first heard them. My mind couldn't comprehend the opulence, the houses and servants and bowing. Not for the man who I had seen gutting fish and planting rice.

It must have been a wonderful time for him earlier in his life: to have survived the great cholera epidemics that killed more than a million people in Nam Kỳ; to have studied and excelled; to have been accepted into the ranks of those that ran the country. With danger and striving behind, my parents must have thought a life of glittering rewards lay before them on their marriage day.

But the glitter hid the decay that lay beneath. A ragged and impoverished country that fell ever deeper into the pocket of the French while its supposed leaders sought wealth and advantage over one another. And in one such power struggle, my father's sponsor in the civil service fell, taking my father and many others with him into disgrace.

A trial was held. It was a mockery.

A charge was laid against my father's sponsor that he had stolen the government's gold for building the Emperor's mausoleum. He was an honorable man, and he committed suicide to protect his family and friends. That was sufficient for his enemies. The man and his supporters had been effectively destroyed; they ceased to care. The charges were allowed to lapse. The stolen gold was a mirage. It had never existed and they knew it.

But stories like the theft of the mausoleum funds gather life like a storm harvests winds. The wealth became the stuff of legend—an emperor's ransom. It had been hidden, the whispers said, and the location known only to a trusted few.

I'm sure that gave my father no more than bitter amusement, until a chance comment, a cruel aside when he was seen by his former colleagues working at the docks, made the stories grow a little more.

There was now one man, just one, came the rumor—a disgraced mandarin, who still knew where the money was hidden. He worked as a humble fisherman in Khánh Hôi, biding his time before he collected it.

Bác Thảo's men came searching through the floating townships for my father.

Lord of the gangs in Khánh Hôi, fierce as a tiger, cruel as death, Bác Thảo ruled the river community, the dock workers and the army of people employed in the construction of the new French Saigon.

There was never any chance that we would not be betrayed, and my parents knew it.

I must have been about six. To me it was just another nighttime on the Mother of Waters and waking to a new home in Ap Long, made from bits of sampan.

Far greater shocks for Lanh and Nhung: born into privilege, having adjusted to life on a sampan and then having to adjust all over again to rice farming. It was not simply that the work was hard and the life unforgiving; the two years immediately before Bác Thảo tracked us down the second time were famine years. As the eldest children, Lanh and Nhung took the brunt of the extra work and ate no more than Tuan or I. I never heard either complain, not even once.

Something of that strength was passed to me, maybe. As my family prepared to say farewell that night, I stopped crying. And as a child, I never cried again, except in the darkness, with no one as my witness.

Chapter 4

I knelt on the wooden floor. It was very hard.

Zacharie and Thérèse Beauclerc, Papa and Maman, sat on a curving cane seat, big enough for a whole family. *Papa* and *Maman*, I said their names over to myself. I mustn't get it wrong. My father and mother would be shamed if I did. They sat on the other cane seats. I had said goodbye to Lanh and Tuan at the stone house in Cholon. I had not cried. I would not cry. I would not.

My parents had bought me the áo dài, the floating, paneled tunic and narrow trousers I saw women in Saigon wear. It was the most beautiful, delicate clothing I had ever worn, like being dressed in butterflies. I stayed very still, frightened I might damage it.

My parents had hired some clothes before we came. They sat, almost strangers to me in their finery, and spoke quietly in French with Papa and Maman.

This house looked as if it was not made of stone, but of wood: a dark teak, waxed and polished till it shone in the light of the lamps. The whole building sat on a slight hill, and at the back it rested on stilts, like the fishermen sometimes made their houses.

White gauze sheets behind me, even softer and lighter than the áo dài, kept insects out of the room and let cool air trickle in, scented with frangipani blossom.

Opposite me, upright against the wall, stood two large elephant tusks. A brass gong, like they had at the temples, hung between them. It was so fine that the room was reflected in the wavy surface, the lights undulating across it as I moved my head.

The other walls had weapons fixed on them, and vases and drums stood in front. So many things in the way. Maybe the house was smaller than it looked from outside and there was nowhere else to keep all these things.

But the worst was the tiger skin which lay in the middle of the floor. Its mouth was open in a snarl and its glassy eyes were fixed on me. It scared me. It became the soul of everything that threatened me at that moment. I tried not to look at it while Papa and Maman asked questions, and my mother and father replied. They spoke of journeys and the trouble in the north, and the words flowed around me.

A woman came in with a jar of cool water and poured more for all of us. She was Chinese. Her hair was plaited, pinned against her head with a shiny clip, and she was dressed in a stiff white tunic and blue trousers.

"Thank you, Aunty," I whispered.

She barely looked at me. Her eyes gleamed beneath low lids like pebbles on the river bed. Her face stayed blank. She gave her head a tiny shake and returned the way she'd come.

Maman spoke of lessons and teachers. My mother kept her eyes down. She had taught me herself. I could speak French. I could read and write too. That was more than any of my friends.

Then Maman asked about my belongings. There was a silence, before my father said: "We agreed that it would be better to start again with nothing."

The talking was over. My father and mother stood. My mother was trembling. I got up too, edging round the tiger. There was an ache that seemed to fill my chest. Surely they could see it?

No! Don't go. Not yet. Just a little more time, a little more. Please.

But we were shuffling awkwardly towards the door, and I didn't dare speak what I felt.

Other people came and held the door open for them.

Was I allowed to hug them?

It was too late. They were outside.

Papa gave my mother a parcel wrapped in red. Then he came back inside and took my hand. I stood there between Maman and Papa. The door closed.

The first part of my life was over.

Chapter 5

We sat back down on the big cane seat.

Fear squeezed my throat, but there were words I had been told to say in French. "I am so very happy, Maman, Papa."

They each took a hand. Their hands were soft and warm.

"We know this is hard for you," said Maman. "It will get better. This will all seem like a dream."

Papa patted my hand. "We think it will be best to start some things straight away." He cleared his throat. "It will help if you have a French name. So from now, we will call you Ophélie. Ophélie Beauclerc. There, isn't that a pretty name?"

"Yes, Papa."

It was pretty, but I thought there was nothing wrong with my name.

"We understand your parents' decision," said Maman. "He is lucky to have the job in Thanh Hóa after all the troubles he has had, but we agree, it is no place for a young girl. Those Can Vuong people are still making mischief and there are those awful Black Flag bandits. Do you understand?"

"Yes, Maman."

My father had no job to go to in Thanh Hóa. The troubles he had described were not the real ones he had. I knew lies were wrong, and even though these were to keep me out of the reach of Bác Thảo, lies feed on themselves.

My father was going to Hué, to see if the passing of time and the evidence of his hardships would soften hearts. He was seeking to join the Emperor's service again, despite everything.

"Anyway, we'll be perfectly safe here." Maman paused. "Now, this has been a big day. You must be tired. It's time you were in bed."

I hadn't had time to realize there was something more to be afraid of. I didn't know what to do with anything.

I had a room just for sleeping. It had a bed. I knew what a bed was. I knew people in stone houses slept in beds. How? Was there a trick to it? What was the white tent above the bed? There was a mirror on a table against the wall. A glass mirror, perfect and cold, reflecting my frightened eyes. There was a tall, empty wooden box standing on its side. A lamp that I must not light. A pot that I understood I was meant to piss and shit in. And the window that I must keep open sometimes and closed at other times.

Too much. Things crowded on me until I felt sick with panic, my hand frozen on the iron latch for the shutters, looking out into the darkness.

That was worse.

Maman's touch was gentle on my shoulders.

"What's the matter, Ophélie?"

"Lights," I said. Lights flickered in the night. One moment they looked close enough to reach out and touch, the next, distant. The ghosts had followed me home from the houses of the dead.

"The lights? What are they making you think of?"

I didn't want to talk to her about the houses of the dead. To name something is to give it life.

"The mountain people," I said instead. Too late, I realized I didn't want to talk about this either, because of the tiger on the floor in the big room, but Maman was waiting and the words spilled from me. "They are *hô con quỷ*. Tiger demons. In the day, they are people and they walk with us. But in the night, they change into tigers. They sit in the dark and watch you, and you can only see them by the light in their eyes."

I had heard this from Minh's father, who had lived many years in Dankia, in the foothills, and he had seen them with his own eyes.

"Of course, but we're a long way from the mountains here, and anyway, I think they're just fireflies near the old Khmer tombs." Maman closed the shutter and pulled me back into the room.

"Well, enough," she said, and helped me strip off the áo dài and put on a simple cotton dress. The dress was too big.

A dress just to sleep in?

I got into bed as Maman told me. It felt very high off the floor. She untied the loose knot in the white gauze tent and lowered it around the bed, tucking it in. She explained that it was a net to keep mosquitos from biting me. But what if I tore it, trying to get out? I watched silently as she put the áo dài away in the tall box. The cupboard, she told me, for all my clothes.

Clothes? To fill the … cupboard?

She paused as she lowered the wick on the lamp.

"I hope we'll be so happy, Ophélie." She thought for a moment, then undid a corner of the net to lean in and kiss me on the forehead. The smell of fruits and flowers lingered after she'd put out the lamp and closed the door.

I lay rigid, unable to move at first.

It was too quiet. The bed was too soft. The bedhead was made of sandalwood, and its subtle fragrance gradually overtook the scent of Maman and the smoke from the lamp's wick. It smelled too different. And I'd never slept alone, never slept more than an arm's reach from my family.

I hugged myself, forced myself to move a tiny bit until I was rocking quietly to and fro.

I am so lucky. I am so lucky. I am so lucky.

Slowly, I calmed. How could I be upset, lying here in such luxury, when Nhung was also alone, somewhere new and unfamiliar, learning to be a maid?

The rest of the family would be far away soon, but Nhung would still be here in Saigon, somewhere close.

I would find Nhung.

Yes, I would be a good daughter to Papa and Maman, and learn things and be happy, or my parents would be shamed. But I would find Nhung too.

It would take time; my world had gotten so much bigger than Ap Long, and so much more frightening.

Eventually, I slept.

I dreamed of the lights beyond my window, but they were not ghosts. I had not called the ghosts. It was Dan, the Year of the Tiger, and they were tigers' eyes, watching me from the velvet night, and they did not blink. I had named them *hô con quỷ*, tiger demons, and I had called them here to Saigon.

And then I dreamed of the Mother of Waters, the wide yellow-brown river that swept everything away.

Part 2 ~ Awakening

醒
悟

Mark Henwick

Chapter 6

Saigon at dawn, the old-timers said, *is like waking from an opium dream.*

Great dragons, formed from the mist off the rice fields, flowed down onto the dark river and raised phantom heads to stare threateningly at the stirring city, with its wide, leafy boulevards and square, pale buildings looming out of the darkness. In the center of the unending landscape of steamy mangrove swamps and flooded paddy fields of Cochinchina, it was Saigon's regular formality that seemed like the strange mirage, insubstantial as dreams.

As Papa and I walked along the Quai du Commerce, the east began to bleed gold into the sky and rob the night of its substance. The mist dragons dispersed. Saigon was allowed to become real for another day.

Our heels clicked at a leisurely pace on the quay's wide stone slabs. He wore his usual white linen suit, ready for work. I was in a slim, elegant dress, pale coffee in color. It was the fashion to be as narrow-waisted as a wasp, but Maman said fourteen was too young to use the corset. Instead, I wore a short jacket to emphasize my shape. My hair was pinned up under a pretty bonnet.

It was early for the promenade, but today I was not concerned about the time, or about fashion. I forced my face to remain calm and composed, but my stomach was more cramped than if I'd been allowed the corset, and for every measured step we took, it felt like my heart beat a dozen times.

The dawn had dispelled the river mists, but guilt and fear lay across my shoulders like a phantom cloak that only I could see.

It was five years since I'd been adopted; my whole world had changed, and I had changed with it. I felt as much French as Annamese, and as much the child of my adoptive parents as of my birth parents.

That was partly the source of the guilt: I was deceiving my adoptive parents because of my fears for my birth parents.

And the fear was well-founded; there was a dagger aimed at all of us.

It took the form of a ship, a French naval corvette called *Victorieuse*, that was en route from Paris.

Every three or four months, a ship would come with important dispatches for the administration of all French interests in the Far East — the protectorates of Tonkin, Annam, Laos and Cambodia, the leased territory of Guangzhou Bay in China, and the colony of Cochinchina.

But this time, the ship also bore a high-ranking envoy with his staff, and it was accompanied by a troop carrier with a battalion of Troupes Coloniales, the marine troops of the Colonial Army. No official explanations had been received.

Since the *Victorieuse* had set out, every ship into Saigon harbor, every telegraph, every conversation had brought more rumors. Saigon was in a fever of speculation. It seemed the future of the French Far East hung in the balance, and something fundamental was about to happen.

Had there been some threat we'd not heard about from Britain or Siam? China? Was there to be an annexation of new territory?

Of course, Saigon was in telegraphic communication with Paris, but those cables passed though British hands, and the British weren't to be trusted. All truly secret communications arrived on naval ships, just never with such a combination of unexplained troops and senior administrators.

Papa appeared aloof from the uncertainty, but he was not. Maman and I could see. We knew the toll this was taking on him, and there was no discussion of rumors allowed in the house.

Mainly my fears arose because the most persistent rumor was about Hué, the imperial capital of Annam, the place to which my father and mother had fled. People were openly saying that the mandarinate was going to be replaced by a council of ministers reporting to a Frenchman, and the mandarins released would be ordered back to assist in the administration of whichever province they had come from.

If my father had been successful in re-entering the mandarinate, they would send him back to Saigon, and Bác Thảo would know. There would be no hiding this time—a poor man can hide where a mandarin cannot.

I'd been having horrible nightmares where Bác Thảo's gangs would flow through Saigon like rats after a monsoon flood, and when they left, my father, mother and brothers would have disappeared.

To make my dilemma more barbed, I knew Papa had enough power in the colonial administration to stop my father being sent back to Saigon. All I had to do was confess to him that my parents had lied when Papa and Maman adopted me.

I believed Papa would understand, and he was fair-minded enough that he would do what was necessary to ensure my birth family would be allowed to stay in Hué. They would be shamed, and whatever status they'd achieved in Hué would be destroyed, but at least they'd be alive. But would Papa and Maman still want me when they realized they had been lied to? No. How could they? It would be the scandal of the year. I would be thrown out.

Which all meant that I should not take this path of confession unless I was absolutely sure there was no alternative. It was possible, for instance, that my father hadn't been able to re-enter the mandarinate. Or that people in Hué knew more of what was actually happening there — that no such proposal to send him back was being considered.

So, in my guilt and fear and doubt, I had hatched a plan to find out as much as I could about what was happening in Hué, and whether my father had indeed become a mandarin once again. All it had needed to progress was for me to tell a lie to Papa. *Yet another lie.*

I'd rearranged my lessons, and I had asked that we could have a walk together along the docks before he started work. We'd had little time together recently, and I let him believe that was the reason. In reality, I hoped to get a few minutes alone here, where there were ships fresh in from Hué and people who might be encouraged to talk.

It was a risk. Bác Thảo remained a danger to me, and if he were to piece together news of an Annamese girl asking about a reappointed mandarin in Hué along with his knowledge of the disappearance of an ex-mandarin from Cochinchina, it might be no great leap for him to work out what had happened.

Everything seemed to be a risk.

27

Unaware of the turmoil in my thoughts, Papa was enjoying the only quiet he would have in the day, spending that time with his deceitful daughter.

We exchanged murmured greetings with the few passers-by. Papa walked with his hands held behind his back, his head up, savoring this peaceful moment.

"And what then, Ophélie," he said, "do you consider his best achievement?"

We were speaking of the Duke of Magenta. News of his death had arrived yesterday on the telegraph and both Papa and Maman were saddened.

They would not think that the duke's best achievement was his Crimean war record, that much I could guess, even though that would be the banner in La Poste, Saigon's main newspaper. My answer was important to Papa, so I put my inner agitation aside and thought carefully.

"His service as president of the Republic," I said. "The balance he kept between the republicans and the monarchists."

"Precisely." Papa was pleased. "And the grace with which he took his leave of the political arena," he added. "Always remember that, too. Except when you die in office, it is the nature of the world that most political careers end in failure. Too often the manner of leaving is all that remains in people's minds."

He was probably thinking on his own position here in the colony.

It had been my parents' plan that the Beauclercs would take me to live in France shortly after my adoption, so I would escape from the threat of Bác Thảo. There had been some delays, and then some more. Months became a year. And a second year. With every passing year, there had been another, yet more vital reason for Papa to stay, and so here we had remained.

For the last eighteen months, Papa had effectively been running the colony while the actual governor was ill.

It was hard work and a great responsibility, but there had been benefits. He'd been able to start many of the important projects he'd always advocated: schools and hospitals here in Cochinchina, and planning for exhibitions of Far Eastern culture, history and industry in France. Papa wanted a display of Indochina at the centennial Exposition Universelle in Paris, which would finally convince the French population at home of the wonderful opportunities that existed for full cooperation with the Annamese and Chinese. His admiration for the people here, and his sense of the shared potential, had become his great passion.

Many people in France still needed convincing.

We turned, without speaking, at La Ronde, the great traffic circle at the central point of the docks, which marked the end of the Quai du Commerce and the beginning of the Quai de la Marine, the naval yard.

It wasn't only that the tall, ironclad sides of naval steamships were uninteresting in their uniformity. Neither Papa nor I cared to pass in front of the government's opium factory, which sat so squat and dark, hard against the naval maintenance stores and in the shadow of the immense coal bunkers the Navy kept.

Papa thought the opium trade was a necessary evil. He said it was a pragmatic compromise that served a greater purpose, not to mention the second largest source of income for Cochinchina, after rice.

As for me, the last few years might have made me appear more French than Annamese, but I believed opium was wrong. That opinion had started back in Ap Long, with Minh's father, and the problems his addiction had caused. Nothing I'd learned since then, from the evidence of addiction in Saigon to my history lessons on the two Opium Wars with China, had made the drug seem more acceptable.

Papa knew how I felt, so we retraced our steps on the Quai du Commerce, to enjoy the more pleasing surroundings and each other's company.

And as I'd deceitfully anticipated, that didn't last.

Chapter 7

"Beauclerc! The man himself. What good luck!"

Luck had nothing to do with it.

The two men who'd waylaid us were junior colleagues in the administration. Given his importance, Papa's days were set out in meetings weeks in advance. There were always officials in the administration or colonials who needed to speak to him urgently. There was nowhere we went in Saigon that this did not happen, and at the docks, it was probably more likely than most places.

If it went according to my plan, Papa would decide they had to continue their discussion at the office, and I would have some time alone, because I'd also arranged for my morning lesson to begin down here.

After making a polite greeting, I dutifully moved a few steps away to let them discuss business.

We had been walking alongside a bulky windjammer, a cargo sailing ship, steel-hulled and four-masted—the *Margareta*, out of Hamburg. The quayside boards had been chalked up, showing its cargo was commercial steamship coal. Customs officers had just completed their inspection and the *Margareta's* captain would now be cleared to trade. Saigon was the busiest port in the South China Seas, with a dozen steamships docked on any given day, and he'd have buyers for his coal before lunch. Already the 'black women', the women and girls who made their living unloading coal basket by basket, were lining up.

Four other men joined Papa's group.

No! If there were too many, and not all in the administration, Papa would not take them to the office.

I skirted around them and strolled on, as if unconcerned, but in truth my heart was in my mouth. It was so hard to arrange moments when I was unaccompanied. Moments when I could do things and ask questions that would not need to be explained with yet more lies.

What could I do now?

The *Margareta* was big—a hundred metres long—and it dwarfed the next ship, a sharp-prowed wooden pinisi out of the Celebes. The pinisi was a quarter of the size of the windjammer, and it had only two masts. Its name was the *Salayar*. The quayside boards left the cargo unstated—they were here to buy. But much more importantly for me, they confirmed the *Salayar's* last port of call was Hué.

This wasn't one of the ships I'd been looking for. I knew that at the far end of the docks, there was a Chinese steamer that had brought a diplomatic delegation all the way from Canton, and which had paused in Hué to allow the diplomats to meet the Emperor. Just being able to speak in Mandarin to the crew might get me some answers.

But I couldn't go down there while Papa was still standing beside the *Margareta*, and glancing back showed no movement in the group around him.

I bit my lip. I had lied and deceived Papa, and now it might all be for nothing. I couldn't bear to go home again without learning anything. The mandarins could be recalled any day, and I had to know what to do.

I strolled alongside the *Salayar*, trying to hide my desperation under a veneer of idle curiosity.

The tall, raised quay was level with the deck. I could see into the ship: the stowed sails made of coarse-woven brown jute; the twin rudders; the dark ironwood planking, decking caulked with coconut fiber and gum; the sharply raked stem and stern, which gave it that wicked prow, like the thrust of a fencer's blade.

The *Salayar* would have shipped spices to Hué's markets; the smell still clung to the ship and tickled my nose.

On the return, they'd be carrying Chinese silks from Hué and maybe they'd be looking to buy cheaper fabrics here in Saigon. And opium, always opium.

I grimaced at the thought, but I had no time to be squeamish. An opportunity was opening up right before me.

The small, ragged crew was stirring angrily on the deck, listening to an argument between the customs official and their grizzled captain standing on the quay.

Tò Laut, these people called themselves — the clan of the sea. *Bugis* was what we called them in Saigon, or sea gypsies. I remembered them well from my early childhood living on a sampan in the floating villages of Arroyo Chinois. To an Annamese child, they were colorful and exciting visitors with exactly the right air of wickedness to make them fascinating.

To the French, maybe they were less fascinating. *Pirates*, some people called them, even though they still welcomed the trade these small craft brought.

They weren't precisely made welcome on the Saigon dockside, but that wasn't what the argument was about.

Though officially it was frowned upon, it was common for customs officials to solicit bribes from ship captains in return for preferential treatment. Being among the first to have their cargos released, or to be cleared to buy and load new cargo, could be worth the cost of greasing a palm or two.

It seemed that the Bugis captain had been moved down the list and was angrily refusing to pay a bribe to regain his place. If I could put him in my debt by helping him, he might agree to give me news from Hué in return. Bugis hated debts and obligations.

All I needed was a bit of luck and boldness, and to put aside my demure French demeanor.

"Is there a problem, Monsieur?" I asked the port official. He turned to me. A short, strong man, with a neat beard shaped like a spade. I didn't recognize the man himself, but I knew his kind. A petty clerk in France, all chance of progress there crushed beneath the stifling bureaucracy. Here in Saigon, he was a big man with a good job, a comfortable house and servants, and probably an Annamese mistress as well.

He bristled at my question, as I expected. As a young girl, it was not my place to involve myself. Papa would be annoyed if he saw me, and his colleagues would be shocked. I hated the thought of embarrassing him, but I had to take any chance of getting news from Hué.

"Nothing to concern yourself with, Mam'selle," the officer said dismissively. "The captain here is confused about the sequence of inspections."

He paused, looking around. "You ought not to be out here alone, Mam'selle," he added. "Where is your escort?"

I had to act quickly before he found someone to take me away—for my own good, of course.

"Oh, the inspection sequence," I said innocently, bending to peer at the chalked numbers on the quayside boards. "I see. This number has been rubbed out and changed."

I straightened up and added, "Perhaps my Papa could help. Monsieur Beauclerc. He's just over there." I waved my hand in Papa's direction. "I'll run and fetch him."

I held my breath, knowing he would recognize Papa and praying I was right in believing that official interference was the last thing this man wanted. Papa would *not* be pleased if I dragged him into this.

The official glared at me. "It's not worth the discussion," he muttered, and waved the closest cargo inspector aboard. The *Salayar* was a small ship; only one would be needed. "Mam'selle." He nodded stiffly and called to his other inspectors, directing them on to the next ship, a steamer out of France, where he'd probably still collect his fee for expediting.

"Monsieur," I murmured at his back, breathing a sigh of relief.

The captain of the *Salayar* had to follow the inspector aboard, but he spared an unreadable glance for me. I quickly touched my mouth and ear, the sign I'd learned when my family had lived on our sampan. *Want to talk.*

He blinked, and made a little upward movement with his head. *Wait.*

He acknowledged the debt. Now I must wait and hope the risk I had taken would pay off.

I returned to Papa's group, which he was trying to disperse.

Monsieur Therriot was reluctant to go. "… but I've been trying so long to get this funding for the Mekong Navigation Association. It's a trifling amount in comparison to the benefits—"

"In comparison to the supposed benefits, which you cannot prove," interrupted Monsieur Champin. Competition for development funds made enemies of them, and made Champin rude.

Papa held his hands up to calm them. "I've made your proposals, which, as you know, exceed our planned resources and have had to be referred. I will not anticipate the response." He shrugged. "Dispatches are coming from Paris. Perhaps there will be something in them for you both."

A nervous shuffle passed through the group at the mention of the dispatches.

The delays in communication and the reluctance to use the telegraph meant no one knew exactly what was happening in the halls of power in Paris until actual directives arrived. People could be promoted, recalled, posted elsewhere. Commercial matters could be sponsored or rejected. Projects might be started or ended—anything. Politics in France was disconnected from the realities of the Far East. French policy in Indochina, they said, was really an argument between the Ministère de la Marine, the French Admiralty, and the Quai d'Orsay, the French foreign ministry.

No wonder it was a time of anxiety for the colonials. For *us*.

"Whatever else is in them, they must require Governor Laurent to stand down," Champin said. "It's not reasonable to expect him to continue in his state of health."

"The man's at the end of his strength," another added. "The dispatches will surely order his return, to convalesce."

"And confirm our friend here in his place." Therriot rocked to and fro on his feet, smiling broadly at Papa and touching him lightly on the arm.

Papa shook his head, unwilling to engage in this speculation.

"But the *Victorieuse* is already late," Champin said. "Now I hear that's because she's gone north first. Why? Why the delay?"

"Of simple necessity, the ship must travel both up and down the coastline," Papa said. "A naval captain has many factors in his decisions. I see nothing to concern us in his choice to visit Tonkin and Annam first."

"So still, one must await the judgment of Paris." Therriot made a joke of it. "And Saigon is the fairest, is it not?"

There was strained laughter.

"It's a sea change," broke in Monsieur Gosselin. I knew him well; he was the father of my best friend, Manon. His eyes were fever-bright in his pale face this morning. "I feel it. A great change. All of us ... change." He lost his thread and frowned in confusion. That happened to him often recently. Manon and her mother were worried. If he had been in the administration, he would have been recalled long ago, but he had always been able to convince the merchant firm he worked for to let him remain in Saigon.

The others were split between embarrassment and amusement at Gosselin's lapse, but at least it served as a break. Papa excused himself for a moment and rejoined me.

"I'm sorry, Ophélie, that was not edifying." He took me by the arm and led me a few steps away from the group.

"You're owned a little by everyone." I quoted one of his own phrases back at him. I was pleased when it made him smile, and I stamped down on the guilt from all my deceptions.

"I must take Monsieur Therriot to the office." He looked around. "Monsieur Song is not here yet?"

"No, Papa."

He continued looking until he spotted a Chinese woman walking toward us from Boulevard Charner. "Ah! Jade has arrived."

Our senior maid, the Chinese woman I'd called Aunty in that first meeting with the Beauclercs, was my constant shadow in Saigon whenever I was not with Papa or Maman. It was an arrangement which neither of us enjoyed, but imposed on us by social expectations.

Jade stopped well short of where we stood. Papa looked as if he were going to call her forward, but I stopped him.

"No," I said. "Don't worry, Monsieur Song will be here soon, and I'm perfectly safe. Jade prefers to keep her distance."

"Well, I suppose it will be alright." He nodded and took a deep breath. "This is a better place for a lesson than some stuffy room. Remind me, what is today's subject for discussion in Mandarin?"

"The docks, shipping and trade of the colony."

"Excellent. If perhaps a little dry."

Therriot was beginning to look impatient, but Papa gestured him to wait. He guided me to a bench and we perched on the edge.

Papa leaned forward and rested his elbows on his knees.

"You hide it so well, but I can tell you're upset by all these rumors and speculations." He held his hand up to stop me denying it.

"We must find something else for you to think about, and, after all, it's your birthday next week," he said, and smiled briefly. "Your French birthday, anyway."

Birthdays were not celebrated in Annamese culture, and in fact, I had no idea what day I'd been born. My adoptive parents had insisted that the French part of me needed an annual celebration.

"Ophélie, you must know what joy you've brought to Thérèse and me." His face was suddenly serious. "We were so worried to start with. What a change for you. What a difficult decision for your family. What if you'd hated us? And yet, here you are; look at you. You are so wonderfully French as well as Annamese. It's more than we could have dreamed. You've been the most dutiful daughter we could ever have imagined."

"It's not duty, Papa." I wasn't lying; I had come to love both sets of parents equally.

I had to bite my lip. I would not cry.

What would they think when they found out I'd been part of a deception? Surely they would hate me?

But not knowing my thoughts, he smiled again. It lightened his face and I wished he would smile more often.

"We may have even less time together after the *Victorieuse* arrives. Thérèse and I think we should make the most of this birthday." He took my hands in his. "You are mature enough to know your mind. Whatever you want, if it's within our power, that'll be your gift."

My heart skipped a beat. I knew what I wanted.

I couldn't ask about my family until I knew what was happening in Hué. But I had family in Saigon: my sister, Nhung.

In all the time since I'd been adopted, I'd found no trace of her. Every time I met a new family in Saigon, I questioned them about their maids. No one knew any maid of that name or description. It was slow, frustrating work trying to discover information without making anyone suspicious.

I couldn't tell Papa the whole truth, but if I told him enough of it …

If anyone could find Nhung, it was Papa.

I couldn't ask them to adopt her, but if she was simply a maid in the same house, how much happier we both could be.

"Well?" Papa interrupted.

This was so important, and so risky. I would have to think it through. And of course, I might need to time it with other truths that I had to tell him.

"I need a little time, please."

"I can see you've got some ideas, though." He laughed, then stood and straightened his jacket. His hand touched my shoulder.

"So solemn! Perhaps a pony?" he said. "Ah! See, a smile! That's like a rainbow—a sign of great good luck and happiness." He laughed again. "Well, enough for now. My regards to Monsieur Song."

He walked away with a wave, collecting Therriot on the way.

Yes, I had great good luck and happiness. In all of Cochinchina, was there a girl as fortunate as I was? A despicable, undeserving girl, who lied to the loving family who'd adopted her, and who lived in comfort in the same city where her sister served as a maid.

My heart felt as if it would break in two. I rocked myself.

I am so lucky. I am so lucky. I am so lucky.

Chapter 8

I waited anxiously, scanning the deck of the *Salayar* and the crowded quay in turn, worried Monsieur Song would arrive before the inspection was finished.

Behind me, people had gathered at the quayside cafés for coffee and hot, fresh croissants. The scents and quiet murmur of voices drifted across. The city was waking. In minutes, it would resume its daily routine: the frantic, invigorating urgency of morning business, which would then pause over a long lunch and resume more sedately in the afternoon, before finally transforming into the renowned nightlife, so I'd heard, which lasted until close to dawn.

In front of me, the brief inspection of the *Salayar*'s hold was finally completed. The inspector walked down the narrow gangplank and away.

I forced my self-pity aside. However it made me feel, I had to try and make some progress.

That was difficult.

The ship was barely thirty metres away, but it might as well have been a mile. It would be unthinkable for a young lady to go on board a Bugis ship. Some gentleman from the crowd in the cafés would run up to 'save' me before I got halfway up the gangplank. It would be a scandal. Jade would report it to Papa and Maman. Difficult questions would be asked. And far worse, the crew might be imprisoned for trying to 'lure' me on board.

I was about to get up and at least walk closer when the crew members emerged and jumped down onto the quay, the captain first among them.

The others set off at a trot toward the market.

The captain sauntered over to sit on the raised rim of a nearby circular flowerbed, one foot folded casually underneath him. He was close enough to speak, but not close enough to attract attention. He made a big show of getting his pipe out, knocking it against the bricks and tamping tobacco into the bowl. His face was polished by the sun and wind, as dark and glossy as the wood of his deck, and about as readable.

He didn't speak.

I knew he wouldn't, unless I did. Bugis approached you, and waited — it was simply their way. If I did not speak, he would feel he'd done what he could and discharged his debt.

Start. Just start.

"Good winds, *Salayar*," I said quietly in Trade. It was a patois, not really a language at all, but it was spoken up and down the coast — more Chinese words in the north, more Malay and Javanese in the south. Everyone had a chance of understanding some of what was said, and my family had needed to use it a lot when we'd lived on the sampan. I hoped I could remember enough of it.

He grunted in surprise at my using Trade. "Winds good no man," he replied in the same language. "Sea good no man. Good come work-work and luck-luck, uh."

He lit his pipe and shifted his weight. "We buy quick. We leave. Quiet, uh. Low-low. Night come, no ship find *Salayar*."

I frowned. What was he talking about? He was sounding like a smuggler. Did he think I wanted something smuggled?

"Opium, uh?" I said.

"Huh." He jerked his chin up. "Can." Which could mean he had before, or he would in the future, maybe, or that he was actually shipping opium now. A Bugis speaking Trade could make evasion an art form.

Maybe he saw something of my reaction in my face.

"Got cloth," he said. "Got Hué silk lot-lot. Buy rice Saigon market. Buy lot medicine. Saigon good-good Chinese medicine. Cheap-cheap rice."

I relaxed and nodded.

"We give clothes like-like us," he said. "You wear, uh. Cut hair. Dirt on face. Come quiet-quiet. Hide in hold. Secret place. No man see. No man catch."

I gasped. He thought I was trying to escape, that I was being held in Saigon by some cruel French master.

There *were* Annamese women who dressed in the French style and were mistresses, though never called that in polite society. They were *demimondaine*. Half of this world, half of another.

"No," I said, falling back into French in my shock. "Thank you, but that isn't what I want."

"Huh." He understood enough of that and looked hugely relieved, taking a deep draught of smoke from his pipe and leaning back. "What want? Hué silk I got. Tò Laut carving I got. Good."

I shook my head.

"What talk Hué?" I asked. I couldn't remember the Trade words for news or Emperor or mandarin. How was I going to ask?

"News, uh?" He laughed, providing me the word. "News yellow girl in white clothes, speak Trade."

Fear spiked through me. News about me had barter value too. This was all going wrong, but I couldn't give up now. I shook my head again. "No talk me. Look for family."

His eyes swung round and looked shrewdly at me before he deliberately turned away again.

"Family, uh?" He puffed another cloud into the morning air and shrugged. "Hué big-big."

"Emperor?" I tried the French word and he blinked. "Man begin work mandarin. Work for Emperor?" I mixed Trade and French.

His eyebrows rose in surprise, but he shook his head. "Mandarin no come dock. Man work mandarin come get bribe."

"Know, uh. But …" I tried to explain myself. "Man come dock, talk. Who do what, who go up, who go down." They must pick up bits of gossip here and there. Otherwise, I had wasted my effort and possibly started another little rumor running—about the Annamese girl in French clothes who spoke bad Trade on the dockside in Saigon and asked about someone in her family becoming a mandarin. At least I hadn't given away the name of Trang.

He shook his head again.

I wanted to grind my teeth, but I had no time for frustration. If there was nothing about my family, maybe there was something about the new administration changes.

"What news change-change? No more mandarin Hué, send home?"

"Uh." He made that upward gesture with his chin. "Mandarin go home soon."

"Sure-sure?"

"Uh."

The rumor was true. Or at least the people in Hué believed it.

Maybe he'd expected me to be happy at the news. Although I kept my face as neutral as possible, something told him I wasn't.

He said something I didn't understand, then seeing my confusion, he tried again in broken French. "All mandarin work Emperor, French make ..." He mimed writing on his palm.

Lists! Of course! The French 'advisors' to the Emperor would know everyone who worked in the court; they'd even know everyone who had applied to work there.

But I held back the sudden hope.

"List belong Hué," I said, mixing French and Trade again, and miming writing on my hand. "No see here Saigon."

"Ah." He made a fist with his left hand. "Hué," he said. Then he put his right hand over it, so the fingers reached all around. "Saigon, uh. List belong Hué come Saigon. Saigon see. Sure-sure."

Maybe.

It *might* be true. Cochinchina was a full colony, Hué just a protectorate. If official government documents came here, they would go to Papa's office, but there might be copies in the central library. That'd be the first place to check, rather than coming up with lies for Papa about why I wanted to see lists of administrators from Hué.

I'd be able to visit the library right after my lesson, if I hurried.

"Thank you," I said in French.

Something had come from this morning's deception. Something I could actually *do* that could confirm what had happened to my family.

He nodded distractedly at my thanks. He was looking past me, frowning up the quay at something.

"Secret, uh?" I said hopefully in Trade, pointing at myself.

"Huh." He wasn't paying attention. I turned to look up the quay to see what he was looking at.

Not far away, I could see the tall, angular figure of the priest, Père St Cyprien, talking to the fleshy Monsieur Riossi, the last of the group that had ambushed Papa. I liked neither of them. The priest had the perpetually sallow face and bruised eyes of someone who slept badly at night. I knew the things that kept me awake, and I couldn't help wondering what it was that disturbed him. As for Riossi, his eyes seemed to follow me around when I was unlucky enough to be in the same room with him.

The pair of them were deep in conversation, waving their hands for emphasis, but slowly coming closer.

"*Tò Dara*," muttered the *Salayar's* captain, and trotted back to his ship, his pipe trailing aromatic smoke over his shoulder. "Bad-bad."

What was that all about?

I wanted to call after him and find out. But young ladies wouldn't do that, and at that moment I saw Monsieur Song striding toward me from the Signal Point at the end of the quay. Slipping quickly past the priest and Riossi, I waved and walked briskly to meet him.

Chapter 9

My *lǎoshī,* my tutor in Mandarin, was Yi Song.

He was a merchant who traded in silks, perfumes and medicines from a modest shop in Cholon, which was the Chinese district of Saigon. He lived in a rambling, airy house, built around peaceful courtyards with water gardens, where scarlet carp drifted beneath the white water lilies and fragrant yellow lotuses.

He spoke several dialects of Chinese, which wasn't unusual, but no other trader I had met also spoke French and Annamese. He even knew some Arabic and Malay, and probably more that I didn't know of.

He dressed plainly, without the embroidered robes or formal hats common to high-ranking Chinese men all around the South China Sea. He also shaved, trimmed his nails and didn't dye his teeth black, all against the fashions of Chinese society in Cochinchina. About the only concession to Chinese fashion he made was to braid his hair in a queue which hung halfway down his back.

His eccentricity extended to his family. His wives and his daughter, Qingzhao, didn't have bound feet. I had even heard them argue with him. I believed it was regarded as something of a scandal in Cholon.

However, despite Song so clearly setting himself apart from them, the Chinese merchants of Saigon all deferred to him.

My friends were sure that must be because he was in the Tong, the sinister Chinese secret society. They were eager to tell me that one day, my tutor would kidnap me and sell me as a slave in China, or worse, somewhere barbaric like Russia, or even Australia.

Let them think what they wanted.

Monsieur Song and Papa shared a vision of Cochinchina. There was such a potential here. Annamese and Chinese and French between them had created the beginnings of a society which would transform the East.

They were not blind. There were huge faults on all sides and much to repair. It would take years of work. And they would need people who were at ease, in language and customs, between all the elements that made up that society.

When circumstances had changed after my adoption, Papa had given up the idea of going back to France and pushing for changes there. He'd replaced that with making changes here instead. It seemed natural for me to fall into that plan and have Monsieur Song tutor me in Mandarin, Chinese culture and philosophy.

If Papa became Governor Beauclerc, and I had not destroyed his trust with my deceptions, I would become part of the mélange of East and West that he could point to.

I wanted, very much, to be able to offer him that.

Maman didn't exactly approve of Monsieur Song, but she couldn't really argue that he wasn't the best teacher for me, and my lessons were coming on well.

And as to those lessons themselves, I enjoyed them, but on the other hand, Monsieur Song tolerated nothing less than my best efforts. I had to put aside the excitement of talking to the *Salayar's* captain, and my eagerness to go hunting lists of Hué mandarins in the library. It was time to concentrate on speaking Mandarin or I'd be in trouble.

We began to walk, Jade following at a distance.

Greetings out of the way, he switched immediately to Mandarin, starting with short, sharp questions about the docks, ships and crews. Where I didn't know a word or phrase, he would tell me and then make me use it in several new sentences. By the time we had rounded the point and walked as far as the Bank of Indochina, I was panicking from the relentless pace of the lesson, sure that the language was going to slip out of my grasp at any moment and I would be left unable to understand a single thing. He always seemed to be able to keep me in that state.

"Good," he said, stopping for a moment in front of the bank to look at all the people walking in and out. Then he turned on his heel. "Now, we will talk about finance and trade."

I groaned silently. It was going to be an even longer walk back.

We were discussing the dangers of indebtedness when we returned to La Ronde. It was much busier now; a constant, noisy swirl of people jostled in all directions.

"But you are a businessman," I said. "You own your business, and you must have borrowed money at some stage. Or perhaps you pay for goods at the end of the month, even though they are delivered at the beginning. That's a form of loan."

"Yes, for practicality, most traders operate like that. For commerce, that is necessary. For my personal life, well," he paused thoughtfully, "I would not want to be in debt to anyone who would lend me money."

What? Did I misunderstand the Mandarin phrase? He wouldn't …

"Lǎoshī! You're teasing me."

His face was impassive, but his eyes gave him away.

We came to a halt.

"An acceptable lesson," Song said, switching back to French.

He looked around until he located Jade, who would accompany me back to the house. She was waiting in the shadow of an awning that a chandler had erected over his shop front.

"Here." Monsieur Song produced a small book from his pocket and gave it to me. "Yuan style essays for you to read. Search for the underlying layers of meaning."

At least it was a slim volume. Lessons with Song were scary but enjoyable; however, reading Ming dynasty literature was simply boring.

"I must return to my business," he said. "Next time, I am minded to try something different again."

He paused for a moment, stroking his chin. "The lesson will be conducted by Qingzhao at the house in Cholon. She speaks more quickly and with less emphasis than I. This will be good practice for you."

"I look forward to it," I replied.

What he really meant was she would be more difficult to understand. Then again, I didn't think she would make me so frantic to keep up with what she said, the way he did. Qingzhao was a little distant with me, but maybe we'd even talk of something more interesting than finance and trade.

A smile touched the corners of his lips. "I will check afterwards. I do not expect you to spend all your time gossiping."

"Yes, Lǎoshī!" Had he just read my mind?

I bit my lip. With his knowledge of languages, here was actually something he might be able to answer for me. "May I ask a question?"

He slipped his hands into the sleeves of his silk jacket and folded his arms. "Yes."

"I heard a word on the docks. I think it might be Trade or Bugis. I wondered if you knew it. The word is *dara.*"

He looked silently at me for a long moment, only the slightest widening of his eyes betraying surprise. "Short words turn up in many languages, meaning different things, and Trade is a mixture of all languages around the South China Sea. It might mean a dove. It would help if you remembered any other words that were said at the same time."

If the Bugis called themselves *Tò Laut,* meaning the clan of the sea, then I didn't believe *Tò Dara* meant the clan of the dove, given the way the *Salayar's* captain had said it.

"Tò Dara," I said.

Song frowned. "Most interesting," he said, eventually. "Bugis, then. The word *dara* means *blood* in their language. The phrase is the name of an old ghost myth of the Celebes." He glanced across at the throngs of workers along the docks. "I must go. Remember, your next lesson with Qingzhao is not for gossip. Not for ghost stories, either."

He turned and strode away, his long paces eating up the distance to the tram stop, his queue swinging like a pendulum across his back.

As I watched, he stopped. There were some street urchins gathered as they usually did on the docks. Monsieur Song gave them something, as he often did—small pastries or coins from his pocket. He spoke a few words to them, and they solemnly bowed to each other before he continued to the tram.

It made me smile, and it was yet another thing that made him unusual. Most Chinese merchants would only chase the boys away.

In all the time he'd been tutoring me, I'd didn't think I'd ever quite surprised him as I had with the question about Tò Dara. That was interesting, but there was no time to waste thinking about it. I wasn't late yet, but it would take fifteen minutes to get to the library, and then however long it took to find if there were documents that listed the mandarins in service to the Emperor before I could hurry home.

"Done," a voice speaking Trade barked in my ear. "Paid."

I'd been so distracted, I'd not noticed the whirl of Bugis that flowed around me in the crowds of people on the promenade. It was a half dozen of the crew of the *Salayar*.

Something pressed against my stomach and for one awful moment I thought I'd been stabbed. My hands instinctively clutched at the object, and I was left holding something hard and weighty, wrapped in coarse jute cloth.

"No owe now." It was the *Salayar's* captain, speaking as he walked away, flanked by his ragged crew. He turned briefly, walking backwards, and jabbed his chest, just over his heart. "Use here. For protect. Saigon bad. Got Tò Harimau. Got Tò Dara. Tall man. Bad-bad."

Tall man. His words chilled me; it was the same name my mother had used instead of saying Bác Thảo.

That couldn't be right.

"Wait," I called, but the *Salayar* had already loosened its moorings in preparation, and the six of them had to leap from the quayside to the deck.

By the time I made my way through the crowds to the spot, they'd poled themselves clear and the current was pulling the bow around.

Immediately, the crew set to raising their lateen sails.

I was shocked to see the *Salayar* was still riding high in the water. They hadn't bought all their intended load of rice and medicine. Something they'd found out this morning meant more to them than their profit for the journey.

Tò Dara? Ghost stories? Bác Thảo?

Maybe *tall man* was just a coincidence and it wasn't Bác Thảo he meant. Bác Thảo himself wouldn't be at the docks early in the morning, would he?

Then who?

I cast my mind back to earlier. The priest and Monsieur Riossi had been standing there together. Riossi was not tall. The priest was—tall and saturnine. A mysterious-looking man.

Père St Cyprien?

No. Surely not. My imagination was running away.

And what was Tò Harimau?

The chances were, I'd never see the *Salayar* again to ask.

Done. Paid. No owe now, he'd said. Bugis didn't like debts, and it seemed he felt his information about lists of mandarins in Hué hadn't been as valuable as my help with the customs officer.

So what had he given me?

I was about to undo the bindings when I realized that Jade had worked her way through the crowd to join me.

"What they do?" she demanded.

I held the Salayar gift next to Song's book and shrugged. "They jostled me accidentally and said something that I didn't understand."

"Bugis," she spat. "Scum."

At least she didn't seem to notice the package, or assumed it was part of what Monsieur Song had given me.

Her eyes were angry as she looked out at the *Salayar,* picking up speed on the river. She looked at me the same way, as if she knew there'd been something happening without being able to work out what it was.

Jade didn't seem to approve of anything—not Monsieur Song, not me, and certainly not Bugis sailors on the dock.

I'd long ago given up trying to change her opinion about anything, so we didn't speak as we returned to La Ronde and took a rickshaw up Rue Blanchy to the library.

My mind was a commotion anyway, split now between the urgency of trying to find news of my father in Hué, and seeking out the meaning of the *Salayar* captain's parting words.

What on earth was going on in Saigon?

A girl brought up on a sampan in Arroyo Chinois, and in the hardscrabble of life of Ap Long, she develops a sense of awareness, a feeling for danger. That sense had been dormant for some time, but I found it returning now. The hairs on my neck prickled.

I found myself anxious to examine the strange gift I'd received, but that would have to wait until I could smuggle it into my room at home, away from Jade's prying eyes. Still, it weighed heavily in my hands as I prepared to search the library for news of my family.

Chapter 10

The ornate longcase clock on the library wall told me I had barely ten minutes left before I had to go home.

Yes, the head librarian had said. The government in Saigon received lists of mandarinate appointments from Hué, but only sent them to the library when their own shelves were full. *No*, they weren't in the general reading section, they were down in the archive.

She'd organized to have them brought up, but the assistant would have to find them.

During my wait, I wasn't having much luck with ghost stories from the Celebes either, and in my hurry, dropped a heavy book I'd taken from the shelves onto the desk.

The only other occupant of the library's reading room looked up and frowned at the noise.

"My apologies, Madame," I murmured.

She was examining the French Cartographic Society's maps of the area between Saigon and Phnom Penh, and comparing them to sketches in a handwritten notebook.

That was uncommon.

But none of my business, and anyway, *uncommon* was probably the same thing she thought of me, an Annamese girl in French clothing, struggling with an oversized compendium on the mythology of the Celebes.

Her gaze passed over the book and came up to my face.

She had the disturbingly intense look of one of the Andalusian flamenco dancers that I'd seen staring out from the painted portraits in the gallery at the Governor's Mansion. Her black hair had probably been pinned up neatly a few hours ago, but clearly resented the restraint, and locks had escaped to frame her face.

The moment passed. She went back to her maps and I skimmed my book.

My trouble was that there was too much. The Bugis island of Sulawesi was a melting pot of cultures and they'd each brought their own myths and borrowed from everyone else. But nowhere did I see any mention of Tò Dara.

With five minutes left, I hurriedly put the books back and returned to the counter at the front to see what had come from the archives.

"This is the compilation of civil administration postings from Hué," the librarian said, sliding a leather folio binder to me—thick, black and dusty. "You'll have to apply to the governor's office if you need something more recent."

"Thank you, Madame," I said. The binding held years of appointments, each year in a booklet, stitched together along the edge. The most recent was four years ago. It was just possible my father would be included in it.

I flipped pages. The book had list upon list, some translated, some still in Mandarin. There were candidates for examinations, results of examinations, sponsors and appointments.

Anyone could become a mandarin in theory, but first you had to pass the difficult examinations. Then you had to have a sponsor in whatever department you wanted to work in. My father had already passed the examinations, of course, but finding a sponsor would be the hard part.

That narrowed it down, but it would still take hours to search through.

I looked up. "Is it possible to borrow this, please? Just for a few days."

The librarian looked surprised, but filled out the form, which I signed.

It was getting late. Not just for me to be home for lunch, but for the library to close as well. However, finding this document had given me an idea. "Is there something similar for maids in Cochinchina? Or at least Saigon? A list of domestic servants in French households?"

She blew her cheeks out. "No. Of course, they try to make an accounting in the census." She shrugged expressively. "Perhaps you could ask at the department of the census in the Secretary General's office."

"One last quick thing, please, Madame."

Madame was unimpressed. Her lunch and afternoon nap were calling her.

"I'm looking for a reference book about the myths of the Celebes."

"Myths?" she said, frowning. "Superstitions?"

"Yes. Something about ghosts that are called Tò Dara."

The librarian looked blankly at me.

"You will not find that here, Mam'selle," someone behind me said.

I turned.

It was the lady from the reading room, passing on her way out. Her head was cocked to one side and her eyebrows were raised as if there was something very strange in asking about Tò Dara.

From her soft accent she was Spanish. She wore a somber green skirt and matching short waistcoat, with a thin spiral of pale embroidery at the sides. Brown boots, with buckles and a pattern tooled into the face, showed beneath the hem of her dress, and her white blouse puffed out around the waistcoat. It was an unusual and dramatic style—a little wild, as if to complement her escaping hair I'd noticed earlier.

She looked to be only in her twenties, but had an air of great confidence about her.

"Emmanuela Cortés." She juggled a leather satchel onto her left hand and offered her right.

I shook it awkwardly, unused to that form of greeting. "Ophélie Beauclerc," I said. "Your clothes are quite wonderful, Madame."

Her lips thinned. "*Como una vaquera.* For comfort." She glanced at the librarian. "Come, I think we are outstaying our welcome."

We were ushered out into the hallway.

As soon as we started walking, I saw that she was actually wearing some sort of culottes, a divided skirt, as if for horseback riding. That was what her Spanish comment must have meant. I'd heard of divided skirts, but this was the first I'd ever seen. My dress suddenly felt so staid. I had the idea that a divided skirt would be regarded as scandalous in French society, but for a moment I wanted to be outrageous and daring and wear one too. Of course, in my position as the Beauclercs' daughter, I could not.

And as if to remind me of that, Jade was waiting in the hall. She stood up and joined us, looking suspiciously at Emmanuela, who just smiled back.

"Ay! *Adelante*," Emmanuela said, as we stood on the steps outside the library. "So, you're looking for stories of the Tò Dara?"

"Yes, I only heard it today. I was curious."

"And now I am, too. It's not a name I've heard outside of little coastal villages in the Celebes. How does a young lady in Saigon hear such a name?"

"Oh, it was just a comment made by a crew of Bugis on the quay this morning. They jostled me and called out some words I didn't understand."

"How strange. Are you sure they were speaking to you?"

At that moment we were interrupted.

"Ophélie!" A Malabar carriage came to a halt on the street in front of us. It was Maman. "There you are."

She told the coachman to wait and stepped down.

"Maman, may I introduce Madame Emmanuela Cortés. Madame Cortés, my mother, Madame Beauclerc."

"Delighted," Maman said. "Do you two know each other?"

Emmanuela's face had paled slightly and her easy use of French slipped a little. "We are just meeting in the library, Madame," she said. "Acquaintances only in passing. I should not keep you."

Maman could see my face fall.

"Do you have an engagement for lunch?" she said to Emmanuela. "Or would you care to join us?"

"I think, perhaps …"

Such an invitation to a stranger, even in the relaxed society of Saigon, was rare and it was difficult to turn down gracefully. Emmanuela had some problem with it, though I couldn't think why.

Maman clearly knew. "I am aware of your argument with the Saigon administration, Madame Cortés, and I assure you that my husband will not be home for lunch, nor will I discuss the matter with you, or with him." She gave that little upward tilt of the head that she did so often. "Come, let's put that all aside. You've just come from Paris, I understand. I would so like to speak of things not to do with Saigon, and we're always eager to hear news from France. Let's talk of fashions. Art. Music. Archaeology even. Anything but politics and government."

Emmanuela suppressed a smile of relief and bobbed her head. "Thank you, Madame. Then I would be very pleased to join you."

"Come." Maman turned to get back in the carriage.

"Let me carry your satchel," I offered to Emmanuela, adding quickly, "May I put my things in there, please?"

She looked quizzically at me, but let me take her satchel, and I slipped the ledger from Hué, Song's book and the *Salayar* captain's gift inside, where no one would see them and ask me awkward questions.

Chapter 11

The house we went to was not the place I'd first met Maman and Papa. That one was out beyond the city park on the Rue de Tombeaux. During the week we lived here in the narrow town house, on Boulevard Bonnard, just down from the statue of the Mekong explorer, Garnier. It was within easy reach of Papa's office and near the center of Saigon.

As we entered the house, Emmanuela and Maman were deep in conversation about the growing commercialism of the art of Alphonse Mucha. With them distracted, I took the opportunity to hang the satchel on a hook by the door and take my secrets to hide in my bedroom.

Although I rushed back downstairs, it seemed that I would have to wait to ask Emmanuela anything about Tò Dara; the conversation had moved seamlessly to the new trend of absurdism in the Paris theater.

Maman missed these things. In fact, it wasn't until we were well into our meal that she steered the conversation in a direction that encouraged Emmanuela to talk about herself and her reasons for being here.

Both she and her father, Professor Orlando Cortés, were archaeologists, working for the University of Barcelona.

Despite being accredited archaeologists with acknowledged expertise in the Khmer empire, the rulers of much of ancient Indochina, it had taken them over a year to obtain permission to search for new ruins. They'd spent that time researching in the Celebes instead, and I guessed that was where Emmanuela had gathered Bugis folklore and myths.

They had had two sets of administration to deal with, and two sets of permits were necessary—one for the colony of Cochinchina, one for the protectorate of Cambodia.

The permit for Cochinchina had eventually come through. Rather than wait for the Cambodian one, they'd set out slowly up the Mekong, hoping that the second permit would overtake them.

As luck would have it, barely two months into their expedition, Professor Cortés had found evidence of a road branching away from the Mekong, and an indication that it would lead to the fabled Kattigara, an ancient port city that had been known as far away as Rome and Byzantium.

"No archaeologist could turn away from exploring that," Emmanuela said, with a smile.

There was a problem; Kattigara appeared to lie across the border in Cambodia. No Cambodian permit had arrived.

Emmanuela had returned to Saigon, and after fruitless telegram exchanges with the administration in Cambodia had instead opted to travel all the way to Paris to get an all-region permission from the government there.

Now she was back with the permit, but in the meantime, communications had broken down with the expedition. She'd expected updates and maps waiting for her at Saigon, as agreed with her father. There was nothing. She had to admit she had no idea where her father actually was.

I understood from the careful way that conversation avoided it, that Emmanuela had requested assistance of some kind from the administration here, and been turned down.

"Anyway, the universities have provided funds for me to rejoin my father, and I shall use them to find him. I have a small expedition prepared, and I will be leaving soon."

"On your own?" Maman said, appalled.

"No. I will have porters and a guide," she replied calmly.

Not what Maman meant at all.

If I'd admired Emmanuela before, I was now totally in awe.

"But now, we must talk of something else," Emmanuela said, "or we will stray into politics and government. I should delay only to apologize for putting you in a potentially awkward situation by talking to your daughter." She actually blushed a little. "I heard the surname, of course, but when Ophélie and I introduced ourselves, I didn't make the connection to Monsieur Beauclerc."

"No matter." Maman brushed it all away. "What prompted you to introduce yourself?"

Emmanuela smiled and gestured for me to take over the talking for a while.

"I was in the library," I began, "researching the mandarinate in Hué after my lesson with Monsieur Song this morning."

I said it that way because I knew that Maman would assume the research was something to do with my lesson. I had to suppress the guilt of more deceptions and go on—this was my chance to learn about the Tò Dara and why the captain of the Salayar had thought it so important that he had to give me something.

"While I waited for the book I asked for," I went on, "I thought it would be interesting to see if I could find out anything about a name I heard while we were on the docks this morning, something about people called the Tò Dara. Monsieur Song just said it was a myth from the Celebes, but we didn't have time to discuss it. I asked the librarian if she knew of anything, but she didn't. Luckily, Madame Cortés heard me and said that she knew about it."

"That's interesting," Maman said. "I understand the Bugis call themselves Tò Laut, and that means clan of the sea, so we just need to know what Dara means."

I spoke quickly, pleased I had that much knowledge. "Dara means blood, so the name is quite sinister."

"The clan of blood," Emmanuela confirmed, and both of us turned to her expectantly.

"It means exactly that," she said, "though you'll never see it written down, so the library is not the place to find out about them. In the Celebes, these things are all part of the oral tradition, tales that mothers tell their children."

"Suitable tales, I hope?" Maman said.

Emmanuela shrugged. "No worse than Grimm's fairy tales."

Maman frowned at that, but seemed interested enough to let her continue.

She started plainly, as if she were giving a lecture.

"It's always been interesting to me, how cultures that have had no historical connection with each other should have myths and legends with such common themes. The Mesopotamians had *lilitu*, and the ancient Greeks had *lamia*, the Annamese had *ma cà rồng*, and the Aztecs had *cihuateteo*. In Europe, we call them vampires," she said, "and in the Celebes, the Bugis call them Tò Dara."

My friends were always interested in scary stories, but I already had the feeling this was more than that. I felt the first shiver of goosebumps spread down my arms.

"The explanations about where these different types of vampire come from, and the advice on what to do about them, varies a lot," Emmanuela went on. "But among them all, I find the Tò Dara are the most frightening. Not because they are terrifying to look at or because of what they do, but because most people don't know they're there until too late."

"Are they invisible?" Maman asked.

"In a manner of speaking." Emmanuela said. "You see, the Tò Dara look like us, act like us. They walk among us, and only a very few people can identify them."

Now I really did shiver. The captain of the *Salayar* had seen one, on the docks, right in front of me.

Maman laughed. "But vampires should be so easy to identify. They have to keep out of the sunlight, do not eat or drink like human beings, they have no heartbeat, their skin is cold, and so on."

"The European version, perhaps," Emmanuela said. "However, the Tò Dara do not share these weaknesses. They appear exactly like us in every respect, until they want to drink your blood. Then they suddenly grow fangs."

"Oh." Maman looked as if she'd bitten a lemon.

"You said very few people can see them," I said. "How do they do that?"

Emmanuela smiled. "That's where it gets a little vague. Some Bugis told me there is a faint scent, so faint you would not think anything of it, unless you had been taught."

"And others?" Maman prompted.

"Well, as it was told to me, some people have a special sight. They see past the illusion, and see the Tò Dara as a hollow shell, a front with no soul, no humanity inside."

I visualized the scene on the docks from the captain's point of view. The tall Père St Cyprien in conversation with Monsieur Riossi. I imagined the priest turning, revealing that he was empty, no more than a mask.

Interested despite herself, Maman asked: "How do you kill them? Is it like vampires? A stake through the heart?"

"A little," Emmanuela replied. "An iron dagger through the heart is recommended."

The Bugis captain had mimed a blow to the chest as he walked away.

What had he given me?

I shuddered, and Maman saw it. "Enough, you'll give her nightmares."

More nightmares, she meant.

Maman changed the subject quickly. "Would you join us tomorrow at the racecourse?" she said. "It's not a real race day. In fact, it's a single race to celebrate the completion of the new stands."

"I'm not sure ..." began Emmanuela.

"Oh, please," I said, and both Maman and Emmanuela laughed.

"Thank you, then," Emmanuela said. "Yes, I would be happy to join you, and I promise, no discussions about the administration."

"Wonderful," Maman said, and began a conversation about the latest fashions that Emmanuela had seen in Paris.

Unable to hold myself back any more, I excused myself and rushed upstairs to my room.

The captain's gift was wrapped in the same coarse jute fabric that the Bugis used for sails. I untied the fiber-twine bindings and pulled the brown cloth open.

A sheath. Inside it, heavy and glossy as a snake, lay the cold, sinuous blade of a kris knife. This was no ceremonial show weapon, either. The blade's edges had been whetted, and the handle was made from curved wood which had become smooth and dark from use.

Its sinister, purposeful look made me shiver, and I guiltily closed the wrapping and hid it again.

For protect, he'd said, miming stabbing in the heart. *Tall man Tò Dara.*

I was in danger from Père St Cyprien? The French priest was a vampire?

They walk among us, Emmanuela had said.

But what if it wasn't the priest?

What if Bác Thảo, the tall man, had been right here on the docks, invisible to me among the crowds? And he was the vampire?

And the *Salayar*'s captain thought I could kill him with a knife?

No. This was crazy!

But however crazy it was, my street sense was tingling. There was a danger to me, here in bright, modern Saigon. I knew it, without being able to see it exactly, or knowing from which direction it would strike.

Chapter 12

The next morning, the crowd at the new racecourse was loud and enthusiastic. They all seemed to be talking at the same time, some of them at the tops of their voices.

I was drowsy from long hours spent the previous night poring over the mandarinate lists from Hué. Every occurrence of the name 'Trang' had set my heart racing. It was not that uncommon a name, but none of them had been my father.

I slipped into sleep eventually with the ledger still open on the bed, only to drift into one of those nightmares that blended my recurrent fears for my birth family with everything that had happened during the day. My family had become hollow, soulless people who stabbed at me with kris knives because I was the monster to them.

Finally, waking in the early morning, I had completed my search. My father had not re-entered the mandarinate, as far as those records went.

Of course, I could ask Papa for the more recent lists.

Of course, I could lie about why I wanted to see them.

But I had to put that decision aside for today. This was a morning for the people of Saigon to celebrate, and I had some time with Papa and Maman at the racecourse. I would be watched, simply because I was with my adoptive father. I must not let my worries show. I did not want to let my adoptive parents down.

When the *Victorieuse* arrived and he became governor as everyone said, the scrutiny would only get more intense. People would watch my every moment. Would that make it impossible to search for Nhung? If it turned out my family wasn't in Hué, would it be impossible to search for them too?

There was too much to think about, and yet time with Papa and Maman was in such short supply, I simply wanted to enjoy what I had, so we were smiling and talking when we arrived at the racecourse.

It did not last. Within moments, Monsieur Champin had elbowed his way through the mass of people to shake Papa's hand and ended up standing right in my way.

"A wonderful idea, Monsieur Beauclerc, wonderful," he boomed. He turned and gestured at the throngs of Annamese and Chinese gathered around their marquees. "With taxes on gambling and opium, we'll be able to fund the whole of the empire in the east."

Papa's smile was strained, but he could hardly argue against the benefit, given how tight budgets were.

The racecourse had originally been a field near the town that the cavalry had used for challenging each other to races. Then it had become a regular weekend hobby for some, and people had gathered to watch. Inevitably, they'd started betting on races. Disputes had broken out, and Papa had decided, rather than trying to make it illegal, the colony would create its first municipal racecourse and tax the gambling. There were now steeply raked stands for spectators and an area with open-sided marquees for people to take refreshment out of the sun between races.

The oval course itself was marked out with simple white-painted wooden rails. I wondered if the rails would be strong enough—the crowd around the Chinese marquees was already spilling out. They were excited—laughing, shouting and betting on the race before we'd even seen the horses.

The Chinese marquees were hung with festive red and gold banners, sky-blue streamers and little flags. They looked much more fun than ours.

Over there, we could see my tutor, Monsieur Song, slowly making his way through the crowds. He waved at Papa, and after making a few more greetings, Papa went across to talk to him in the quieter space between the marquees.

Maman was deep in conversation with her friends, so instead I tried to speak to Emmanuela. No such luck; she was too popular with a lot of the men.

"Ophélie! Where are you going?"

I'd found two of my friends instead: Rochelle Champin and Manon Gosselin.

Rochelle was petite, with dark hair and eyes. She was a very sweet person, and about as different from the abrasive character of her father as she could be. Manon was blonde, lazy, messy, absolutely irrepressible, and simply the best friend I could wish for.

"I was trying to speak to Madame Cortés."

"You know her?" Rochelle asked, wide-eyed and a little shocked, speaking with her hand over her mouth as if someone might be listening to us.

"Yes," I said, pleased to have surprised her. "She came to lunch yesterday."

"She's scandalized the whole town with those culottes she wears," Manon said, clapping her hands together. "It's wonderful."

"She's wearing a dress today," I pointed out.

"Yes, but look how she's making up for it."

Indeed, although it wasn't her fault that so many men wanted to talk to her, I could see some angry, sideways glances at her. Whatever my friends and I might think of her, Emmanuela was not popular with the ladies at the racecourse.

"Well, anyway." I shook my head. "She'll be leaving soon. She's setting out on an expedition to meet up with her father, Professor Cortés, somewhere along the Mekong or down in the jungles near the coast. The gossip will die down."

Or other gossip would swamp it. Gossip like what on earth was going to happen in Saigon when the envoy from Paris finally arrived.

But my friends seemed less impressed by Emmanuela's bravery and flair than I was, and they steered us to another topic so they could start teasing me.

"He finds you interesting. I know it," Manon said, pointing out where Alain Sévigny was standing, talking to some of his friends.

I doubted it. Alain was the elder brother of Chantal, the most popular girl of our age group, so we'd had some opportunities to meet. But he was nearly eighteen, and he was so handsome it made my heart ache. It wasn't as if I were the only one who thought so. I suspected my friends were teasing me to cover up their own feelings.

As it happened, we didn't have the chance to spend a long time on that topic either.

The buzz of conversation changed and quietened, rippling out from someone who'd just come in. In a minute, everyone around us had turned and stopped to listen.

It was the Chief of Police, Meulnes, and he was agitated. He was a small, energetic man from the south of France, dark skinned, with black, wiry hair. His face was now flushed and his hair slicked down with sweat from wearing the white pith helmet the police used. He accepted a drink gratefully and downed it in one draught before speaking again.

"I have hunted them in the jungle, and I tell you, without a shadow of a doubt," he said, shifting his weight from foot to foot. "There was a tiger in Khánh Hôi last night."

The words made me feel cold, even in the humid heat of the overcrowded tent.

I'd always been scared of tigers. They'd been a real threat, living in the village of Ap Long. They'd taken farmers in the fields, on the paths, even from the little bamboo houses.

And stupid as my superstition was, I still avoided walking on that tiger skin in the weekend house on Rue de Tombeaux.

"Another attack? This is incredible," one of the men said.

"My God! How many dead?" asked another.

"Four men mauled to death," Meulnes said. He thrust his arms behind his back and squared his chest. "It's all under control now. I've had squads with rifles checking every hiding place and every building in the whole area."

"Did you find anything?"

"No tigers," Meulnes replied with a grimace. "Beyond the signs where the men were killed in the warehouses down on the Arroyo Chinois, there was nothing."

"How could that be?"

"They can't just disappear!"

Meulnes shrugged, but before he could answer, another man spoke.

"They can swim," he said. I recognized him; he was a big plantation owner, probably in town just for the opening of the racecourse. "I saw that for myself when I was up in Kon Tum province last season," he went on. "The tiger might have swum down the arroyo. It could be anywhere now."

There was a bubble of speculation and more questions, cut through by a new speaker.

"No. They wouldn't swim in the arroyo."

I recognized the voice, of course. It was Monsieur Gosselin, and he had that glazed, fevered look about him.

"Oh, Father! No, please. I beg you. Not now," Manon said under her breath. She pressed her knuckles against her mouth and tears suddenly gleamed in her eyes.

"Where's your mother?" But as I said it, I saw that Madame Gosselin was already making her way through the crowd. Manon started forward as well. I went with her, unsure what I could do, but wanting to support her.

"We are blind, we colonials," Monsieur Gosselin said, waving his finger at the crowd. "We come here so full of civilization and knowledge, so full we think it shines out of us and lights up the darkness. But it just blinds us. Blinds us. The truth is, the tiger does not need to swim the Arroyo to get away, because this is no ordinary tiger. No ordinary tiger would come into the city."

Madame Gosselin reached his side and began to whisper urgently to him, pressing him toward the exit.

The crowd parted. Most of them knew Monsieur Gosselin. There were some embarrassed smiles, some anxious faces. Many thought he'd just spent too long here in Cochinchina, and were probably calculating when they should leave.

He turned. Maybe he was speaking to the crowd, but his eyes caught mine. In that moment, it felt as if the two of us were alone.

"A tiger demon," he said. I heard him as clearly as if he had spoken in my ear. "Hô con quỷ. You have called it here."

Memories of that first night of my adoption flooded my head. I'd looked out from my window at the Rue de Tombeaux. There had been the lights by the old tombs and it had been Dan, the Year of the Tiger. I'd named the lights hô con quỷ, the tiger demons from the mountains.

And I'd dreamed that by naming them, I had brought them to Saigon.

Chapter 13

"Please, Ophélie," Manon was saying. "We'll be fine. Just let us look after him."

I didn't speak. I managed to lift a hand to wave goodbye and they were gone.

I found myself alone. Rochelle had been called away by her parents, as if just being close to the Gosselin family was dangerous.

Tiger demons. In Saigon. My fault.

No. I stopped myself sliding into that spiral. Whatever my rational French education argued, my instincts told me that, although there *were* tiger demons, it was nonsense to blame them on myself.

Were they a danger to me?

The captain of the *Salayar* had said that Tó Dara were what threatened me, not tiger demons. And Tó Harimu, whatever those were.

All I wanted was for my birth family to be safe from Bác Thảo, and for me to be a good and dutiful daughter to two sets of parents.

I took a deep breath and turned back to hear what Chief Meulnes intended to do about these attacks.

"How have you left the situation in Khánh Hôi?" This was from Riossi. As well as being a director of the Opium Regie, the government regulator of the opium trade, he was also a director of Messageries Maritimes, the company that dominated the French shipping trade and ran the commercial side of the docks in Saigon. This was their base in the South China Sea. I'd seen it before; anything that threatened smooth operation of the docks made him furious.

"It was touch and go down there," Meulnes answered. "I've had to leave most of my squads in the streets where everyone can see them; otherwise there'd be no coolies working today. Not on the docks and probably not on the building sites either. Question is, how long can I keep that up? What happens tomorrow, eh?"

"We can't let the docks close," Riossi said.

"I understand, but as you must realize, this is the worst possible time," Meulnes said, and he looked around until he found the gaunt, sallow face of Colonel Durand, the regimental commander of the Colonial Marines here in Saigon. He made a stiff little bow. "Colonel, I must officially request the assistance of your troops for peacekeeping tomorrow."

Durand's mouth twisted downwards. "They're not policemen. There are risks with using them like that. Would it not be better to delay the execution?"

There was a sudden silence in the whole group. This execution had been the talk of the town, amongst adults at least, but quiet talk. Private talk. Not out in the open like this. Maman absolutely refused to tolerate any mention of it, even in the house.

"A delay would make it look as if we've lost our nerve," someone muttered.

There were pursed lips and nervous glances.

The execution had sharply divided opinion in the colony. That was partly because the condemned prisoner was a woman. But it was worse than that; it was to be a public execution, to take place right in the middle of Boulevard Charner.

The thought made my stomach churn. I didn't know what she'd done, but that poor woman, to be executed in front of all the jeering crowds!

She was also Annamese, and this was all to show that French law and French penalties were to be applied throughout Cochinchina. The justice department and the police had decided a public example would help emphasize that. It was a difficult balancing act they attempted, with the potential to dissuade criminals on one hand, and on the other, to cause a riot.

Papa returned at that moment.

"I believe this is neither the time nor the place for this discussion," he said, taking Chief Meulnes and Colonel Durand aside. "Both of you, please attend a meeting at my office immediately we finish here. We will discuss this and all aspects of public order over the next few days."

They nodded acceptance, and everybody else was distracted by the announcement that the pre-race celebrations were about to start. The crowd split up into murmuring groups and moved toward the fence around the track.

I hung back. It was sure to be a colorful spectacle, with fireworks and lots of banging gongs and drums. But there was also a dragon dance. I couldn't even think of that without remembering my brother Lanh. It must have been when I was seven or eight and I'd asked him to tell me stories of Sai Gon. He knew I liked my mother's tales of how the first Annamese emperor had been descended from a dragon and so he told me how dragons sometimes danced in the streets of the city. How vividly my young imagination had painted pictures from his words, and how he'd encouraged it, until I really believed in dragons.

Would I ever see Lanh again? Any of my family?

Right now, I didn't want to be thinking about that while every day brought the *Victorieuse* closer, with its cargo of upheaval for Indochina and threat to my birth family.

I was so preoccupied, I didn't notice Emmanuela until she was right beside me.

"Are you well, Ophélie?" she said. "You look upset."

I was usually better at hiding my emotions.

"It's silly," I said. "I'm upset about Monsieur Gosselin ..." I stopped abruptly, and suddenly, I just wanted someone I could tell the truth to. Someone older and wiser and sympathetic, who was not Maman or Papa.

Emmanuela was looking at me, her eyebrows raised.

"Please don't say anything to my parents, Madame Cortés," I blurted out, "I mean the Beauclercs, but ..."

"Call me Emmanuela, please. I had enough of formality in Paris," she said, taking my arm and leading me aside. "Of course, you have two sets of parents. The celebrations remind you of your birth parents, somehow?"

She was so perceptive.

"It's the dragon dance. It reminds me of them." I paused. I would not cry. I would not. "I'm sorry. You should take the chance to see it. It's spectacular."

"I will, but only if you come with me."

She refused to go without me, and I didn't want her to think I was just a silly young girl, upset about nothing, so I followed her. She had no trouble getting men to make way, and we ended up right on the rails.

Somehow, while the firecrackers were exploding, she got me to explain that I had believed real dragons danced in the street because my brother had told me so.

"Ah. I had a cousin who told me things like that when I was small," she said. "I was so gullible. He told me of the *xana*. What would you call her? A nymph, perhaps? She was very beautiful, this nymph, and she granted wishes. She lived in the great fountain of the old castle ruin that was near our village. I would come back from the ruin all covered in scratches from the espino, the thorn bushes, that grew there. My back would be burned from the sun, because I would lie on the edge and look into the fountain pool all afternoon."

She laughed. "I never saw my beautiful nymph, but I still went."

As she spoke, the drummers came out onto the track, spinning and kicking and beating their drums. We caught a glimpse of the dragon—just a flash of gold and red before it hid again at the far end of the field.

She kept prompting me as the dancers progressed, and I told her how I used to think that Saigon was the center of the world, the biggest city imaginable, and how the people who lived in Saigon must all be dragons who lived in stone houses.

I spoke much more freely than I normally did. There was something about the way she listened while we watched the celebrations, something about the way it felt; it was as if we were isolated from other people by the noise.

I had to stop myself in the end. I wanted to pour out everything—the rumors of changes in Hué, my dilemma about talking to Papa, finding Nhung, the kris knife that the captain had given me, Bác Thảo, my sense of some undefined threat, all of it. I desperately wanted someone to advise me, but that would be unfair to Emmanuela. She had her own concerns, and I should be asking her about them, not talking about mine.

Then the dragon came out where we could see it clearly. It was good enough to get a gasp from Emmanuela.

I'd been right, the dance was spectacular. The dancers made the whole dragon body ripple and twist as they chased the drummers to and fro. The body stretched half the length of the field, and seemed to fill it with bright red and gold.

Everyone loved the show, clapping and cheering when they finally left the field.

Quickly, the racecourse quietened down, and the horses started to arrive. I knew Papa would expect me to watch the race by his side, but I had time for one question that had been on my mind.

"Thank you so much for telling me about the Tò Dara yesterday," I said. "But there was one other name like that I heard from the Bugis ..."

"You are full of surprises," Emmanuela said, laughing again. "What was this name?"

"Tò Harimau."

She frowned. "What a peculiar conversation you must have overheard," she said. "In any event, that's a Bugis name, but it refers to an Annamese myth."

"Oh? Which one?" I asked.

I spotted Maman making her way toward us.

Emmanuela turned to follow my gaze and smiled in greeting. "The one your friend's father, poor Monsieur Gosselin, was speaking about," she said to me. Looking toward Maman, she was oblivious to my reaction as she continued: "You know, the legend of the hô con quỷ. Tiger demons."

I stood there silently in shock as Maman and Emmanuela spoke of the dragon dance, unaware of my reaction.

I could explain Monsieur Gosselin's words away. The man was ill. But the captain of the *Salayar* was not, and he'd thought Saigon was dangerous enough that he'd not waited to fill his hold with cargo here.

Tó Dara. Tò Harimau. Bác Thảo.

Was I completely surrounded by threats? What could I do? Who could I turn to?

I felt like I was drowning, but I wasn't given time to do anything about it.

A touch on my arm made me jump.

"Ophélie, you know this young man, don't you?"

Papa was at my side. And with him, Alain Sévigny.

My brain refused to function.

I knew I should say something, do something, but I couldn't move.

Papa looked puzzled, but smoothly continued to cover up my hesitation. "Alain seems to know something about the horses, so I've asked him to join us for the race."

"Oh, good," I managed to say.

How stupid I sounded. Even Alain was looking puzzled now, but he was quickly distracted as Maman introduced Emmanuela to him.

And in the middle of everything else, the pang of ridiculous jealousy did more to clear my head than anything I could have done to myself.

There was a space reserved for us with a good view of the finishing line. Papa guided us there just in time to see the horses paraded before us.

"There, now, you see," Alain said. "This fellow's a grand cavalry horse. Look at him, you can see the weight of the bones, and the power in his hindquarters. But he's too big, too muscled for the distance. The next one, however, with the blaze all the way down to his nose. That's Lighthouse. Deep chest, but lighter body. He's the one for this race. Sure winner."

"You are so knowledgeable, Monsieur Sévigny," Emmanuela said.

Alain flushed slightly.

I turned away and looked at the horses.

They'd reached the end of the stands and were circling back for a second view.

"Well, place your bets," Papa said as they approached the starting line. "I'll give you good odds on your horse being in the first three."

He even had a notepad and a pen ready. No real money would change hands; he did not approve of gambling. I suspected his real reason for joking was to draw me out of myself.

I knew I needed to respond.

I thought carefully. Of the horses I had seen, one was especially beautiful. It was called Touchstone. Another had the lovely name of Dancer's Dream. They were the two I liked.

"I don't want to bet on being in the first three," I said. "I want to bet on winning."

"Mmm. More risk with that bet," Papa pointed out.

"More return too, Monsieur Beauclerc," Alain said, and in a stage whisper to me he went on: "If I might advise you, Mam'selle Beauclerc, put lots of money on Lighthouse to win."

"No," I said. "Dancer's Dream and Touchstone."

"But they run in the same race," Papa said. "Only one can win."

"I know. I can't decide."

"Hmmph." Papa very deliberately wrote the names in his notebook.

Everyone laughed and we gathered on the rail to watch.

Alain stood next to me. He touched my hand to attract my attention and pointed out racing things, like the slight benefit that the horse on the inside track would gain. It was foolish that even in the heat of the morning, I thought I could sense the warmth from his body.

These thoughts were not only inappropriate for Mademoiselle Beauclerc, which I could overlook, but trivial in comparison to the larger events going on around me. This realization did not help and my hand continued to tingle, even after the horses started racing.

As it turned out, Lighthouse won.

Alain shrugged off congratulations, and he seemed to sense that I was upset.

Papa shook his head and hissed dramatically through his teeth. "You lost everything," he said mock-sadly. "When you back two horses to win in the same race, Ophélie, that's the most likely outcome."

If only it were all about horses.

Chapter 14

Why was it so difficult to find the right vegetables today?

The market churned with people this morning, bright and noisy. There was lots of smoke from small charcoal fires as food sellers fanned the smell of beef noodle soup and grilled pork across the crowds.

But I had to find the sweetest, most tender bamboo shoots or Maman's lunch would be ruined. The stall traders couldn't seem to understand. They weren't usually like this.

Jade hated the market. She was muttering and cursing in Cantonese behind me. I could feel the anger like a heat radiating from her. It was like being followed around by a badly made stove.

"*Măng*," I said, using the Annamese name.

The Chinese stallholder wrinkled his face in bafflement, showing his gold-lined teeth. He saw my French dress and my Annamese face, and that confused him so much he couldn't understand what I was saying.

"Eh?" said the Tamil man in the next stall. He was chewing betel, and the red juice made it look as if he were bleeding from the mouth.

Next to him, a hunched Annamese woman was selling her farm produce. She sat on the edge of the road, surrounded by woven baskets of her wares.

"Go," she said in Trade, waving me away. "Busy-busy."

"Mam'selle, cannot," Jade said. "Go back now. Late."

I could never do anything without dragging her along like a sea anchor. Imagine what I could achieve without her. And what had I ever done to deserve the way she treated me? The frustration of it all boiled over.

"Why do you hate me, Jade?" I said, over my shoulder.

"You fight against the will of heaven," she said, sounding like the priests at the temple. "The child must bear the burden of the parents. If the will of heaven is for you spend your life in the gutter, then that is what must be. You cannot escape, not even by being sold. To try is only to bring your bad joss with you and spread it to others."

Joss. Luck, fate, karma.

I lived a life that was partly French now. I was educated. I should be able to laugh at the word, but it chilled me.

And what was Jade doing speaking to me like that?

I turned around, but there was no one following behind me. All I could see were the indifferent faces of the crowd, jostling their way through the bustling Chinese market.

And at that moment I saw *her*, as I always prayed I would one day.

"Nhung!"

She was bending down to judge the ripeness of some fruit from a stall three rows away, her hair plaited in her special knot and lying down her left shoulder on her blue shirt.

"Nhung!" I ran through the market. People didn't have time to get out of my way, and I bounced and twisted through the crowd. I lost sight of her. The people were too tall.

Workers delivering sacks of fruit and vegetables shouldered me out of their way. Women balancing baskets of fish and eels on their heads blocked my view. Stallholders shouted out prices and waved samples of their wares in my face.

She wasn't at the fruit stall when I got there.

Ignoring the shouts from the stallholder, I climbed onto his cart and looked around wildly over a sea of blue and white tunics and straw hats.

People were starting to notice me. Tall, shadowy figures formed into groups and began to move through the crowds to where I was.

There! I saw Nhung again and I dived back into the crowd.

Five stalls away, then three. How was it she couldn't hear me calling?

I was breathless by the time I caught her.

"Nhung," I panted, touching her arm. She turned.

It wasn't her. The strange woman's mouth was full of blood. Where her eyes should have been, there was nothing but darkness.

I woke with my pillow damp from my tears.

∞ ∞ ∞ ∞ ∞

I can't back two horses in the same race. And I can't do everything at the same time for everybody, or I will achieve nothing.

Every possible path felt like the most bitter betrayals of one side or another. Or everybody.

Sitting in my room, I tried to think clearly.

My most achievable aim was to track down Nhung. I could go to the Secretary General's office and ask about the census of domestic servants. If that didn't work, I could reveal only a tiny bit of the truth and ask for Papa's help.

But Nhung was safe, living as a maid. My birth parents would not be safe if they were sent back to Saigon.

As I walked downstairs to breakfast, I finally resolved that the next step I had to take was for me to ask Papa to allow me to inspect the government's documents on the Hué mandarinate.

I would make up an interest about the working of the Emperor's court. Only if the documents showed my father was there would I need to take it to the next step and start confessing this nest of lies. I would need to start soon. The *Victorieuse* was closer every day, and not all my wishing would hold it back so much as an hour. It had probably visited Hué already. The mandarinate might be being dismantled right now.

Nhung, my dear sister, I'm so sorry. You have to wait. This is my fault for not doing enough, quickly enough. I promise I will find you as soon as I can, but I must look to the lives of our parents first.

It was too late to do anything this morning; Papa was ready to go to the office. I would start tonight when he came home.

All the rest, the threats to me, vampires and tiger demons—what could I do, really? I would find a way to carry the kris knife with me, hidden in a bag. I would try and find out more about these monsters and why they threatened me. I had to override the growing fears of my intuition. What could threaten me in the bright, open boulevards of modern Saigon?

However I worked it around, all my plans and reasoning sounded pitiful and desperate and inadequate to me.

"You slept late. Are you all right?" Maman asked as I sat at table.

"Yes, thank you, I'm fine really. I just didn't sleep well last night."

"So much going on," she said, patting my hand. "The new racecourse. Your birthday coming. This humid weather while the monsoon is delayed. The Harvest Ball to look forward to. It's hardly surprising you're sleeping badly."

I nodded.

"Have you thought about your birthday present?" she asked. "Your father suggested a pony, but I think he was joking."

"Of course he was." I tried to smile. "I'm still thinking. It's important."

I will beg for your forgiveness when I confess my lies, I thought, and turned my head so she couldn't see the shame in my face. *Forgiveness would be my most special gift.*

But too much to ask. Far too much.

I could hear the door to Papa's study open, and he called out that he was leaving for the office. Maman stepped into the hall with him. I heard them talking quietly about a telegram from France that had just arrived.

Something was making them concerned. I couldn't hear what it was about, but I could hear the tone of their voices.

I couldn't use that concern as another excuse to delay. However that first step turned out, I had to take it tonight. I couldn't put it off any longer.

As for today, it would feel endless, I knew. And that feeling of slowness would last right until the time came for me to start asking my questions of Papa. Then it would feel as if everything had happened too fast.

Monsieur Song had told me that the Chinese philosopher, Lao Tzu, had said that only unhappiness comes from thinking too much about what had been and what might be. I needed to live today in the present.

It was Maman's coffee morning at the Café La Ronde. My friends would be there as well. I wanted Maman to enjoy her day, not worry over me. I needed to let simple pleasures fill my time; to be Ophélie: dutiful, demure and appropriate daughter of the Beauclercs.

However much I wanted to be Bian, and to think about my plans, my failings, my premonitions and my nightmares.

∞ ∞ ∞ ∞ ∞

Half an hour later, we took a rickshaw. Maman told the man who pulled it to take a longer route, up to the Secretary General's office, along Rue d'Espagne and down Blanchy, but whichever way we went, we had to cross the wide expanse of Boulevard Charner, and I couldn't help but look down the length at what I knew would be there.

I could see the pale uniforms of Colonel Durand's Marines already forming lines in front of the courts, and beyond them, the gathering of the crowds who'd come to witness the execution. They were like a restless sea, still relatively quiet now, but building even as I looked, and full of foreboding.

The guillotine had been set up on a raised wooden platform during the night. It was much larger than I'd imagined. The whole apparatus gave off a sense of ominous finality that reached right down the boulevard, and drew my eyes to it.

As we passed, they were testing to make sure the blade was falling freely.

It thudded against the stops and I flinched at the thought of what that would mean in a short while.

Despite my resolution about filling my day with simple pleasures, I started to ask: "Maman, what crimes justify such an execution—"

"Hush, Ophélie," Maman said, taking my hand. "Ladies do not want to know about these matters. You must not discuss it, or even think about it."

I had tried asking before, with the same result.

But as the rickshaw completed the crossing of the boulevard, I could not help but take one last glance down at the gathering crowd.

They *were* like a sea; a sea starting to surge against what held it back, and even from the top end of Boulevard Charner I could hear the chilling anger rising in the multitude of voices.

Maman squeezed my hand and spoke brightly, as if nothing was happening. "Now, we will need to make plans soon. We're having cousins from France coming to visit. They'll be on the steamer that should arrive this week."

I answered in kind. "That'll be interesting, Maman. Are they touring, or will they be staying with us?"

"They'll be staying at our town house until they arrange their own accommodation. They're not on a tour; he's been posted here by his company for six months to review their Far Eastern operations."

"Oh. What are their names?"

"Yves and Blanche Fontaudin. Blanche is my cousin. She's from the branch of the family based in Toulouse. Unfortunately, I was only really familiar with the Bordeaux side of my family. All I know about them is that Yves works in the clothing industry."

"Will Blanche know all about the latest Paris fashions then?"

Maman laughed. "There's more to clothing than fashions, but she'll know more than us, that's for certain."

We started to talk about the new styles that Emmanuela had described, and that conversation lasted till we arrived at the Café La Ronde.

The café had tables spread out along the street in the shade of the scarlet-flowered flame trees. Where the shade was patchy, they'd grouped wide green parasols, except in the very center, where there was a small fountain which sparkled in the sunlight.

Maman turned to the right and joined her friends.

I stood in the sun for a second, enjoying the cool water of the fountain with the tips of my fingers.

The table of daughters was to the left. I looked across, out of the corner of my eye.

There were four girls there, heads together and voices lowered, dressed in the latest Paris fashions for young ladies. The adjustment for Saigon's climate was limited; the cloth was paler and lighter, without shawls or capes. All the cuts were, to my eye, a bit severe, but mercifully without the frills and ruffles of last year. Bonnets and hats had also become more restrained.

Thankfully, my clothes would not make me stand out. As the only Annamese girl adopted into the French society of Saigon, I didn't need anything else to make me unusual.

In truth, my early acceptance was probably partly thanks to Papa's position in the government. But over time, I'd felt that the color of my skin mattered less. In fact, I was not really much darker than some girls whose families came from the Mediterranean coast of France.

Still, I could never quite forget that I was different from the others.

Nearest to me at the table were Rochelle Champin and Manon Gosselin. I had no worries about their welcome.

The other two were Phèdre Riossi and Chantal Sévigny.

Black-haired Phèdre was the daughter of the unpleasant Monsieur Riossi, the man with the eyes that followed me around. She was as spare as her father was fleshy, but shared his Corsican olive skin. She wore her hair with an unfashionable fringe, like a curtain she could hide behind. I'd always found her odd and moody.

Beside her sat Chantal. Since the Revolution, we hadn't had French queens, but no one had thought to tell Chantal.

As always, Chantal was turned out in the prettiest dress, this one an embroidered pale green that went well with her golden hair. She'd kept her fingerless white lace gloves on, against the custom here in Saigon. Her pale complexion and bright blue eyes made some people compare her to porcelain, but from my experience, porcelain didn't have the right sharp edges to properly describe Chantal.

How did one family produce both Alain and Chantal?

I was pleased to see that Manon seemed to have recovered from yesterday at the racecourse; she saw me and waved enthusiastically. "Ophélie," she called, bouncing on her chair. "Come, sit with us."

I caught a glimpse of Madame Gosselin frowning. Yes, young ladies were not supposed to wave and call like that, however good it made me feel.

I walked across and took the offered chair gratefully, with a smile and a greeting for them all.

Chapter 15

In contrast to Manon's welcome, the atmosphere at the table was subdued, with an underlying tension.

"Well," Chantal said, after quiet greetings were completed. "Perhaps now we can learn something about what changes the *Victorieuse* brings?"

I had a strong feeling that this was *not* the topic they'd been furtively talking about when I'd arrived at the café.

"You all know the Beauclerc household rules," I said, trying to make light of the questions. "No rumors are discussed, ever."

I'd told them that often enough, but the imminent arrival of orders from Paris about the naval ship had raised the tension enough for Chantal to keep pressing, with the quiet encouragement of the others.

"We've had enough of rumors, we want to know," she said. "Surely the man who's going to be the next governor must have some idea of what's happening?" Chantal arched an eyebrow at me.

"The dispatches are secret until they are delivered by the navy." I shrugged. "The alternative would be to summon him to Paris first, which is impractical, or send details by telegraph, which is not safe."

"But surely!" Rochelle said. "There's so much at stake. They have to realize that in Paris. *All* our families are so concerned ..."

She was right. Obviously the people most affected were in the colonial administration, but changes would ripple out to everyone in Indochina.

I still couldn't do anything about it. It was frustrating, but if my friends had a better idea of what it meant to my families, *both* of them, perhaps they wouldn't press me so often.

A waiter brought me a coffee which gave me a moment, and then there was a welcome distraction provided by another arrival at the café—Alain Sévigny.

He walked in and stopped to greet his mother and her friends.

I was careful not to look over there, especially when Manon nudged me. I did notice, from the corner of my eye, just how good he looked in his casual suit. But then, he was the sort of man who would look relaxed and well-dressed in any clothes. His friends, even those who were older than him, looked like boys borrowing their fathers' jackets and trousers in comparison.

Only Phèdre was uninterested. One of the few things she'd ever said to me in private was to claim she thought Alain's face looked cruel. That was ridiculous. It was nothing more than a hint of coolness, which many successful men showed.

Anyway, Papa warned me against judging people on their looks.

Chantal didn't appreciate that her brother had become the center of attention. She liked it even less when he came across to say hello to us as well.

As etiquette dictated, especially with the mothers looking on, he began with his sister, greeted all of us, and did not stay long.

Rochelle and Manon were very friendly in their responses.

Phèdre dipped her head and peered through that fringe, muttering in answer.

Almost immediately we'd said our hellos, his raffish friends came to collect him and he left, wishing us a pleasant morning.

Everything as dictated by polite society. I wondered if Madame Sévigny or Maman had noted that he'd stood closest to my chair and rested his hand on the back.

Surely such a thing might be intentional, and if so, what did he mean by it? That he was attracted to me?

Rochelle murmured, "See? He looked at you for longer than any of the rest of us."

Not for the first time I wondered whether I was at a disadvantage. I understood the rules of etiquette and courtship, the peculiar signals you were allowed to give in French society, and the way that young ladies and gentlemen were expected to practice. But they made no sense to me. There seemed a difference between being born to them and adopting them.

Alain's gaze *had* lingered on me, perhaps.

It was frustrating; what exactly was I to make of that? It was one of those things I thought Annamese society did better. But I was expected to follow French rules, and Rochelle's teasing needed a response.

"Nonsense," I replied. "He was here only to be polite, and he was. You and Manon, however, were very forward with him."

Manon laughed. Chantal looked up sharply.

"What were you thinking of when you came in," Manon changed the subject hurriedly, "standing with your fingers in the fountain?"

"That you had your heads together like conspirators," I said to the group as a whole. "I wasn't sure you wanted to be interrupted."

Manon giggled and Rochelle blushed. Phèdre peered at me, her eyebrows raised. Was she surprised I had noticed? Anyway, I knew I was right; there had been something they were discussing and my instinct said they wouldn't have been discussing it if their parents had been listening.

Was this another puzzle of French society's rules and expectations?

I didn't want to be singled out as different. I didn't want to be unable to make friends among French people of my own age.

Would they tell me what this secret was?

How should I react if they did?

"Do you know this ideogram?" Chantal said, bringing out a piece of paper with one of her pencil sketches on it. "It's the French sign for justice."

It was an outline of the guillotine, cleverly drawn to look like a Chinese character.

"I don't think it's a matter for joking," I said.

"Because it's a woman?" Rochelle grimaced as she looked down at the paper.

"Because a person will die today, put to death in our name." Turning away, I ordered another coffee from the waiter.

"That makes it sound as if we're responsible," Phèdre was saying, "but when you say 'in our name', you mean in the name of every citizen."

"You can't hide behind that," Manon said.

"We passed Charner on the way here." I interrupted before they could start a futile argument about responsibility. "People were gathering there already. They seem angry."

"We passed there too," Rochelle said. "The locals really seem to have picked up on this."

"Are they against it?" asked Phèdre.

"No." Rochelle shook her head. "It didn't look like that at all. Quite the opposite. It looked as if they wanted to kill her themselves. It looked dangerous, but they have the army there. It won't get out of hand, will it?"

"They wouldn't let us out of our houses if there was any danger of a riot." Manon dismissed it with a shrug. "I don't even know what she did, but it must have been awful."

"Something about kidnapping, I think. Horrible."

"We're not supposed to even ask about it," Phèdre said. She rolled her eyes and the others nodded.

All of us had been told it wasn't a subject we should show any interest in.

Like a magician with a card trick, Chantal flipped the guillotine sketch over, revealing a government pamphlet on the other side.

"These posters about it are all over the market and docks," she said, "but I can't read them."

Manon and Rochelle stared at the pamphlet as if it were a scorpion. Taking a pamphlet on the execution was something young ladies, duly warned by their parents, would simply not do. Rochelle's eyes flicked over to her mother sitting on the other side of the café.

"We shouldn't," she said.

Phèdre sneered, but Chantal held up one hand to stop her.

"You can always go for a walk, Rochelle. Honestly, we wouldn't think any less of you."

Rochelle blushed and dropped her eyes. "I was just saying."

"So why can't we read about it? Apart from the fact we can't actually read it." Chantal waved her hand languidly over the pamphlet, her eyes fixed on me.

"It's in Mandarin, isn't it?" Manon said. "I can't read Mandarin."

"Ophélie," Chantal murmured, "you read Mandarin, don't you?"

I nodded unhappily. Too late, I saw where this was heading.

"No one will know." Chantal tossed her head. She slid the pamphlet across the table. "Ophélie?" she said slyly, her voice lifting at the end in a way that made me think of a fishing hook.

I sighed. I *did* want to remain friends. Even, in a strange way, with Chantal. "I'm not that good at reading this kind of Mandarin," I said, "but I'll try."

We all leaned forward around the table, five conspirators now.

"Let me see." I scanned the heading. "Her name is Madame Cao. She's aged 52." I peered at the public clock on the building across the road. "She's to be executed on the hour."

Only minutes left to live. What's going through her mind?

I tried to concentrate on the words and not think of the person behind them.

"She's a widow and ... um ... you know these aren't the sort of words I get taught. I think this is saying she is or she used to be a prostitute. Poor woman." I frowned. "And an owner of some brothels."

"That's not all they're saying she's guilty of, is it?" Rochelle asked.

That would hardly have been enough. Protected as we were, we still knew there were places that soldiers and sailors went for women. You couldn't execute people for running them.

"No. Her crimes ..." I stopped again.

That can't be right. Surely not.

"What? What does it say?"

"It says she's been convicted of kidnapping." My voice dropped and my heart began to beat more quickly. "Kidnapping over a hundred girls from small towns and distant farms, smuggling them into Khánh Hôi and selling them into prostitution."

Manon gasped.

I followed the text further. A sour taste filled my mouth. "It says there were auctions. Children as young as nine put up on the block and sold."

"Oh, God," said Rochelle, muffling it with a hand over her mouth.

Manon was staring down at her lap, blinking. Even Chantal looked pale.

"Kidnapped? It definitely says kidnapped?" Phèdre's question cut through the shock.

I checked the characters. "That's what it says."

"Well, they would say that, wouldn't they?" she went on.

"What do you mean?" Chantal said.

"I bet some of those girls were sold by their parents. I heard farmers sell their daughters to become maids. Now they're being asked by the police, of course they'll say the children were kidnapped. I bet some of them even knew what would happen."

"Phèdre! How can you say that?" Manon said.

"It's just something these people do. I suppose it's understandable when times are hard and girls can't do as much work in the fields as boys. Family doesn't mean the same thing to these people as it does to us." Phèdre waved her hand, imitating one of Chantal's gestures. "Present company excepted, naturally."

I couldn't raise my eyes.

Bình tâm. Bình tâm. It helped to speak to myself in my own language. *Keep calm. Keep calm.*

She didn't mean it. Surely.

And the growing dread kept me translating, looking.

No! I don't want to ...

But I could not stop.

The pamphlet was cheaply printed, and dominated by the text I'd already read. There was a small blurry picture in the bottom right-hand corner.

A pain blossomed in my chest.

It could be anybody, couldn't it? I was just imagining I recognized her.

Beneath the picture was the woman's full name, in Chinese and Western writing, and in the Chinese style, with surname first.

Cao, Kim Lein.

Kim.

It was as if I'd been hit with a whip. I forgot Phèdre and the others. I leaped up, ignoring the startled questions and I ran, gathering my dress as best I could, my elegant boots threatening to break with every desperate pace. Maman's call followed me, but I barely heard it.

Kim is a common name.

There were tens of thousands of women named Kim in Cochinchina. It couldn't be Aunty Kim, because that would mean I'd been living a lie within a lie. It would mean that Nhung suspected, all that time ago, what was going to happen to her, and she said nothing, because she thought my opportunity was worth more than her sacrifice.

Kim is a common name.

It would mean that Minh's mother knew, snatching him away from us that day in Ap Long. *Don't talk to them* she would have told him. *Don't catch their bad luck.*

And my birth parents, not born into that poverty, not able to even comprehend that people would do such a thing.

But not Nhung. She'd known.

Nhung undoing her hair and hiding her face. Beautiful, gentle Nhung. *Never say that, little sister. Never say you hate me, whatever happens. Promise me.* Saying nothing, hiding her face in shame at what she had to become, just so that I could have my chance at a better life.

As I ran, the truth froze inside me like a glacier, squeezing my chest until I thought my heart was going to burst.

I had to find Nhung. Papa would rescue her, wherever she was, whatever had been done to her. But only Kim could tell us where she was. I had to ask her.

I heard the crowd long before I saw them. A terrible, seething noise like a vast, angry animal. I turned the corner and Boulevard Charner was blocked with people, as solid as a wall.

Colonel Durand's Marines had formed a square surrounding the tall, stark outline of the guillotine, high on the platform. There was a long board behind the guillotine, and a knot of people there, so I couldn't see what they were doing. Figures in colonial white uniforms stood facing a man on the platform, who was reading from a sheet of paper. No one could possibly hear him.

Around the guillotine and the officials, there stood a double line of Marines. I could only see their red faces and white helmets above the crowd that had gathered to witness French justice.

The courts had wanted to send a message to the people of Cochinchina with this execution and it had worked, in a way. The pamphlets posted all over the city had created a lurid picture of her crimes. The people of Saigon had responded far more angrily than they'd anticipated.

Whatever poisons of frustration and anger they held in their lives had suddenly crystalized into a single hatred, focused on this one person. Few of them could have been personally affected by these crimes, but it ceased to matter. She stood as a symbol for everything wrong that had been done to them, and the crowd heaved against the line of soldiers, howling abuse at the condemned.

"Witch," they yelled. "Demon. Whore."

Other words—worse—some of them I didn't know, harsh words in all the languages and dialects used in Saigon, thrown like rocks at the woman on the platform.

I was tossed from side to side, fighting to get through. Sometimes they saw my clothes and fell back, surprised to see a French woman was in the crowd with them. Mostly, they didn't notice me at all. My dress was torn, my hair pulled. Fists and elbows struck my face, intentionally or not. I tasted blood in my mouth.

"Keep clear, keep clear," the officers behind the line called out, marching up and down, their hands gripping their ceremonial swords or running anxiously over their pistol holsters, as if to reassure themselves. "Steady, men, hold steady there."

The soldiers themselves grunted with effort as the crowd pushed and surged against their lines. There was movement on the platform. The man with the paper had finished. The noise redoubled.

I squeezed through to the front and, like a cork coming out of a bottle, I was hurled against the line of soldiers. My face slammed into an unyielding chest and a brass button cut my cheek. I pushed back to create a tiny space.

"I have to get through," I screamed up at the Marine.

"No closer than this. No further, Mam'selle."

"You don't understand. I have to speak to her! She knows. She knows where my sister is."

It was as if I were speaking another language. He wasn't listening, or he couldn't hear.

"No further, Mam'selle," he repeated. His eyes were focused on the crowd behind me, but as I was pushed against him again, he staggered and was forced to use one arm to bar my way.

He looked down, and I could see the puzzlement in his face. What was this Annamese girl doing, speaking French and dressed as a Frenchwoman in torn clothing? Why was she struggling to get closer to an execution?

The noise reached a peak. It had become a mindless, baying sound, beyond words or thoughts.

I twisted my body, bent my legs. I was much smaller than him and not trying to keep in line. I slipped out of his grasp, through the gap between him and his neighbor, past the second line. I sprinted forward to the platform.

"Mam'selle, no," they shouted after me, horrified, unable to leave their lines.

I was just in time. Not for my purpose, but in time to see the swift fall of the dark blade. In time to hear the hiss of the descent suddenly ended with utter, thudding finality.

An officer caught me and started to pull me back. It was too late.

Unaware I was right below him, the executioner reached down into the basket and lifted up the head by the hair for the crowd. Her eyes were still open, glazed, looking right through me. Her face twitched spasmodically and blood poured from her cleanly severed neck, but there was no mistaking the features of the woman I'd known as Aunty Kim.

Part 3 — The Right Path

正

道

Mark Henwick

Chapter 16

I'm like a poison. A disease. I spread bad joss to everyone around me.

The wooden floors had been polished that morning until they gleamed. The lemon scent of the polish overwhelmed the creamy, wild-honey smells of the sandalwood and rosewood furniture and the peppery perfume of the potpourri. Fragrances which had become familiar and comforting over the last five years.

The salon at the back of the house on Boulevard Bonnard was quiet but for the measured tick of the longcase clock against the wall. The screaming in my head didn't count.

A murmur of voices reached me from the hallway. Maman talking to the Marine officer who'd brought me home. He lingered, concerned he'd somehow failed in his duty. A doctor had already come and gone. He'd declared there was nothing wrong with me and prescribed rest.

I couldn't rest. I couldn't close my eyes without seeing that head, the blank gaze, the bleeding from the stump of the neck. The horror of it chased my guilt around in circles inside my head.

If I'd put more effort into finding Nhung.

If I'd found Kim before she'd been caught.

If I'd been able to make her tell me where Nhung was.

I heard the front door open, a deeper voice asking a worried question. Papa had returned from his office, called by one of the servants. It got worse and worse.

All because of me. All because of the stupid, stupid idea that I could delay Kim's execution and somehow get her to tell me where Nhung was.

I'd made a fool of myself and I would live with that. I'd made a spectacle and I'd have to live with that, too.

But in drawing attention to myself, I might have endangered both sets of parents. Who could say what Bác Thảo knew and heard? What he might find out if he started listening to the unusual gossip?

And how was I going to explain myself to Maman and Papa now?

If I told the truth, I shamed my birth parents and exposed their lie.

If I lied, I continued to shame myself and I was being disloyal to Maman and Papa, and so I still shamed my birth parents.

There was no option that was not a betrayal.

I had to tell the truth.

Why would Maman and Papa want to keep me, once they knew?

What would I do?

I heard the front door open and close again. The Marine officer was gone. There were whispers outside and I braced myself. The salon door opened. Maman and Papa came in.

I sat with my head down, clutching at my knees, not even able to look them in their faces. I was paralyzed with fear and shame.

"Ophélie." It was barely audible. They sat either side of me. Each pried a hand away from my knees and held it between theirs.

I'd expected anger and shouting. I sat shivering, half expecting to be beaten for what I'd done.

This gentleness was worse.

"I'm so sorry," I said, staring at the floor. "I've brought shame to the family."

"No, you haven't," Maman said. "We should be the ones apologizing."

"What?" I looked up, blinking in confusion. "Why?"

"My darling, darling daughter." She looked down and stroked my hand. Her voice caught. "We always knew there was something."

She was crying!

"Something we thought you must have been told to keep from us," Papa said. "Yet, while you were doing so well, we decided to let it be. We told each other we didn't want to upset you. We told each other that time would heal everything." He cleared his throat and looked away, his mouth a thin line and his jaw tense. "This was the counsel of cowardice."

"All this time," Maman said, "you've been striving so hard to be what we wanted and we've been so proud, Ophélie, *so* proud. But we've never thought enough of you, or your real needs."

"No! Maman, Papa, this isn't your fault." I closed my eyes. "It's mine."

"Foolish girl." She pulled me against her and kissed my head. "To think you're alone. To think you must bear your burdens in silence. That's what family is for. There's no fault here, no blame, except ours."

"Come. Tell us," Papa said. "Share this burden. Then we can decide what we must do together, as a family."

I couldn't hide things from them now, but twice I started and stopped; the feeling I was betraying my birth family was squeezing my throat.

I tried for the third time, but at that point there was a knock at the front door and Jade let someone in.

"A moment. I'll send him away, whoever it is." Papa went out.

But the visitor didn't leave. Instead, Papa came back with Chief of Police Meulnes, who looked very grim.

Chapter 17

"I'm sorry to disturb you at this difficult time, but you see, I have a profound problem," Chief Meulnes said, once we were all seated again. "Mam'selle, I'm sure there is a good explanation for what you did on Boulevard Charner, but unfortunately, already it has been reported to me that people are saying this was a protest against the government and the legal system."

"That is ridiculous!" Maman said, glaring at him.

She voiced the anger I felt. An anger that as Ophélie, a young lady in polite society, I was not supposed to show. I struggled to restrain the part of me that was still Bian. That my love for my sister, my guilt, my fears, my grief should be thought by others to be no more than play-acting for some stupid political statement was almost more than I could bear.

"I agree," Meulnes replied. "A foolish rumor. Nevertheless, we must counter it."

"But a child, upset at—"

Meulnes held up his hand to stop her. "Not any child, Madame. Not even really a child any longer. A young lady at a formative age. And also the adopted Annamese daughter of the man who is governing

Cochinchina. She is in a unique position, greatly visible, with a corresponding potential to do harm."

"She had no intention of harming anyone, and it had nothing to do with the government of the colony," Papa said, his voice clipped and controlled.

"Of course. As I said, these words are a foolish rumor," Meulnes responded. "But I most strongly recommend, Monsieur Beauclerc, that I am able to leave here with a statement of facts that will satisfy our friends, and stop our enemies making anything more of this." He shifted uncomfortably. "Among other matters, as you know, the whole colony is anxiously awaiting the arrival of the *Victorieuse,* perhaps bearing the determinations of our future."

Chief Meulnes rose to his feet, apparently unable to contain himself. He took a position in front of the windows, facing us.

"Already there is unrest," he said, waving his hands. "On top of that, I must now report to you in your position as acting governor: I have come directly from an emergency meeting with Colonel Durand. Just one hour ago he received telegraphic orders from the Ministère de la Marine to place his regiment at the highest level of alert, short of martial law. All leave has been cancelled. I understand formal notification is now being copied to your office. No explanation has been forthcoming."

"This is outrageous!" Papa said. "We must question the Quai d'Orsay immediately. By what authority—"

"Monsieur, naturally we have tried to get further explanations by telegraph and we find that communications with Paris have been closed. As have connections with Hué and Tonkin. After the last orders to the Colonel, neither the Ministère de la Marine nor the Quai d'Orsay is available to enlighten us."

He cleared his throat.

"As you know, this sort of information about the Marines cannot be kept secret and it will be like throwing dry timber onto the firestorm of rumors about the mission of the *Victorieuse.* Monsieur Beauclerc, we must defuse as many of these rumors as we can to prevent the flames getting out of control."

"But the Marines on alert?" Maman said. "And more troops coming with the *Victorieuse.* What on earth is happening, Zacharie? Do they think there's going to be a revolt?"

"Absolutely not." Papa dismissed that. "If it were that sort of trouble, we would be the first to know. And besides, there would be a full deployment of troops and calling up reserves, not a single extra battalion sent from France and diverted up to Hué. No, it's a precaution, or a show of strength, but for what?"

"Indeed," Meulnes said, rocking on his heels. "It must be a precaution, but that will not be the calm assumption that will spread in the rumors. So you see my point, it is so very important that nothing adds to this."

He put his arms behind his back and looked meaningfully at me. "Even an action that was entirely innocent."

Maman and Papa also turned to me, and my heart sank.

It was one thing to screw up my courage and speak the painful truth to them. It was something else to say the same things in front of the Chief of Police.

"It is your decision, my daughter," Papa came to my defense. "Only if you feel you can tell us."

Chief Meulnes scowled, but said nothing.

"This story may be a danger to other people," I said to them, my voice very small, "if it's heard outside this room."

They all frowned.

"Oh, come on," Meulnes said.

Papa glared at him and he shut up.

Once I started, it just poured out. I began with my birth parents, their full names and the high position my father had held. The false accusations about the funds for the Emperor's mausoleum. The trial. My parents' friends deserting them, everyone terrified of the contagion of bad joss. My family's disgrace and ruin. Being born on a sampan on the Arroyo Chinois. Then the rumors about my father and the mausoleum funds. The gangs searching for us in Khánh Hôi.

"The disgraced mandarin and the Emperor's gold!" Meulnes, still standing, grunted quietly and nodded, his mouth turned down. "This, I have heard."

My mother kept pressing my hand between hers.

I continued with the tale. The escape to Ap Long. A life of planting rice in paddy fields.

Then it got harder. The renewed threat from Bác Thảo. My parents' desperate plan. And the arrival of Madame Cao in Ap Long.

"I can see now," I said, my head bowed in shame. "The villagers in Ap Long knew what Cao really was. But they didn't say! They didn't want anything to do with us. Like my parents' friends in Saigon, they didn't want to catch our bad luck by helping us."

I had to struggle to keep going. "My father and mother, my brothers … I'm sure they didn't know. They believed she was going to be a maid and the money my parents received was a share of the recruitment fee. But now I understand, my sister knew," I whispered, pausing to take a shaky breath. "Nhung knew and yet she didn't say anything because my parents needed the money for the second part of their plan. She didn't say anything because she thought her sacrifice would let me escape."

My heart ached and my eyes stung, but I made myself go on.

The return to Saigon. Buying clothes for me. The pretense of hiring clothes for my parents to make them look well off. The lies about my father's employment in the north, when the real plan was for them to travel to Hué. Then the *Victorieuse*, bringing rumors of changes in the mandarinate that might return my family to where Bác Thảo could threaten them again. The ledger of appointments in Hué I'd borrowed from the library in a vain search for mentions of my father.

I didn't speak about the *Salayar*, or the Bugis captain who'd given me the idea about the ledger. I didn't speak about the kris in my bedroom and the warnings about the Tò Dara, or my suspicions about Père St Cyprien. I needed to keep it as simple as possible. Although Chief Meulnes had listened without much interruption, I knew, from his expression, I'd already said things that he didn't believe.

Papa saw it too, and demanded he explain.

"Very well, Monsieur." Meulnes put his hands behind his back and tilted himself forward like a schoolteacher in his class. "I have no doubt that Monsieur Trang and his family were chased from Khánh Hôi by a gang, and that a gang eventually discovered that they were hidden in Ap Long. Maybe it was even the same gang. But this 'Lord of Thieves', this 'Bác Thảo'; he doesn't really exist. He is the Annamese bogeyman. They blame Bác Thảo for everything: if they can't pay their debts, it's Bác Thảo's fault; if they steal something, it's because Bác Thảo told them to."

He shook his head in exasperation, his voice rising. "The tales of Bác Thảo go back years. He is ageless, and to listen to these tales is to fall into a tangle of myth: Bác Thảo is Moi, from the mountain tribes, a sorcerer of course, like many of the Moi, and he can change his shape by this sorcery. Oh, yes! He becomes a tiger at night! This is the man we must arrest for the killings in Khánh Hôi yesterday!" He sighed and raised his hands in exasperation. "I regret that Monsieur Gosselin has now spread this ridiculousness to the French community."

He started rocking on his heels again, his leather boots squeaking quietly.

It was clear that neither Maman nor Papa liked the way he was speaking and he retreated a little.

"I apologize," he said, more calmly. "I do not wish to be rude. However, as Chief of Police, I am very well aware that we have a surfeit of gangs in Khánh Hôi. We have street thugs. We have the Chinese and Annamese 'societies'. We have Tongs and Triads. They are inevitable here in the Orient, and sufficient to keep my men thoroughly occupied. We do not need a 'tiger-sorcerer' as well."

"I see no need for anything about this Bác Thảo, or false accusations of stolen gold to be any part of what we say about this," Maman said. "Nor any unnecessary details about Ophélie's birth family."

"Incidentally, this is the first we've heard of this," Papa said.

"And it makes absolutely no difference to us," Maman said immediately.

Meulnes nodded. "But of course, that is your private matter, Madame. For me, I am required only to speak to the governor, or acting governor." He made a little bow and gesture in Papa's direction. "So, by definition, I will not tell others any of your family's private matters. There remains, however, the public matter. We have a decision to make, of how much of this should be the official version. The background? Well, it lends much credence to the story of why your daughter ran up to the guillotine."

I looked up at Meulnes. "I just wanted to ask her where Nhung was."

I could not bear to look at Maman and Papa.

Papa rose as well now, and started pacing the length of the room.

"We say simply that Ophélie thought this woman, Cao, should be made to say where her victims had been sold, and to whom," he said. "Make a mention of some family member kidnapped. A relative. A distant cousin."

Meulnes made a thoughtful humming noise without actually agreeing.

"And this, I believe, now calls for an initiative from the government on policing of these kinds of matters." Papa stopped and took up a matching posture opposite Meulnes, arms behind his back.

Meulnes stopped his rocking and went very still. He cleared his throat again. "I see," he said.

"The law has rightly shown that these crimes are unacceptable in any section of society, but that is wasted unless it is reinforced with action," Papa said. "Madame Cao's collaborators must be brought to justice, and they must be required to reveal those who purchased slaves through this disgusting enterprise, or they will face even harsher sentences. Once we have those connections, the police will follow them to their utmost ends. We will rid Cochinchina of any stain of slavery, sexual or otherwise."

"Monsieur, this is laudable," Meulnes held up his hands as if to ward off the pressure from Papa. "But this is hardly the time for this initiative. The colony is in a state of alert. The *Victorieuse* is expected at any time, and carries orders that we cannot anticipate. Beyond that, there are practical considerations of police budget and manpower. This is not to mention enormous difficulties with cultural differences and expectations in the various races throughout the colony."

"I understand your concerns, Chief Meulnes." Papa was equally adamant. "I allow there must be a consideration of practicality and timing, but a colony though this may be, it is also part of France. Ultimately, there must be one law for all."

"Monsieur." Meulnes bowed his head. The Chief of Police took orders from the governor; there was a point where that was the end of it.

"As to the rest," Papa said, "I would request that we all carry on as normal. When asked, we give the barest details—that we should indeed have taken more information from this criminal to help prevent other crimes like hers."

He fixed Meulnes with his eyes. "You and I will meet shortly and discuss the detail of our plans in this regard."

Meulnes took his dismissal and left, bowing to us politely, even if his face told a different story.

Papa checked his pocket watch.

"I must return to the office," he said. "Meulnes is a difficult man, but determined and thorough. I think good things may come of this. As for us, we put this behind us."

"As far as everything else is concerned, yes," Maman agreed. She'd not let go of my hand the entire time. "But it breaks my heart to think of your sister, Ophélie."

I started to apologize again for everything.

"What can we do, Zacharie?" Maman said, stopping me. "It will take some time for you and Meulnes to get the police to start searching, and he's right, there are constraints."

Papa frowned and stared at his shoes in thought. "There's a team of inspectors working in the Customs Department, the Opium Regie. Regulating the opium business, essentially." He grimaced in distaste. "They're not policemen, of course, but they have rights to enter and search premises."

"Will there be a problem about using them?"

"Well, it'll need to be set up carefully. Riossi will help me in exchange for some consideration for his concerns." Papa tried to speak neutrally, but the set of his jaw told me what he thought of Riossi's concerns. He went on, his eyes focused in the distance, his voice becoming more thoughtful. "It must be seen to be about all the victims, not just Ophélie's sister. Once it gets going, we'll also need accommodation for the women, even if it's temporary; we can't just turn them out onto the streets. Food, clothes, practicalities like that. Maybe the Sisters can help. Then some way of communicating with their families." He stroked his jaw in silence for a while. "It's an enormous project, but it's entirely justified, and I think it can be done."

"It was what I thought I might ask of you for my birthday present, Papa: to find Nhung. I know it's too much. I know. But there is nothing else I could possibly want, not while there's a chance that Nhung is …" I couldn't go on, and Maman squeezed my hand again. "Please, just find her, and free her."

"We will do better than that," Maman said firmly. "Zacharie, we must adopt Nhung."

I gasped.

"Of course," Papa said, as if there'd never been any doubt. "There is no other solution."

He left, and I lay for a long time with my head against Maman, hardly daring to believe how lucky I was.

Chapter 18

Carry on as normal. The next day was my Mandarin lesson at Yi Song's house in Cholon. With the Chief of Police's comments about unrest, I half-expected to be kept at home. However, a note from Monsieur Song had arrived reassuring my parents it would be safe, and stating I would be met at the tram stop and escorted.

I wasn't entirely sure whether I felt relieved or not. I didn't want to leave the safety of the house, where no one could see me and ask me about the execution, and yet there *was* a reason I wanted to go to Cholon. One that was nothing to do with learning Mandarin.

So I set off, feeling nauseous with apprehension. How many people I passed would know it had been me at the execution? What would they think?

I didn't really want to meet my friends, not even Manon. They'd be full of questions, or worse, they'd shy away from me.

As ever, Jade was close behind me. As ever, silent and radiating unhappiness.

I tried to ignore her and concentrate instead on the gentle hiss of the southerly wind as it blew through the leaves of the trees that lined the roads. It brought the smells of the old market to me: food and people, spices and incense.

I took the side streets to avoid walking down Boulevard Charner. The roads were less busy that way, though it still felt as if everyone was looking at me.

The tram to Cholon went from a station next to the Arroyo Chinois, beyond the market, so it wasn't possible to stay on quiet streets the whole way. My mouth felt dry as we walked past the three great open-sided halls of the old market, but the only voices that called out to me were street sellers naming their wares and prices.

Another time, I might have paused, but every shouted *Mam'selle* felt as if it might lead to questions about Boulevard Charner. So instead, I walked quicker, sure that there were eyes following me until we arrived at the tram station. I bought tickets for Jade and me. We had timed it well. We got on board straight away and sat together silently for the brief journey to Cholon.

The change from the center of Saigon was always startling.

The name Cholon meant *big market*, and that described it well. Instead of broad European-style boulevards and trees, shops and cafés, there were old, narrow streets, mazy, with storerooms that doubled as shops and homes. Every building seemed to sell something, and peasant traders sold on the roadside from woven baskets they'd carried in from their farms. The streets were crisscrossed with canals, some wide and thick with sampans and junks, others smelly, choked with silt and spanned by humpbacked little bridges.

Cholon was busy and loud and colorful and noisy. To French eyes, it was rough. Certainly, much of what the administration did not want to see in the center of Saigon ended up here. French people didn't come to Cholon during the day. During the night, only French men would come, looking for gambling, drink, opium and other nighttime entertainment. Ophélie was out of place here. Jade, in her smart white tunic and trousers, also looked as if she didn't belong. She'd been unhappy in the center of Saigon. If I could see a difference in the level of her unhappiness, I would say that Jade was more unhappy now, in Cholon.

Qingzhao was waiting for me at the tram station, alone. I was surprised. I'd expected some of Monsieur Song's servants, but his daughter evidently thought her presence was enough. Certainly, she would be known in Cholon, I reasoned, and there would be few people who would want to offend Yi Song.

Qingzhao didn't bother to greet me in French—we were immediately talking in Mandarin, and not the direct, informal way that Monsieur Song used, but the layered and decorative language of the court.

"Could we pass by the temple of Quan Yin?" I asked her once the formal and elaborate welcome was complete.

She studied me solemnly as we began to walk.

"The Goddess of Mercy hears the cries of the whole world," she said. "You don't need to visit her temple to pray. She hears the murmurs of every heart."

"The lady hears everyone, everywhere, but I do not," I replied, trying out Monsieur Song's manner of turning questions aside obliquely.

She actually smiled, as brief as a flash of sunlight on water, but she changed direction and we headed for the temple, continuing to talk in Mandarin.

My mood lifted as we went. Whether it was because I was concentrating on speaking Mandarin, or because Cholon didn't care what went on in Saigon, or even that I was with Qingzhao, I didn't know, but the feeling of being watched so closely felt much less here.

The part of me that was Ophélie was still out of place. But the part that remained Bian, on the other hand, loved Cholon and relaxed a touch. Foolish, given that the streets of Saigon should be much safer for a young lady.

The route to the temples took us through a lane of roadside food sellers, where the air was thick with the acrid smoke of small coal braziers, fanned over the passing crowds. Cooks shouted out their specialties and prices. We were jostled as we walked, but it was only that everyone was so busy and intent on their business. I managed to smile when I heard Jade swear in Cantonese behind me, as someone trod on her toes.

At the end of that lane was the spice store where my parents had left me with my brothers while they made the final preparations for my adoption. Seeing my discreet interest in the store, Qingzhao paused in the shade of their awning to see how many of their spices I could name in Mandarin.

The store was owned by the same men, but their eyes passed over me without recognition, of course.

Then, with our journey resumed, a few minutes later we were in the temple district. There was more space here; it was an oasis in the relentless churn of Cholon.

Qingzhao and Jade sat at the entrance to the temple, in the shade, letting me walk on alone into the broad forecourt.

On the inner wall of the forecourt stood a statue of the goddess. Her tranquil gaze looked down over many worshippers; she was a popular goddess. Next to her was the door into the main temple.

But I wasn't here to pray.

In the middle of the forecourt, apparently the object of the goddess' contemplation, was an old crumbling limestone wall, standing alone. It was about twenty meters from end to end. It had originally been intended as a spirit wall—a feature to prevent evil spirits from directly entering the temple. Maybe it still fulfilled that function, tatty as it looked. The community repaired and re-plastered it every year, yet within days it looked again like it did now, almost as if it were alive with the wings of a thousand birds. It had become a prayer wall; pinned to it with small iron nails, practically covering it, were pieces of paper, all fluttering in the breeze.

It had many names. The French called it the Wall of Petitions. Across the top, out of reach of most people, monks had written their name for it in broad Chinese ideograms—'Words in the Wind'. Every time they repaired the wall, they rewrote the name, and every time, someone added something. This time, they'd made it read like a Chinese poem.

Prayers; words lost in the wind.
Yet hope rises like the sun.

I blinked and my throat felt tight, but I had no time to dawdle. I started scanning the little papers, trying not to read the heartbreaking words.

"May I help, young lady?" An old beggar bowed by my elbow. He spoke in formal Annamese. His tunic was threadbare, but clean, and his face darkened by the sun. His thin hair was neatly tied back with a bow. An old clerk who'd lost his position, maybe, and who now made a pittance reading for those who could not. Normally, there would be two or three like him, offering to help in return for alms.

Still, did I look as if I couldn't read?

"Thank you, Uncle, but no." I pressed some centimes into his hands and returned to searching.

Saigon and Cholon were huge and sprawling, growing every year. They met like two big rivers running together, churning where they touched, but Saigon was stronger, pushing the boundary back year by year. Poor people built ramshackle houses wherever they could, and not a month passed without some area being cleared of them, often without warning, for Saigon's relentless expansion. Families were split, people went missing, newcomers searched for relatives. Here, they posted their desperate calls, in among the sad petitions for help from the goddess: the son who'd fallen ill; the father who wouldn't stop spending his money on opium; and the landlord who was cruel.

The last things my elder brother Lanh had said to me on the night I was adopted were whispered instructions on how to check and speak the words in the wind in our own secret way.

A way he'd learned from Nhung.

He'd said it would mean that, however far apart we became, we'd never be lost to each other if we could visit here.

Each little page was a prayer, the monks said. With each flutter, the prayer flew up to the goddess. Surely one would come back down to me.

I'd visited Cholon with Papa, and managed to persuade him to bring me here to the temple on just four occasions in the five years since I'd been adopted.

I had used those opportunities to look for messages, but I hadn't really believed there would be anything. I'd thought the rest of my family were in Hué, and Nhung was a maid in Saigon somewhere. That I'd be more likely to find her in the old market by the tram station.

The guilt of not understanding what had happened to her was like ice in my blood.

All that time—

"I can help you search."

I looked at the beggar again. Maybe it had been a mistake to give him money before I went looking. On the other hand, four eyes are better than two, and I couldn't take too long.

"Find me a prayer with *zhèngdào* at the top." I sketched it in the dust to make sure he understood. "With the rest of the message in Annamese."

"The right path." He murmured the translation of the ideogram, and his broad forehead wrinkled. "Most unusual." Then he shrugged and shuffled to the far end of the wall to start looking.

Anyone could see the prayers, and if they saw one from my birth family, that news could make its way to Bác Thảo, so Nhung had told Lanh that any message we left had to be cryptic.

At least I could ignore any that didn't have zhèngdào at the top.

But there were no messages waiting for me under the ideogram for zhèngdào. I met my beggar helper in the middle of the wall. He turned his mouth down and shook his head.

With a sigh, I pulled out a message I'd written at home.

It was in the code I'd been told to use: Chief Meulnes had *not* persuaded me Bác Thảo didn't exist; quite the opposite.

Could it work?

If Lanh had got the code right … *if* Nhung was ever allowed out … *if* she managed to get here in the next few days before the message was covered by others or blurred by rain …

I realized that the hope that she would see my message grew smaller with every *if*, but I had to try.

Under the zhèngdào character, I had written two simple lines in Annamese.

> *Beloved elder sister, come back to me.*
> *There is no night so dark that dawn will not follow.*

There were many others who wanted to use the wall, but finally I was able to give my message and donation to one of the monks. He picked a piece of paper that had faded away in the sun and replaced it with mine. I watched as it started fluttering, one lonely wing beating in a whole frantic flock. Feeling foolish, I tried to steer it on its way with a half-remembered prayer to Quan Yin.

The beggar clerk was still at my elbow, reading my prayer. "Maybe tomorrow," he said, and pointed at the line written along the top of the wall. "Hope rises like the sun."

He smiled, making his face compress into a net of wrinkles, fine as a spider's web. I felt sorry for him; he couldn't have been long in his current state of poverty—his teeth were good, his eyes were still clear, and he seemed in remarkably good spirits.

My street instinct, the Bian side of me, had a different reaction, but I dismissed it. I couldn't see enemies in every face that passed me by.

I gave him a few more centimes and hurried back to the patient Qingzhao.

Chapter 19

"I'm sorry that took so long," I said as we continued through Cholon.

"No matter," she said, waving to dismiss it. "It's busy. She's always popular. It's human nature; we feel we have to appeal for favor to the gods and goddesses, but unfortunately we know what we really deserve, so we beg Quan Yin for mercy, and not Quan Ti for justice."

I laughed. It was true, the God of Justice was very fierce, and his temple was much less visited than the Goddess of Mercy's.

For the fifteen minutes it took to get clear of the tangle of Cholon streets, we spoke about the Confucian puzzle of the meaning of justice as seen by two people on the opposing sides of an argument.

It was a relief to enter Yi Song's house, but only because it was cool. The language lesson continued without break.

Jade left us, and we walked on into the main courtyard, sitting down in the shade beside the pools of languid carp, where silent servants brought us fragrant jasmine tea in the shade of the Hoa Sua trees.

I tried to be careful and drink politely, mirroring Qingzhao. I had always been rather nervous of her, and unsure of what she thought of me.

There was no time to dwell on that—she continued our conversation relentlessly, leaping from subject to subject. Even when we had a break, and stood to do some of her leisurely Chinese exercises, she still spoke Mandarin, instructing me in how to follow her movements.

I was exhausted in mind and body when it came time to collect Jade and return home.

"It has been an interesting morning," Qingzhao said, on the walk back to the tram, as we approached the station.

Then she finally relented and spoke in French. "You continue to make excellent progress."

"Thank you. As you say, a very interesting morning. Will I be meeting you for the next lesson, or will Monsieur Song send a note to arrange it?"

"No need for that." She smiled, and her eyes flicked to one side. With a start, I was suddenly aware he himself had joined us.

He greeted me in Mandarin, and I groaned internally. Apparently, my lesson wasn't over yet.

Monsieur Song and I boarded and sat together on the tram. Jade followed and sat across from us, staring out of the window.

"It's fortunate that Jade speaks no Mandarin at all," he said. "I have something important to tell you, which you will want to keep secret."

I blinked. "Lǎoshī?"

What was this?

"You face enemies. However, I suspect you look for them in the wrong places and as a result, there are some you don't see at all."

We had never spoken like this in our lesson. I felt a spike of fear.

"I don't understand."

"No." He cleared his throat. "You visited the Quan Yin temple this morning, and left a prayer on the Words in the Wind."

I'd been with Qingzhao all day, but he could have heard that from his servants who'd spoken to Jade.

"Yes," I replied. "A message rather than a prayer."

"A message to whom?"

Should I explain about my birth family?

I trusted Yi Song, and he was a friend of the family as well as my tutor.

"My sister," I said. I hesitantly began to explain about my family, but he held up his hand to stop me. His features softened.

"I am sure I can predict much of your tale from what I know already. Let us discuss it at the next lesson." He sighed. "Today, I am only accompanying you on the tram journey, and there is merely time for a warning on a different matter."

"What warning, Lǎoshī?"

"Words in the Wind is used by many families who are looking for each other, as you and your sister are. However, cryptic messages placed there have other uses. For example, those that wish to regain control of this country from the French by force use it to communicate without meeting."

I gasped. I remembered my brother Lanh's enthusiasm for the mysterious rebel groups up in Tonkin. But surely there was no sympathy for them here, down in the south?

"The Black Flags?" I guessed. What did this have to do with me?

Monsieur Song shook his head. "They are long gone, but others have taken their place. The important thing is that the French know about them, and they watch the wall."

"But it's just a message for my sister."

"And it's clearly in some sort of code. It could mean anything. They look for such messages."

"I can't believe—" I stopped. "The beggar clerk!"

I should have followed my instincts with him.

Monsieur Song nodded. "An informant of the Deuxième Bureau."

My jaw fell. This wasn't just the police—it was the sinister secret service agency.

And he was saying that I was a subject of their suspicion.

My fury drove out the shock. I wanted to scream with rage. It was bad enough for Chief Meulnes to come and tell me some people were speculating that my running up to the guillotine had been a political statement. Now France's security forces thought my attempts at finding my sister were a danger to the colony.

"I shall go straight to Papa and—"

"No! Please calm yourself," Song said. "It would do no good to discuss this with Monsieur Beauclerc. The Deuxième Bureau does not answer to the colonial administration."

He raised his hands in exasperation. "In fact, the way these organizations work, I believe it would make things *worse* if your father were to make representations on your behalf. They would become more suspicious of you, and of your father as well."

Worse and worse. Papa's unstinting efforts for all the people of the colony should have made him above suspicion. Now stupid rumors about me ...

And of course, the Deuxième Bureau will hear the rumors that Meulnes reported as well. They will see these as proving ...

"So this faceless bureau can come here," I snarled, "answerable to no one, not under the control of the administration, they can form ridiculous, unfounded suspicions and start investigations of anyone —"

"Mademoiselle Beauclerc," he interrupted sharply, "you are not 'anyone'. Please, be calm."

The Bian part of me subsided. His rebuke was well aimed. Ophélie Beauclerc had duties and responsibilities, and had to act in a way that Bian would not want to.

Silenced temporarily, I glanced at Jade, and was relieved to see she'd fallen asleep and heard nothing of our conversation or the tone in which I'd spoken.

Still seething inside, I folded my trembling hands in my lap, looked down, and spoke meekly. "What should I do then, Lǎoshī?"

No one else witnessed it, but I was well aware I had also been disrespectful to my tutor in letting my anger show. My meek voice was part of my apology.

"Do nothing," he said, his voice kindly. "The Bureau is too busy to spend time on a single obscure message, no matter how unusual your position in the colony. However, I would strongly counsel that you do not visit the wall again."

It had always been unlikely that a message on the wall would reach Nhung. I knew that. But knowing it did not lessen the frustration and anger I felt that, for the second time in two days, I might be accused of somehow rebelling against the colony.

That my innocent actions might damage Papa's authority in Cochinchina.

And that, remote a chance as it was, another way to find Nhung was closed to me.

But Monsieur Song was not finished.

"I will make sure that the message is replaced regularly and any response comes to you discreetly," he said. "Please, keep this our secret."

"Thank you, Lǎoshī!" I looked up. "But wait, won't that attract suspicion to the person who visits the wall?"

111

He smiled. "The agents of the Deuxième Bureau are clever, but they also overlook what is always before their eyes."

I recognized that was one of his replies that responded to a question without really answering it. Would the monks help him? There was no point in pursuing it; he would only get more obscure.

"Thank you," I repeated instead.

He smiled.

However, the Bian side of me refused be completely silent. I went back to something he'd said earlier. "You said 'enemies', Lǎoshī. Where else should I be looking?"

The tram began to slow with a squeal, then came to a juddering halt. We were at the terminal already.

He stood and ushered me out.

"The answer to that is complex," he said, "and deserves a long and uninterrupted discussion. Your next Mandarin lesson will provide an excellent opportunity."

I didn't say what I was thinking—that it would certainly be more interesting and important a discussion for me than shipping, trade and banking.

"I will send a note to your house, arranging for us to meet again in two days," he went on. "In the meantime, concentrate on your family here, and on the events in Saigon. You should definitely not spend your time worrying about matters such as the Tò Dara, which are no threat to you."

Oh!

There was no time to pursue that. He bowed his farewell and I had to match him.

As he walked away, a pair of street urchins joined him, trotting to keep up with his long strides.

I had to laugh as he produced a little white packet of pastries for them to share, like a conjurer.

And it suddenly struck me that his earlier words might have been much more informative than I had thought at the time. What would be easier for most people to overlook than a street urchin? Even the Deuxième Bureau.

Was there a reason he befriended the urchins? Did he have a network of unseen little spies?

On the other hand, I was stubbornly not going to agree with his dismissal of the Tò Dara. He might think that a civilized French mademoiselle should not be paying attention to a Bugis myth, but however I appeared to the world in my elegant French dresses, with my maid following me like a shadow, I was not that far removed from a street urchin myself. Bian still lurked inside me, and street urchins survived by trusting their sense for danger. I'd just had a lesson in the folly of ignoring that sense with the beggar clerk who was really an agent for the security police. I wouldn't make the same mistake dismissing the Tò Dara, even if my tutor said that other enemies were more threatening.

How many enemies did I have?

How did Monsieur Song know more of them that I did?

And why?

I gave myself a mental shake and began the walk home, barely noticing that Jade was behind me.

It looked as if it would be the most interesting Mandarin lesson ever in two days' time, but I felt overwhelmed with everything. It threatened to become too much. It was time to concentrate on what I knew *now* and what I could do *now*.

For Nhung: even with Yi Song's help, the Words in the Wind were never going to be a sure way to contact my sister, but Papa had already concluded an agreement with Monsieur Riossi of the Opium Regie. As part of their normal work in visiting opium dens, the Regie's inspectors would look for women who'd been kidnapped or who were being kept as slaves.

What could I do to help?

Papa had once told me he never relied on orders transmitted by impersonal letters through the branches of the administration, especially important ones. He made a point of meeting the people who would need to carry out those orders.

I should do that with the Opium Regie inspectors. As soon as possible. It was too late today, but I'd seek them out tomorrow.

And for the rest of my birth family: if I was going into the colonial offices tomorrow, then I could also ask Papa for access to the government's internal library, where I could find the latest information from Hué on the mandarinate.

A thought struck me as I walked away from the tram station. After so long being unable to progress, suddenly, I had clear aims that would take me steps closer to rescuing Nhung and finding out what was happening with my family. There was a sense that clouds were lifting, and progress could be made, which allowed a feeling of hope, followed by a real belief.

I would do this. All that was required would be work and patience.

And above it all, I felt a tremendous relief; the weight of lies that had been crushing me was lifted.

My adoptive family knew the truth about my birth family, and they hadn't thrown me out. Quite the reverse.

Contemplating this wonderful good fortune drove out the anger that had threatened to engulf me when I learned that the secret service spied on the Words in the Wind.

I was so bound up in these happy thoughts and the dazzling anticipation of genuine progress that I completely lost awareness of my surroundings.

Chapter 20

"Mam'selle!" Jade called out urgently from behind me.

I looked up and I was surrounded by a mixture of people from the market. Chinese and Annamese, Malabar and Singh, traders, merchants, peasants and fishermen. *Lots* of them. More even than the busiest of Cholon. They were pushing, looking over their shoulders toward the market, trotting hastily away from it, and as my head came up, some signal seemed to spark through the crowd. Like a flock of startled birds suddenly taking flight, they began to run, to surge and jostle in panic. In moments, there was no possibility of moving anywhere but the direction the crowd was going, no possibility of thinking about anything but keeping my feet.

To fall would be to die in the stampede.

They were as rough as the mob that had watched the execution, but unlike them, they were moving in a direction, like water from a burst dam they fled from the market.

Just as I thought I would fall and be trampled, we exploded out from the narrow side road onto the wide Boulevard Charner and the pressure eased. I managed to get out of the most frantic stream, but I couldn't see Jade. I couldn't see *anyone* I knew in the frightened faces around me.

What on earth is happening?

A black-clad arm reached out and held me, pulled me sideways into the shelter of a doorway.

I screamed in shock, but no one from the crowd spared me so much as a glance.

I screamed a second time as I looked up into the face of the man who had pulled me out of the flow: Père St Cyprien.

"Mam'selle Beauclerc," he said solemnly. "Are you injured?"

"No," I managed to say, shaking from head to foot. "Just startled."

Was this the tall man that the captain of the *Salayar* had meant? Was the priest Tó Dara? A blood-sucking, soulless monster?

Monsieur Song said there was no danger. He *hadn't* said there were no Tó Dara, and how could he be sure that there was no danger?

If there *were* Tó Dara, who was it? Who had the Bugis captain seen on the dock?

Even with a lack of other candidates to suspect, I couldn't be sure about the priest. The Bian part of me sensed something dangerous about St Cyprien, but not enough to make the Ophélie part forget her manners.

"Thank you, Père," I said, with a bob of my head. "What's happening? Why are they running?"

"I don't know," he replied, "but you're safe here with me."

Not safe, my street sense contradicted him.

St Cyprien looked even more pale and haggard than ever, those features always accentuated by his stern black cassock. His face floated above the white collar, dominated by his large nose and his bushy gray eyebrows. His eyes were a watery blue. He habitually squinted against the sun, even here, in the shade cast by the buildings. His eyes were restless, continually passing over my face and then sweeping the area around us before returning.

He licked his lips, hurriedly, like one of the tree lizards. "That was a brave thing you did at the execution."

I flinched at the reference, but I would have to talk about it to someone eventually, and here we were, not a minute's walk from where the guillotine had stood. I shuddered.

"It was foolish, Père. I just thought she might say where all her victims had gone. I mean, right at the end, when she was standing in front of the guillotine. I thought …" I stuttered and left the sentence dangling.

He nodded, as if it wasn't foolish at all. "It was a good thought, and a Christian impulse."

His Adam's apple bobbed up and down nervously. "The considerations of men and women change when they are faced by their imminent mortality," he said.

He spoke quietly, and I had to lean forward to hear him.

"Death speaks to us all in our last moments. I believe that to be condemned to death and facing your imminent execution is, strangely, somewhat similar to a state of grace. Thinking becomes clearer. The Devil's temptations and diversions are put aside."

As he spoke those words, he looked as if he'd forgotten me and everything else around him. His face relaxed.

Then he blinked and squinted again.

"Who knows?" He cleared his throat and continued. "Madame Cao might have recanted and given up her evil conspirators. Certainly, confession would have lightened her burden, and then it would have been a very good thing that you'd done, in the eyes of the people and the Church."

St Cyprien lifted his circular black hat and passed a trembling hand across his sweaty brow. "Your steps are slow, coming to the Church, my daughter."

We'd spoken about this before. I'd been brought up with a blend of Buddhism and Confucianism. I wasn't comfortable with that anymore, but neither did I feel ready to commit to the Catholic Church, despite attending with my parents.

When I didn't answer, he touched my arm and then withdrew his hand quickly, as if he'd found the contact painful.

"I will speak to your mother. Come and see me at the church," he said. "Mam'selle!"

It was Jade, and for once, I was enormously pleased to see her.

"Stupid people. Stupid army," she said. She explained what she'd heard: a minor scuffle between traders had resulted in an overanxious lieutenant leading his Marine squad into the market with their rifles ready. Everyone had assumed something terrible was happening.

It had all been for nothing. Already, people were drifting back to the market.

I thanked the priest for his help.

"Good day, Mam'selle," he said abruptly, turning to walk quickly away, his black robe flapping around his ankles.

There had been a dispensation for Catholic priests in Cochinchina to wear cooler white robes instead of black, but Maman told me St Cyprien wore the black as acknowledgment of, and atonement for, his sins.

I wondered what sins were included, and what sensible reasons I could give for keeping away from him, and never, ever being alone with him in his church, whatever he said to Maman.

Chapter 21

The nightmares came with renewed vigor in the next morning's pale pre-dawn.

I woke, sweaty and twisted in my sheets, struggling with questions which drifted like grey phantoms in the shadows of my room.

The suppressed and formless anguish about my birth family was now edged with a painful possibility; I might see them again. But how would they feel about me?

I didn't want to think what Nhung had gone through while I lived in comfort. Was *still* going through. My nightmares would flee with the dawn. Hers would only begin again.

How could I excuse how long it had taken to rescue her? Or my stupidity in not understanding what had really happened that last night in Ap Long? How would her awful experience have changed her?

What would she think of me? I was no longer simply Bian. What if Nhung didn't like Ophélie?

And my birth parents who had sold me, intending I would live in France. Would my remaining here in Saigon bring shame to them?

Shaken with nightmares, in the uncertain light, I couldn't call my mother's face clearly to mind. Or my father's. However strongly I tried to hold onto them, they were fading like dreams. In fact, when I thought of 'parents' now, I usually meant Papa and Maman.

I was no longer the Bian who cried silently at night so that others wouldn't see my weakness, but neither was I completely Ophélie. The next step in my life seemed to have so many different directions it could take.

One set of paths led me back to Bian. On the other set, my birth family's faces faded away to nothing, and I became entirely Ophélie. It weighed on me like a cold stone in my chest.

I sat sleepless at my window and watched the sky deepen into fiery rose. The sun floated up out of the east and the day rushed up on me, indifferent to my worries.

My plans had changed yesterday evening at dinner.

Papa had long promised that, when my Mandarin was good enough, I would have to exercise it in his office, where there were many jobs such as translating for trade delegations. I wasn't ready, but the world didn't wait on me. The government's interpreter had taken ill yesterday, on the very day an important trade delegation had arrived from Canton. They had no interpreter of their own, and a group of French merchants were eager to speak to them. I'd agreed as soon as Papa asked me.

It was still early when I accompanied him to the City Hall—so early the delegations had not arrived.

While I waited in the main hallway, I was surprised to see Emmanuela hurrying in.

"Oh, Ophélie, this is good luck," she said. "I was afraid I wouldn't be able to see you to say goodbye."

"No! What's happening, Emmanuela? Where are you going?"

We'd only just met and I really enjoyed her company. There was so much she'd done in her life, so many places she'd seen. I had so many things I wanted to ask her about.

"There's a Navy barge going up the Mekong. It may be the last for a while, and they've agreed to take me," she said. "I'm just in to register the journey. It's fortunate, really. Reliable transport is difficult to arrange, and this is my best chance to go and find my father."

"Of course." Despite my disappointment, I understood. "I'll miss you."

I knew, as Ophélie, I shouldn't like her so much. Too unconventional, too outgoing, too outrageous for polite society. All the things the Bian side of me liked, along with her breezy confidence and the spell she seemed able to cast over young men.

"I'll miss you, too." She smiled and drew me aside while others passed down the hall. "Now, I don't know if anyone has spoken to you about what happened on Boulevard Charner, but I want you to know that what you wanted to do was very noble. Don't let others tell you anything else."

So the official story had reached her ears. That was good and bad. Good that what Chief Meulnes considered would be acceptable had got out there quickly. Bad, because it wasn't the whole truth, and I hated that there were new lies I had to hide behind even with her. I really wanted to tell her the whole truth, before it came out in some other way.

I had the feeling that she would not judge me. Unlike many in Saigon.

There wasn't an opportunity now. The front doors opened to admit the Cantonese delegation, ushered in by the colonial official in charge of the meeting.

"*Ay! Ay! Adelante!* Good luck," Emmanuela whispered as we kissed cheeks.

Maybe when she returned, I would tell her the truth.

She bowed politely to the Cantonese.

"Take care," I said as she left to register her Mekong trip with some functionary in the building.

I turned my full attention to the delegation.

Oh, yes, good luck is what I need.

The group was clearly from the more traditional culture of mainland China. All of them were in glossy silk robes and ornate hats—the more senior, the more gorgeous. The important among them also grew their fingernails, and favored long Confucian beards. The whole group had deliberately blackened teeth. All these fashions had been described to me by Monsieur Song and Papa, along with the protocol of who I should talk to and how.

I hoped I could keep it all in mind.

I bowed deeply and was introduced by the French official.

He was nervous that the delegation would be offended because the Saigon administration didn't have a man available to translate, or that I wouldn't be capable. As it turned out, no one paid my gender any overt attention. On the other hand, the Cantonese spoke Mandarin so quickly and with such a heavy accent, within the first few minutes my stomach was already tied in knots and my hands were trembling.

At which point, Monsieur Gosselin arrived with three other French traders.

Oh, no!

I hadn't realized he would be in the meeting.

What if he starts talking about tiger demons?

But he was all business, and completely lucid, as if nothing had happened at the racecourse.

We moved to one of the airy meeting rooms and sat down. Monsieur Gosselin and the others wanted to talk business right away, and I had to restrain them while the Cantonese delegation were served tea and conversation consisted of polite observations about Saigon and Canton.

All too soon, that was over and the talk turned to trade opportunities.

Soon, I had no time to worry about him as I struggled to keep up. It was lucky that Monsieur Song and Qingzhao made their Mandarin discussions so difficult; it prepared me for the business negotiations I had to translate that morning.

By the time everyone declared themselves happy with the matters they had brought up, I felt shaky at the sustained effort.

"Mam'selle," one of the junior Cantonese tried out his French, "you speak Mandarin good, like teacher when I boy. In Canton. When I young boy learn Mandarin." He held his hand out to indicate a child's height. "You very correct, like teacher. Very clear."

He explained what he'd said to the others in Cantonese, and then again in Mandarin. The younger ones smiled. The leader nodded solemnly.

I took it as a great compliment, and the French merchants were pleased too. Monsieur Gosselin patted my hand. Everyone bowed, the junior members of the delegation tried out shaking hands with the French, and finally the two delegations went their separate ways.

As soon as they were out of sight, I collapsed ungracefully back on a chair.

Thank you, Lǎoshī. Thank you, Qingzhao. I have not disgraced myself, or your teaching.

Tempting as it was to sit there and relax, I couldn't dawdle.

Lunchtime was fast approaching and if I delayed, the Opium Regie inspectors would be out for hours. I could come back in the afternoon, but that was the time they usually conducted their inspections, and also the time I had mentally put aside to visit the government general documents library, where they stored the latest communications from Hué.

If I met with the inspectors this morning, I could have all afternoon to look through the lists of officials employed in the mandarinate or undertaking the examinations.

I walked quickly to the next building, the Customs office, where I found I was in luck—Messieurs Picardin and Valois, the Opium Regie inspectors, were in their office and available to see me.

The two men were amiable and bewhiskered, both rather overweight and slow moving. They clearly enjoyed talking, but they were also nervous about giving offence when they discussed what they would be doing.

"It will be easy to include this task, Mam'selle," Picardin said, "and we will likely get some results. You understand, many of the establishments we regulate as part of the opium licensing …" He paused and wobbled his hand, uncomfortable with what he had to say. "They are inclined to be diverse in the … ah … entertainments they offer."

"We apologize," Valois said. "This is not a topic we normally discuss with ladies."

"I understand. Please don't be concerned on my behalf. What you are doing is much more important than my modesty, Messieurs."

Picardin beamed.

"We are confident of success, if not immediately, then relatively soon," Valois said. "There is …" He hesitated and the pair of them exchanged a glance. Picardin made a moue with his expressive mouth and the tiniest nod for Valois to continue. "There is a new proposal to increase this small department. The addition of two gentlemen who have been languishing in the Department of Roads and an increase in the number of our Annamese assistants."

"Excellent news! I admit my surprise." I looked down modestly. "I hear so often of financial restrictions." Meaning that almost everyone petitioning Papa in my hearing was told that there was no more money until a new budget was introduced. A budget that would have to wait until the current governor recovered from his long illness, or a new governor was installed, or the *Victorieuse* brought some unexpected bounty.

From the corner of my eye, I saw another glance between them.

Intriguing.

"Yes ..." Picardin said, but there was a little shared shrug and they moved the conversation away from the funding.

I stayed and talked with them about the 'project' as they called it. Having got over the awkwardness of offending my modesty, they were delighted to have someone interested in what they did.

They knew the official version of why I'd been at the execution of Madame Cao, and obviously they knew Papa had requested their new task from Monsieur Riossi. They had been told, or deduced, that unspecified 'relatives' of mine might be among those kidnapped by Cao and her organization.

Giving them Nhung's name was out of the question. Everything else aside, however discreet they were, it would become plain that they were looking out for someone. Bác Thảo would hear. That would be dangerous for Nhung.

Instead, Papa's requirement was for them to collect all the names and submit them to the colonial office, where the reports would be copied to the documents library. The girls themselves would be taken and housed in temporary barracks with the Sisters of Saint Paul.

I would check every report and I would visit the sanctuary every day until we found Nhung. The inspectors assured me that, once the project was up to speed, they would be able to visit every opium den two or three times a year, and adding houses of prostitution would not delay them or compromise their primary task. The first complete sweep would be completed within a matter of months.

"Such hard work and such a large project," I said, as I prepared to leave, much later than I had thought I would. "You are to be commended for being willing to include this in your duties. I am most grateful to you both, and to Monsieur Riossi."

They shrugged, almost bashful now, as they followed me out and closed their office behind them.

"It's not so much," said Valois.

"And it needs doing, Mam'selle," said Picardin. "The new staff will help enormously. Thank goodness the funds ..."

He stopped and they both looked embarrassed.

Valois licked his lips and cleared his throat. "We know Monsieur Beauclerc doesn't approve of rumors, but in this instance ..."

"You will attend the Harvest Festival Ball of course, Mam'selle?" Picardin said.

"Yes, of course."

The Harvest Festival Ball was organized by the governor's staff. When they'd started the tradition, they'd chosen the name and the date to coincide with the Annamese festival Tết Trung Thu. That was a harvest celebration, but in addition, it was a festival for children, and in keeping with that, the Harvest Festival Ball was the only one of the governor's balls where younger people were also invited.

For my friends, it was the social highlight of the year. I was always there with Papa, and I got him to ensure my friends' families were on the invitation list.

"Well, then, you will know it soon," Picardin said. He leaned forward, tapped the side of his nose and whispered, "We heard yesterday. We will have a new governor announced at the ball, and that is why funds are suddenly to be made available."

I left the building in a daze, taking my leave of them on the steps, where Jade was waiting impatiently for me.

I walked back home with a spring in my step and a smile on my face.

Jade must have thought I'd been hit on the head and lost my wits.

But Papa would be governor, and then soon, *soon*, I would be reunited with Nhung. She would be free. I put aside my childish nighttime fears about whether she'd like me or not.

There was a letter for me waiting at home, from Alain Sévigny. I read it in the privacy of my bedroom. He had such beautiful writing. It was almost calligraphy, and I had to trace the characters with a finger, imagining the way his hand had moved to form them.

The letter itself was about the Harvest Festival Ball. Alain was thanking me for ensuring that the Sévignys got invitations. He hoped I didn't think it too forward for him to request a dance with me.

No, not at all.

I hadn't asked Papa to include the Sévignys with a mind to Alain being there. I was only trying to make sure that all my friends' families got invitations, and it would have been spiteful to exclude Chantal's.

I hadn't expected a letter of thanks from her, let alone from Alain.

Of course, he was just being polite.

I shouldn't read anything into it, I thought, as I traced the loops and curls of his words.

And nothing would come of it, certainly not if Chantal had her way.

Chapter 22

I already knew my Mandarin lesson the next day would be most unusual, but even that anticipation did not prepare me for what happened.

We started early. Monsieur Song sat with me in the dining room at Boulevard Bonnard and began by listening patiently while I explained the complex story of my birth family in Mandarin.

I was nervous, but I trusted him, otherwise I wouldn't have been saying anything. I trusted him more than I trusted Meulnes, and so I also told him about the meeting with the Chief of Police and what had been said there.

Song had a different kind of knowledge about Cochinchina, about things the French dismissed because they didn't fit into the accepted European view of the world. Things like hô con quỷ, the tiger demons. Did he believe in them? Would he confirm that they were here, in Saigon? Was Bác Thảo real? Was he a tiger demon? Could Song help me? Would he?

When I fell silent at the end, he leaned back and sighed.

"Chief Meulnes is not a fool, but he is wrong this time," he said.

I felt relief. And a chill in my bones. "In what part?"

He didn't answer directly. Instead, he got up and walked to the windows.

As usual, during the day they were open and covered with gauze curtains.

He seemed unsure how to proceed. I'd never seen him like that before.

"He's wrong about much of what you already suspect." Monsieur Song waved his hand. "Not only is Bác Thảo real, but he's also the most powerful gang leader in Khánh Hôi, and I can assure you, he has not forgotten the stolen funds for the Emperor's mausoleum, nor has he forgotten the name of Trang."

"But it was all made up—nothing was stolen," I said, arguing against my own fears. "The mandarins didn't really believe in the theft, and that must be accepted now, otherwise why would my father believe it was possible to get back into the mandarinate?"

Monsieur Song pursed his lips. "Only the mandarins who made up the story know for sure that it is false. You might be right about it being widely accepted as false, but you cannot be sure. Your father might not have wanted to depend on that understanding of the situation. He might have changed his name and applied under a new identity. He could have relied on no one recognizing him after the passage of time." He nodded thoughtfully. "To be sure, the senior mandarins take little or no interest in juniors."

I'd spent yesterday afternoon at the City Hall and I was about halfway through the lists from Hué. If my tutor was right, then I would need to go back and check all the lists again for all candidates for the examinations, regardless of their names. Suddenly it was a more difficult job than I had originally thought.

"I understand, Lǎoshī."

"That is my guess, but there's another possibility." My tutor grimaced. "There might be mandarins who *still* believe the stories that the gold was stolen, and also that your father was part of the group responsible. Your father might exploit that. He might get one of those to sponsor him, if he is brave."

I frowned. "Why would they sponsor him, if they believe he stole it?"

"Precisely because of that. They would do it in the hope of discovering where the gold is hidden, and stealing it for themselves," he said, his tone neutral. "The quality of the mandarinate is not what it once was."

A maid interrupted what I was sure would be a lecture on the decline of the Annamese administration by bringing us hot water. As he usually did, Monsieur Song made the tea, and talk was not permitted while he did this.

"The core of the problem is what to do about Bác Thảo," he said when we had our cups. "Everything else can continue as you have started. To be harsh: you will find your parents, or you will not. You will find your sister, or you will not. But you cannot help your birth family safely while you are threatened by Bác Thảo."

"Surely the police can arrest him," I said. "Can you think of a plan to persuade them?"

"That's not so simple." Song returned to the window. He stood there, sipping his tea and looking out thoughtfully through the gauze curtains.

I joined him and waited. It was always difficult to know what he was thinking, but this morning, I sensed a reluctance to tell me things.

"These curtains allow the light to come in, the breeze to flow. Flies and insects are kept out," he said. "The French also like to keep things out of the mind. Things that do not fit with their view of the world. Few listen to Monsieur Gosselin, and he is an ill man. Yet, in his muddled ravings there's often truth."

I felt another chill along my spine.

He turned abruptly to me. "Do you trust me, Bian?"

"Yes, Lǎoshī. But I am Ophélie now."

"You are both," he said, guiding me back to my seat at the dining table. "The part of you I want to talk to is the Annamese, the *Bian*, and I think we will do so through some of the ritual heritage that we share."

While I sat, he brought a candle on a small metal tray from the side table and placed it in front of me.

He lit the candle.

From my folder, he took a piece of blank paper, the broad-nib pen I sometimes used to draw Chinese ideograms, and the pot of ink.

"Describe to me the three realms," he said. "Briefly."

I was puzzled why he asked, but this was an easy question about Chinese mythology that we had spoken of before.

"Well, the three are Tiantang, Yang Jian and Ying Jian. Tiantang is heaven, a place of repose for those souls that have earned it. Yang is the living material world all around us, the world we perceive with our senses. Ying is the spirit world, the world that passes through Yang but is not perceivable to us, although our souls exist in both Yang and Ying."

"Excellent." While I spoke, he had been writing with deft strokes. "How could you perceive the spirit world?"

I blinked. What was he doing? "In the myths there might be a guide," I replied. "Or dreams, perhaps. Or a spell that allows you to talk with the spirits."

"That would be more than we need," he said. "More than we have the time for. All we need are spirit eyes, for the passage of flame across the paper."

He put the pen down. The writing on the paper made no sense to me. There were symbols for 'safe' and 'passage' and 'eyes' that I picked out, but some of the others I didn't understand.

"What are we doing?" I said.

"Opening your spirit eyes. Do you still trust me, Bian?"

"Yes."

"Then you will be safe." He stood just behind my chair, one hand on the back. "I am here. Now just watch the flame. Watch."

He reached across and touched the paper he'd written on to the flame and placed it on the metal tray.

"See how it sways, how it grows." His voice dropped.

The flame did sway. And it grew.

"See the curl of the smoke in the air," he whispered. "So slow."

It was so quiet here in the dining room at Boulevard Bonner. I could hear the sound the candle flame made as it danced on the wick. The crackle as the paper burned.

All so slowly.

The smoke that drifted from the flame's tip swirled up in the air, producing fantastical shapes.

Shapes that seemed to grow familiar.

A mask? Of my own face?

It *was* like a mask, it *did* look like me. It was almost transparent at the edges. In the center, where the eyes would be, it was a deep grey, the grey of swollen monsoon clouds.

The mask drifted toward me, or I drifted toward it. I closed my eyes and gasped as it touched my face. It was cool, like water, like a mist or spray, touching my skin so softly.

When my eyes opened again, the world was not the same.

Here was the dining table, the side table. There were the chairs, the pictures on the walls, the chandelier above us.

But the light was different. It was as if everything now gave off its own light. As if everything was, at the same time, both solid and yet no more substantial than smoke.

I drifted like a ghost and I passed through the gauze curtains. They were no more a barrier to me than if I'd been smoke and air.

There was no sun in the sky, no moon. No day, no night. Everything had its own light, everything was both hard edged and intangible.

I realized my eyes were seeing the Ying world, the world of spirits that flowed around and through the Yang world, the world of the living.

And at the same time, I knew this was madness. Impossible. Irrational.

I floated. It felt as if I were falling, in a nightmare, and yet, in the way of dreams, I never hit the ground.

There were people on the streets. I could see both Yang and Ying aspects, but the Yang, the face that the living world saw, was indistinct to my spirit eyes. The Ying spirit hovered around the same space, tethered in some way, but pulling to one side or the other. The spirit faces were clear and mobile, unrestrained and expressive, whereas the Yang faces were wooden and obscured. Many of the Ying faces were distorted and grotesque, and for those, their pale spirit bodies were tainted with colors that suggested strong emotion.

I swooped past them, drawn towards the offices of the colonial administration. Through the walls and inside.

There's Papa.

Although his living face was indistinct, I knew it was him. His spirit body was calm and sat easily within the boundaries of his living body. It was pale blue, as pale as the sky at noon. His Ying face looked calm and resolute, with his eyes looking steadfastly forward.

But around him was a different scene. The building seethed with others who were not at all the same as him.

Their Yang faces were also calm, their movement as stately as lawyers through a courtroom, but their Ying faces screamed, and their bodies glowed with suppressed emotions.

Are these my father's enemies? So many!

I could not hear their spirit screams, nor the measured words of their living mouths, but a darkness seemed to leak from them and it gathered in every corner of the building, until it overflowed, trickling out of windows and doors like a fog.

There, beside Papa, was Monsieur Therriot, who had greeted us on the docks. I recognized him from the way he had of touching my father's arm to emphasize a point, or to stress that he was supportive.

His Yang body was green and twisted back on itself, almost as if it were a knotted rope, and the face looked bitter, the eyes sliding back and forth, only looking to the sides.

Envy?

I wanted to stay and find out more, but whatever had drawn me to the building now drew me away.

Up. Out.

There on the street, I saw Monsieur Riossi and Père St Cyprien talking together.

Stay. Stay.

But I was flying upwards. I had barely a moment to observe them, their outer faces calm and their inner spirits in turmoil. I had no more than a glimpse, a sense of redness, then I was too far away.

I paused high above Saigon, above the Ronde, in the middle of the docks, looking south to the Arroyo Chinois, where the face of the water was nearly covered with sampans. On the far bank across the Arroyo from Saigon sat the dark warehouses and choking, lawless streets of Khánh Hôi. To my right, a kilometer or two down the Arroyo, was Cholon.

My spirit view was different from up here. Time passed more quickly than it had below, and I couldn't see individuals on the streets; instead, I saw movement like rivers. People flooding into Saigon from Khánh Hôi and Cholon to work on the new buildings as the architects extended the reach of the city. Those people at the end of the day, flooding back. I was seeing the pulse of the city.

I swooped down, so quickly my breath caught in my throat, down to the point that the flows of workers separated, at the first bridge across the Arroyo Chinois. Left to Khánh Hôi, straight on to Cholon.

Spirit time slowed again, so I could see individuals in the flow, and I passed like a ghost among those that walked over the bridge to Khánh Hôi. No one soul looked worse than others I'd seen elsewhere in the city, but overall, as an accumulation, there was a darkness that hung about them, that slowed their movements, weighed them down.

As I lingered, I saw where that darkness came from — almost all that crossed the bridge carried a brand on their spirit faces. On some, it was no more than a blur, but on others, it was clear enough to see that it was an image of a tiger.

I was pulled deep into Khánh Hôi, through the warren of narrow streets, turning always in the direction the darkness increased, where the brands were more and more visible, until I came to the heart of it.

The tall man. His Ying soul was a tiger, and while I watched, the Ying and Yang bodies of the man moved like smoke, shifting, passing through each other, reforming, until they'd exchanged places.

The tiger turned its lambent eyes on me, full of fury.

I wanted to scream, but a ghost has no breath.

"Ophélie? Ophélie?"

I heard Maman's clear voice as if I were underwater.

I gasped, sucking air into my lungs like I'd been holding my breath the entire time. I was not in the stifling passages of Khánh Hôi. I was sitting in the dining room at Boulevard Bonnard, with a cooling breeze coming though the gauze curtains. In the center of the table, a candle burned on a metal tray. At the foot of the candle lay the ashes of a piece of paper, with the last wisp of smoke escaping from it and vanishing.

"There you are." Maman opened the door and put her head around it. "My apologies, Monsieur Song, but we'll have to curtail this lesson. Our cousins are about to arrive from France. The ship has been sighted on the river."

She went back out.

My mouth moved with questions to ask, but it seemed an age before my voice worked.

"Lǎoshī! What? How? What have I just seen? Was that real?"

"Sometimes, to perceive the method is to lose the substance of the lesson."

We spoke in Mandarin still.

"Think on this deeply," he said. "We will speak further, but not a word to anyone else at the moment. We should be in a much better position after the Harvest Ball."

Clearly, he'd heard something about the announcement that Papa would become governor, but that was as much as I could get from him.

At the door, he bade us both a good day in French and left, his long queue swinging like a pendulum across his back.

Chapter 23

It was more difficult than I'd expected to find our cousins, the Fontaudins, in the crowd of people disembarking from the steamer *Toulouse*.

Passenger ships at the dock came in all sizes, and the only way to get people off them efficiently was one of the cumbersome, whitewashed gangplank assemblies. These iron and wood constructions were wheeled across and winched up until their long boards formed a footway from the deck down to the dockside. There were iron railings to hold onto and canvas panels draped on either side so people couldn't see you slipping and stumbling. The Toulouse already had the biggest gangplank against her side and the first passengers were gingerly making their way down, the whole thing flexing and swaying beneath their feet.

Knots of people waited on the dockside, and a swarm of coolies ready to carry the luggage down.

There were lots of returning colonials on the *Toulouse*; they were the easiest to spot and the quickest to leave. They'd either have friends meeting them or, with a whistle, they'd have their luggage loaded in a cart to follow them, while they were whisked away in a Malabar carriage.

There were new government officers, wide-eyed and nervous, wondering whether they'd made a mistake going for a Saigon posting. They'd thought they'd gotten used to the heat on the ship, but it was a different matter on the dockside. I could see, between their doubts and the assault of noise and color, they were left with the sinking feeling they wouldn't cope. They were easy to spot, too; they wore the tropical suits they'd been advised to buy in France, and which were all subtly wrong. If they stayed, they'd learn to cope and they'd soon be dressed more comfortably, and for a fraction of the cost, from local tailors.

There were travelers on business, straining to see the company officials sent to meet them. That was the group where the Fontaudins should have been.

Then lastly, the pleasure travelers, unsure and gruff with the coolies, most of them with far too much luggage.

I couldn't see anyone who I thought could be the Fontaudins. What would they be like, these cousins?

Maman was beginning to worry. The last few passengers were coming down the gangplank. There was no one on the dockside who was obviously searching for us.

"Look, Maman, Papa," I said, pointing. "On the side of those trunks."

A team of coolies were carrying three large, grey-green trunks down the gangplank. On the side, the name 'Fontaudin' had been clearly stenciled in square, white letters.

And then, as the disembarking deck emptied, they finally made their appearance.

Blanche Fontaudin was a tall woman. She was brown-haired, heavy set and pale. Her lips were pinched tightly. A double necklace of pearls swung from her neck and her powder-blue dress was the severest, most elegant cut I'd ever seen.

The reason they were last quickly became apparent. On the deck, Blanche was able to support herself with a stout walking stick and the arm of her husband. On the gangplank, she required assistance and Papa ran up to help.

Her husband, Yves, was plump and jolly. His skin had gone pink from the sun and his thinning, light brown hair was combed back. He wore a white suit that was far too stiff and looked uncomfortable.

Nevertheless, he was laughing as, between them, he and Papa maneuvered his wife down the swaying gangplank and onto the safe, stable ground of the quay.

I hung back slightly as Maman greeted them.

"Hello! Hello! Wonderful to be here at last. Splendid," Monsieur Fontaudin said loudly, and he kissed her on both cheeks.

"Thank goodness, we were getting worried," Maman said. "How are you?"

"This heat—my God, I'm going to melt. How do you stand it? Other than that, we're fine, absolutely fine. Sorry about the delay. Just needed the gangplank to be clear."

"This is our daughter, Ophélie." Maman beckoned me forward.

"Monsieur, Madame," I said, and bobbed.

"Well, yes. Hello. Hmm." He blinked at me. "So, you are Ophélie. So, ah, grown up." He swiveled around. "Blanche, just look at her."

"I have eyes, Yves," she said. "Can we kindly get out of this sun?"

"You wait right over here," Papa said, guiding them to the shade of one of the trees. "I'll get the Malabar to come to you." He strode off.

"That leg seems painful," Maman said. "Did you fall on the ship?"

Madame Fontaudin shook her head. "An old injury that gets worse with the heat. I have an excellent doctor at home. No chance of that here, I suppose. I'll just have to make do."

"Perhaps it will settle with rest, now you're on firm ground," Maman said. "Here's the carriage now."

∞ ∞ ∞ ∞ ∞

Madame Fontaudin retired to her bedroom without lunch. Monsieur Fontaudin thought himself a great raconteur, and regaled us while we ate with stories from France. Finally, he, too, retired for the worst of the afternoon heat.

Papa had to return to the office, and I took the opportunity to accompany him. It got me away from the Fontaudins, and by walking with him, Jade as well.

Was it the aftereffects of whatever had happened with my tutor in the morning? Either it had stirred up my imagination, or I was catching glimpses of people's spirit souls.

Surely just my imagination.

As Maman said, there was a lot going on, and having Jade's constant disapproval was wearying. As for the Fontaudins, I had gone down to the docks excited to meet these relatives. From their unenthusiastic welcome to their general cool disregard of me, I'd quickly moved to actually disliking them and hoping they quickly found their own house to stay in.

In contrast, working on Hué lists in the quiet of the library through the afternoon was a welcome relief and an opportunity to think.

Despite not liking him, I'd listened carefully to Monsieur Fontaudin over lunch. For someone who worked in the clothing industry, in Toulouse, way down in the south of France, he was eager to show he had his fingers on the pulse of the capital.

It was clear, he said, that the government in Paris was going though one of its periodic reassessments. Finances were being husbanded, budgets were being cut, and every department's watchword had become 'efficiency'.

That we already understood. Papa had commented to me over the last few months that every communication he'd received from Paris included the word 'efficiency' as if it were a mantra.

But Monsieur Fontaudin went on.

According to the rumors, he told us, the Quai d'Orsay had suffered some defeats against the Ministère de la Marine, and there was some disquiet about Cochinchina which must be held against the administration.

Papa waved that away. Rumors were not to be heeded. His length of service would speak for him, and the income of Cochinchina was going a long way to supporting the entire French presence in the Far East. They could hardly ignore that.

And although I could not repeat rumors in front of Papa, the inspectors at the Opium Regie had told me he would be announced as governor at the Harvest Ball. That would provide security against the bickering between the departments in Paris.

Chapter 24

Boulevard Norodom was the widest and most splendid of Saigon's boulevards. It ran from the Botanical Gardens, past the old Citadel, right up to the gates of the Governor's Palace.

To feel the heart of trade that beat at the center of the South China Sea, you would go down to the Quai du Commerce and the Old Market, down to the shops and brokers that clustered in the streets from the Ronde to Boulevard Charner.

To sense the awe of the French navy, you would visit the Quai de la Marine, be dwarfed by the ironclad ships, and gaze in wonder at the mountainous coal bunkers next to the imposing bastion of the arsenal.

To see the majesty of the French empire, you simply came to the Governor's Palace.

It was set in formal gardens, facing Boulevard Norodom across a lush, circular lawn big enough to ride a dozen carriages around. It was the embodiment of France in the Far East, an echo of the recently deceased Duke of Magenta's proud statement: *J'y suis. J'y reste.* Here I am, here I will remain.

From where we were waiting, I could cast my eyes over the triple tiers of the building. Every detail was in harmony, from the upward sweep of the pale stone staircase, through the cloisters of arched windows, up to the crowning Louis 16th cupola; all designed to project a sense of the divine right of French imperial power, of agelessness. Of inevitability.

In the middle of the circular lawn, the dying light of the setting sun highlighted the French tricolor, hanging limply from the tall flag post.

The day had seemed to last forever but now we were finally —*finally*— on our way to the Harvest Ball. Papa had arranged for a Malabar carriage to deliver us right to the doors, but that meant we were in a procession of them, and had to wait our turn.

I was excited. The whole of Saigon had exploded with the celebrations of Tết Trung Thu, the Harvest Festival and Children's Festival. So many lanterns glowed, the house and street lights seemed dim. Dragons and lions danced in the streets, chasing bands of drummers while children ran, laughing and playing, between them. Every trader seemed to be out selling mooncakes to the crowds.

And *soon*, this evening, it would all be crowned by the Harvest Ball.

The palace had begun to use electric lights, and these had been switched on by the time we finally drew up to the stairs.

"Monsieur, Madame, Mam'selle." We were greeted politely, and quickly ushered through the lofty, marble-floored passage to the huge reception room with its deep red and gold carpets.

It was filled, side to side, with a sea of faces and a froth of the most fashionable dresses; stark, formal jackets; and military uniforms. Ladies' throats and fingers dripped with jewels, and officers' chests with medals, until they rivalled the chandeliers with all their glitter. All their voices were joined together in one hum, like a huge hive of bees.

Among the guests, Annamese servants in loose blue trousers and starched white tunics passed silently, bearing trays of drinks.

I attempted to take a glass of champagne, but Papa swopped it for a tall, cold mango juice with sprigs of mint.

If I'd waited just another minute, he would have been too occupied by the swirl of people asking him for news of the *Victorieuse*, or clarification of some rumor. He shrugged off all the questions, but made a supportive comment for every person's concern.

I could not help him with this task, and moved away to search for my friends.

I found Manon and Rochelle talking to Phèdre Riossi.

Their conversation was about the *Victorieuse*. I greeted them, but didn't join in.

139

Tonight, Papa would be announced as governor, and at last some of these rumors would be laid to rest. It couldn't happen soon enough for me.

I wondered how it would be done. Governor Laurent himself would have to make the announcement, surely. I couldn't see him here. Was he well enough? I searched the faces.

But at that moment, the orchestra began to play, and a stir went through the crowd.

I watched as gentlemen approached ladies for a dance, noting the way an elegant lady, not far from where we stood, took her time before inclining her head gracefully, with a small smile. She laid her hand on his arm and allowed him to lead her to the floor.

That's how you do it.

From the corner of my eye, I saw Phèdre sneer and fade back toward the wall.

There was a tap on my shoulder.

"Now, young lady, are you too old or too young to dance a gavotte with your Papa?"

"Neither, Monsieur," I said and was about to make a grand curtsey, then I remembered and tried tilting my head slightly like the lady I'd watched. Gracious, not arrogant. It was difficult to get it just so.

Rochelle stifled a giggle, which I'd make her pay for later.

Papa took my hand and led me to the floor, our steps quickly taking up the rhythm of the dance so we arrived at the others already in time with them.

The gavotte was not my favorite. It was old-fashioned and stuffy, but so what?

Round and round, flap hands, bow and step. It was really the silliest dance, and even Papa couldn't help but laugh as we bobbed and twirled.

At the end he bowed. "Alas, now I must return to duty," he said, making his eyebrows wiggle. "I have every lady in the colony keen to whisper in my ear this evening."

I curtsied formally and returned to where I'd left the others, but they'd dispersed. Those that had missed the gavotte now had a simpler two-step to navigate.

I took another juice drink from a tray and looked around the ballroom.

I couldn't see the governor yet, but it was difficult to be sure with so many here.

By the far wall, Colonel Durand stood, surrounded by Marine officers. He was speaking, but every so often his eyes swept over the room, as if he were watching everyone. He saw me and I could not mistake the anger in his eyes.

Was it because I'd slipped through the cordon of his Marines at the execution? Or simply because I was here?

I looked away.

Much closer to me was Monsieur Riossi. His eyes also swept the room.

I shivered. I *was* obligated to him. This was the man who had agreed to let his inspectors search for Nhung and the other girls who'd been sold into prostitution. I *had* thanked the inspectors, and I was safer here than in many places; we were in a ballroom with hundreds of onlookers. Nothing was going to happen. I should be mature enough to thank him. It was the least I could do.

His eyes swept back across the room and held mine.

I smiled and took a step. Immediately, he excused himself and walked over to me.

He made a little bow. "A dance, Mam'selle Beauclerc?"

I had only wanted to talk, but I was trapped now. To refuse would hardly be the opening for me to thank him. The dance was halfway over anyway.

"Monsieur." I tilted my head again and laid my hand on his arm.

He moved smoothly, dancing well despite his weight. His right hand held mine and his left pressed lightly on my lower back. He smelled of strong, scented soap and expensive cigars.

My vision, or my hallucination, if that's what it was, had given me a glimpse of threatening redness in his spirit soul, him and St Cyprien, but I refused to let that dominate my thoughts, or to give in to my street sense about him.

Instead I spoke. "Have you had an opportunity to enjoy the festivals in the streets today, Monsieur Riossi?"

He had, and we had a civil and unremarkable conversation until the end of the dance.

"I wanted to take the opportunity to thank you for allowing the Regie inspectors to assist with my father's project to rescue girls," I said, as he escorted me out of the dance area. "It's a cause close to my heart."

"Naturally it is, Mam'selle," he said. "And I am pleased if it gives you pleasure. Such little favors exchanged make the world so much more enjoyable for all."

Someone waved at him. "Ah! You must excuse me. Thank you for the dance."

He moved off.

The words were so vague and probably just his way of speaking. I shouldn't see hidden meanings.

I rubbed my hands together, surreptitiously wiped them on my dress.

Rochelle joined me as the orchestra struck up a Viennese polka. They seemed determined to start off the evening with a different dance of every kind. The polka was much more my sort of dance, but it seemed the gentlemen were occupied with others.

Phèdre also appeared, quiet as a ghost beside us. Behind her curtain of hair, she looked impassively out over the dancers.

"Did you enjoy dancing with my father?" she said.

"He dances well." I tried to deflect the question.

"Yes, he's very sure in his moves."

She looked as if she might have said more, but Rochelle interrupted. "I swear Chantal's wearing a corset."

I picked her out, near the center of the floor, dancing with an elderly man. She was certainly moving stiffly.

"Who's that dancing with her?" I asked.

I was surprised that it was Phèdre who answered. "His name's Janin. He has a huge rubber plantation, up past Binh Long, right next to the border."

"How old is he?" Rochelle asked.

"Old enough to remember when gentlemen wore wigs to a reception," Phèdre said without expression. "And he's sorry they don't still."

Rochelle and I smothered our laughs. Yes, Monsieur Janin was old and very bald.

The polka wound down to its end and many of the dancers left the floor.

"I believe I have already put in a request for the pleasure of this next dance, Mam'selle?"

I spun round and almost fainted. Alain Sévigny.

Chapter 25

I caught myself, managed to incline my head graciously as I'd been practicing that evening, and let him take my hand to lead me toward the dance floor.

What would it be? Another polka? Something old like a cotillion? I hoped not; that was almost as stuffy as the gavotte. It was all right to laugh while dancing with your father, but less so dancing with the handsomest young man in the room.

Whatever the dance, I was never going to forget this. My first dance, other than with Papa and my parents' friends, or obligations like Monsieur Riossi.

My first real dance, I thought, though that was silly.

My first dance with Alain.

We reached the center. There was a slight, expectant hush and the first notes came: a horn, so clear and pure, I bit my lip. It couldn't be! Then the strings quickly followed and the beautiful music swayed through the room. Strauss. *An der schönen blauen Donau*. A waltz! My *favorite* waltz, my dream dance.

"Ophélie?"

Heart in mouth, I turned toward Alain and placed my hand gently on top of his shoulder. His hand slipped behind me and—two, three, one, two, three—we floated away across the floor.

I swallowed and remembered to breathe.

"This is my favorite dance, my favorite music." It felt as if I had to squeeze the words out of my chest.

"Really? Mine, too. I was surprised they let it be played." A smile played about his lips. "Some people say it leads to decadence."

One, two, three. One, two, three. Do not think of decadence. De-ca-dence. One, two, three. He has such lovely, languid eyes. The same blue as Chantal, but not sharp.

"They say decadence becomes fashionable toward the end of a century," he said.

"Well, only a few years now. Do you believe there's something in the numbers?"

"No." He laughed. "Rank superstition, but people think there's significance in the numbers and therefore, there's significance."

"Well then, what will the end of the century mean for us here in Saigon?"

"Who knows exactly?" Alain said. "There's a new century coming. What some call decadence is just a chance to sweep away old restrictions and traditions. A chance to reinvent the world as it should be. Starting out right here, in the furthest part of the republic."

I'd never had much chance to speak with Alain privately before, if you could call speaking on the dance floor private. He spoke with an excitement and passion in his voice that was intoxicating.

He leaned closer and his voice dropped. "I hear there will be an announcement about the governor, right here at the ball. With your father in charge, perhaps that will signal the start of changes."

Of course, if the Regie inspectors knew, others might also know that Papa would be announced as governor tonight.

But I must not speak of rumors, so I just smiled.

We turned and Colonel Durand brushed past, dancing with Rochelle's mother.

Alain noticed that I looked away.

"What's wrong?"

"Colonel Durand. I think he doesn't like me."

"Perhaps. You can't expect everyone to like you."

"No. I suspect he doesn't like me because I'm ..."

"Because you're Annamese? Yes, there are many like that, here in Saigon. But why worry?"

"What do you mean?"

"He's just posted here." Alain gave a tiny shrug. "In a few years, he'll go back to France and become a bore, telling wildly exaggerated stories of the 'hardships of Cochinchina'."

"Another will replace him."

"And another, and another. But they come and they go. Saigon will remain, and eventually the Durands will not come."

I wanted that with all my heart.

"Maybe. What about you, Alain? Your father's the city architect. They'll run out of the need for more civic buildings eventually."

He laughed again, freely, easily. "No, never. And this is our home now. I know, we weren't born here. My family is French, but my father has poured his heart into making Saigon what it is. How could we leave?"

"You really feel that way about it?"

"Yes! Look at the city. This is the Paris of the East, and without the numbing rubbish that goes on in France. A place for new starts. A place to experiment. A place that's exciting. Why on earth would I leave?"

We turned again, dancing closer that we strictly should have.

It could be, it really could. Enough dreamers to dream, and the dream would be the new reality. Sweep away the old.

I tilted my head back, feeling a little drunk. Chandeliers spun like constellations of stars above me. For one glorious waltz, I believed we could dance our cares away.

Papa would become governor.

One-two-three. One-two-three.

I would be reunited with my sister, and Papa would protect my birth family if they returned here. He would have Bác Thảo arrested and thrown into prison. His enemies in the administration would not dare move against the governor, and by the time he finished his term, it would be the new century and things would be different.

In Papa's words, France itself would finally wake to the glorious possibilities of the East, to embrace its dynamic peoples, to reinvigorate itself and, as a unified new state, to become once again pre-eminent in the world.

145

I would work beside him, and beside others who shared his dreams.

One-two-three. One-two-three.

There were threats and problems and puzzles here in Saigon, yes, and not just for me personally, but for all the people. Those threats might be stubborn. But we would defeat them all, and even if we could not eradicate them, well, we were young and strong and full of life, and we would outlive them. With people who believed in the dream they were building here, nothing was impossible. We would inherit this wonderful city and we would sweep all the problems away. Nothing was impossible. Nothing.

One-two-three.

Alain and I …

The music faltered, stopped, and couples on the floor stuttered to a standstill while voices called out questions. A buzz of speculative conversation broke out.

There were men in naval uniforms, plain working uniforms, stopping the orchestra and clearing a space on the stand.

Victorieuse, someone said behind me. Another voice took it up.

A gong sounded and the buzz quietened, became a murmur.

Then Governor Laurent walked in, and there was absolute silence.

Most of the people here, like me, hadn't seen him since his last official engagement months before. I could see my shock echoed in all their faces.

His skin was pale and loose, as if his inner body had shrunk. His uniform, heavy and bright with gleaming medals, was hanging off him. He leaned heavily on a walking stick. In his left hand he held a piece of paper.

I'd met him and remembered most the lively, piercing green of his eyes. Those eyes were now dull and clouded. He raised them to the assembly without expression, and I wondered if he could actually see anyone. Were we just a blur to him?

Yes, I wanted Papa to become governor, but not like this.

Governor Laurent looked at the piece of paper in his hand and frowned. The paper shook.

"Mesdames and Messieurs." He stopped, and looked around again.

His walking stick trembled. His left hand closed, crumpling the paper, and then moved across to steady his right.

"My friends and colleagues," he started again, more strongly. There was a sigh, like a breeze, that passed through the grand chamber, and his eyes seemed to clear a little.

"I came out to this colony twelve years ago, full of a sense of purpose, full of a vision, a dream for all the people of Cochinchina that I know many of you still share. A dream of a dynamic, exciting part of France, where we would light a great beacon, and call out to the young and adventurous. A wonderful, wonderful dream. But those of you who are as old as I, know only too well that dreams may die, and if they do, the body soon follows."

There was a sharp intake of breath throughout the room.

"To fulfil that dream was my sacred mission," Governor Laurent said, "and my last duty for the republic, but I have fallen far short. The body you see before you will not much longer bear the rigors of this task. It is time for me to step down, and this should be no surprise to some of you. I have resigned my post and will return to France on the *Victorieuse*."

He sighed and looked down as if to gather his strength.

"The world does not stand still, will not stand still. *You* cannot stand still, and thus, you must embrace the change. If you accomplish your goals only to find they are redundant, it is as if you did nothing. And so I leave you, my friends and colleagues, to carry forward such ideals as may fit in the new vision, this new and higher purpose. I will not advise you further, for the way ahead is dark to me; I have dropped the torch and cannot see."

He turned to look at the group behind him briefly.

"It remains for me only to introduce you to the herald of this new vision, the envoy from Paris who has, this very hour, arrived on the *Victorieuse* with his family. He bears the authority of the Quai d'Orsay and the Ministère de la Marine. His name is Monsieur Andre Hubert."

People stirred and craned their necks to see.

Governor Laurent walked to the back and sank into a chair. He leant forward and rested his head on his stick; his speech looked to have exhausted him.

Taking his place in the center was a man I assumed to be Monsieur Hubert.

He was new to the East—his cheeks were red and sweaty with the heat, his jaw covered in a dark, pointed beard. His hair was combed straight back and shiny with pomade.

Behind him stood a woman I assumed to be his wife, and next to her, a boy and girl of about my age.

When Hubert spoke, his voice was strong, but too even, as if he were shouting.

"Thank you. Good evening, Mesdames and Messieurs. I apologize for interrupting your entertainment, but a wide gathering offers such an efficiency of communication that I could not forego doing so."

There was a stir among the guests, many of whom probably recognized the political watchword—'efficiency'—from Paris.

I immediately didn't like Monsieur Hubert, and I didn't like what I felt lurking behind what he was saying.

"It is also perhaps suitable that we use these festivities as a marker, an end of an era if you like. The era of adventurers and light responsibilities, the era of trials and testing of new ideas, in short, the era of youth. Yes, it is time, time for change, time for our colonies to reveal their maturity."

People shifted uncomfortably. In the Far East, only Cochinchina was a true colony. And for someone just off the ship to be saying *our colony* hit a false note.

The feeling I had that something was wrong was growing with every sentence he said.

"The time has come for Indochina to stand separately as a responsible part of the Republic. Long intervals between orders from the Quai d'Orsay or the Ministère de la Marine, and conflict in directions, all those are a thing of the past. For the majority of civil matters, Indochina will effectively govern itself as a new entity, the Federation of Indochina."

Someone clapped and was hushed.

What did this mean? Papa? I looked around, but I couldn't see him.

"Practical concerns mean that the Federation must have an administrative capital as well. After much consideration of the strategic issues, we have chosen Hanoi as the capital, where the Governor of Indochina will reside."

Shouts of disbelief were quickly silenced as he continued without pause.

"Cochinchina, Laos, Cambodia and Annam will be ruled by lieutenant governors. Let me assure you, there is no slight intended on Saigon. It is simply that Hanoi is more populous, closer to China, and also the harbor of Haiphong is better suited."

Where was Papa? I should search for him, but the droning voice continued.

"I will take time to meet with many of you in the coming days, starting with the outgoing administration. I know the rest of you will join me in taking this opportunity to thank them. Normally, we would have a full parade and ceremony, but I'm sure we can all understand that Monsieur Laurent would wish to return to France for therapy by the quickest possible route, and the *Victorieuse* must leave in two days' time."

Of course, we could all see that the governor, *already Monsieur again*, wasn't able to wait on ceremony.

"It remains only for me to formally relieve Monsieur Laurent of his duties," Hubert said, "and, at the same time, to accept the honor of the position of Lieutenant Governor here in Saigon for the remainder of his term."

No! No!

I stumbled through the room searching for Papa.

Maman was already at his side when I joined them. They stood alone. His face was pale, but composed.

"… a deliberate and calculated insult," Maman was saying. "I'd like to leave now, Zacharie."

He nodded, but remained silent. As a family we turned, seemingly ignored by the room.

I looked back. I couldn't see Lieutenant Governor Hubert or his wife; the press of people around them was too thick.

I could see his children, though, standing to one side. Chantal Sévigny was talking to them, welcoming them to the bright, new Saigon. Monsieur Hubert's son was clearly dazzled by Chantal. Not so the daughter. For Alain was also there, and she had eyes only for him, as he had for her.

Part 4 ~ Unravelling

败落

Mark Henwick

Chapter 26

No one in the house at Boulevard Bonnard slept well that night.

I dozed, jerked awake by nightmares of Lieutenant Governor Hubert marching through the streets, banging on doors and shouting. People came drifting out of their houses as if sleepwalking and fell into step behind him, their Yang faces becoming indistinct, their Ying faces bearing a sorrowful brand I could not quite see.

And behind Hubert, in the middle of the street, Alain danced with a young woman.

One-two-three. One-two-three.

Her head fell back when they spun, and she laughed.

Whenever I woke, I heard the creak of floorboards as Papa paced, and once or twice a murmur of unhappy conversation.

I finally got up before dawn to an exhausted silence in the house, and went out. I didn't wake Jade. I needed a little time, a little space without the constant abrasion of her anger.

Saigon was physically unchanged from yesterday: it still had broad boulevards lined by trees, and the pale buildings along them were emerging from the night. I could hear the sound of insects; the scurry of lizards hunting them; the familiar, waiting quiet; the feel of the city gathering itself to spring forward into another day.

Workers were already picking up the litter of lanterns and paper from the festival last night.

But the Saigon dawn that the old-timers said was like waking from an opium dream—that had become a fear of waking to a nightmare for me.

With Papa denied the governorship, how much would go wrong?

They had to retain him in a senior position, that was obvious. His knowledge of the colony, how it ran, why things were done a certain way—all of that was invaluable. But there was a huge difference in power between the man at the top of the administration and those who advised him.

He might not have the authority to protect my birth parents, for instance. Papa could advise the lieutenant governor that Bác Thảo should be arrested, but his word would carry less weight than Chief of Police Meulnes, who didn't even believe in Bác Thảo.

It was lucky the project to rescue the girls from slavery was mainly divided between the Opium Regie and the Sisters of Saint Paul. Of course, the lieutenant governor might not add the resources of the administration behind it, but at least it could proceed slowly. I could still hope to be reunited with Nhung.

And I could still check the mandarinate lists. Maybe my father had not rejoined the mandarinate in Hué. Maybe all my concern about my birth family being sent back here was groundless.

But for Papa: I feared for all his projects. Behind the words at the ball last night I heard the phrases about 'adventurers' and 'new ideas', the watchword of 'efficiency'. Papa would need to fight for everything, and some things he would lose.

I arrived at the docks as the eastern sky paled.

At the bakery near the Ronde on the Quai du Commerce, I bought an armful of hot croissants, the first of the morning's output, and had them wrapped in layers of paper so they'd stay warm. We had salted butter at home, and it would be the work of a moment for me to get coffee percolating. Nothing else would be needed. This would be a difficult day for Papa, and I hoped a good breakfast could help start it the right way.

The day seemed to hurry after me as I returned quickly. The east deepened into fiery rose. A few lazy puffs of hot wind came up out of the south, carrying the tang of the distant sea. The city stirred around me, full of distant calls, the scurry of traders intent on the best places in the market, and the clatter of the Malabar carriages.

I had turned off Boulevard Charner, and I was almost trotting along Boulevard Bonnard when, through the morning sounds, came one I eventually realized was directed at me.

"M'zelle. M'zelle."

It was like the chirping of a cricket.

I turned. A street urchin was chasing after me as fast as his little legs could carry him.

I stopped to let him catch up.

A message from my tutor? Was I right he used the urchins?

In my concern for Papa, I had forgotten that many of his hopes for the colony were shared with Monsieur Song. The arrival of the new lieutenant governor had an effect that would reach down into Cholon as well. In fact, it would reach the whole colony. The whole of Indochina was waking to the new regime today.

The boy reached me, and made me sorry I had moved so quickly. He looked very out of breath.

I couldn't understand his French, and he was Malabar rather than Annamese or Chinese. We settled on speaking Trade. His name was Hamid.

"Come wall night," he said, pointing one finger down, meaning this last night.

Wall?

He was holding a piece of paper crumpled in one grimy hand. He held it out to me.

"For you," he said. "You M'zelle B'clerc."

My heart skipped a beat. The wall? The Words on the Wind?

I knelt so we were on a level.

"For me?" I said, not daring to believe, as I took it. "Sure?"

"Sure-sure," Hamid waggled his head, full of confidence. "Got chop."

Chop. The ideogram at the top.

Could it really be?

I unfolded the paper and there it was, in stark strokes: *zhèngdào; the right path.*

Beneath, in the rushed and careless script I recognized from years ago, was written in Annamese:

> *Little sister,*
> *Not this way, but another.*

I will come to you.
Speak of me to no one else.

Lanh! My elder brother had been at the Words on the Wind in Cholon last night.

Chapter 27

Despite my parents' thanks for the fresh croissants and my efforts in preparing the meal, breakfast was the most awkward we'd ever had together. Fortunately, the cousins were not up yet; their presence could only have made it worse.

Maman and Papa didn't notice my preoccupation, or thought it was from entirely the same source as their own. The conversation moved in jerks and stops, some of it obviously continued from their nighttime discussions.

Maman was still angry, and she was angry enough to suggest leaving the Far East completely. Then she would apologize, and sit without talking for a minute.

Papa was still shocked by it all. One minute he'd be silent, the next he'd be listing reasons why the work he'd started was so important to the colony, and how the new administration would need him to maintain progress.

Before we'd even finished eating, a message arrived from the lieutenant governor. Papa was required to attend a meeting at 8 o'clock. It was an acknowledgment of sorts, that his must be the first meeting of the morning.

Earlier, I'd sent Hamid, my urchin messenger, back to Cholon with a croissant, some centimes and a request for me to speak to Monsieur Song today. It was a huge relief to hear my tutor at the door, after Papa had left and before the cousins had come down to their breakfast.

Maman waved me out. I felt guilty I was leaving her alone with them, barely ameliorated by the sense that they might be easier for her to talk to without me present.

Jade, of course, followed me, a dozen steps behind. My parents had assumed she'd been with me buying the croissants, but she knew I'd escaped. She wasn't going to say anything, but it didn't make her happy. Not that anything seemed to.

Song and I spoke in Mandarin. My tutor had already heard the first reports of what had happened at the ball, and he listened with a grave face as I recounted every detail I could remember about Lieutenant Governor Hubert.

"This is a considerable blow to the whole community," he said when I finished. "There is no hiding that."

"But you and Papa can both still work toward your aims. It'll just be slower and harder, won't it?"

Monsieur Song hummed, and didn't answer directly. When he spoke, he was obscure: "A man who has far to fall, falls far," he said. "And much of my authority, my power, comes from people knowing whom I work with. If it is the same man, but a lower position, I am reduced as well. We must see what the new lieutenant governor intends for your father. But in every possible path, this will make many things more difficult."

"It's all wrong," I said.

"That's the way people are," Monsieur Song said. By that time, we had walked past the theater, and arrived at the Ronde on the docks. "Let us talk of other things. You have received a message from the Words in the Wind."

"Yes! My brother." Lanh had told me not to tell anyone, but my tutor knew already, and I trusted him. "He says to not use the wall, and wait for him."

"A suspicious or cautious man, and perhaps justifiably." Monsieur Song nodded as he looked around at the bustle of dockside Saigon. "He is alone, then, or your parents would have sent the message. It will be interesting to see what he has to say."

He turned so we walked along the Quai du Commerce.

"If I can help, I will," he said. "But in any event, we will have to wait."

"Could we not find him?"

He raised an eyebrow. "How?" he asked.

"With the spirit vision. I saw Papa, I was *drawn* to him. Would that not work with Lanh?"

"Ahh." Song chuckled. "We must talk a little about the vision, too."

"It was real, wasn't it?" I said. "I saw how many hidden enemies Papa had, and then at the ball, I saw the way all the people who'd pretended to be his friends deserted him."

"Clearly a true vision then."

I had the feeling my tutor was being evasive.

"So, the rest of it is true as well. I saw Bác Thảo. I saw he *is* a tiger demon, and he *does* change shape—"

"Indeed, Bác Thảo is what you call hô con quỷ in the Annamese language."

I shivered. "In my vision, he looked at me. The tiger, I mean. Could he sense me? Does he have the power to see into my spirit vision?"

He frowned and we walked on a minute before he answered.

"The spirit vision is not quite as straightforward as that. It may show you what others say, and it may show you some things you believe. What significance should you give to Bác Thảo looking at you?" He hummed before going on. "I believe it means that he knows of you as a possibility, as a ghost, if you like, a suspicion, that might haunt his mind. It does not mean that he actually saw you. You should not fear that."

"Well, good. But if he is a tiger demon, surely we should be able to prove it to the police. If he is as bad as he seems from what I've heard and from what I saw in my spirit vision, then he should be imprisoned or executed. The laws apply to everyone, monster or human."

"The laws the French apply have no concept of people who shift their shape, or people who practice the spirit arts, or others who do not fit into the narrow shape that the French call 'real'. And to call them 'monsters' is to fall into the trap that many people would, a trap of fear and misunderstanding."

He was using a mixture of Annamese and Mandarin. For magic, he used the Annamese *ma thuật*, spirit art.

159

"What should we call them? The people who practice ma thuật, or the hô con quỷ, or the Tò Dara?" I was mixing languages to name them all as well.

"You need only concern yourself with hô con quỷ. But they are not demons, and whereas Bác Thảo is a monster, not all shape-shifters are. That distinction would not be easy for many people to make. Would you not feel responsible if innocent shape-shifters died due to panic among humans caused by your revelations?"

There are other shape-shifters?

"I would, Lǎoshī." I knew that was the only possible response.

"Good. The Bugis' name is better. They call them Tò Harimau, which means no more than Tiger Clan. People who happen to be different, but still people underneath. Some may be monsters, but it is not their shape or instincts or spirit art that make them so."

Bugis. We were walking along the docks. Close to where the captain of the Bugis ship *Salayar* had leaped up and returned to his ship, muttering ominously about Tò Dara.

My tutor had dismissed the Tò Dara before, and I didn't want to raise it bluntly again, but what if I approached it obliquely? Should I tell him about the kris knife? Surely he would agree that the Tò Dara were monsters?

I didn't get the chance.

As I was about to speak, I sensed Monsieur Song growing tense, and we were interrupted by the approach of a Chinese man who I didn't recognize.

He was short and unremarkable. His hair was tied back in a queue and his clothes were those of a wealthy man, but not ostentatious. He rolled a little as he walked, and he squinted, as if his eyesight was not good, but I had the impression his eyes missed nothing.

He spoke in Mandarin—the sharper, quicker version that my tutor used in lessons.

"I went to your house, Song. I was surprised to find you were here, and who you were visiting."

"Had you warned me of your visit, Zheng, I would have greeted you."

The lack of welcome and the tone used told me plainly that there was no friendship between them. It seemed Zheng was a visitor from far away. Perhaps he didn't realize how important Monsieur Song was in the Chinese community.

"The path you chose has ended. None of this would have happened if you'd agreed to our plans. Now, you waste your time," Zheng said. "We have much to discuss."

"Unless you're on the path, it's unwise to declare it's ended. Yes, we must discuss, so long as it remains a discussion."

Monsieur Song turned his back on Zheng deliberately.

"Excuse this person's lack of manners, but I regret I do have business I need to attend to." He looked around. "Jade will accompany you back to your home, and I will try and visit your father, perhaps tomorrow."

He left with Zheng.

Jade and I returned to Boulevard Bonnard.

I was hoping that I might have some time with Maman. An opportunity for a quiet conversation in the salon.

But I heard the voices raised in anger from the hall. Papa was back already, and I'd never heard him so furious.

Chapter 28

Her duty done for the moment, Jade disappeared to the back of the house.

I should have gone in. I would have, but I heard my name, and froze outside the door to the salon.

"... part of the problem, don't you see? Even, maybe, the core of it."

That was Monsieur Fontaudin. His wife was agreeing with him.

"Ridiculous!" Maman.

"No, Thérèse, believe us," Madame Fontaudin said. "You've been here so long, you're out of touch with attitudes back home. I assure you, whatever your motives, adopting an Annamese girl has made people doubt your judgement. Please listen to us."

"You're not saying that this all came about because we adopted Ophélie? You've met her! How can you say such a thing?"

"No, no, no." Monsieur Fontaudin tried to calm Maman. "It's not all due to that. Not at all. But you have to admit, Zacharie's list of projects would utilize the entire revenue from Cochinchina for the benefit of the native population. That's simply not —"

"It's for the benefit of the *whole* population," Papa said. "French, Annamese, Chinese, everyone. Can't they understand? And it's all investment. A healthier, more educated citizenry must lead to improvements for the whole country. Tell me that's not the policy in Paris."

"For France, and French people, yes."

"How can you say Ophélie is not French?" That was Maman.

I had never heard my adoptive parents so angry.

"It's not important what I think," Monsieur Fontaudin said. "Not important. I'm merely passing on what the family have asked me to pass on. We had a family meeting, you see, and, given we were coming out here, I was tasked to pass this on to you. To explain that, despite the family doing what they could at the Quai d'Orsay, their lobbying is having less and less effect."

"You've been here, without a single visit home, longer than anyone anticipated, and of course, the family was tremendously excited when they learned you might become governor," Madame Fontaudin said. "But that gamble has not paid off."

"You must look at this as an opportunity," Monsieur Fontaudin said. "Hubert has ordered you back to France. You must use that, of course! Go! Go straight to the Quai d'Orsay and make your case. Make it well enough and who knows? You might return as governor for the whole of Indochina."

"But taking this girl ... this adoption ... to Paris will only give enemies an opening to attack," Madame Fontaudin added.

I felt sick. I felt as if I'd been spat on and slapped.

Of course I knew there were people who couldn't get over the fact I was Annamese—Phèdre Riossi for one. And that it was not necessarily something you grew out of. But the thought that my adoption was turning my parents' family against them, that enough people in the Quai d'Orsay, who'd probably never even met an Annamese person, regarded my adoption as proof of faulty judgment ... that was vile.

It felt like I was trapped in one of my nightmares. I hurried away and found Jade.

"I'm going out again," I said abruptly.

On Boulevard Bonnard, we walked past the statue of Garnier, the Frenchman who'd explored the Mekong. Then down Rue Blanchy, commemorating a Frenchman who made a business out of farming peppers in Cochinchina. That took us to the Ronde, where the traffic circled around a statue of Admiral Rigault de Genouilly, the French naval commander who had captured Saigon forty years ago.

None of it was new to me, but all of it looked different after what I'd heard.

I sat at one of the shaded tables of a cafe and looked into a swirling cup of coffee as if answers might be found there.

I tried to put my hurt feelings to one side.

What would Maman and Papa do? What *should* they do?

Papa's mission was far more important than me. His projects would benefits hundreds, as soon as they were finished, and thousands or millions in the future. All he had to do was persuade the politicians in Paris, and to do that, he needed to go back without me.

Because despite living and behaving as a Frenchwoman, I was not French.

It wasn't the color of my skin—many Corsicans were darker, for instance. It wasn't the language—I would defy any person to tell I was not French from only hearing my voice. Was it the tiny fold in the corner of my eye? Their shape?

Those defined me?

Did I truly want to be part of a society that thought that?

Was I somehow untrustworthy because my instinct was that all the people who lived in Cochinchina were citizens? Did that mean Papa was untrustworthy as well?

What if the politicians did not agree with Papa, whatever he said? What if the damage had already been done, simply by adopting me?

I was unable to find any answers. I blundered instead from imagining one dreadful scenario to another. I could wear a veil in France like a grieving widow, obscuring my face. Or I could hide at the family home in Bordeaux while Papa visited Paris. I could stay in Saigon.

But if I was the weakness that others would exploit, what did it matter how disguised I was or how far away I hid?

Wouldn't it be better for his cause if he reversed the adoption?

I bit my lip, hard.

Of course it would.

My birth parents sold me out of love, hoping that I would escape, so far away that their misfortune would not follow me. I hadn't gone very far at all, and now I knew what I had to do to prevent that misfortune that still clung to me from attaching itself to my adoptive parents.

I had to let them go, without guilt, because I loved them.

Whatever the cost to me. However much it hurt. And it hurt.

I spilled the coffee in my rush to get up. I had to do something. Anything.

With Jade trailing behind I walked quickly back toward the center of the city.

I didn't have a clear plan, I just needed to be too busy to think about being abandoned.

It was a surprise to find myself in front of the City Hall, and yet it was the ideal place for the distraction I needed. I could go to the documents library and finish reading the ledgers of all the appointments to the mandarinate in Hué and see if I could tell what had happened to my birth family from that.

That was exactly the right level of concentration I needed.

There was a guard on the door; not everyone could go in of course. I normally went in with Papa, but the guard would recognize me.

He did, but that did not help.

"I am sorry, Mam'selle Beauclerc, but I have orders. Only people on the list may enter the building without a letter of invitation from someone who works here, or a written authorization from Lieutenant Governor Hubert."

"But I don't want to see anyone, I just need to go to the documents library."

"I understand, Mam'selle, but the documents library is inside, and my orders are very clear. I don't know why this is necessary." He shrugged and ran his thumb down the edge of the list he held, then shuffled the pages as if he might find my name elsewhere. "Perhaps it is just temporary. You could try again next week."

It wasn't his fault.

I walked away, a scream building up inside me. Not even a full day in Saigon, and Hubert had torn my life at the very foundations. I felt like an empty sampan on the river, spinning idly, a captive of the current, drifting and directionless.

What else would he destroy?

There was the familiar kick of guilt as I came to think of my sister, Nhung, last. The agreement Papa had with Monsieur Riossi. Surely, Hubert would not stop that? He would not prevent the inspectors rescuing girls who'd been sold as slaves. There was no saving for the colony that he could point to. It was all incidental to the inspectors' work and the caring for the girls would be by the church.

I ran.

"Mam'selle!" Jade called behind me.

The Customs Office was only in the next block.

There was no guard on the door, and the crack of my heels as I ran down the marble-floored corridors echoed behind me. Heads came out of offices to see what was happening.

The inspectors' office was open and they were startled when I rushed in like a madwoman.

"Monsieur Picardin, Monsieur Valois, please tell me that you haven't been ordered not to search for kidnapped girls."

"Mam'selle, please, calm yourself."

Picardin pulled up a chair for me and closed the office door carefully. Valois poured me a glass of water from a tall decanter.

I accepted the glass numbly. The looks on their faces told me the answer to my question.

But it was not that clear-cut.

"There are no orders, but, umm …" Monsieur Valois foundered, his hand circling as he tried to reach the correct phrase.

"An indication, no more," supplied Monsieur Picardin. He squeezed his thumb and finger together as if picking up something small.

"Yes, the budget," Valois said. "It appears it is too small to allow the increase of this department by two new inspectors. The fellows we wanted from the Department of Roads, they will be deployed elsewhere. There is, therefore, not the anticipated spare capacity."

"Nothing else?" I said. "Just no increase in the team?"

"Ahh …" Picardin wobbled his hand.

"A request for more detailed reports." Valois pursed his lips and nodded his head thoughtfully.

"An acute interest in what we do. The efforts we put in," Picardin mimed offering something and then taking it back, "and the financial results that return from that activity."

"It could be construed as a requirement for evaluating our request to increase the size of this department," Valois suggested.

"Yes." Picardin frowned.

Or it could be a way of telling them to concentrate on what they were paid to do, couched in language that only a civil servant would understand and could be denied later.

"This change in opinion on your budget and interest in your work, it comes from Hubert?" I said. I could not grant him *Monsieur*, let alone his official title.

"From the office of the lieutenant governor, certainly," Valois said carefully, emphasizing his elevated rank. "Monsieur Riossi did not elaborate."

Hubert could not command everyone in the colony to do as he said, even if he was the lieutenant governor. He had to work with people who were in positions of authority. He would have put this to Riossi as a request for Riossi to implement.

"I could talk to Monsieur Riossi," I said. "He is the director of the Opium Regie. Hubert cannot tell him how to run his department."

They sat back abruptly, both of them.

"Mam'selle." Valois spoke slowly. "It is best not to take this to the director."

"He is a very busy man," Picardin said.

They exchanged glances.

"Very busy. Very important." Valois licked his lips. "Not someone who should be approached ... casually."

"This is no casual matter for me," I said. "I should go right now."

Picardin went to the door and peered out into the empty corridor before closing it again. He stood with his back to it, like a sentry.

"We understand, Mam'selle Beauclerc," he said. "We will do what we can for the girls on this project, and we do not know what that will be, but we both advise you ... both of us ... and please, do not repeat this, Mam'selle ... we advise you most strongly not to seek assistance from our director."

"He can refuse to even see me," I said, "if he is so busy —"

"Mmm. Or he could accept, and agree," Valois interrupted. He dabbed at his forehead with a handkerchief. "As a favor."

"And request ... favors in return," Picardin said. He did not look at me as he spoke.

Favors. The word was swollen with meaning.

Chapter 29

I left the Customs Office, silent with shock. With Jade following, I walked back to the house on Boulevard Bonnard.

I had no doubt what they wanted to warn me about, what favor Monsieur Riossi would require in exchange. Behavior of his that they had clearly seen before.

I shuddered in the heat.

Those eyes of his that followed me. And his words at the ball—*little favors exchanged make the world so much more enjoyable for all.*

I knew it had required the fullest extent of the courage of Messieurs Valois and Picardin that they had told me as much as they had. If I did nothing, they would not put any real effort into finding girls who had been sold into prostitution, whatever they had just said. They might find it horrible, but it was not their job, and they had been told to concentrate on what made the Opium Regie so profitable for the colony. And Riossi would make certain they knew that, because it was something to hold over me. It was entirely possible that Hubert had made no specific demands about the Opium Regie, that Riossi had just seen an opportunity.

His daughter Phèdre's little comment at the ball—*he's very sure in his moves.*

A warning? From Phèdre? That if he wanted something, he would find a way to get it?

I'd lost myself in my thoughts, and finding myself back at the house, I stopped to look around me.

Each block on Boulevard Bonnard was wide, effectively two roads separated by a series of small, rectangular parks in the center. Each little park was shaded by trees and there were benches you could sit on. Gardeners kept the parks clean and tidy.

What a restful, elegant place to live.

What a contrast for my sister. What did she look out onto? Did she even have a window?

Five years she had endured horrors while I lived in luxury; while I lived the lifestyle *her* sacrifice had bought me; while I enjoyed the privileges that *her* lifestyle paid for every day, even now.

Even right now.

I felt physically ill, unsteady on my feet.

"Mam'selle?" Jade wanted to go inside.

I nodded and walked into the house, my footsteps dragging, still feeling dizzy.

The Fontaudins had gone out, leaving Papa and Maman to discuss what they were going to do.

They looked up with a start as I entered.

"Ophélie! Are you all right?" Maman rushed across and hugged me.

"It's nothing, Maman." I made myself smile and look up at her. "A little faint in the heat."

She didn't believe me, but she poured me some water and we sat on the sofa. Papa stood with his back to the window. He looked as pale as I felt.

"There is bad news," she began reluctantly, and I took her hand to stop her and comfort her, as much as I was able.

"I've heard. All your projects, Papa. I'm so sorry."

He nodded sharply without speaking, his eyes fixed on the floor between us.

"And we are to return home immediately," Maman said. "To France, I mean."

She gave a brave smile. "I have wanted to show you Bordeaux for so long," she said brightly. "It will be a marvelous holiday, and there are so many of the family to meet."

"Maman, I know," I said. "I'm sorry, but I could not help overhearing from the hall when I came back from my lesson with Monsieur Song. I heard what our cousins said about me."

She stiffened. "No, Ophélie—"

"You mustn't misunderstand," Papa said.

"I don't," I said. "It's very clear to me. This is nothing to do with us as a family, or what you feel. It's not even really about me."

Papa came and sat beside me as well, just as they had done the day of the execution. That felt so long ago. Today, they were not comforting me; I was trying to comfort them. But I didn't know what to say, or how to say it.

"Other things are becoming clearer to me, too," I said, finding words in the dark. "We've talked so often, Papa, about duty."

His breath caught, and I wanted to stop so much, to not cause him more pain, but I knew if I did stop, I would never start again.

"I feel you have a duty now, both of you. It's a higher duty. A duty you owe to all the people here in Indochina, not to one person. Not to me."

"No," Papa whispered.

"It means you have to go back to France and you have to persuade the Quai d'Orsay of the necessity of your projects. They have to see that the schools and hospitals are needed. Then you have to persuade them to restart the committees with the leaders of the Annamese and Chinese and Malabars, so that the people here understand that these are their projects, that they are French. Then hundreds, or thousands, will benefit."

As I spoke, intending to comfort them, I reinforced the decision that I hadn't even consciously taken, to stay in Saigon. I also realized that I was not going to speak about the meeting I'd had with Valois and Picardin. Papa could do nothing and it would only distract him.

He needed to go to Paris. Maman needed to support him. I needed to stay here.

There was a feeling of inevitability about this, of implacable fate, crushing down on me. I wasn't fated to go to France. If I had been, we would have gone long ago.

As I spoke, what I needed to say became clearer to me, and at the same time, I felt separate, as if I were looking into the salon, seeing my body sitting on the sofa, hearing my voice talking.

"But we must do this together," Papa was saying.

I shook my head. "They don't see your vision yet, and they won't, if I'm there to distract them, or to provide a way for enemies to question you. You have to win the arguments with logic alone. And you need your families in Bordeaux. They have supported you all this time. Let them support you once more without having their attention diverted by me."

"But we can't go back without you," Maman whispered.

"You have to," I said. "I will stay here this time. Next time will be for the Centennial Exhibition, and we'll all go together."

I felt a chill. It was bad joss to claim that. Had I not just had the thought that I wasn't fated to go to France?

We discussed it as the morning turned to noon. We discussed it over lunch. We discussed it as the heat of the day reached its zenith and the Fontaudins returned. It was one of those disjointed arguments full of stops and starts, where the end never seemed to be reached. But I sensed, in their jangling, painful sentences, the same feeling that was in my mind. There was an inevitability about this—they would return to Paris and I would wait for them here.

Chapter 30

When I went to my room late that evening, I turned the lights out and sat by the window, staring out over the boulevard.

What could I achieve, when Maman and Papa were not here?

Staying in Saigon would help them with the situation in France, even they saw that. But what could *I* really achieve?

I would be here for my brother Lanh to contact me.

He would have news of our parents, and I might be able to help them, if they had to return here. Surely I could find some friends who would take them in? That would give them some small measure of safety from Bác Thảo.

And then there was Nhung.

What could I do?

Maybe Lanh had already found her and rescued her? That was a pleasant dream for a few minutes, but I knew it was just a dream.

Which led me back to Riossi.

I couldn't leave Nhung wherever she was. Monsieur Song might try to help, but his reach did not extend over all of Saigon, and he had his own troubles, I could see. I couldn't wait for Papa—even the best of all possible outcomes would be months away while he travelled to Paris and back. I couldn't *make* Valois and Picardin search for her in the meantime, and I had even less chance of persuading Police Chief Meulnes.

The one way remained, and Riossi sat, like a spider, waiting for me on that path.

Outside, there were gas lamps lit in the little parks along the middle of the empty boulevard. In the faint light they cast through my window, I watched my indistinct reflection. It floated in the glass pane like a rootless Chinese ghost.

I didn't want to be like that—to drift, insubstantial and powerless, always outside, looking in. I wanted to be *strong*, strong enough to make people do things. Or was that only a dream too, like my brother Lanh rescuing Nhung?

A dream. Were all dreams nightmares, in the end?

I dozed fitfully.

I dream a child rides upon her sister's hip. She lives where life is fair and rules are certain; she knows that good will follow virtue. It is her time of innocence. Of pure and simple joys. Of sharing.

My sister was a shadow behind me in the glass of the window, out of reach of my fingertips, her hair hiding her face. But the lamps on the boulevard had been extinguished and there were no images in the glass that I had not dreamed there.

The child lives in a hut of palm-leaf woven with bamboo. Saigon is a dream of stones and silk, a city waiting, soft and heavy with tales, peopled with dragons that dance in the streets. Somewhere in the darkness, waiting for her. A city where innocence is far away and long ago.

I undressed.

We want you to be happy, my birth mother had said. *Free of the tall man, free of our shame.*

I took my kris knife from its hiding place and laid it in my lap as I sat before the window again.

The handle was worn smooth with sweat and use; the blade writhed like a pale serpent in the night. But the knife was innocent, whatever it had been used for. Innocent, and full of wisdom.

The child lives a dream of Saigon, but the right path is full of lies, and dreams must end. She must waken.

Just a little more time, a little more. Please, she prays.

I caressed my forearm with the sinuous blade of the kris. It was soothing.

Riossi.

What exactly will he want? How much? How will I hold him to any promise he makes?

The blade whispered of monsters in Saigon. Creatures that changed to tigers, creatures that drank blood, and creatures that sought power over others.

My tutor was right. It was not their capabilities that made them monsters, but their actions. And in those, humans could be every bit as evil as monsters.

I dream a child is no longer a child. An innocence is put aside and a mark is made upon her. Others read that mark and the word they speak is ugly.

Her sister cries.

I only made you promise not to hate me, she says. Do not do this.

I jerked awake.

I told her I loved her. If they called me a whore for rescuing her, well, that's what they'd called her for five years. I was as old now as she'd been when she decided my opportunity was worth more than her innocence.

Whore.

I knew there would be no turning back.

Ophélie feels sick. The strength has leaked from her limbs.

I stood and rested my head against the glass of the window.

Bian is strong. Bian understands that the knife is innocent. Bian understands that nothing is done but we do it ourselves. We alone can choose the paths we walk.

Just a little more time. Please.

But the sky was growing lighter, moment by moment. Prayers would not hold back the day.

Will it hurt?

I turned the blade of the kris so that it pressed against my flesh.

Yes. It would hurt. More inside than out.

They say Saigon at dawn is like waking from an opium dream.

But I'm waking to a nightmare.

I will find a way to speak to him and persuade him to search for you, whatever it costs, as soon as Maman and Papa have gone. I promise you, my sister. I will find you. I swear to you.

The knife broke the flesh, and a thin line of blood sealed my vow.

Chapter 31

After breakfast, Maman arranged for a message to be sent to the Gosselins, and a Malabar carriage to take us there mid-morning.

She was concerned, naturally, as Monsieur Gosselin was not always well. However, Madame Gosselin was a strong and capable woman, and Manon was my best friend. Their house on the far side of the Governor's Palace was spacious and pleasant. It never crossed my mind that there would be any other place that I should stay, or that our request would be refused.

The first sign of a problem was that there was no message returned. It was not significant in itself. This was not Paris, with the absolute formality that one had to be invited with an exchange of letters before visiting.

The carriage arrived and we set out.

We were quiet. We crossed Boulevard Norodom right in front of the gates to the Palace, and Maman would not look out of the window.

I was more concerned with wondering how I would be able to carry out my plans without the Gosselins realizing what I was doing and stopping me. That was, if I had the courage of my nighttime convictions. Everything I'd decided on in the dark of my room seemed harder to accomplish in the light of day.

Manon saw us arrive. She rushed out of the house as we got down from the Malabar and she threw her arms around me, in tears.

I thought she was upset for me, for what had happened to Papa, but as I patted her back, her mother came out and I realized she'd been crying too.

We were invited into a house as cheerless as our own at the moment.

A fresh pot of coffee was delivered as we were ushered into the salon. I knew the Gosselins' servants and had always spoken with them. This time the maid hurried past in silence with her eyes downcast.

"I'm so sorry I didn't reply to your message, Thérèse," Madame Gosselin said, when we were sitting. "And, of course, I've heard about your news. I'm truly, truly sorry. I know how much his projects meant to Zacharie. To all the people here. It is a travesty, what has happened."

She put her coffee cup down and clasped her hands tightly in her lap.

"I'm afraid we also have had bad news," she said, with an effort to speak levelly. "We, too, are being sent back immediately."

"I'm so sorry," Maman gasped. "But why? What reason?"

"My husband is not well. We all know this." Madame Gosselin stared fixedly at her hands. "It comes and goes. In truth, it affects no one else."

The upstairs floorboards creaked as someone walked above us. It was the master bedroom—Monsieur Gosselin, I assumed. Neither Manon nor her mother looked up.

"However, the lieutenant governor has decided that it damages the colony, that he should sometimes be seen to be unwell by the ... by the natives," Madame Gosselin continued, her eyes flicking across at me in a sort of apology. "He says that it damages respect for France. That we must seek treatment in Paris."

"This is outrageous!" Maman said. "That man! What does he think he's doing? Your husband doesn't even work for his administration."

"Yes, we said that too." Madame Gosselin sighed. "However, in serious matters of health, the government can enforce repatriation apparently. We have no basis to refuse."

She dabbed at her eyes.

"The *Victorieuse* leaves tomorrow, and we must be on board, or be arrested and taken to the ship. There is no time for anything. We will have to leave half the packing to a shipping company. And what am I to do with the servants? They have been with us since we came. They deserve better than to be turned out. What can we do for them?" She shook her head and went on more quietly. "I'm sorry, I know these are all things you face as well."

We did, but Maman had decided her cousins should stay and look after the house on Boulevard Bonnard, so we were better off in many respects. I hated the idea of the Fontaudins in our house, but there was nothing for it.

Maman explained why we'd come, even though it was now clearly not possible. When she said that I would be staying, Manon wanted to stay with me, but Madame Gosselin did not know how long it would take for her husband to be cured, if ever. She ruled out leaving Manon behind.

We left their house shortly afterwards. Time did not pause for tears, any more than it paused for prayers.

The Malabar had waited for us and Maman gave the driver another address, where my other good friend, Rochelle Champin, lived with her parents.

But it was desperation and we both knew it. The Champins' house was small and Madame Champin didn't feel she could accept the responsibility. She wrung her hands and wouldn't meet our eyes as she listed everything that made it impossible for me to stay there.

I could tell Rochelle was disappointed, but she wasn't the sort of daughter who would let it show in front of her mother.

When we left the Champins', Maman told the driver to take us back to Boulevard Bonnard. My parents had many more friends, but Maman's faith in them had been shattered by the events at the ball.

"Perhaps I could stay at Monsieur Song's," I suggested as we rolled away.

"Nonsense," Maman said. "Cholon is not an acceptable place for a young lady."

She stirred uneasily in her seat.

"I understand he is a very good tutor to you, Ophélie, but honestly, if it were only down to me, I wouldn't accept you even visiting him for lessons. Whatever his merits on other matters, whatever the truth of his position in the Chinese community, he lives there with his wives and concubines. That is his business, and his culture, but it's not an appropriate place for you to be."

"Yes, Maman." There was no point arguing with her. "Where then?"

She sighed. "I know it's not what you would want, but the best solution at the moment is for you to stay in our house with the Fontaudins to look after you."

Chapter 32

It was the day the *Victorieuse* departed. It was early; another pre-dawn gathering of mist dragons slid off the Saigon river as the sun turned the eastern sky pink. Taller quayside buildings began to glow as the light caught them, but it still felt chill and dark beneath the imposing ironclad bulk of the corvette. The navy ship loomed alongside the Quai de la Marine, tall and indifferent to the petty concerns of the people gathered before it.

I didn't care how it looked or how brave I'd been before; I clung onto Papa and Maman.

I'd never had the chance to hug my birth parents, to tell them how much I loved them. And yet I was finding no comfort in this parting embrace.

Don't go. Not yet. Just a little more time, a little more.

I felt sick and numb at the same time. My heart was pounding so hard, I could feel it in my throat, but Maman said I looked so pale.

Time was running out.

They'd carried ex-Governor Laurent aboard on a stretcher an hour ago. In the gaslit darkness, he'd looked exhausted, struggling to acknowledge farewells.

The Gosselins were ready to go aboard. Monsieur Gosselin looked utterly bewildered and lost. Taking him away from the place he loved seemed to have exactly the wrong effect. Madame Gosselin rushed around for both of them, making sure everything was in place, that she'd said goodbyes to all their friends.

"I'll write," Manon said through her tears, still hugging me as her mother plucked at her sleeve. "I'll write every week."

"You won't," I said. "But try to write every month. I will treasure each word."

And I would. Letters from Manon would be hopelessly tangled with her exuberance and so precious to me.

The family made their way carefully up the wobbling walkway onto the deck. Their former servants clustered on the quay and waved, some of them crying.

Then, finally, there was just Papa, Maman and me in the shadow of the *Victorieuse*.

The Fontaudins had bid their farewells to my parents and left us to our grief in private. Madame Fontaudin had needed to rest her hip, so they sat and waited for me outside one of the cafes on the Ronde.

Maman had been right about the majority of our friends in Saigon; few of them had come to say farewell. The Champins did. A half-dozen others. But now that they had all gone, there was one final friend: Monsieur Song and his daughter, Qingzhao, approached.

We exchanged formal bows and greetings with the Songs. Then Song offered Papa his hand to shake in the Western manner.

"I am most upset at this parting," he said seriously, as he and Papa shook. "I am even more upset at the behavior of this new regime. Hurry back, my friend. Saigon needs you."

There was silence for a minute. Whatever Papa might say privately, it was shocking to hear the opinion said openly by my tutor, and yet it was true. Whatever the reasons for the lieutenant governor's actions, perhaps to 'put his stamp' on the new administration, he had damaged so many things in such a short time.

"I will need the full backing of the Quai d'Orsay," Papa said. "But I have every intention of returning to repair these problems."

"Ophélie is staying behind with our cousins," Maman said. "Will you be willing to continue giving her lessons?"

Monsieur Song first looked surprised and then glanced briefly over at where the Fontaudins sat waiting.

"Of course," he replied.

"We don't wish to impose a burden on our cousins," Maman said carefully. "They don't understand the communities here like we do. I wouldn't want them to be concerned about where Ophélie goes for lessons. Could you come to our house on Boulevard Bonnard?"

My tutor paused before replying. "So long as I am welcome there."

There was such an undercurrent. I wasn't sure whether Monsieur Song was not pleased that I was staying, or not pleased that it would be with the Fontaudins.

The Songs exchanged glances. They both slipped hands into their sleeves and their faces smoothed. It made me think of the surface of a pond after a single breath of wind has rippled across and died away.

They bowed once more and left us.

"Boarding!" A seaman shouted from the top of the gangplank.

It seemed such a brief time since Papa and I had walked down here and spoken of the Duke of Magenta, and how most political careers end in failure. Papa looked somehow less alive than he had then. His shoulders were lower and the spring was missing from his step.

He saw my look and straightened up. "It'll not be long, Ophélie. In just six weeks, your mother and I will be back in France. Then we'll clear up the misunderstanding at the Quai d'Orsay. We'll send you telegrams. It'll take four months, six at the most, and we'll be together again, here in Saigon, on this very spot."

He blinked and swiveled round as the last of their luggage was being carried aboard on the long, springy gangplank.

"Hey! Look out there. Careful with that," he called.

He passed one hand across his eyes and then rubbed his hands together briskly.

"I must check that they're getting them to the right cabin."

"Papa," I said and hugged him. "I love you. I'll miss you so much."

"No more than six months, my daughter. I love you very much." His voice had become tight. He gave me one final squeeze and hurried away up the gangplank, leaving me a few more precious moments with Maman.

She was looking so pale.

"I love you, Maman," I whispered. "It'll pass quickly."

"Ophélie, my beloved daughter," Maman replied, "this day of all days, I cannot lie to you." She looked down and her hand clutched at the gold locket where she kept tiny locks of our hair knotted together. When she spoke again, her words came slowly, and stumbling. "I feel a … a shadow in my heart and I fear for us all."

Her words chilled me. I seemed to feel it then, as well. Some horror we'd all overlooked, one that was in plain sight. "Maman—"

"Hush, hush, my girl. Let me speak while I still can." She took a deep breath. "Children grow on the foundation laid down by their parents. Unless that foundation is firm and constant, how difficult is it for a child to grow to be upright and strong? I'm sick with the knowledge we've failed you, Ophélie: not just Zacharie and me, but both your sets of parents. We couldn't give you that time of careless innocence that children need, and without which they grow bitter and suspicious. For the right reasons, we've made all the wrong choices. Now, we are stuck. All we can give you is our love and our hopes."

Tears gathered in her eyes. I hugged her wordlessly.

"Boarding!" came the call again.

"It's only a few months, Maman."

A tearful smile trembled her lips.

"I know you will grow up to be fearless, my precious child, but may you also grow up to be true. I wish, with all my heart, you find an easing of your burdens, and you come to your fulfillment, whatever that may be." She kissed my forehead. "I love you. May darkness never dim the light that shines in you."

"Aboard! All aboard!" A seaman was hanging over the railing and calling out. "Last call."

One final, awkward hug that I wanted to hold forever, and then Maman was last up the gangplank before they swung it away.

Then the cables were being winched in and the bow eased out into the current. The river never seemed so swift as it did that morning, when the *Victorieuse* slid around the first bend and took them out of my blurred sight.

Part 5 – Darkness Falls

黑

暗

中

Mark Henwick

Chapter 33

When I could no longer see any part of the grey corvette I turned away and looked for the Fontaudins.

We hadn't started off well, Maman's cousins and I. My life was going to be awkward enough without complications at home. I had to remind myself we hardly knew each other, and they knew nothing about Saigon and Indochina. I should give them some leeway.

Never make an enemy you don't have to, Papa had told me many times. It was very sound advice.

I sighed; I would find some compromise. It would not be such a burden. I needed some freedom to proceed with my plans to find my sister, and, while not exactly there in place of my parents, the Fontaudins would be regarded as my guardians by French society. I needed to respect that. I would have to charm them to pursue those plans while keeping my home life tolerable and as respectable as it could be, on the surface.

Very well.

I had to pause as a squad of soldiers marched along the docks. It seemed they had not been stood down yet, after the precautionary alert in preparation for the changes to this region brought by the *Victorieuse*.

It sounded a strange note in the clear Saigon morning.

What did they think would happen? A revolt? The changes hardly seemed to matter to anyone outside of the French colonials.

Not my concern.

The Fontaudins were sitting under the awning outside the cafe where Rue Vannier met the Ronde.

"Thank you for waiting," I said, slipping into a seat opposite them. "You are so kind to agree to all this at such short notice."

Despite the early hour, I noticed Monsieur Fontaudin was drinking absinthe with his coffee.

"Oh, it's nothing. Nothing," he said. "A grievous week for you. A terrible blow for Zacharie and Thérèse. Terrible."

Madame Fontaudin's mouth was a thin line. "We must go back to the house now," she said. "If my hip gets worse, I won't be able to face those stairs."

"Oh, one moment, my dear," her husband said, as he took another sip.

"Hurry up," she replied brusquely, and turned to me. "Get a carriage. One of those … malaback things."

"Malabar," I said. "We call them that because the drivers mainly come from the Malabar coast of India."

"I don't care why you call them these outlandish names. Why are you still sitting there?"

"Blanche," Monsieur Fontaudin remonstrated gently.

His wife turned her face away.

I went outside and waved. There was a Malabar just discharging his passenger on the other side of the Ronde, and he trotted his horse around quickly.

"M'zelle." He beamed, pleased to pick up a new fare so quickly.

"For Boulevard Bonnard, please. It will take a moment for my … guardians to arrive." I nodded in their direction. "The lady needs help to climb in."

"Yes, M'zelle." He jumped down, still beaming, put some steps on the ground and stood ready to help.

Monsieur Fontaudin finished his absinthe and helped his wife to her feet.

She gripped her stout walking stick and began to make her way towards the Malabar.

"God! The heat, and it's early yet," Monsieur Fontaudin said, wiping his pink brow with a handkerchief. He held her right arm at the steps.

As she paused, the driver reached out.

"Keep your filthy hands off me," she spat and made a swing at him with her stick.

He jumped back, shocked.

"He was just trying to help," I said.

She ignored me, banging her stick on the floor as she entered the carriage.

Monsieur Fontaudin shook his head in embarrassment and followed her in.

I stayed outside and apologised quietly to the driver.

His face had gone completely blank.

"It doesn't matter, M'zelle," he muttered.

I wanted to walk home, but I made myself get in and we set off.

Bình tâm. Keep calm.

Give them time. They are adapting to Saigon. Charm them.

"So, what are your plans for the future, Ophélie?" Monsieur Fontaudin asked.

"Do you mean until Papa and Maman come back, or for ever?"

"You shouldn't assume the Beauclercs will come back for you," Madame Fontaudin cut in.

I blinked.

"What do you mean, Madame?"

"Hush, Blanche," her husband said. "This isn't appropriate at the moment."

"Nonsense. The sooner she understands, the better." She raised her chin. "It is not kindness to be unclear on this. She is not French, and she will never be accepted into real French society. Not even here, let alone in France."

I couldn't believe what I was hearing.

"You were a ploy, nothing more. A move that seemed clever at the time. Who better could understand the Asian question than a man who had adopted an Annamese girl? Who was better qualified to lead the colony?" She sniffed. "Well it failed."

"This is outrageous!" I said. How dare she?

"Is it? Monsieur Beauclerc works for the Quai d'Orsay. He will go where they tell him to. They are certainly not going to send him back here. You're a fool if you believe they would."

"Blanche, this is needless, and you do not know these things for sure," he said.

"Oh! Fah!" She snorted and turned to look out the window.

Monsieur Fontaudin made a calming gesture with his hands, as if he were trying to put out a fire. "It is true that Zacharie must heed the orders of the minister, but I see no reason they will not return him here, Ophélie. Eventually. You must be patient, I think. We must be patient and careful with the money, and so on. That's all we can say now. That is all."

Careful? What does he mean?

Papa had left more than enough to maintain the house on Bonnard, and it wasn't as if they were being charged to stay there. Monsieur Fontaudin had a job while he was here in Saigon, and a good income from it. This was all ridiculous.

Still … what if his company ordered Monsieur Fontaudin back to France before Papa returned? I didn't need the Fontaudins to look after me, but it was not acceptable in society for a young lady to live on her own.

None of which possible complications excused Madame Fontaudin.

The rest of the trip passed in an icy silence, and as soon as we were home I left to meet with Rochelle, Jade in tow. There was no point returning until my temper had cooled.

Could there be truth in what she said?

Who would I trust to tell me?

Chapter 34

Coffee with Rochelle was a somber affair. We spoke with every effort to be normal, but it was clear to me how much we both missed Manon. It was Manon who would continually bounce the conversation to a new topic before we'd quite finished the last. Without her, the talk seemed to slow, almost stuttering to a stop.

I was ashamed that it was a relief when Rochelle said she had to return home.

I stayed at the table, watching her collect her companion, an Annamese woman they called Belle, and set off down the street at a leisurely rate.

They walked together, talking. Not like Jade and me.

I could see Jade looking across from her table, but I was not ready to go back and face Madame Fontaudin yet.

I waved at the waiter and asked for La Poste, the main Saigon newspaper, to read.

What are they making of all the changes?

It was the third day since the ball, and the lead article was still full of the implications of the new colony of Indochina. Much of the text echoed what had been said by Hubert already: better structure, clearer purpose, responsible management.

I wondered if others saw through the text: the cancellation of projects to relieve the poverty of the people; the emphasis that Indochina would fund itself from the output of Cochinchina—rice and opium. A whole page was given over to the responses of planters and merchants.

They were all for it. There were voices raised against some of the changes, but they were small and tucked away in the corners of the page.

The last page featured an interview with the lieutenant governor himself. A modern style interview, where they quoted passages from him verbatim, as if he were talking directly to the reader.

I was about to cast it aside, but the word *tigers* caught my eye.

I have thrown aside a mountain of misguided projects and useless, meaningless tasks. Here's one that defies belief: an investigation requested of the police to chase down gangsters who can turn into tigers at night! A girl, adopted by a French family, claims to be hunted by one of these—a terrible gangster by the name of Bac Thao, a man a hundred years old or more, and all because her father stole some gold from the Emperor.

No. This is the end of the 19th Century. This is a land governed by France. A land we will govern with clear heads, with intelligence and rationality. We will cast aside old superstitions and the moldering past. We will bring this land into the modern age. That is how we will bring the most benefit to the great numbers of people under our rule.

Meulnes.

The police chief was the only person who knew my story and could have told Hubert.

For the second time that day, I was trembling with anger. My hands were clumsy with it, making the act of paying far slower than it should have been.

I stalked out of the cafe, the newspaper clutched in my hand.

It was not far to the police headquarters on Rue Lagrandiere, and early enough that Meulnes would not be gone to lunch.

By the time I got there I was thinking more clearly, so I was amazed when I was actually allowed into the building and shown into his office.

I was still angry enough that I slammed the paper on his desk.

To his credit, he winced visibly.

"Mam'selle Beauclerc. Please. Take a seat."

"You promised to keep this confidential!"

"No, Mam'selle. I said to you, most carefully, that I am required only to speak to the governor."

"So you told Hubert everything?"

"Lieutenant Governor Hubert asked specific questions of your family, and I was constrained to answer them. He has access to notes and messages passed between your father and me. He would have found out if I had refused to speak about a matter that we referred to."

"He deliberately mocks me, in a newspaper article, and he might as well have had my name printed!"

"That, I cannot control, and for what it's worth, I regret his behavior," Meulnes said. "In his defense, he thinks no harm can come from it. He simply doesn't believe there is anything in the story."

"And neither do you," I said. "Yet all your disbelief will not protect me. Even if you don't believe there can be someone real called Bác Thảo, you admitted there are gang lords who know the story about the gold. They will hear of this article."

Meulnes shrugged. "That's true. Yet what I believe has no impact on this matter. There is nothing I can do, no resource I can spare that the lieutenant governor will not find out about." He shifted in his seat, moved the large blotter on his desk a fraction to one side. "Should you be harmed, we will of course act with the utmost vigor."

"That will be such a comfort to me."

The sarcasm was a mistake, I saw.

His voice became harder. "You should consider your position, and those of your adoptive parents, very carefully."

I gasped. "Is that some form of threat?"

"No, Mam'selle, not in the sense that I am issuing a threat," he said. "But there are many dangers to you that you seem not to be aware of."

He paused a moment before continuing. "You must realize that words spoken in Saigon sound different in Paris. We talk to each other through the artificial constraints of telegrams and dispatches. There is no subtlety as there is in talking face to face. Meanings are lost. What may be the truth in Saigon ..." he shrugged again, "may have no more weight than a rumor in Paris. And vice versa."

"I don't understand, Monsieur. What truths and rumors are we talking about?"

He sighed and pressed his hands flat down on the blotter.

"It is the nature of these things when a politician falls out of favor, that those who cause it will seek justifications for their actions."

"You are saying there are allegations being made against my father?"

"Indeed. The matter of your adoption, for instance. There are questions raised over the legality."

"Governor Laurent himself signed the papers. Are you saying that he broke the law?"

"Perhaps. I am not an expert in that kind of law. Certainly, there were questions put to me by Lieutenant Governor Hubert, as to whether you'd been bought and sold, like chattel. And if there are such questions here, what will Monsieur Beauclerc face in Paris? Eh? Monsieur Laurent is in no fit state to support him, or defend his actions, not even to counter the claim he was already too ill to govern when this took place."

"That's just false, and you know it. This is monstrous!"

"It is politics, Mam'selle. But yes, it is also monstrous." He got up and went to the window, where he began rocking on his heels as he often did. "Nor does it necessarily stop with allegations directly against Monsieur Beauclerc."

Everything was spinning out of control. I had come in with a legitimate complaint about the newspaper article. Now the chief was talking about lies being spread about Papa, or about me.

"What do you mean?"

"I am aware of questions raised about you and your Chinese tutor," Meulnes said.

"What? Me? And Monsieur Song? What possible questions could there be?"

He ran a weary hand through his hair. "Out here, in Saigon, we understand certain things about life in the East. That, for instance, the indigenous population is familiar with strong rulers and personal rule. Happier with that structure. That they see our system of courts and laws, where plaintiffs are faceless and equal in the sight of the law, almost as a weakness."

I made to interrupt, but he waved me to silence.

"Now, Monsieur Song is a good man. His rule of Cholon is benevolent. I understand this, and I'm willing to work with him for the good of all communities. But describe the situation to someone in Paris and that man will call Monsieur Song a gang lord. They would have trouble seeing the difference between descriptions of Monsieur Song and Bác Thảo."

"He's nothing like that! He's a respected man and a leader of his community."

"More accurately, he is a leader of the Cholon Harmonious Societies." Meulnes spoke on over my protestation. "Even I, with years in service in Cochinchina, have trouble telling the difference between a Harmonious Society and a triad or a tong. Certainly, in the end, they must all maintain their position with illegal force."

"I am sure Monsieur Song would be better able to argue this with you, if he were here. I simply don't believe it. Why do you say such things?"

"Why indeed, Mam'selle? You seem to think I am trying to damage Monsieur Beauclerc, his friends and you. I am not. In fact, I am doing what I can to protect you. And I am not lying."

"Protect me? You haven't even been able to keep my name out of the papers."

"What I *have* been able to do, Mam'selle, is keep as many facts as I am able out of common knowledge. Facts which would be used against you and Monsieur Beauclerc."

"Such as?"

"I have been able to hide all mention of your sister from the lieutenant governor and others. Imagine what Monsieur Beauclerc's enemies in Paris would make of it if they could say your sister is a prostitute."

"But she had no choice! She was sold; she's a slave. My parents were tricked."

"I must assure you, such details would not make a difference to the people in Paris who would wish to say these things."

He raised his hands to quiet my protests.

"Please, this is not the matter at hand. I am not about to make any information available that I do not have to. I merely mention it as an aside. For Monsieur Song, well, there's nothing that we can say or do that will change things. But for you, Mam'selle, I have a warning. If you were to make complaints and people were to go looking for ways to discredit you, they would find them. Not from me, but they would find them. And in discrediting you, they would also discredit Monsieur Beauclerc."

"What could they possibly find?"

"Rumors. Suspicions. But serious ones." He tilted his head. "You are aware of the Deuxième Bureau?"

"The secret service. Of course. Why would they—"

I stopped. They'd seen me at the Words on the Wind in Cholon. Monsieur Song had warned me that it was used by rebels. I hadn't been back, but as Meulnes said, a mere suspicion here in Saigon might be regarded as the absolute truth in Paris. Papa might be confronted with this 'fact', and in the time it took for the truth to be discovered, the damage would be done.

If he was going to have a fight just to get posted back here, as Madame Fontaudin suggested, it would become an impossible task if there was a flow of more 'rumors' from Saigon. I understood what Meulnes was saying: that bad as it was, making a nuisance of myself would certainly make it worse.

I took a deep, despairing breath. Saigon wound its coils around me, tighter and tighter.

"There is nothing in the Deuxième Bureau's suspicions," I said. "I want no part in rebellion. I was looking for messages from my family as countless others do."

Meulnes just shrugged. He clearly didn't suspect me of treason. And yet, as he said, what he believed didn't counter the power of this lie.

"And so much for being a secret service," I said. If Meulnes had heard it, who else might have?

"They are indiscreet," Meulnes acknowledged.

Never make an enemy you don't have to.

I had come close to making an enemy of the police chief, and that would be a mistake.

I dropped my head. "I'm sorry I shouted at you, Monsieur."

"Your situation is not easy," he replied. "Please remember that neither is mine. My duty has requirements of me. And my advice to you is to sink out of sight. To do nothing. To be unavailable for people to use you in their political schemes. To hope to be forgotten."

I looked down. It was good advice. Ophélie would take it. She understood about being a meek French girl. About not causing a fuss. Bian was a different matter.

"Thank you for your advice," I said. I made to rise, but paused. "Would you speak the truth to me about my father, Monsieur Meulnes? My adopted father."

Meulnes frowned at me.

"Yes, of course."

"How likely is it that he will be able to return? If no one ... ferments other rumors to damage his case."

The police chief returned to his chair and blew out a long breath.

"He will return. The East has a way of getting into your blood, eh? Whether he remains in the administration is a matter of politics beyond my ability to predict."

It was a fair answer, and he liked that I had asked him. It seems I had avoided making an enemy of him.

"I see. Thank you for your honesty," I said. "Is there anything I can do that will help him?"

"Nothing." He looked to the side, embarrassed. "Forgive me, but you are just a girl, and not even French in the eyes of many."

I left the police headquarters under a boiling monsoon sky. A sense of hopelessness hung over me.

Just a girl. Not even French. Helpless. A liability.

If I did nothing, Papa might still face impossible obstacles preventing him returning in a position to carry out his plans for Cochinchina. If I made a nuisance of myself, they would whisper that his adopted daughter was a traitor. And if I followed the only path to find Nhung that seemed open to me, they would call me *whore*, and they wouldn't whisper.

And somewhere out there, Bác Thảo would be hearing news of me and dreaming about the fortune in the Emperor's gold that he had chased for so long.

Threats loomed from every side.

Chapter 35

I could not return home yet. In my current state, one comment from Madame Fontaudin and I would lose control. Even the Bian side of me realized that everything could be made more difficult if I gave the Fontaudins cause.

Be invisible, Meulnes said. *Hope to be forgotten. Do nothing.*

I couldn't. *Nothing* was not acceptable.

An hour ago, I might have asked my tutor for advice. Now? Was my tutor a gang lord? Did Papa know of this? How could he not? Or was Meulnes mistaken?

Without advice that I trusted, I had to be realistic. I couldn't help my birth parents, and there was nothing I could do to help my adopted parents. I couldn't hide from Bác Thảo.

The last remaining action left to me was to help my sister.

I swear to you.

I had sealed that oath with my blood.

I didn't know how to do what was needed, but every journey starts with the first step. And it was easier that Maman and Papa weren't here to witness.

I looked up; as if they'd known in advance, my wandering feet had brought me to the office of the Opium Regie, where Messieurs Valois and Picardin had warned me against asking favors of their boss.

There would be no turning back, once I started down this path, but what else could I do?

Hide for six months and pray that Papa would return with some authority?

If he no longer worked for the administration, what could he do? I would have waited six months for nothing.

My legs felt weak.

Ophélie cringed at the thought of the shame she would bring to her family. Bian had made an oath.

I'd walked past the entrance. I needed a little more time.

No!

I turned around suddenly, startling Jade.

I ignored her. My breath came short and my heart raced as I entered the building.

Only to be confronted with the same arrangement that I'd seen at the City Hall. A guard stood in the way.

"I've come to see Monsieur Riossi," I said. My voice sounded weak.

"He's not expecting you, Mam'selle." The guard looked at his list.

"We didn't make a specific appointment." I held my hands together to stop them shaking and looked up at the guard. "I'm sure he'll see me, if you ask him. Would you ask him for me? Please?"

I smiled.

Was there a particular way I needed to smile? How would Emmanuela smile? I couldn't imagine a guard stopping her from going in.

The guard rocked back. He pursed his lips. "Ah. Well. In any event, he is out." Then, after looking around first, he leaned forward and whispered. "He's seldom in the office, Mam'selle. Look for him at the Messageries Maritimes in the early evening. Or catch him at lunch."

"What a good idea. And where does he lunch, Monsieur?"

He huffed. "Hôtel de l'Univers has the best restaurant in town. If you don't find him there ..." He glanced around again. "Come back and speak to me. I'll see what I can do."

"Thank you, Monsieur. You've been most helpful."

Still trembling, I turned away. I made myself look back over my shoulder at him and smile.

It had been difficult and not so difficult, at the same time. There would be far worse to come.

And still, I'd been defeated at the first step, if only temporarily. Out onto the street, dazzled in the harsh sun after the darkness in the entrance to the Regie, I wondered where to go next.

"M'zelle! M'zelle B'clerc!"

It was little Hamid, the urchin who'd brought me Lanh's message from the Words on the Wind. He was trotting across the road toward me with something in his hand.

My heart stuttered.

Lanh had said not to use the wall, but he hadn't said how he would contact me. What better way than to use the urchins, especially if he knew which one had brought me his message from the wall.

Or was it a message from my tutor? What would I do, if it was?

"Hello, Hamid," I said and knelt to be level with him. He had a huge grin on his face.

I could hear Jade's snort of disapproval, but she didn't say anything, thinking Hamid was just another beggar and I was a fool to talk to him.

"Got message," Hamid said in Trade, handing a piece of paper across out of Jade's sight. "I come quick-quick find you."

"Thank you," I said in French and then switched to Trade. "Not got little bread now. Here coin. You buy good food."

He took the coin. It would be enough for a meal from a stall in Cholon. His eyes grew wide.

"Thank you," he sang in French and decided to leave before I changed my mind. "Thank you. Thank you," came drifting from him as he trotted back the way he'd come.

I unfolded the piece of paper.

It was Lanh's writing.

Under the ideogram for the right path, he'd written hastily in Annamese:

Be by the banh xeo food stalls on Crocodile Creek at the start of the second watch

There was no Crocodile Creek anymore; it had been filled in and covered by the market, but people still used the name. Second watch was the old Annamese way of telling time. It started at 9pm.

How would I do that? How would I get out of the house in the night, without anyone following me? How dangerous would it be?

That was Ophélie speaking. Bian would find a way.

A little seed of hope pushed its way through all my despair at being powerless. Maybe Lanh could do things I could not. Find Nhung. Get our parents to somewhere safe.

Yes!

Lanh was clever and capable. He could go places I couldn't. No one would be watching him and Bác Thảo wouldn't know he was here in Saigon.

All I needed to do was sneak out of the house and down to the market.

It was scary. I couldn't tell if that was my street sense warning me, or just the reaction to Ophélie thinking about wandering the streets of Saigon alone at night.

No matter. I could not turn down this opportunity.

What luck that there had been a guard on the door of the Opium Regie, that Riossi had been unavailable. Maybe I didn't need to commit myself to a course of action that would shame me for life, and damage Papa's plans for the people of Cochinchina.

I returned home, determined not to provoke a scene with Madame Fontaudin.

That determination was sorely tested. Nothing would be good enough for the woman. I sighed in relief when she went upstairs to rest from the heat after lunch.

The afternoon passed, slow as an overloaded bullock cart. Thunder growled away to the east, but no rain fell in Saigon.

Monsieur Fontaudin had been told to take some time to acclimatize, so he was not at work. He complained of the heat even more than his wife, but he also seemed very distracted and restless. In the late afternoon, when it had cooled a little and businesses would be open again, he announced he would be going out.

Madame Fontaudin was still resting from the heat in the bedroom, so he and I were alone in the salon. He stood and patted his pockets.

"I need to go to the bank," he said. "No need to disturb Blanche. Let her rest. Just some of these silly formalities one has to do. Nothing to concern anyone."

He was sweating profusely and his gaze flicked around the room, anywhere but me.

What is wrong with him?

Not all Frenchmen could stand the heat, and it looked as if Fontaudin might be one of those who couldn't. I shouldn't make too much of it; he wasn't as bad as his wife. He certainly was under no obligation to explain to me why he was going out.

I should be thankful for small mercies. I could relax alone for a while, think about Lanh and plan on how to leave the house without anyone noticing.

"Should I arrange for a carriage?" I asked.

"No. No need. I will walk to the corner and take a rickshaw."

He fumbled and fussed for another minute before leaving, carrying a small file of papers.

In the quiet that followed, I found some grease to put on the hinges of the front door and checked each step of the stair for creaks.

Soon after Monsieur Fontaudin returned, still red-faced and evasive, Madame Fontaudin came down the stairs, banging the floor with her cane and complaining about her hip.

As often happened with French people newly exposed to the heat, she had no appetite for an evening meal. When Monsieur Fontaudin declared he had business meetings over dinner and left in a rickshaw at six, she decided to retire to the bedroom again. *My bedroom*, she said and it was like the screech of rusty hinges to my ears. That was my parents' bedroom.

But nevertheless, it seemed luck was going my way.

At eight o'clock, I changed into clothes that my tutor had provided for me to do exercises in. They were dark, made from a tough cloth and shapeless. I tied my hair and hid it down the back of my shirt. I would look like hundreds of other Annamese walking through Saigon in the evening, and to a casual glance, people would scarcely be able to tell if I was a boy or girl.

Lanh might recognize me. I was sure I would recognize him.

At quarter past eight, I crept out onto the landing and listened. There were no sounds from my parents' bedroom.

Carefully, I went down the stairs. There was a lamp in the hallway. The rest of the house was in darkness.

I moved the lamp so that less light shone on the front door and slipped silently out into the breathless night.

There were people strolling along Boulevard Bonnard, even people I knew. No one noticed me as I scurried down the road. In these clothes they didn't even look at me. My confidence grew with every step. Putting aside worries of being caught, I started to look forward to seeing my brother again. We would have so much to say. I would need to be careful to get back home before dawn.

Why was Lanh being so secretive? Did he think he was an embarrassment to me? Or was he hiding from Bác Thảo?

Or was it something else?

The market was a very different place at night; it was much quieter and full of shadows.

The stalls were almost all food vendors at this time. They were lit by hissing hurricane lamps and the glow of the coal fires they used for cooking. Food sizzled and the stallholders rattled their pans as they called out their prices. Clients ate and moved on, like a river running through the streets.

I was too early. It would look odd if I just stood and waited, so I bought a banh xeo, one of the fried pancakes full of shrimp and pork and egg. I kept my face averted as I paid, but the sweaty stallholder paid me no attention beyond what was necessary to hand across the pancake and wave his hand at the bowl of spicy sauce.

I squatted down, resting against the front of a closed shop across the street from the stall, and ate my food.

It had been five years. How would Lanh have changed? I imagined him taller. Smiling to see me. Laughing. He had always been too serious when we'd lived in Ap Long.

I finished and wiped my hands on my pants. More clients came and went. A young woman in a hurry. An old man, his stringy chest bared to the sweltering air, eating as he shambled on down the street. A couple of dour, stocky men in dusty work clothes, who stood not far from me to eat their pancakes.

Bullock carts' wooden axles squealed as they made their way down to the Arroyo Chinois. Tall Malabar carriages rattled by. Some soldiers wandered past.

Then a Malabar came to a stop right in front of the banh xeo stall I'd bought from. No one got out and I couldn't see inside it.

Was this Lanh?

But as I stood to look, strong hands grabbed me from behind. My arms were pinned by my sides. Another hand gripped my jaw; I couldn't shout. I could smell the banh xeo spice on the strong, dirty fingers. A sack dropped over my head and I was lifted into the carriage.

"Silence," hissed a voice, speaking Annamese.

Chapter 36

Stupid girl.

To wander blindly around in Saigon, dressed like an Annamese youth, the very day that Bác Thảo found out who I was from the newspaper. They must have been watching the house and couldn't believe their luck when I just walked out.

Stupid, stupid girl.

I didn't struggle on the floor of the carriage. They'd only tie me up.

Pretend to be too frightened to move.

There might be a chance when we stopped, if I wasn't tied up. The Malabar couldn't cross the footbridge into Khánh Hôi. There were always people walking over the bridge. I'd run away from my captors. Even if they caught me, they'd have to drag me across the bridge. Surely someone would stop them if I fought and screamed?

Maybe. Maybe not. Better not to be caught. Dive into the creek.

The journey didn't take long. I could feel the carriage rocking as the road changed and became more uneven. The smell of the Arroyo Chinois made its way into the carriage.

But it was too quiet. The footbridge was a busy, noisy area.

Where were they taking me?

We lurched to a stop. The door opened and I was pulled out roughly.

I tore at the sack over my head and kicked out hard.

They had expected it. My kick missed. I couldn't even get the sack off.

I could hear them laughing as they held me and pushed me inside a house. The door banged behind.

I was forced down onto the floor and the sack was taken off.

They loomed over me. The two dusty workers from the market.

One held a piece of paper in front of me with the zhèngdào characters and Lanh's message.

What?

"Don't fight," he said.

His accent was northern.

"Who are you?" I said. "Why did you bring me here? What do you want?"

"Shut up. Wait."

I was still angry, but there was a glimmer of hope; they didn't seem to be Bác Thảo's thugs. Unless he'd caught Lanh and found a copy of his message.

I asked more questions, but they ignored me. One slipped back outside. The other kept the door open a tiny amount, so he could look through and watch his companion.

Are they criminals? Looking out for police?

Perhaps it was too early for hope.

I heard a soft sound and spun around. Another man had come in the room, and he sat down on the floor across from me.

We were lit only by a single, dim lamp. He was an older man, maybe forty or fifty, round-faced, thin but strong, dressed in plain workers' clothes like the two who had kidnapped me. He looked Chinese rather than Annamese to me. His face was expressionless, but I saw a cold intelligence in his eyes. He was watching me closely.

"Your brother is here," he said. His accent was also northern, but he was well educated, unlike the other two. He startled me by switching to French, which he spoke well, but stiffly. "You may talk to him after I have finished."

"Who are you?" I asked. "What do you want with me?"

"It's better for you that you don't know my real name," he replied. "Call me Thiêu. As for what I want, that has greatly changed since your brother and I set out to come here."

The name he'd given meant 'burn' in Annamese. It had an ominous sound to my ears.

"What do you mean?" I said. "What has changed?"

"When we set out, you were the adopted Annamese daughter of the Frenchman who was going to be Governor of Cochinchina. Now? I admit, I'm only speaking to you because brother Lanh believes you may still be of some use."

"Use?"

"To the patriots of Annam."

Revolutionaries! The secrecy. The lookout at the door.

"You're the Can Vuong." I made a wild guess from discussions with Papa about the unrest in the north of the country.

The man's mouth pursed in distaste. "We have no interest in returning this country to the emperors who abandoned it, like the fools in the Can Vuong. We are the Party of the People."

He used the Annamese words to name his group —*Đảng Vì Dân*.

I had never heard of them, and he saw it. He was irritated, even if he hid it well.

"You have heard the words of the American president, Lincoln?" he said. "A government of the people, by the people and for the people?"

"Yes, of course," I replied. It was a favorite of Papa's.

"Are we not people, too? May we not have the same aspirations?"

Naturally my brother, always filled with the sense we should have pride in ourselves as a people, had fallen in with revolutionaries. At the same time, it hurt me. It sounded as if he'd only considered returning to Saigon because his party thought it would be useful to recruit me as a spy in the governor's house.

That wouldn't have worked. However much I loved Lanh, however much I might support the idea that Annamese should be ruling themselves in Cochinchina, and however much I was torn between my love for both my families, I had to draw the line somewhere. I would not have spied on Papa.

But these revolutionaries were dangerous. Not as bad as Bác Thảo, but equally capable of killing me if they felt I threatened them in some way. Could Lanh protect me? He seemed to be junior to this man. I had to be careful, for his sake as well as mine.

"I can't think what use I would be to you now, Monsieur Thiêu," I said meekly. "But I would still like to speak to my brother, please."

He looked silently at me for a minute before he nodded. "Very well. I will let him explain our purpose here."

He leaned back and rapped on the flimsy wall.

Lanh came in. After five years, I knew him in an instant, though he'd changed so much. He was taller, stronger, but he moved differently, more cautiously.

I wanted to hug him, but something told me that would be wrong with Thiêu watching, so even though my heart ached to do it, I stayed where I was while he sat on the floor next to Thiêu.

"Elder brother," I said respectfully in Annamese and bowed. "I am pleased to see you."

He nodded, his face stiff. This was not the Lanh I remembered. He'd been animated, enthusiastic, quick to anger, quicker to forgive. Easy to read.

"Even though the Frenchman is gone, you still have a chance to do something useful," he said.

I could hardly believe his first words to me. Five years and this indifferent sentence—it was like he'd slapped me.

"Not even a greeting? And what about our parents?" I said angrily. "Have you nothing to say about them?"

He shook his head, as if to dislodge a fly.

"They're not important."

I gasped. "Lanh! What has happened to you?"

"They are safe. Is that what you want to hear?" Lanh said. "He failed to get back in the mandarinate in Hué. He borrowed money and bought a small farm. As far as I know, he's still there. I don't care. I left to join the struggle against the oppressors. I no longer acknowledge the people you call parents."

"How can you—"

"Listen to me, Bian. You've been living like a French girl. Good food, good clothes, a nice house. Just like the mandarins, and all of it on the backs of the people. The rest of us are no more than beasts to the French and the court." He spoke quickly, angrily, his sentences full of stiff phrases, as if he'd learned them by rote. "Your father wanted to go back and join the mandarins, to be part of the cesspool of corruption and treason around an Emperor who collaborates to keep our people downtrodden, just so long as *he* was all right."

"So long as his family was all right, you included," I snapped back. It was bad manners for me to argue with him, especially in front of strangers, but I could not stop that coming out.

He looked surprised, as if he hadn't expected his little sister to argue back.

We had both changed. I knew from Papa that these new revolutionaries put aside the Confucian family order, the obedience of the son to the father, of the daughter to the son, and so on. They said that was all the sort of superstition and bad culture that made us weaker and easier for others to dominate.

Lanh had put those traditions aside. If he did not acknowledge a need to be respectful to our father, then I didn't need to be respectful to my elder brother.

But arguing with him about it was not going to work, however much I wanted to. I needed to be clever. It sounded as if my birth parents were safe. I could think about what I might do to help them at a later stage. What I had to do now was to get Lanh's help for Nhung.

I must appear to submit to him and mention Nhung when he might be more receptive.

I bowed my head. "I am sorry. I will not argue with you about your decision."

Even if it's as sensible as Jade telling me I can't escape my bad joss.

Lanh grunted.

"We know about Beauclerc. He was better than most," he said grudgingly. "The party thought he was good enough to send Thiêu and me here to talk with him. But he's gone, and Hubert is not the same."

I kept my head dipped. I wasn't going to disagree with that last comment.

"So now, we must do things for ourselves and not expect to recruit any of the French to our cause."

"I still don't know what I could do to help," I said.

Or what I might want to do. There were many things wrong with French rule, but if Thiêu was an example, I doubted the 'Party of the People' would be better.

I saw an exchange of glances between Thiêu and Lanh. Evidently, from my words, I had passed some minor test, because Thiêu nodded, and Lanh continued.

"Your tutor."

I blinked, surprised. "Song? You think I might influence him?"

"You might, but we are not at that stage yet. What we need now is an introduction."

I frowned.

"Song does not allow us to enter Cholon openly," Thiêu said. "He does not respond to our messages. We will not creep around like thieves."

Yet Lanh had crept in to send me a message on the Words on the Wind.

"He probably thinks we are like the Can Vuong," Thiêu went on. "You need to convince him that we are not. That we are more like him."

Even if my tutor was a gang lord, I doubted that he was anything like Thiêu, but something about the man frightened me, so I kept silent.

"Instead of fighting each other, we should unite," Lanh said.

I nodded as if reluctant.

Careful not to be too accepting, too quickly, I pretended to let them convince me over another hour of talking about how bad things were for the Annamese and Chinese, who were the rightful owners of this land, and how much better everything would be if their party were in control of it.

I didn't dare let my true feelings show.

One thing I did not doubt was that they fiercely believed they could improve things. Thiêu believed it with a deep passion. He'd chosen his nom de guerre well—he burnt with that passion, and the flames had a hypnotic quality. I'd never met a person like him, but Papa had warned me about them.

To live as they do, these fanatics, they give up many things. They expect their followers to make the same sacrifices.

Lanh was not quite so fierce and absolute, but I could see he was gradually falling under the spell of this man.

And I remembered another thing that Papa had said: *this kind of fanaticism needs them to regard their enemies as less human than they are. They are capable of unbelievable cruelty because, in their own minds, there is no cruelty in hurting lesser beings.*

That was what my street sense told me about Thiêu. Even with Lanh here, I was in danger. If I wasn't part of their party, I was not truly human in their eyes. They seemed to have no awareness that it was the same fault they accused the French of.

It was as if the spirit vision that Song had shown me had returned to my eyes. I could sense the frightening rage beneath Thiêu's calm exterior. I could also sense his arrogance. He expected to find a submissive Annamese girl with a spark of spirit that he could bend to his party's purposes.

Bian knew, if he saw what he expected to see, I might be safe.

"I will explain your messages to my tutor as well as I can," I said finally, bowing my head again.

So, whatever he was, I'd have to go and see Song.

And if he was really the head of the Chinese gangs in Cholon?

Now I was over the shock of Meulnes' accusation, I found it less upsetting. Maybe I was becoming numb to such things.

If Song *was* powerful, maybe he could kidnap Lanh, for his own good. Maybe he could think of a way to find Nhung. But if his tutoring had all just been a strategy to help an understanding with Papa, why would Song want to help me now?

So many things to think about. So many dangerous paths.

But whatever the truth about my lǎoshī, I trusted him more than I trusted the Party of the People.

"Good," Thiêu said, bringing me back to the conversation here. "You should do anything to persuade him."

I kept my head bowed in case they could somehow see my thoughts, and watched them beneath lowered eyelids.

"You advised me well," Thiêu said to Lanh. "Your sister is the sort of girl that we could use to spy on the French. They will find her attractive."

Lanh went pale, but his face showed nothing.

I felt a shock, down in the pit of my stomach.

Bình tâm. Bình tâm, I said to myself. *Keep calm. Keep calm.*

I'd learned to school my face when Phèdre or Chantal tried to provoke me. And I suspected this wasn't aimed at me; it was a test for Lanh. Thiêu was watching him, not me.

I couldn't allow myself to be sidetracked by Thiêu talking about me as if I were a whore for his revolutionary party, any more than I would have responded to Phèdre suggesting my parents deliberately sold Nhung.

Given what I'd planned on doing with Riossi, Thiêu was closer to the truth. I felt a little sick, but it was far more important to get their help for

Nhung, if I could. I couldn't leave it for another time. And now was a good time to get Thiêu's attention off my brother.

"I must ask something in return," I said.

"I don't make bargains," Thiêu said, but his cold gaze came back to me. "But tell me what you think is so important."

I hated him then, even more than I feared him.

"My brother has disowned our parents, but his elder sister is still family," I said. "She needs help."

I explained what I knew—how 'Aunty Kim' had tricked our parents and what she actually did with the girls she bought or kidnapped.

Thiêu made no comment. He was watching Lanh again.

I'd fallen into a trap, putting Lanh through another test.

But Nhung! His sister! He can't ignore her.

My elder brother's face was frozen. His eyes would not meet mine.

"The only sisters and brothers I acknowledge are in the party," he whispered eventually.

They let me go shortly after that.

I found I was down by the Arroyo Chinois, a couple of alleys away from the footbridge to Khánh Hôi. I hurried back to the market.

It was just as it had been before. Everyone going about their business, heedless of me.

I supposed I was lucky. Apart from a few bruises, they hadn't physically hurt me at all. But in my mind, I couldn't stop hearing Lanh's voice. *The only sisters and brothers I acknowledge ...*

It was because Thiêu was listening. He didn't mean it. Not Lanh.

But at the moment Lanh and the Party of the People were just another group who wanted to use me for something. There was no help for Nhung from them.

I would talk to Riossi tomorrow. I heard the distant chimes from the cathedral and corrected myself: today.

Nothing is done but we do it ourselves. We choose the paths we walk, and there is no more time. I swear to you, my sister.

It was strange. A numbness had leaked into me.

If Thiêu had suddenly appeared in my life a month ago, I wouldn't have been able to do anything.

If my story had leaked out to Bác Thảo a month ago, I would have been frozen in fear.

But now, it was as if everything that had happened was preparing me. *For what? What is coming that is worse?*

I was so bound up with thinking about that, I almost got caught.

A Malabar was coming slowly up the boulevard. Too late, I realized it was stopping in front of my house. I was already reaching for the front door when Fontaudin stepped down from the carriage.

I was saved by the fact that he was drunk. His foot slipped on the step and he sprawled onto the ground.

My first instinct was to help him, but another man was immediately behind him and I couldn't let them see me dressed like this and out in the road.

I slipped quickly into the house, closing the door silently. The lamp had gone out and I stood in the darkness.

From the window, I could see Fontaudin getting slowly to his feet, helped by the other.

"Far too much to drink, Yves," his companion said. The voice was thin and harsh. Hadn't I seen him getting off the ship when we met the Fontaudins?

"I'm fine," Fontaudin mumbled.

"Well, let your head answer to that tomorrow," the man said. He was frowning. He sounded irritated. "You need to get to work, earn some money. The sooner the better, eh?"

"I told you, I can pay you," Fontaudin said loudly, slurring his words. "Just a bad run of cards … won't last forever."

I heard a creak from above and fled upstairs, but not so quickly that I missed a last rejoinder from Fontaudin's companion: "Neither will my patience."

I skipped the noisy steps, crossed the landing and was inside my bedroom, leaning against the door, heart thudding, as I heard the answering thump of Madame Fontaudin's cane at the head of the stairs.

Fontaudin was a drunk and a gambler. Papa had left him in charge of his interests here in Saigon.

Chapter 37

It was hardly surprising I slept badly again.

Nightmares about tigers that crept into the house while I slept. A city full of people with their faces hidden behind stiff white masks. Terrible fanged monsters that seethed out of the sewers like spirit vipers and filled the air with their hissing.

In the twilight before dawn, I sat at my window, caressing the flesh of my arm with the sinuous kris knife and watching the sky bleed and congeal into a thunderous, aching bruise of a storm cloud that spanned the whole horizon.

The monsoon season was late, and it gathered itself slowly above Indochina.

It needed release. I dreamed I had a magic knife; that I could reach up and cut the cloud; that the sweet, cool rain would fall and cleanse the earth.

I dozed through the morning, not bothering to go downstairs. The Fontaudins didn't care. The whole house remained quiet, as if everyone were holding their breath.

It lasted until late morning, when I was roused by the sound of shouting and angry voices. Slamming doors.

Then silence.

Had I dreamed it? Perhaps I'd heard an argument from the boulevard outside?

It wasn't important. Riossi would be going to lunch soon.

I dressed carefully, and left without anyone noticing. I took a parasol in case that storm cloud burst. And to shield me from the view of others.

My hands were trembling and I could barely feel the street beneath my feet.

I crossed Boulevard Charner and Rue Catinat to arrive at the side of the Hôtel de l'Univers. I slowed down in the shade of the trees lining the street. At midday, most colonials were inside. No one was watching me. No one was noticing whether I looked nervous or guilty.

Could I do this?

My heart thudded in my chest, pulsed against my throat. I felt sick to my stomach.

What if one of my friends sees me?

I could claim to be walking down to the Ronde. For the exercise. Without a chaperone.

I *wanted* one of them to see me. It would give me an excuse to not go in.

None of them were here.

The arched Italianate windows on the upper stories of the hotel looked down at me like rows of disapproving raised eyebrows.

My sister does not have a choice of what happens.

I turned at the end of the street. Roads ran away from the Ronde like the spokes of a wheel. The main entrance to the hotel was in the next street. Right in front of me.

Breathing as hard as if I'd run there, I walked up to the doors.

No going back.

Servants opened them, smiled and bowed as I passed. I looked straight ahead, concentrating on forcing my trembling legs to carry me in that direction without stumbling.

Through the lobby.

No one paid me attention. Perhaps they saw only my clothes.

A short passage and the restaurant lay ahead.

After the bright light outside, it seemed dark. The room was tall. Huge punkas softly waved above the tables, keeping the air stirring.

Guarding the restaurant was a heavy wooden lectern, and behind the lectern was the maître d'hôtel, a Frenchman, who was carefully writing names into a large book, his concentration total.

He looked up, startled, as I neared.

"Madame?" He recognized me and gave an embarrassed cough. "I beg your pardon. Mam'selle Beauclerc. Welcome."

His smile was broad and empty as the sky in the dry season. He craned his neck to look behind me, failing to see who was bringing me to his restaurant.

"Monsieur," I replied.

"How many in your party, Mam'selle?" he asked, flicking the page back and holding his pen ready to write the answer in.

My mouth felt dry.

"Actually, I'm here alone to meet with Monsieur Riossi."

The man blinked and laid his pen down carefully beside the ledger. He did not raise his eyes to look at me.

"Is Monsieur expecting you?"

Obviously not, otherwise he would have told you.

A few minutes ago I'd been begging fate that I would have an excuse not to come in here, but now I had forced myself this far, I wasn't going to be denied by the gatekeeper. I'd never get up the courage to try again.

"Yes," I replied and walked past.

"Oh! Mam'selle. No, no. It is forbidden to interrupt."

He had to scuttle out from behind his lectern, so I was in the middle of the room before he caught up.

The restaurant was almost as quiet as a library, and the maître d'hôtel was making enough of a commotion that Riossi could not fail to hear. I was far enough into the room that he could see me as well. He sat beside a gauze-curtained window on the far side.

He looked up, his face unreadable, and made no sign. The maître d'hôtel was right at my elbow. The hotel was famously protective of its patrons' privacy. Without Riossi's invitation I would not be allowed to join him, and I wasn't sure if I'd have the courage to do this again.

What if I'd misjudged everything and made a complete fool of myself?

After all, what would a rich, urbane, married man like Riossi want with an inexperienced Annamese girl like me?

"Please, Monsieur Riossi," I said quietly. Too quietly for him to hear, but he could see. He smiled and stood, his open hand indicating the unoccupied chair at his table.

Without so much as a blink, the maître d'hôtel's demeanor changed. He snapped his fingers and two waiters were laying a place for me in the time it took me to walk there.

Riossi held my chair for me. I sat, clasping my hands in my lap to hide the trembling.

"Thank you," I said mechanically.

"My pleasure," he replied easily, returning to his seat.

A waiter poured a large glass of iced water for me, and the maître d'hôtel handed me the menu.

"You are well?" Riossi said.

"Yes, thank you." I took a long drink of water. I couldn't look at him yet. "I trust you are, too."

"Yes. It was an immense shock for us all, at the Harvest Ball," Riossi said. "I could scarcely believe what was being said, let alone the manner in which it was delivered. I wrote to your father along those lines, but his leaving was so rushed he may not even have read it. No matter."

Why did he need to bring that up?

I couldn't respond angrily.

I can't antagonize him. This is Nhung's only chance.

"I'm sure he'd wish me to thank you for your concern, Monsieur Riossi." I looked at the unopened menu in my hands. I had no appetite. "I really didn't ..."

"This is a restaurant. Whatever did you come here for, then, if not to join me for lunch?"

My heart stuttered. Was I mistaken? *No.* I could see it in his eyes. It was a game.

"I came to ask a favor."

He raised an enquiring eyebrow. I sensed he wanted more than that. He didn't want me just to ask; he wanted me to beg.

I tensed beneath the table where he couldn't see.

It's only words. So far.

"I came to beg a favor," I amended humbly. "Not really to eat."

"Come now." He smiled at me, but there was a predatory look in his eyes. "I'm sure we can come to an understanding," he paused meaningfully, "but of course the civilities must be observed. Forgive me for pointing out that you've arrived in a state of some trepidation, Mam'selle Beauclerc. It's to be expected. You are very young, very inexperienced in the ways of the world, and very worried. I understand."

He opened his hands and indicated the room. "We are merely having lunch. That is, unless you just sit there while I eat. That would be noticed. It would even be impolite."

I have to do this the way he wants.

"Very well." I opened the menu and tried a polite smile. My face felt tight.

"Good, good." He was quick to reward my agreement, but he hadn't actually expected me to choose my meal. He nodded at a waiter, who approached silently on felt-soled slippers.

"We'll both start with the cream of chicken soup," he said. "Then for Mam'selle, the medallions of fish. I'll have the beef ribs in juice. Seasonal vegetables for both of us."

The waiter bowed and took our menus. He hadn't even glanced at me the entire time. I did not have an opinion on what I wanted to eat, or if I did, it was only to be expressed through my male companion.

How many times had Papa managed to deflect this when we were out, without me even noticing?

Now, I was on my own and saw it clearly.

The maître d'hôtel appeared silently behind me and poured me a glass of the wine from the bottle in the ice bucket beside the table.

"A bottle of the Latour to go with my beef," Riossi said. "Open it now and let it breathe if you would, Jacques."

"Of course, Monsieur."

A tilt of the head, a bow, a small smile. *Monsieur has immense good taste. The perfect wine for his meal.*

"I'll leave the Muscadet for you," Riossi said. "It's an excellent accompaniment to your fish."

I sipped it, to please him, and looked at him through my eyelashes.

He was not as ill-looking as some Frenchmen became in the heat of Indochina—all gaunt and yellow. Neither had he become immensely fat and pink, as others had. He was fleshy, but not uncommonly so. His skin was as dark as mine, like many of the Corsicans. His hair was black and neat. His eyes brown. His hands clean. His clothes elegant.

He is not repulsive. I must school my face.

"It irritates you," he said, making my heart skip a beat wondering what he was going to say. "The way the waiters ignore you; it grates, doesn't it?"

"Yes, it does."

"I thought so. You see, we are not so different, you and I," he said. "We're both outsiders."

"You're making fun of me, Monsieur Riossi. They bow and scrape to you."

He snorted. "No. They bow and scrape to money and power and influence." He waved it away. "We must stick together, we outsiders. Look out for each other. Help each other."

His voice lowered and he leaned in, nodded towards the other diners.

"They're whispering among themselves even now. It's quite ridiculous and hypocritical. You know, all these men have mistresses, and yet when they see two friends having lunch together, they call that a scandal."

Yes. They would be talking about me already. There was no going back.

"But we're not like that," he said. "You see past the petty moralities that fog their views. You're a serious young woman with important matters on her mind, and I respect that. I am touched that you should come to me for a favor, as a friend."

"Thank you, Monsieur Riossi."

"Hmm. But if we can be friends, we cannot be always *Monsieur* and *Mam'selle* in our private conversations. You do not ask *Monsieur* a personal favor. We can be Ophélie and Bernardu to each other. That's more friendly, is it not?"

"I ... yes, naturally ..."

It caught in my throat. Young French women did not call gentlemen by their first names—it was improper and far too intimate. Once I had crossed that line, it was an admission that we were to be more than 'friends'.

Riossi was watching me carefully. He pushed delicately. "It would make me very happy to hear you call me by name, Ophélie," he said.

I paused, taking a breath. *Nhung.* I was doing this for my sister. "Yes ... Bernardu."

"Good."

"Why do you believe you're an outsider, Bernardu?" I spoke now in the familiar French form, *tu* rather than the polite *vous*, which I would never have done with another man of his age.

I could see he was pleased; it was another move in his game. He believed he was guiding me, herding me gently into a position where there was no retreat.

Perhaps that was important to him, that feeling of power.

"I am Corsican," he replied, "and the French do not believe we are entirely French."

"But Saigon is full of Corsicans, and don't they group together and regard French as outsiders?"

"Indeed they do. But I'm an outsider to the Corsicans as well. My wife is from Paris. I am not to be trusted." He raised his eyebrows and chuckled.

I'd never met Madame Riossi, who seldom ventured outside of her house, and here I was with her husband. My shame was intense.

But Nhung did not have that privilege. I swallowed it.

"I think you would see it differently," I said, "if you looked through my eyes."

He laughed.

"Yes, I see that I might. Nevertheless, we are all outsiders to them, and I meant what I said, that we should work together and do favors for each other. Do you agree?"

"You are right, Bernardu," I replied and bobbed my head.

The waiters served our soup.

It was strange. I wanted him to be uncouth. Rude. Perhaps I wanted an excuse to be so mortally offended that I could leave.

It seemed that once I had acquiesced to the intimacy of using given names, using the familiar *tu* with him and agreeing to the unvoiced implications of *favors*, he was satisfied for the moment. Certainly, nothing truly improper happened while we ate. Riossi was charming, his conversation light and witty. He gave me plenty of opportunity to speak. He listened to what I said, and with my tongue loosened by the wine, I spoke too much.

I could not help but speak about the Fontaudins. Riossi shook his head, and commented that Monsieur Fontaudin would not last the period envisaged by his company.

"If he does not run out of health, he will surely run out of money!"

But he would not be drawn on details.

As they cleared away dessert at the end, my fears returned to me. Was I making a fool of myself? Was he sitting there laughing at me?

However, business began over coffee.

"I believe you wish my inspectors to add to their duties," he said, sipping his coffee and watching me over the rim of his cup.

"Yes," I stuttered, caught off balance by the sudden turn in the conversation. "The situation is abominable. The Sisters are ready to help. It is such a little thing for Messieurs Picardin and Valois to help so many out of a slavery that should never have been allowed to happen in the first place."

"Something we *ought* to do." Riossi smiled. "For the good of the many girls caught in this web, despite the wishes of our new lieutenant governor."

My throat constricted. I could not answer.

"You haven't come here for the good of the many, my little Ophélie, have you? You haven't come here to rescue some distant cousin either. It's much closer to home, is it not? We're not so different, really — Corsicans, Annamese, French. For such bravery and sacrifice, I would look for a reason close to home. Perhaps within the immediate family." He pursed his lips thoughtfully. "A sister?"

He knew.

"Nhung," I said quietly. The anger returned, cleansing me of everything but my purpose. "Her name is Nhung. Yes, she's my sister."

"Good. I like that we will be honest with each other, should we become the best of friends," he said.

"What … what do you expect of me? For us to become the best of friends?" I cleared my throat, my heart in my mouth. "What must I do, Bernardu?"

"Ahh. Well." He tossed his napkin on the table. "We cannot rush these things."

I opened my mouth to protest, but he continued.

"We should first demonstrate a …" he rolled his hand, "… a commitment, don't you think? A token of willingness and ability. A little secret for us to share. This is how one does these things. It will ensure we understand and trust each other."

I looked up at him, my hands hidden underneath the table again.

He took a cigar from his pocket and a waiter immediately appeared with a lighter.

We sat in silence until it was lit. He blew a cloud of smoke that danced in the gentle wash of the ceiling punkas, then he leaned forward, his voice smooth and low, his eyes bright as a serpent's.

"I'll tell you what," he said. "This evening, my inspectors will visit one of the largest brothels in Saigon and test the procedure Monsieur Beauclerc suggested. Tomorrow, you and I will meet and discuss the results, and our next steps."

Steps. Like a dance.

What had Phèdre said? *He's very sure in his moves.*

I took a last sip from the full wine glass to ease my throat. "Thank you, Bernardu."

"Who knows, we may be lucky and find Nhung on the first attempt." He smiled again. "And if not, you will, in any event, see I am able to do these favors for you."

"And in return?" I asked. "My sign of commitment?"

He took out his wallet and found a piece of paper. On the back, he wrote in neat little letters and handed it across.

"Tonight, at midnight, go to this place and ask to see Madame Phan. She will expect you, and she will guide you to a little gift from me that will be waiting there for you. A little secret to keep me in your mind. That is all. If you are certain."

Chapter 38

As I took the paper from him, a man rushed into the restaurant, ignoring the attempts of the maître d'hôtel to detain him.

The newcomer ran up to our table.

"I apologize, Monsieur Riossi." He gathered himself and spoke more quietly. "A situation, at the docks. It requires you. A carriage is ready outside."

"Wait in the carriage for me," Riossi said.

The man hastened away, apologizing again.

"I apologize, Ophélie. Power is not all privilege and pleasure. There are responsibilities as well." He stood up and moved around the table to lean over me. My left hand rested on the tablecloth and he covered it with his.

"This was a delightful lunch," he said. "Thank you for joining me. I am truly sorry that it took such an awful situation with your sister to bring us together, but you know, I feel we would have become friends anyway, and enjoyed each other's company. The situation merely precipitates matters."

"Yes, Bernardu." I looked up at him.

"So pleasant to hear my name on your lips." He breathed in deeply. "The lunch is on my account, naturally. And don't worry. Together, you and I, we'll find your sister and free her. Enjoy your afternoon."

His hand squeezed mine briefly and then he strode away.

I shivered.

My earlier fears were groundless. I had not misjudged the situation, and he had not been sitting there simply indulging me. He had communicated his desires, despite not actually voicing them outright.

I understood. His 'token of commitment' from me would show him that I could get out without being stopped by the Fontaudins, and, as importantly, that I would do it. Perhaps tomorrow we would move to the 'next steps'.

Another little tremor passed through me.

No poor girl raised in a single room with her whole family grows up entirely ignorant of sex. For that matter, my French friends knew more than their parents suspected. We were all of an age of awareness and potential, but none of us, not even Chantal, had turned that uncertain knowledge into experience.

And so the heart of it, the true power—that was a mystery.

I would be his whore. I repeated that. *Whore.* I needed to make myself used to the name, so it lost its capacity to hurt me. And, while I was his whore, his inspectors would search for Nhung alongside their other duties.

But how long would this work? How fascinated was he? What if he grew bored with me?

Against my better judgement, I finished my glass of wine.

I would discover this power. Riossi would remain fascinated for as long as it took for his inspectors to find Nhung. That was my responsibility.

As for my finding enjoyment in it … perhaps that was what he needed to believe. Perhaps, if I learned to convince him of that, I would find part of the key to this secret power.

And I would not be put off by his challenge—this first demonstration of my resolution and ability to visit somewhere at midnight.

The piece of paper was an address in Cholon, one of the riverside alleys called Mat Hem. Did he really think I wasn't brave enough to visit Cholon after dark?

I felt a little fear, and an exhilaration at the same time, possibly helped by more wine than I was accustomed to. I had taken the first step. Already, if he kept his word, there would be one less brothel that Nhung could be captive in by this time tomorrow.

On the other hand, people at lunch had seen me with Riossi. The gossip would start today and I would soon have to practice not caring about it. It couldn't be helped.

Tonight, I would visit Cholon.

But this afternoon, I had another urgent destination: the bank.

Fontaudin's drunken discussion in the road last night and Riossi's comment about Fontaudin today had me very worried.

At the bank, the worry blossomed. The assistant manager paled at my demand to view the details of the account set up for me by Papa.

"You should be accompanied by a responsible adult," he said, peering through the door to see if there was someone there.

"I presume you think that would be Monsieur Fontaudin," I said. Papa had needed someone to elect as a trustee in his absence, and Fontaudin had been right there and available. A member of the family. Someone to trust.

"He is the nominated party. I can't show you the statements unless he is in attendance," the man said. He fiddled with his little round glasses, taking them off and squinting. Perhaps he thought if he couldn't see me, I would go away.

I demanded to see the manager of the bank, and after further prevarication, I was eventually admitted to his spacious office.

"I fail to understand why you will not even show me statements," I said, impatiently cutting the formalities as short as I could. "What possible requirement or advantage would there be to having another adult present?"

"Well, to explain matters," he stumbled. "These are not—"

"Is the manager of the Bank of Indochina unable to explain the intricacies of a simple bank account to me?"

His mouth opened and closed.

"The truth is, Mam'selle … this is most irregular. I had assumed you were informed. Most irregular."

"What?"

He found something fascinating on the glossy desk between us.

"You no longer have an account," he said abruptly. "It has been closed and the balance moved."

"To Fontaudin's account?"

"No, but I cannot reveal the destination account. That is confidential to the parties involved." He stood, tugged at his jacket. "I understand this comes as a shock, but we have acted entirely within our rules. You must raise this with Monsieur Fontaudin."

"I certainly will."

There was nothing more I could do at the bank and no sensible target there for my anger.

On Boulevard Charner, of course Madame Sévigny, mother of Chantal and Alain, happened to be passing. Of course, she immediately saw I was unaccompanied.

It all seemed so trivial, as Riossi had said—all these petty proprieties that people kept uppermost in their minds while they walked the clean, tidy streets and the horrors seethed out of sight.

I ignored her. Another meaningless blemish against my character. It would not be the first, or the last. Certainly not the worst. I couldn't afford to care.

I stormed into the house and found both of the Fontaudins in the salon.

He looked unwell. Good.

"Where have you been?" Madame Fontaudin shouted at me, before I could say anything. "How dare you go out alone?" She shook her walking stick at me. "No wonder the servants have left. It's your fault. Tell her, Yves."

She banged her stick on the floor with such force I could see the marks in the wood.

"You really should not be out—" he began.

"The servants, you idiot! Those arrogant, stupid, superstitious fools that my witless cousins left for us to look after."

"Ah. They've gone," he mumbled.

The shouting that had woken me this morning. I had dismissed it as unimportant.

"They disobeyed me!" She emphasized every word with another bang of the stick against the floor. "They *argued* with me."

Jade was sullen, without a doubt. She had argued with Maman, too, but she'd not left because of it. The sight of Madame Fontaudin's red face and the fury with which she was striking the floor gave me a clue to what had happened.

"You hit them, didn't you?"

"Of course I did! What else was I to do? How do you expect obedience from them without discipline? Who do they think they are?"

"They are servants, not animals!" I said. "We pay them, they work. We hit them, they leave."

"Well of course, *you* would side with them. Yves! Tell her! She has to be more respectful."

He floundered like a fish out of water.

"And anyway," she went on before he'd actually said anything, "it's *you* they blamed. You bring bad luck or something."

She snorted. "I could almost become superstitious, seeing the trail you've left behind you."

"Indeed, perhaps it was some of that bad luck that took me to the bank today."

Monsieur Fontaudin gasped. He looked to struggle to his feet and escape, but his wife clutched at his arm.

"What?" she said. "What are you talking about, girl? Why would you need to go to the bank?"

"To check the money in my account. I found it's no longer there. Neither that money nor the funds that my father left to pay for the upkeep of this house, where you're living for free, remain."

The loss of the second account was a complete guess, but I was sure I was right.

"What?" she said.

He looked even sicker and tried to get up again.

"Your husband has stolen the money from both accounts to pay off his gambling debts."

"No, no," he said, waving his hands. "Merely a convenience, to collect them in one account, you see."

"Yves? What is she talking about? What money?"

"If the money has been simply moved to your account, Monsieur Fontaudin, then we should walk down to the bank now and you can prove it to me. And then you can transfer it back, as it is not convenient to me for it to be in your account."

"How dare you?" Madame Fontaudin spat. "He has no need to walk anywhere to prove anything to you. Sit down, Yves."

He sat, refusing to look at me.

"Thieves," I said and walked back out.

In minutes I was in the Central Post Office, which sat in the square by the cathedral. From there, telegrams could be transmitted around the world.

But not to ships at sea.

I stood inside the beautiful building and closed my eyes for a moment.

It was hopeless. I could try and send a telegram to all the ports where the *Victorieuse* might be stopping, but the navy did not announce where it would visit. If my parents had gone on a commercial liner, then that company would have transmitted a telegram to their offices in the next port, but on a naval corvette, Papa and Maman were out of touch for six weeks.

I would send a telegram to the family in Bordeaux to wait for their arrival. I had plenty of time to compose it. I would tell him what had happened, and then that he should instruct a lawyer and immediately continue on to Paris to present his arguments for the development of Indochina to the Quai d'Orsay. I was going to have to emphasize that he must not delay on either task.

There was the smallest possibility that the news about my behavior in Saigon would arrive in Paris only after he persuaded the Quai d'Orsay to post him back here, with the authority to proceed on his projects.

It was the best I could hope for.

What else could I do now?

There was no point going to Police Chief Meulnes. As the appointed trustee of the funds in the bank, Fontaudin had broken no laws. He was entitled to dispose of the money as he saw fit.

Who else could I even talk to?

Chapter 39

I sat in the library during the hot afternoon. As the sun dipped, I walked through the city. The western horizon turned into a lake of fire which painted the bases of the lowering clouds with blood.

By the time I returned to the house, I was ready for another confrontation with the Fontaudins. I could not back down; it was a matter of principle. I would not let them chase me from my parents' house.

But the house was empty, silent but for the sounds of my heart beating and the air rushing into my lungs.

I changed into my Annamese peasant clothes, and hid some small coins in a little pouch. I didn't take too many; Cholon, especially at night, wasn't as safe as Saigon. Thinking of those dangers, I also took the kris knife from its hiding place. I couldn't carry it openly and I'd never thought of fighting with a knife, but the kris looked threatening. Maybe that was all I'd need. After some thought, I fashioned a sling from some leather strips and hung the knife and sheath down my back, under my shirt. I searched through the house and found an old conical straw hat, the type every peasant had. It lay on my back, held with a string around my throat, and it hid the knife.

Enough. I slipped back out into the boulevard.

Last time I'd gone out like this, I'd been so excited about meeting Lanh, I'd not really noticed how much I changed my identity when I changed my clothes. Colonials didn't see me. Annamese and Chinese didn't care. There were people who looked at me: the soldiers and police. There were more of them than usual, groups on corners, watching all the Annamese and Chinese who passed them.

There was a feeling in the air I hadn't noticed earlier—a restlessness, a charge, like before a storm.

The tram station was closed. Police stood outside. I walked past and continued toward Cholon. I could walk along the Arroyo Chinois. It wasn't that far. I still had lots of time.

But a few minutes later, I saw more police on the road ahead. People were being stopped and questioned.

My street sense prickled. *Danger.*

I was carrying a knife. If that were discovered …

I turned into one of the alleys and doubled back.

It wasn't late yet; I could go back to the high road, the one that went through the old Khmer tombs. It wouldn't add that much to the journey.

But instead, I found myself in a large group of workers heading back down the arroyo to where it emptied into the Saigon river. I kept to the middle of the group, head down, looking around carefully.

Even more soldiers now. We passed the end of the alley where the Party of the People had taken me. There were police knocking on doors and questioning the people living there.

What had happened? Was it a coincidence, or were they looking for Lanh and Thiêu?

Had Lanh gone?

I couldn't stop. I kept glancing back until I suddenly realised where the group I was hiding in was headed: the Khánh Hôi footbridge. No one walking in this direction was being questioned, but the soldiers were watching everyone.

It was too late for me to leave the group.

But *Khánh Hôi*. Where Bác Thảo ruled.

I felt sick as we walked over the bridge.

I told myself it was ridiculous. Even Manon and Rochelle would have difficulty recognizing me, let alone a gang lord who'd never seen me. I was just another Annamese girl. It was a good disguise.

As soon as I was on the Khánh Hôi side, I made a right turn, back along the creek. If I followed this road and crossed one of the bridges further down, I would be in Cholon.

At least there were no soldiers on this side.

Neither were there any street lights. The dark mouths of every creekside alley in Khánh Hôi seemed to be reaching out toward me as I trotted by. I could feel the hot, stinking air flowing out of them, like the breath of dead things. Just its touch made me feel unclean.

It was a relief of a sort when I reached the end of Khánh Hôi. No more alleys. Fewer people. But the road became a dirt track I could barely see as the last glimmer of lights from the town died. There was no moon; the sky was black with muttering clouds. I stumbled as I hurried.

Beside the track, sampans covered the creek, stirring on the uneasy waters. The odd shout from the sampans or suspicious glares from people who loomed suddenly out of the night had my heart in my mouth the whole time.

Why hadn't I gone back and taken the high road? I didn't like the tombs, but this was worse.

A group of young men drinking on a sampan and lit by a single lamp watched me go by, like hungry dogs watching the butcher's cart.

Just as I started to get really scared, I saw the lights of Cholon and heard the sound of voices from their night market carrying across the creek.

I hurried over the first bridge, which took me to the edge of the market. I bought *bot chien*, a little rice cake, from an old Chinese woman. It was cheap, and the sort of food I could afford with the coins I had.

"Aunty," I said politely. "Where is Mat Hem, please?"

She squinted at me through the smoke from her cooking fire. She didn't speak, but tipped her head to the northern end of the market, then turned away and spat.

I recognized the gesture. She wouldn't speak, or show me exactly, because that would bind my fate with hers. I should not be going to Mat Hem, in her opinion. And if I did go there anyway, the fate that waited for me would find some tenuous thread of karma that linked back to whoever had sent me, or guided me, on the way. She wanted no part of it. She spat out the thread, as she saw it.

Superstitious foolishness, but a little cramp of fear clutched at my stomach.

I had to ask twice more before I finally stumbled into the entrance of an alley that ran up the hill, away from the creek. It was dark, apart from a big lantern hanging outside a building halfway along. In comparison to the market, this narrow alley was quiet. But not silent. A sewer ran down the middle of it, sealed with iron gratings, and through that, I could hear the trickle of water and the rustle of cockroaches swarming below.

I'm crazy. This isn't safe.

Heart in my mouth, I edged into the alley and let the darkness swallow me.

Was Riossi laughing at me? Or was there something worse, something evil going on? Was I offering myself up to my own kidnapping?

I froze at a noise ahead. A man, a European, well dressed, emerged into the light of the lantern.

There was a murmured exchange of Chinese and French voices and then the man walked toward the entrance of the alley, his heels scuffing.

I pushed myself against a wall, deep into the shadows.

What if he recognizes me?

Stupid. It was so dark, he wouldn't recognize his own family in this alley.

Still, I stayed where I was, trying not to breathe so loudly, and to not think about the rats and cockroaches.

Was Riossi trying to test how brave I was—or how insane?

As soon as the Frenchman left the alley, I walked quickly toward the lantern, moving to the middle of the alley, close to the scuttling sewer, away from the shadows.

Riossi's note said the House of the Red Door in Mat Hem.

Closer to the lantern, I saw a moon gate sealed with a red-painted door. This had to be it, even though it looked strange. On either side of the gate stood carved columns, about my height and the thickness of my leg. The tops of the columns glistened, as if they'd been anointed with an oil. A floral fragrance wafted from them, fighting against the smell of the sewer.

I knocked timidly on the door, and after a minute it opened to let a large Chinese man out.

His head was completely shaved. He leaned on a chang gùn, a carved wooden staff, that was as tall as he was. His plain tunic was gathered by a belt, from which hung a set of large iron keys.

"What do you want, boy?" he said, speaking Cantonese.

"I need to see Phan," I replied in Annamese, hoping he'd understand. My Cantonese was not good.

He stepped forward and peered at me. "Not a boy," he grunted, still in Cantonese. I didn't catch what he said next. Something about work. Was he asking if I wanted work, or saying Phan was busy working?

"Not want work." I switched to Trade. "Want see Phan. She know, she wait, I come."

He grunted again, but after looking down at me for a long minute, he stepped to one side, allowing me to pull the door open and go through. He closed it behind us and I could hear the scratch of the key as he locked it.

I stood at the entrance to a small courtyard. The middle was given over to a pink-blossomed frangipani tree standing on a little island in the middle of a round carp pool. Along the sides of the courtyard were raised wooden walkways. There were doors, evenly spaced in the walls, and lamps hanging at the corners.

The man jerked his head to indicate a room to the side, and I went in.

It was a plain room without windows. In one corner, a woman with grey streaks in her hair sat on cushions beside a small table. She was painting in the courtly Chinese style—a young girl looking down at a frangipani blossom floating in a stream.

She looked up as I entered.

"Mam'selle Beauclerc?" she said in French, her eyes sharp and her pronunciation surprisingly good.

"Yes." I shifted my weight uncomfortably under her gaze and indicated my clothes. "I thought it would be safer to dress like this."

She tilted her head and looked at me thoughtfully.

"That depends on what you wish to be safe from." She made a last stroke with her brush and placed it in a bowl of water. "I am Madame Phan and you are Monsieur Riossi's friend, come to see my house."

I shrugged. "I don't know why I'm here. This is some kind of test, and …"

I wanted to talk. I wanted to explain why I was doing what I was doing. To ease my fears. To justify myself. To persuade someone else that my reasoning was sound.

All of those.

I couldn't expect anyone's blessing, but if I could have their understanding …

"It is a test, after a fashion. Are you sure you want to go on? You could leave now," she said.

"I have to go through with it."

."Whatever it is." She wiped her hands on a cloth and stood.

It was halfway to a question, but I said nothing in response.

"Very well. Walk with me. Walk softly. Do not speak."

She took the small lamp from the table and we went into the courtyard. I followed her around the walkways to a door on the opposite side, and we went through that.

Inside there was a narrow staircase, bare and leading down into more darkness. The only light was from her lamp and she had the wick turned down as far as it would go.

A faint smell of incense floated through the still air, masking other scents. Something salty, sweaty, sour. Something smoky. And a distinctive whiff of flowers. Someone was smoking opium.

Was this an opium den? Why send me here?

Madame Phan walked down to the first landing. Our shadows leaped around the stairwell as she turned. The stairs continued down, but she chose instead the passage leading to the right. The corridor was completely empty, as was the next on the left. Everything—floors, ceiling, walls—was wooden. It was like being inside a box.

Halfway down that corridor, she stopped.

There was a sound of music, voices and laughter, very faint. It seemed to come from all around us.

There was nothing I could see, but she reached up and moved a flap, uncovering a tiny hole in the wall. She put her eye to it briefly, then stood back. She put her finger to her lips and then waved me forward to look.

I frowned.

Riossi's test is to spy on people?

The room I looked into was not brightly lit. There were soft seats and green plants everywhere. Some men, Europeans, played musical instruments in the corner of the room; others sat and took drinks being offered to them by women. Women who were half naked.

I jerked back from the peephole.

Madame Phan held her finger to her lips again.

She slid the peep flap back into place. She walked around the corridors back to the staircase, and down another level.

I looked at the stairs leading up and out. I should run now and pray the guard would let me out.

A brothel. I was in a brothel.

Riossi's test was ... what?

Is he here? Is that his idea of a 'gift'?

I followed numbly, down to the next level, steeling myself. Nhung had lived in a place like this for five years. My cowardice shamed me.

There was no conversation or laughter seeping in from the rooms here. Instead, there were faint moans and cries from all around us.

There were three peepholes for each corridor in the square. Three rooms each side for three of the sides. On the first corridor, Madame Phan looked and rejected the first two. At the third, she motioned me to look.

The only light in the room came from a candelabrum on a side table. It showed a European man slouching naked in a big chair. A Chinese girl knelt on the ground between his legs, head in his lap.

I jerked back again.

I knew that the physical love my parents shared was not the whole spectrum of what people did. I knew about brothels. I knew there were other things people did.

This was my test. Did that mean Riossi expected this from me? Would I have to do what I'd just seen for him to agree to search for Nhung?

Madame Phan gripped my wrist as she pulled me onward.

Three more peepholes on that level. Six on the next.

Girls on their knees, on their backs, on their stomachs. Arranged in whatever position the men wanted them. Doing whatever the men wanted them to.

And ... inviting them. Encouraging them. Urging them.

Somehow their voices made it worse.

I was feeling sick when Madame Phan opened a door at the end of the last corridor and waved me inside.

Now? Is he here? Is it my turn?

Chapter 40

For all the jangling of my nerves and pounding of my heart, the room was empty.

It was furnished as a bedroom, and in the middle there was a curtained, four-poster bed. I pulled the curtains aside hesitantly, still not absolutely sure that Riossi was not there.

He wasn't.

On the bed was a box with my name in Riossi's handwriting on the lid. There was no other written message. Another puzzle for me to work out. I opened it. Inside was a gold chain bracelet. I lifted it up into the light. Real gold, but not a bracelet; it was an ankle chain.

I ran the links gently through my fingers.

Its beauty did not hide its function. It was a fetter, a shackle.

What had he said? *A little secret to keep me in your mind.*

It was more than that; it was a reminder he would have a claim on my body. It was a sign of ownership.

But Nhung had no options. No choice to wear the chain, or not.

Swallowing hard, I put it on my ankle and let the pant leg fall back to hide it.

Madame Phan silently guided me back up the stairs to the door, where the guard let me out.

As I hurried down toward the faint light at the mouth of the alley, I heard the brothel's door lock behind me.

And steps following me.

My heart raced and I looked back over my shoulder.

A shadow. A shape that loomed in front of the lantern. Big. As big as the Chinese guard in the brothel. If I screamed, would the guard come back out?

I couldn't be sure, so still looking at the man behind, I sprinted away. Straight into the second man waiting in the darkness at the mouth of the alley.

He twisted me around, clamped an arm over my face to muffle my scream.

I bit him, hard. I kicked back and caught his shin.

He swore. "You'll pay for that, bitch."

Mandarin! Not Bác Thảo's thugs from Khánh Hôi. Not the Party of the People either.

His arm shifted under my jaw, holding it closed.

I struck backwards with my elbow, hitting him in the ribs. Not hard enough.

The other one, the big man who'd chased me down the alley, punched me in the stomach.

I coughed and tried to double over, but the man holding me had trapped one of my legs. I couldn't get air in my lungs, but I still struggled.

The big man reached out and gripped my shirt, jerked me forward and slapped me hard across the face. Once, twice. I saw stars.

My shirt was tough. It didn't tear, but two knot buttons slipped their loops.

He stopped.

I gasped as he jerked more buttons loose.

"He only told us to catch her and take her back," he grunted.

The other one laughed. "He didn't say we couldn't enjoy it, eh?"

His free hand pulled my shirt open, grabbed my breast and pinched.

I tried to twist away, tried to scream, but neither worked.

"We've got time." I could sense him looking around. "Here?"

"Down near the creek," the big man said. "We won't be disturbed."

He thrust his hand into my pants.

I still had one leg free. I kicked him in the groin.

He crouched and swore, but he'd been too quick to turn away and I hadn't really hurt him.

"It seems you hardly need my help." A familiar voice sounded from behind me.

Surprise made my captor's grip loosen a fraction as he swiveled to see who it was. I twisted desperately, freeing my jaw.

"Qingzhao! Run! Get help," I screamed.

She didn't. She stood calmly at the entrance of the alley, leaning on the old chang gùn I'd seen her use for exercises.

"You!" the big man spat. He drew a long blade from a sheath on his belt. "After we're finished with you, we'll let you crawl back to Song and tell him we have his little toy. He does what Zheng says or we send her to him a piece at a time."

Qingzhao laughed. "Your stupidity continues to be unbelievable. You come here to Cholon, to our own territory, and try to tell us what to do? When that fails, you sneak in at night and try to threaten us?"

"She will die slowly if Song doesn't obey." He pointed at me with the knife. "You know how painful we can make that."

He *hissed*. His mouth seemed to go hazy, and for a moment I thought I saw his teeth had been filed down to points.

What?

But my captor took that moment to jerk my head further back while he drew a blade of his own.

"Stupid." Qingzhao shook her head, still speaking calmly. "You're right *here*, not safe in some fortress up the river. And the only way out is through me."

What was she doing? She couldn't fight them.

She lifted her staff above her head, idly spinning it between her fingers, one-handed.

"You think we're afraid of that?" the big man sneered.

The man holding me laughed. He moved again, forcing me behind him. I turned, carefully, shifting under the grip around my neck.

Qingzhao did not answer the big man. A look came over her face, an eagerness, almost like hunger. Her chang gùn spun faster, flickering in the light from the lantern. There was something strange about the blur it made. The noise. How big was it? How could she spin it like that?

Even the big man faltered as he edged closer. As much as he tried to hide it, the spinning chang gùn worried him.

The man who held me also seemed drawn by the flickering circle. I took a chance, shifted some more.

Qingzhao put up her other hand, and with a *crack* the chang gùn came to an abrupt stop against her palm.

It now had gleaming blades sprouting from the ends, each as long as my forearm.

"Huh?" The big man was still looking at the staff, open-mouthed, when Qingzhao sprang at him and slashed.

He yelled and leaped back.

They'd both moved faster than I could blink.

I twisted some more, reaching behind me underneath the crushed straw hat, and tore my kris knife from its hiding place.

"Hold still, you stinking bitch," my captor yelled, pushing me down. He thought I was just trying to escape.

I stabbed him in the thigh as hard as I could.

He screamed and let go, but as I tried to get away, he punched me. His blow was like being kicked by a horse's hoof. I collapsed. My head reeled and the whole alley around me was a black mist of confusing shadows.

The big man was shouting something, staggering, swaying, his arms windmilling. My captor limped away, tugging at the kris buried in his thigh. Light glittered on Qingzhao's blades.

I tried to get to my feet. Couldn't.

Seeing double. No strength in my limbs.

There was a thud. A spray of something warm on my face. A body fell in front of me. It ended hideously at the neck, which was spurting blood. A second later, the head rolled out of the night. It was the big man, still looking shocked.

I vomited into the gutter and passed out.

Chapter 41

I was in a rickshaw. There was a little coach lamp swinging from the awning. I could hear the soft thudding of the man's feet as he pulled us along a dark road.

Someone was cleaning my face with a wet cloth.

Qingzhao.

I jerked up, gasping as if I'd been held underwater. The movement made me ill again and I had to hang my head over the side. Qingzhao held my hair out of the way and patted my back. Mercifully, the man pulling the rickshaw ignored it.

"What happened?" I said, when I finally stopped. "Those men ..."

"You don't need to worry about them," she said.

"You ..."

"I killed them. Yes." She tilted her head at me, as if sensing revulsion. "They were going to rape you. And me. Then they were going to torture you and finally kill you."

I slumped back against the seat.

"That was clever, and brave, to stab the man holding you. And foolish." She held up my kris knife, turning it one way and the other, so the blade seemed to slither like a snake in the lamplight.

I took the knife, nearly dropping it. I'd stabbed a man. I knew I should be revolted at the violence, but I wasn't. In fact, if I hadn't been crouched at his feet, I'd have stabbed him in the stomach. I would have killed him, if I'd known how. My parents would be appalled, but now I realized Qingzhao didn't need to justify to me *why* she'd killed them.

How, maybe she could explain that. How one slim woman beat two men. And that staff. The way it had spun, and had suddenly grown blades. Was it magic? She was Yi Song's daughter. Was it one of those staffs like the fables said the Monkey God had? Was there some truth in all those tales?

The staff itself was right there, on the other side of Qingzhao, jammed between her hip and the side of the rickshaw. Just a staff, no magic blades showing.

Qingzhao did not seem about to discuss it with me. When she spoke it was about something completely different.

"You will not find Nhung in Cholon's brothels, Ophélie," she said quietly, taking my hand in hers. "And searching for her like this is too dangerous. You're so lucky you started in Cholon where I could reach you. You must stop."

She must know everything her father knew about me, but she didn't know the whole truth. She thought I was looking for Nhung myself; she didn't know about Riossi yet, that I'd been in Cholon to prove myself to him, and to get him to use his inspectors to search for Nhung. The shameful secret behind my visit to the brothel would come later.

What would she think of me then?

My head was aching abominably.

"I don't understand," I muttered. "I'm not complaining, but how did you even know where I was?"

She laughed.

"You don't think the street urchins' favorite lady can sneak into Cholon without us knowing? Even in disguise."

I frowned. The urchins' favorite lady? Nothing seemed to make sense tonight.

"You need to rest," Qingzhao said. "We'll get you home, to bed, and you'll feel better in the morning."

"I can't go home," I said, and took a deep breath. I couldn't face the Fontaudins like this—turning up in the middle of the night, holding a knife, dressed in Annamese clothes with blood all over them and worst of all, feeling like my head was going to split.

She insisted I tell her about them. How the bank had admitted Fontaudin had taken the money. His drinking. The conversation with his gambling friends. His wife's treatment of the Malabar driver and our servants.

"We heard some things about the Fontaudins from crew on the ship," she said when I finished. "It seems they weren't exaggerated. You're right, you can't go back to your house while they're there. You can stay with us in Cholon instead."

She was just about to call to the man to turn the rickshaw around.

"No. Wait," I said. "We're nearly at the old house on the Rue de Tombeaux. I'll stay there tonight. I have clothes in the cupboard and at least it'll be my own bed."

The truth was, I was scared of the thought of staying with my tutor, who could use magic and might be a gang lord, and his daughter, who killed with a staff that sprouted blades. People who used magic, and hid it, but not from me. Why? I just wanted to sleep so this headache would go away, not worry whether I'd be turned to stone or something.

And I needed to see Riossi tomorrow. I wasn't sure they'd let me, even if it was the only way I'd find Nhung.

Qingzhao looked silently at me for a long minute.

"You're right, we're nearly there," she said eventually. "You can sleep there tonight, but my father will come and talk to you tomorrow. If his enemies think you're a way to get to him, then you're not safe alone."

"Who are they? These enemies?"

"My father will explain," she said.

"Qingzhao, I know you and your father must use *ma thuật*. He's shown me the spirit world. I saw Bác Thảo in my vision. I know about the Tò Harimau, the people who can become tigers, and the Tò Dara, the vampires. I've seen you use a magic staff. You don't have to keep secrets from me."

She said nothing, just looked at me.

"The big man you killed," I started, and immediately slowed down. It sounded so ridiculous. "There was something about his mouth, his teeth."

She sighed. "I will still let my father explain it all, but yes, those men were what you call Tò Dara. Not that all Tò Dara are like that, any more than all Tò Harimau are like Bác Thảo. For more than that," she held up a hand as I began to ask another question, "you must wait to talk to him."

Actually, I didn't really want to talk more about it tonight. On top of everything else, I had confirmed that there were more monsters in Saigon who were a danger to me. The captain of the Bugis ship *Salayar* had warned me, and I'd actually used his kris knife against one of the Tò Dara. I shuddered. Monsters with fangs who drank blood.

I definitely didn't want to think more about that tonight.

I hoped I would feel better tomorrow. More able to deal with everything then.

But Qingzhao was not finished.

"What is your real reason for not wanting to go back to Cholon with me?" she asked. "Is it because I killed those men? Are you afraid of me?"

"No!" My head throbbed. I couldn't face making up more lies. It was too complex. "No, not because you killed them. Yes, I'm afraid of you. A bit."

"But I wouldn't hurt you. Neither would my father. Surely you know this."

"Yes, why would you save me, only to hurt me later? It's stupid. I don't know. I don't understand." I put my head back and looked up at the night, unable to face her. "Why did you save me? Why would Monsieur Song want to protect me?"

She started to reply in Mandarin, switched to French, and back to Mandarin, seemingly exasperated by not finding the right words. "Because of our connection with you and your family. Because we're your friends, and that's what we do."

"Even if I'm no use to you anymore?"

"Oh, Ophélie." Her voice was gentle. She stroked my forehead. "What have people been telling you?"

I closed my eyes. It hurt too much to focus.

"That he's the gang lord of Cholon," I said. "That he only tutored me to become friends with Papa and strike some kind of a deal with the French to give him more power."

"And yet, your father is on his way to France and here we are, still helping you." She sighed. "He will explain it better. Of course it helped that he was your tutor, but our fathers respect each other and worked together for something they both believed in."

She spoke to the rickshaw man in Cantonese, telling him we were going to the house off this road, and not down into the center of Saigon.

He grunted and nodded. His pace never changed.

"As to the rest," she said, and sighed again. "My father is not a gang lord, but he insists on rules that the gangs in Cholon follow. That's how I can tell you that Nhung is not in Cholon. No brothel in Cholon is allowed to purchase girls as slaves."

"The gangs in Cholon … why do they obey him?"

"Because he is stronger than they are. Again, if you want to know more, you'll have to wait to speak to him."

He is stronger than they are. Not *we*. Not some gang that he runs. All the gangs in Cholon. *He* is stronger.

He'd only shown me the spirit world so far. His daughter could make a wooden staff grow metal blades. I wondered what he could do if he were challenged.

But he had been challenged.

"That man Zheng they spoke about … Zheng wants your father to do something?"

The rickshaw reached the house and the man turned up the drive.

"My father will tell you when he thinks you need to know, but just as the colony here suffers from meddling by distant powers, so do we."

More to think about when I felt better.

I stumbled getting down from the rickshaw. Qingzhao caught my arm, peering at me.

"I'm not sleeping well," I said, trying to shrug it off. "I'll be all right tomorrow."

She paid the rickshaw man and returned.

"Do you have the key?" she said.

"No. But there's a window at the back that doesn't close completely. I have to climb up to the porch."

"*You* have to sit right here."

She left me on a step, with my head bowed. It was only after she'd been gone a while I noticed she'd left her chang gùn next to me.

I shivered, and put one careful finger out to touch the carved wood.

Nothing. Certainly no magical blades jumping out.

"Anything you don't understand can seem like magic," she said from behind me. I snatched my hand away guiltily.

"Sorry," I said.

And I kept having to say sorry over and over. I was so tired and my head hurt so much I couldn't manage anything. She stayed and helped me undress, bathe and get into bed.

"Don't worry about the Fontaudins," she said, stroking my head. "My father will send messages to Monsieur Beauclerc and arrange for a lawyer to act on your behalf in his absence."

Just having her there was strangely comforting, and lying down eased the pain in my head.

She turned the lamp off and stayed beside the bed for the brief time it took for me to fall into a deep sleep.

Chapter 42

I woke to an empty house and sweltering heat.

I had a moment of panic. It was nearly midday and I had so much to do!

Had Riossi kept his word? I didn't want to see him until I knew, so I would first go to the convent. The plan had been that anyone rescued would be sent to the Sisters of Saint Paul.

If he'd kept his word last night, I needed some way for him to contact me. For the *next steps*, as he put it. He wouldn't know to send messages to this house out on the Rue de Tombeaux so I'd have to send a message to him. Then I needed to visit Boulevard Bonnard to rescue some of my possessions from the Fontaudins.

And I needed to meet with Yi Song.

I found a brief note from my tutor on the table in the hallway:

It is better that you sleep. I will return later.

Letting me sleep on had helped. I was rested, but rushing only brought the headache and dizziness back again. I had no money for a carriage, so another hour passed before I reached the convent.

Riossi had been true to his word; there were some rescued girls there, and the sisters greeted me as if I were a hero that made all this happen.

What will they think of me when the rumors of me and Riossi start?

Whatever happened later, they were welcoming now, and let me talk to each of the girls.

The girls themselves were dull-eyed and listless. They looked shocked, still scared, as if everything was a huge trick and they would find themselves taken back to the brothel. Those that would talk had terrible stories of being tricked or kidnapped and then finding the horror that awaited them at the brothel. There had been no mercy, no respite, and disobedience was harshly punished. One had been badly beaten yesterday for not doing what she was told. She held herself stiffly and cried quietly while she spoke.

None of them knew Nhung.

And there was nothing of the joy I had hoped they would be feeling.

One named Tuyet voiced their feelings. "I'm a whore," she said in a voice that echoed a quiet desperation. "It wasn't my choice, but people don't care about that. It means I can't go back to my village. My parents don't want a daughter who's a whore. I can't get housework from the French because I'm a whore. No man will want to marry me. I don't have any money to buy a farm or a store. What choice do I have but to go back to being what I am—a whore?"

Two hours later I left the convent, feeling sick and depressed.

They *were* better off, however they felt today. Even if they went back to prostitution, at least they wouldn't be slaves.

It hadn't seemed that long, but it was late in the afternoon already.

I had to shade my eyes. Even with the clouds dull and heavy overhead, it felt too bright. The air was still and the humidity stifling. The shade of the trees along the roads didn't offer their usual respite. The streets were quiet. Saigon suffered under the weather's assault.

Surely it couldn't be much longer before the monsoon broke?

I sat on a bench, trying to piece my day back together. I couldn't think clearly. What did I need to do next?

Boulevard Bonnard. Yes. I needed to go home to get my possessions.

I couldn't carry them all to the house on Rue de Tombeaux, but I had some money in my bedroom. I'd pay a Malabar to take a trunk. One trunk would be all I would need. Enough to give the lawyer time to force the Fontaudins out of the house and get the money back. Or until I went to stay in Cholon. Because monsters were hunting me, and Cholon would be safer.

I was half asleep and Saigon seemed all part of a dream, where spirits flew, dragons danced, tigers roamed and blood-sucking monsters walked through the unknowing streets.

My thoughts flapped and swirled around like crows rising into the sky.

Darkening monsoon clouds built above my head, and I dreamed again of reaching up and cutting them open, releasing all the rain. It would be warm, the rain, like blood splattering on my face.

But I couldn't reach the clouds. I woke and rubbed my arm. It itched where I'd cut myself and I remembered the shock: that strange, sick fascination, because it had felt good. It'd stopped all the whirling, confusing thoughts, and focused them down into one, straight, pure, red line.

It'd been a release.

Again, it whispered, and my head throbbed. *Again.*

Nothing is done but we do it ourselves.

I just wanted to lie down and sleep, but I forced myself to my feet and turned my reluctant steps towards Boulevard Bonnard.

Chapter 43

He was out. She was home and came out from the salon as soon as I closed the front door behind me.

"Where have you been?" Her voice was shrill. It made my head throb more.

I was in no mood to be polite. "You don't care, so why would you want to know?"

"Don't talk to me like that! I'm your guardian."

"No. You were my guardian. You chose not to behave as a guardian. You are no longer my guardian."

"Listen to me, child!" She followed me slowly, hampered by her hip, as I climbed the stairs. "You don't understand."

I ignored her. There was a travel trunk above my cupboard which I brought down. It would be big enough.

"What are you doing? Listen to me!" she repeated, raising her voice.

"I'm listening. You don't need to shout. I'm packing."

"Packing?"

"I'm leaving this house, temporarily." I swung round. I couldn't loom over her, unfortunately; she was far taller than me. "Just enough time for you to find other accommodation."

"What?"

I took clothes from my cupboard and laid them inside the trunk.

Bending over made me dizzy. I missed part of what she said next. Something about money and expenses.

"Money wouldn't be a problem if it were still in the bank," I said. "There was enough in there for all three of us to live comfortably."

Shoes. Hair brushes and other toiletries.

"Your servants stole money from us," she said.

I was having problems controlling my temper. Naturally, Madame Fontaudin would never be guilty of anything. It would always be someone else's fault.

"You're mistaken." Miserable as Jade was, she was honest.

"You can't go off," she said. "We need help in Saigon. Servants —"

"You had servants and money to pay them, and I fail to see why I should help you get more. How would you pay them anyway?"

Undergarments went into the trunk. I wasn't folding now. I just wanted to get out as quickly as possible. I threw in my jewelry; I dared not leave that here. Some books.

I took my money from the drawer. Very important. Too little.

She was still talking.

"What?" I must have misheard her; something about helping them.

Her voice had changed.

"You could help us," she repeated. "You know the prices in the market, how to shop and haggle. You can cook; Thérèse told me that. I can't do anything ... this hip is too painful. You can see that, can't you?"

"You want me to be your servant? For free, no doubt. Tell me, what money should I use to go down to the market? What will I use to pay the oil bill? That's due this week."

I slammed the trunk, closed and locked it, my head swimming, my fingers slippery with sweat.

There was no way I could carry it, even only half full. I dragged it to the stairs, pushing past her.

"And if you can't even walk with me to the market, who would be my chaperone?" I said as I pulled the trunk over the first step and it landed with a bang on the second.

Not that I wanted another Jade.

"Well, I suppose you don't really need a chaperone."

For one moment I thought she meant I was old enough to look after myself. That was stupid of me.

"It's not as if you're French, after all," she went on. "You're Annamese. You don't have to be so concerned with your reputation. Not like a French girl does."

I slid the trunk down another stair. Another. Another. I concentrated on how each bang seemed to reverberate through my head and not on how much I hated her more with every word she spoke.

She struggled on the stairs as I reached the bottom. The trunk rested on the floor, but the banging went on.

It was knocking on the door. A messenger. One of my tutor's urchins, who handed me a short note.

"Thank you," I said, kneeling down and giving him a coin. "Could you call a Malabar to go to Rue de Tombeaux, please?"

"Malabar. Rue de Tom'," he said and ran off down toward the corner where Bonnard crossed Charner. At least one person wasn't feeling the heat today.

"You can't just go off on your own," Madame Fontaudin said, coming down the last step. "What will I say to Thérèse?"

"Yes, it'll be a difficult conversation, telling her what happened to the money."

She had gone past the wheedling, back to being angry.

"I have my duty to my cousin. If you leave, we'll have to inform the police," she said. "They'll come and find you."

It certainly would be a problem, if I had to hide like a criminal, but I doubted it would come to that.

"Since you're so sure I'm not French," I said, "do you know what law it is that applies to Annamese girls leaving home? The one that says the police have to take me back?"

She didn't, naturally.

"You're being completely unreasonable! This is all a misunderstanding."

"A misunderstanding? Maybe the lawyers will clear it up."

I waved the note from my tutor.

"Lawyers?" Her eyes widened.

"They will be in contact regarding the disappearance of the money, and the terms of your staying here in this house."

She gasped and covered her mouth with a hand.

There was a jangling sound like little bells.

I had heard it so seldom, it took a while to remember what it was. The telephone that Papa had installed in his study. It was for the office to talk to him, but of course anyone who had the number could call us.

Who would call?

I picked up the peculiar instrument and held it awkwardly to my ear and mouth, as I'd seen Papa do.

"Beauclerc residence," I said.

"Ophélie!"

Riossi.

I cleared my throat. "Bernardu."

"My dear girl, thank goodness! I never believed you would go to Cholon after seeing the police on the streets last night! Now Madame Phan tells me you dressed as a boy and went anyway. How resourceful! But also excessive. I would never have asked you if I knew it would be dangerous."

Riossi's idea of dangerous was getting stopped by the police. He had no idea how truly dangerous it had been, and I wasn't going to tell him.

"You kept your word, Bernardu. I keep mine. In all things."

No matter how I felt about him, he *had* kept his word and he was the only way I was going to find Nhung.

He was silent for a second, and when he spoke again, his voice sounded deeper.

"Join me this evening at the Continental. They've opened a private room for gambling tonight. I feel lucky."

"Very well. What time?"

"Seven. Plenty of time to eat and place a few bets, before we go elsewhere."

It was just after five now. Two hours.

"Good. I'll see you there."

I ended the call and closed my eyes.

Tonight. And any night, whenever he calls for me.

As long as he kept his inspectors searching for Nhung.

That's not the way to think about it.

I had to find a way to make him so eager for me, that the work of his inspectors wasn't a concern for me. Even that he would increase the number of inspections and find Nhung sooner. That *he* would be the one worried that *I* might break our agreement.

That's what I should be thinking of.

How? What works like that on men?

What if I offered some of the things I'd glimpsed in the brothel last night?

Although it felt wrong to even think of asking them, perhaps one of the rescued girls like Tuyet could advise me what I needed to do. No time today. Maybe tomorrow.

"Who was that?" Madame Fontaudin asked, breaking across my train of thought.

"A private call. Not your concern."

"It was a man!" she said. "And you called him by his given name. I heard you. You're seeing a man. Does Thérèse know of this?"

"Maman is not here. Do please write to her and explain everything that's going on. Be sure to include the servants, the money problems, and your new address."

Chapter 44

The arrival of the Malabar served to finish our conversation.

The driver took me to Rue de Tombeaux, and he carried my trunk into the house.

I bathed in cold water and changed into something pretty.

I read my tutor's letter more carefully. He'd contacted a lawyer on Papa's behalf and that lawyer would be talking to the Fontaudins. But he'd also contacted Madame Phan, and he knew or guessed my desperate plan to find Nhung. He instructed me to wait and talk to him.

I couldn't. He might be the effective ruler of Cholon, but his power didn't extend to Saigon. Or Khánh Hôi. Bác Thảo might rule there, but he would not prevent the French authorities from inspecting brothels.

I made my way slowly down to the center of town.

Naturally, this happened to be timed exactly right to meet my friend Rochelle, who was taking the opportunity to stroll. The air outside was no cooler than it had been earlier, but it would be even hotter inside the houses.

"Ophélie. Where's Jade?" She peered over my shoulder.

"Madame Fontaudin dismissed her," I said. "I'm alone."

"Oh." She looked uncomfortable, not quite sure how to react to meeting one of her friends on the street without a chaperone. Making

Rochelle uncomfortable tended to make her talk more, and today was no exception.

"You know, they say a storm is rushing up from the coast to bring the monsoon, at last. This heat! The humidity! It can't last. It's driving people crazy. I mean, have you heard about all the trouble in Khánh Hôi?"

"No."

We fell into step.

"It was like when Police Chief Meulnes came out to the racecourse. Remember that? They've seen tigers again, just across the arroyo. Not just one. There have been patrols of armed men crossing the Khánh Hôi bridge all afternoon."

Dare I feel a little spark of hope?

"Did they shoot any tigers?"

"No. Belle says she heard there were lots of dogs killed." Rochelle nodded at her companion, who'd dropped a few paces behind.

It would have been too much to hope for that Bác Thảo would fall victim to something so mundane as a bullet.

Could you even kill Tò Harimau with a bullet?

Qingzhao had cut off the Tò Dara's head last night. Was that what it took to kill them? The captain of the *Salayar* had said a knife through the heart. Would a bullet do as well? Was there a difference between killing Tò Dara and Tò Harimau?

I'd have to ask Yi Song ... except it might be too late for that now. He would want me to go and stay in Cholon with him. But I needed to be here, to keep Riossi's inspectors searching for Nhung.

"Are you alright, Ophélie?"

I blinked.

"No. I'm not. Fontaudin has stolen the money Papa left for looking after the house. He paid gambling debts with it."

"Oh, my goodness! Are you sure?" She put her hands to her face. "That's awful. What are you going to do? It must be so awkward."

"It's not awkward anymore. I've left the house. I've moved to the Rue de Tombeaux."

"Your parents' old house? Alone?"

"Yes."

I could see she was scandalized.

What did I want? Some understanding, possibly even sympathy, but I wasn't going to get it from little Rochelle. I could see her edging away.

"It's late. I must get back," she said.

It wouldn't take long for her to hear about Riossi and me. When she did, that would just confirm the attitude toward me that I saw forming on her face. Living on my own, I was already no longer an acceptable friend. She would not grasp that, if I had only one power, that I would use it, regardless of the cost. This might be the last time we spoke.

"Goodbye, Rochelle," I said.

She blushed and turned away quickly.

Would Manon have stood beside me? Or Emmanuela? I didn't know, and it served no purpose wishing they could be here. I would have to make do with what I had.

I crossed the road and a minute later, I walked into the foyer of the Continental Hotel.

It was clear which room they had put aside for the night's entertainment; a buzz of excited conversation cut across the normally sleepy hotel. I had no maître d'hôtel to avoid, but heads turned when I came in. I saw some frowns, and some familiar faces.

Alain Sévigny for one. "Ophélie. What a pleasant surprise." He beamed at me.

I walked by him. "Not an emotion I share, Sévigny."

He was startled into silence. I could have stopped and asked him where Mam'selle Hubert was, but I no longer cared about this pettiness. I had more important business.

But I couldn't see Riossi.

What I did see was beyond belief and overwhelmed me with anger.

Fontaudin. Sitting at a table, facing away from me, drinking and playing cards.

I couldn't walk past. I knew I should, but I couldn't.

"Really, Fontaudin, whatever are you using to finance your gambling?"

A ripple of shock swept outward.

He staggered to his feet clumsily, spreading cards and spilling drinks. He was already drunk.

"How dare you?" he blustered.

I ignored him. "I do hope, Messieurs, you are not loaning him money," I said to the others around the table. "The bank account has already been emptied."

"This is slander," he said.

"Well, instruct a lawyer. You'll have to anyway, since one has been instructed to act on Monsieur Beauclerc's behalf, for the return of the funds you have taken."

Others spoke now, all at the same time. I hadn't expected such a concerted reaction.

"Who's brought the girl in?"

"Is she old enough? She can't just walk in here!"

"Are Annamese allowed?"

"Maître, take this girl out. Out! Right now!"

Chapter 45

The maître d'hôtel and all the others arraigned against me were answered by one voice.

"Mam'selle Beauclerc is here with me, as my guest."

Just in time.

"Bernardu." I turned and smiled at him as brightly as I could.

"Come Ophélie, let us leave these people to their baccarat."

He steered me to the far end of the room, followed by the glares of the men at the table I'd disrupted. We sat next to each other at a round table, bare but for the starched white tablecloth. Waiters fussed and brought us ice-cold champagne at his instruction.

"I was worried at first that I'd embarrassed you," I said when they left us.

"And now?" he asked, raising his eyebrows.

"I can see you enjoyed it," I replied. "Something in your eyes."

His face was sober, but the expression could not conceal his amusement.

"How observant you are. Clever as well as beautiful. Yes, they are ridiculous, and Fontaudin chief among them. To be bad at cards is no real fault. Neither is it a fault to be fond of drink. To falsely believe yourself good at cards and confound it with drunkenness while playing is pathetic."

He sighed and looked less amused.

"This is not the group I was hoping to see here when I invited you, but anyway, alas, events have overtaken us."

"What do you mean?"

"The docks are in uproar, and there are more ships approaching. I will have to return to the Messageries Maritimes in half an hour."

I sipped champagne to ease my throat. It seemed I would escape another day.

"How awful," I said. "What is the cause? Tigers again?"

"Oh, those are some of the stories, but that's just what they are — stories. No, the real reason is the new lieutenant governor's desperate need to show his regime is in control by flooding the city with police and soldiers." He snorted. "On the one side, we have stories of rebels hiding in Saigon and on the other, tiger demons in Khánh Hôi. And all because Hubert is ignorant about Indochina and painfully unsure of himself."

A pair of rumors I happened to know were true for once.

He turned to me, serious now.

"Last night ... I would not have held you to your promise with soldiers on the streets."

"I had no means to judge that, Bernardu. It is important for me to show you that my word is good."

"You've certainly done that." He leaned closer, and his voice softened. "It adds to your allure."

"Why am I so alluring, Bernardu?" The question had been fermenting inside me and it seemed to come out on its own. It was a fair question. Was everything he did no more than a ploy to take my virginity, after which he'd walk away? But it wasn't the right question to ask now: it betrayed how unsure I was. I had to cover my clumsiness.

"After all," I went on quickly, "you could have an affair with any woman you desire. It's not as if I'm the governor's daughter or ..." I looked down, "or especially skilled."

That seemed to work, even better than I'd hoped.

"You are young yet, to truly see yourself as others see you." He chuckled, and emptied his glass. "You will learn. Your allure? Yes ... you are that exquisite blend of the exotic and the familiar: the mysterious, unreachable Annamese and the relatable, accessible French. Not like the

257

women of the demimondaine, a bit of this and that, but truly able to be all of both. Unique, certainly in Saigon. There is not one of those," he nodded at the tables of gamblers, "who is not burning with envy of me."

I could hear the rich satisfaction in his voice when he said that.

He'd mentioned at our lunch how he'd felt excluded by the mainland French in Saigon because of the bias against Corsicans, and by Corsicans because he'd married a woman from Paris. I got a glimpse of how much he built himself around that sense of injustice, that exclusion. They could not exclude him now, with his powerful positions in the Opium Regie and Messageries Maritimes. He was a man they had to defer to, to accept in their clubs and societies. What better revenge, what better way to further emphasize his position over them by having a mistress they desired and could not have?

Maybe my position was not so precarious as I feared.

"Did you like my gift?" he said.

"Of course! Thank you. It's so pretty. Naturally, I'm wearing it now, for you."

The tablecloth fell all the way to the floor. From the waist down, we were hidden from the room. I had a very good idea what he would do when I said that, and I was right.

His hand brushed down my side and lifted the bottom of my dress.

I thought of the girls in the convent this morning. Of Nhung. They'd had no choice and no benefit from what they'd had to do, which was far worse than this.

I am so lucky. I am so lucky.

I felt his fingers on my ankle and stilled the reflex twitch that would have pulled me away from him.

I am so lucky.

I took a deep breath and angled my legs towards him.

His fingers found the chain, tugged it gently before letting go.

"You like it?"

"You're not talking about the chain, are you?" I drank more champagne. "I confess, it excites me, the forbidden."

He liked that. He liked everything I'd been doing and saying. His breathing deepened and his eyes took on a hungry gleam.

"It scares me as well," I said. It was the truth. I needed to tell him as much truth as I could, to better hide the lies.

That, he also liked. His voice softened. "To be scared and still resolute. You are remarkable. Your young mind is full of the unknown now, Ophélie, which quite naturally, you fill with fears. You are scared of outrages, as if sin was original. It's not. You will come to see it as normal. As something ... everyday. Like having lunch or dinner with me. And then you will come to find enjoyment in it."

"I'm sure I will," I said. "I need to tell you, I won't be staying at the house on Boulevard Bonnard. I can't go back there until I get the Fontaudins out."

Then I had to explain to him my visit to the bank, and my decision to stay alone at the Rue de Tombeaux.

I could see his interest at that news. No doubt he had an apartment somewhere in Saigon where he could conduct his liaisons, but to use an elegant house instead ...

I didn't want to spend time talking about that. He would have to go soon. I needed to see if there was a way to speed up the hunt for Nhung. To see if he had a lust for gold as strong as his lust for me.

"My only concern is the danger," I said. "Rue de Tombeaux is a little out of town."

He frowned. "What danger?"

But I recognized the man who'd just entered the room and was heading for us. The same man had interrupted us at lunch.

"Ah. Another time. I think the Messageries Maritimes await you, Bernardu," I said. "Will I see you tomorrow?"

"Yes! Come to the Hôtel de l'Univers for lunch." He stood and bent his head over my hand. "Then I will take the afternoon off," he murmured, looking keenly into my eyes. "The docks be damned."

"I'll be there," I said. "I look forward to it."

He and his colleague strode off, their heads together and deep in conversation already.

I let out a breath and sat back in my chair. Riossi was intelligent, powerful and rich. If I could relax a little, I'd probably find him entertaining as well. Champagne certainly helped with that. He wasn't coarse. He didn't smell. He seemed sensitive.

I felt almost cheated. He should be easier to hate, though hating him would serve no purpose.

On the other hand, he was married, old enough to be my father, and it wouldn't do to get on his wrong side.

Having been held off by all the adrenaline of dealing with Riossi, my headache now returned.

I poured myself more champagne. I read somewhere that alcohol dulled pain.

Tomorrow, I would return to the plan that had crystallized in my brain. I would tell Riossi about the danger of Bác Thảo, and about the Emperor's gold. I would not tell him the story was false. Instead, I would say that I was too young to know anything about it, but my sister …

Would that work?

Would Riossi protect me and speed up the process of finding Nhung?

Would he make me promise not to walk away when Nhung was found?

Why wouldn't I? As Tuyet had said today, what other options are there for a whore? Thanks to Fontaudin, I had no money, no means of support for myself, let alone my sister as well.

What about Papa and Maman returning to find me Riossi's whore? What would I do then?

I would have to deal with that when it happened. I had no other choices.

The headache redoubled in intensity. My whole body seemed to throb in time with my pulse, until I felt faint.

I needed to leave, but everything seemed so far away.

The gauze curtains beside me stirred gently. I realized they'd been moving for some time while I sat there. I felt sweaty and then chilled, almost as if I had a fever. Too hot. Too cold.

How long had I been sitting here alone?

The curtains billowed out suddenly, reaching into the room with ghostly hands.

The buzz of conversation dipped. It had been still all day, but now the wind had a floating voice, and there came the faint sound of distant drums.

I shivered.

A man stood up from one of the tables and went to the main window.

He peered out and jumped as he was enveloped in a searing light that hurt to see. There was a crash like cannons firing and he staggered back into the suddenly silenced room as if he'd been shot.

Chapter 46

I laughed.

Another one of Rochelle's rumors had actually turned out to be true; the storm was about to break over the city. The monsoon had finally come to Saigon.

Now I really needed to get home; carriages and rickshaws wouldn't be out if the storm was as bad as it sounded.

I made my way across the room and the lobby beyond, ignoring the looks from all sides.

"Not good, Mam'selle," the servant holding the hotel's front door said, looking into the wild night. "No Malabar."

Streetlamps were out, but I could see the trees along Rue Catinat, thrashing in the wind. It was already raining. It would only get worse, and I couldn't stay here.

Rue de Tombeaux was out of reach. There was no way I could make it that far. The headache was making me ill and I had no strength in my limbs. I would have to creep into the house at Boulevard Bonnard, covered by the noise of the storm. I'd barricade myself in my room and leave at dawn before the Fontaudins realized I was there.

I shrugged and the man reluctantly held the door open for me, gripping it with both hands, and closing it quickly behind me.

The wind buffeted me as I made my way along the front of the Continental. I crouched down, with my hand out to take some stability from the hotel.

All I had to do was cross Catinat and Charner. Walk a little way down Bonnard. Surely not such a difficult thing?

I was reluctant to leave the partial shelter of the hotel, but it was raining harder every moment I hesitated, and I was drenched already.

The wind strengthened even more as I set off across the wide Rue Catinat, making me stagger. By the time I got to the huge square at the intersection of Charner and Bonnard, the world had disappeared into a maelstrom. I knew the statue of Garnier was to the side, but I couldn't see it. I couldn't even see the other side of the square, and as I crossed it, I was knocked down.

Shapes hurtled past me in the night—branches torn from trees, sacking from the docks and markets, bamboo shutters, sun blinds that had been ripped from shopfronts, chairs, tables, a lady's parasol, people's hats, books. A child's toy. They flew past and vanished as the storm shrieked above Saigon. Sheet lightning flared above, showing glimpses of the angry bases of towering clouds. Thunder sounded so low I felt it in the ground. The boulevard was running ankle-deep in water already.

This was no ordinary storm. It was as if the monsoon's delay had gathered all the wind and rain to unleash on Saigon in one blow.

I got up, stumbled, and immediately fell again. Again.

Where was the other side of Charner? I could see nothing. I wasn't even sure I was crawling in the right direction.

I was too weak. There was no point going on. If I stayed down, at least nothing more would hit me.

I knelt and cried.

It was too much. The force of the storm was beyond me, like the forces that moved beneath the surface in Saigon were beyond me.

I was nothing, a girl with no power, not even to find my sister. No one here cared. No one would help me, except in payment. And Riossi was a man of the world; he would see through my plans and discard me as soon as he'd had me. The French would not want me. *Too Bian, too Annamese.* The Annamese would not protect me. *Too Ophélie, too French.* Yi Song wouldn't want me after I'd decided to go to Riossi. Neither would my parents.

Only Bác Thảo wanted me. He would find me and kill me, trying to find a treasure that didn't exist.

"No!" I screamed into the storm, my words snatched away in the wind and lost in the night.

A momentary easing of the downpour showed me a glimpse of the corner of Charner and Bonnard that I was trying to reach.

Was that someone standing there?

Bác Thảo? More Tò Dara come to kidnap me?

Too small.

I screamed again, wordless, lost in the tumult.

If that were Nhung, sitting there on the roadside, waiting for me, what would I say? *It was too hard. I couldn't cross the road. I gave up.*

Bian would not give up. I'd made an oath. If Ophélie wanted a reminder … I tore the arm of the dress back and scratched at the thin healing scar until it bled again. Blood swiftly disappeared, washed away by the rain.

It took a little of the madness with it, and brought a chilled calmness.

The only way to be sure to fail was to not try at all.

I would go on, until I could not. Until I died, if necessary.

Despite that calmness, I couldn't remember crossing the remainder of the square. There was no figure waiting for me, not there and not on Bonnard either, which I must have crawled down on my hands and knees, cowering from the storm. It hurt to try and focus my eyes. Sight and sound blurred together in the meaningless pandemonium.

I found myself at the front door of the house. Then inside. There were no lights on, no movement. It was blessedly quiet and still after being outside. Puddles gathered at my feet.

I moved slowly up the stairs until a step creaked loudly and I froze.

There was no answering sound.

I looked back down to check if I'd miscounted steps, but I couldn't see.

After a few minutes, holding onto the banister, I took another step. Silence. Another.

Finally I was in my room, actually shivering with cold.

My clothes were ruined, torn and filthy. I stripped them off with difficulty, all the material wet through and sticking together.

I had left some shifts in a drawer earlier. I used one to dry myself and another to put on. All I could think about was sleeping until the pain in my head subsided. Just bed.

But there was a light under the door and I'd forgotten to block it. It opened and Fontaudin stood there.

"You whore," he said, slurring words and swaying from side to side. "You think you can embarrass me like that, then come sneaking back into the house?"

"Get out, Fontaudin! Get out of my room. Get out of my parents' house. Get out of my life."

"Little bitch. I'll teach you a lesson." He swung at me, but he was still drunk.

I slapped him hard, but the shock of hitting him jarred through my body and my head. It felt like lightning behind my eyes. I reeled as if he'd struck me. We both stumbled and Fontaudin grabbed at me to steady himself. He got a fistful of my shift. It tore.

"You let Riossi have you, eh?" He shook me. "You think he'll protect you? A man like him doesn't care what happens to his whores when he's finished."

I struggled, twisting and turning and kicking.

The shift tore some more and Fontaudin pushed me back toward the bed. I felt it press against my knees. I couldn't allow him to push me down onto it.

I struck at his body, swinging wildly. It had no effect. His arms blocked me.

The door was thrown open and his wife stood there, lit by the lamp in the corridor, her face distorted with rage.

"You slut!" she screamed. "Your lover throws you out and you think you can come back here and seduce my husband. You're all alike. Whores and sluts, all of you."

Fontaudin jerked back, allowing me to get my hands up and scratch at his face, trying to get his eyes.

He stumbled away, letting go completely. "She scratched me!" he shouted. "I'm blind! The bitch scratched my eyes."

I overbalanced. I was determined not to fall backwards onto the bed, where I'd be defenseless. Instead I staggered and crashed against the window, hitting my head. The storm's thunder crashed outside. More lights in my head. Strength was leaking from me.

I slid down the wall and collapsed on the floor. I couldn't see clearly. Everything became dark and monstrous.

Madame Fontaudin loomed over me. She had her cane gripped in both hands. She raised it. The grip was like the head of a hammer. Ugly. Threatening.

My arms and legs wouldn't work. I couldn't even put my hands up to defend myself.

This shouldn't be happening. I can't let this happen. There is so much I need to do.

The cane came down. Again. Again. Agonizing, stunning blows to my head. I tasted blood. A great blackness descended and crushed me beneath its heel.

Part 6 – Revenge

復
仇

Mark Henwick

Chapter 47

It's cool on the lake.

Misty veils of morning hide the shorelines, and the sun is no more than a silver glimmer in the east. Silence drops like dew from the innocent sky. A breeze, carrying scents of the sea, tugs at my hair and plays with the shining silk áo dài I wear.

I step between sacred lotus blossoms, dainty as a butterfly, walking on the lake. The deep water dimples beneath my feet.

"It's so beautiful." I breathe the words. "So peaceful."

"It is." I hear my lǎoshī speak, but I cannot see him.

"Why am I here?"

"Because you're dying."

"Am I? Truly? I'm sorry. But it's not so bad, then."

"No." He sighs. "Sometimes death is so much easier than life."

"Are you dying too, Lǎoshī?" I feel I should want to cry, but there are no tears left. "You sound so close, but I can't see you."

"No, I'm not dying."

"Oh. That's good. What happened to me?"

"You were struck on the head, very forcefully, many times."

Memories flare like lightning in the night. The Tò Dara in Cholon — the one who punched me and made me feel so sick. The Fontaudins — the cane coming down out of the night, remorseless. I gasp and stagger. My feet sink into the lake.

As I cry out and start to fall, a hand grips my arm, steadies me.

I can see him now, his tall body bent over me. He's holding me while I get my balance. He's angry about something. He looks much fiercer here than the Monsieur Song I remember.

But everything's alright. It doesn't matter anymore. After all, I'm dying. It's over.

My feet float upward and break the surface of the lake again. The ripples fade.

"Perhaps you should go now," I say, when I feel steady again.

"In a while," he says. And then, quietly: "You could come with me."

I'm not sure I want to. Even thinking about it makes my feet feel as if they're sinking back into the lake.

"I suppose this is part of the spirit world?" I say, thinking about things that are *here*, not back *there*. I move away from him and spin around as if I were dancing.

"Not really. This is something you made." He moves, quicker than my eye can follow, catches my hand, and circles around me, right in the middle of the lake.

"You should let me go," I say.

The mists on the lake seem a little darker at one point. Is that the shore, there? It calls to me.

"I will ask you a few questions first," he says. "Then, if you tell me to leave you, I will go."

"Is that a promise?"

I remember promises I made to people. Was it a long time ago? There was a promise, like an oath. And another, like a bargain which had rules. I did something. Someone did something in return. Whatever happened to those? Why did I make promises?

Nothing matters.

"Yes, a promise, but we must hurry." His hand grips me tightly. "Bian, would you come back with me to be with your parents again?"

"I let them all down," I reply, shaking my head. My birth parents. Better off never knowing I'd failed after all they sacrificed for me. My adoptive parents. I can't remember, but I know I was ashamed, back when I wasn't dying. Too ashamed. I don't want to go back and have to explain to them. I don't want to think about it at all.

"What about your whole life ahead of you. Does that not draw you?"

I shake my head again. It seems so distant.

"Would you come back to rescue Nhung?"

The lake is suddenly cold and dark and soft as mist. I'm sinking again. He's holding me here; otherwise I would fall in, and it *hurts*. Everything rushes back in, so blurred and bright, it burns.

"Yes." My voice is thin and shaky. I have to force the words out between sobs. "I promised. I made an oath. There's only me left to save her. But I'm dying. How do I get back, Lǎoshī? Can you cast a spell on me? Do you reach in and pull me back?"

He sighs.

"I misled you before, and now we face the consequences while time flees like the morning mist. I am not an Adept, not a user of the spirit arts. I have some abilities, but I cannot cast spells that would cure you. I cannot save you, but I can change you so that you can save yourself, if you want to strongly enough."

"Nhung needs me. I don't care what happens to me if I can only save her. She gave up everything for me. Yes, I want to save her. I want *that* strongly enough."

But what does he mean? Change?

"What would I change to?" I ask.

He doesn't answer directly. "I must warn you, it's dangerous. Many do not survive." His eyes are red, but his grip is tight. "Injured as you are now, and unprepared, there is great danger. But you are young, so there is hope. And if you survive, you will become strong enough to rescue your sister without making these bargains."

Danger?

"What is danger to someone who's dying?" I say. "But tell me, Lǎoshī, tell me the truth now. Change to what?"

His head bows and raises again. "What you think of as a monster."

It comes to me then and I struggle in vain. Who would be so strong that all the Chinese gangs of Cholon would fear him? Who but the gang lord of Khánh Hôi? The tall man. My tutor is Bác Thảo in disguise!

But I'm wrong. His lips draw back. His teeth blur and the canines grow sharp and long.

I look into his face with dread and truly understand. This is not Bác Thảo. This is the monstrous, evil Tò Dara the Bugis captain of the *Salayar* warned me about, on the Quai du Commerce, so very long ago.

To 'cure' me, he wants to make me like himself.

A monster.

And yet, I promised.

It's as if Nhung stands beside me again, letting her hair fall across her face.

Whatever happens, she whispers.

She gave herself for me.

There is no other way. I find I do have tears left.

"Yes," I say.

The lake is so dark now, I can't see, but I can still feel. I feel a pain like my head is splitting open. A coldness, creeping over me. A stillness that I somehow recognise. That stillness is the end of my life.

I feel my lǎoshi is holding me cradled in his arms. My real body. My spirit body.

And I am *him* in some way, as well.

His strength flows through me. His warmth holds the stillness away. His breath seems to fill my lungs. His blood seems to stir in my weakening veins.

I can hear his heart so clearly. It's so slow and heavy, like the distant sound of cannon on the breeze when the navy practice out at sea. Mine is a feeble counterpoint.

I can't move. Some animal instinct wants me to struggle, but my body refuses.

Maybe it's too late.

Am I already dead?

Is this a dream of life?

Does consciousness linger for a while before slipping away?

But it does not slip away. It's as if his mind is holding me like his arms are holding me. As if there are two people in my head at the same time. I'm frantic with panic, but he's so calm, so sure.

Two minds, two sets of sensations.

My skin is cold and clammy to his touch.

His breath on my throat.

Run! Get up and run away!

"Calm," he says quietly. "The pain will be gone soon."

And something needle-sharp grazes my skin.

Fangs!

I try to speak, but it's too much. I'm falling. It's too late.

A scarlet flower blooms in my throat. A flower of pure fire. But it's not painful. Not at all.

What's happening?

Pleasure pours into me, soaking up the pain in my head, burning away the chill in my limbs, until there is nothing else.

I grasp this sensation as if it were a lifeline and I were drowning. It's life itself, this pleasure. I pull it to me. Cling onto it. My whole body sings while his fangs are buried in my throat. I sense he's taking my blood from me, giving me in exchange this pleasure, this fire. It consumes the dark, it consumes me, until I seem to be nothing but smoke and light.

And slowly, an exhausted sleep falls over me like a net, so entangled with visions or dreams I cannot tell what is real and what is not.

Sometimes I skim the surface of the lake and I know I'm dying. Sometimes I wake to sunlight filtering through a screen and I know I'm alive.

Sometimes I know I am becoming a monster that kills for blood. Sometimes an angel who can cure people of sickness and injury.

I lose all track of time.

Through the drifting nights, Qingzhao sits beside the bed and whispers cool words to me as I burn with fevers.

This is your time of trial, she tells me. *We call this 'crusis'. If you survive, you will be Athanate. Not vampire, not ma cà rông, not Tò Dara. Athanate. It means undying.*

The human world glimpse us only through the dark glass of myth; we Athanate are a people hidden in the illusion of the world, she says. *No longer hidden to you.*

I float up to the ceiling and look back down at the body and soul that is me. I see things about myself.

There is now a monster inside me that can kill for the pleasure that comes with blood, just as there is an angel who can heal.

It's up to me to choose.

Chapter 48

I wasn't even half awake. I couldn't tell whether I was still dreaming.

I heard distant bells. Was it Sunday? Maman and Papa would be at church. Should I join them, or was I already too late?

Too late, the bells spoke.

The wind blew in, cooling the tracks of tears on my cheeks, and I knew this was not Boulevard Bonnard. Ophélie's dream of Saigon was gone; my life as Ophélie Beauclerc was gone. The *maya,* the veil of illusion over my world, had been torn.

That cooling wind brought the distant smells of street cooking and charcoal fires. Temple incense and stagnant canals. The rich fragrance of lotus mingled with the sweet perfume of the Hoa Sua trees from the courtyards outside my room.

The smells of Cholon. Of House Song.

Not an ordinary house. No longer just the rambling, airy building where my tutor lived, because threaded through the jumbled sounds and scents and dreams came another, deeper awareness, subtle as the whisper of silk in the night.

I *belonged.*

This was my *House.*

I was a monster. My eyes flew open, and for a moment, my heart hammered in my chest like a tiny bird might struggle in the cage of your hands.

Today ...

I sat up, clutching the edge of the bed. Put other concerns aside.

I am alive.

Hold onto that thought.

My injuries were healed, even if I was still dizzy at the moment. And nothing said I *had* to become a monster. I could be Athanate and not be a monster.

Calm.

In the medley of scents was one that human noses would struggle to pick out: it was coppery, with an overtone that somehow made me think of cool, swift rivers.

Humans would struggle, but I could now discern it easily. To me, it was a balm. It was the unique scent that identified House Song among Athanate communities.

And underneath the scents and sounds was another sensation, as intangible as that word on the tip of your tongue, as powerful as that sense of being a part of something larger.

That was also part of what identified House Song.

Between them these scents and sensations told me that, while I was no longer completely human, I was home, and my Master, Yi Song, was near. Just outside. Waiting.

It was time. I stood up slowly and moved carefully, dressing in simple Annamese clothes. As I'd been instructed yesterday, I wound a black velvet strip across my eyes.

Fingers trailing the walls, I walked out of the room and down the passage. I turned at the end. A few tentative paces forward. I heard the space of the courtyard and felt the heat of the sun. My feet explored the steps down to the ground, where I stopped, sensing someone in front of me.

Both the scent and the touch in my mind that identified House Song had the subtlest of variations. An Athanate had to be able to identify every member of her House by those two senses alone.

Today's test started now.

A flare of panic. What if I got it wrong?

I locked my hands together to hide the trembling.

"Greetings, Xiu," I said, and bowed.

I could hear the sternness in his voice as he replied. "Greetings. Please attend Master Song."

Much more panic now. Still blindfold, I had to find him in the courtyard, hidden among the trees and ponds.

They are not trying to make you fail, I told myself.

I knew roughly where my tutor was; I could sense him, a bit like the way I could have sensed my father when we lived on the sampan. It was as if the whole world moved a little when he was near, as if it all tilted a fraction in his direction.

My feet crept along the ground, feeling the texture of pebbles, rock slabs, earth and grass. They were not trying to make me fail; there were no traps on the way.

I stopped when I could hear his heartbeat. There was no other like it, for me.

"Greetings, Master." I bowed.

"I prefer *Lǎoshī* to *Master*," he replied. "The name has served us well; let's continue with it."

"Yes, Lǎoshī." I bobbed my head again.

"Sit."

I sat down beside him, like a child beside her father.

Athanate did not have children. New Athanate were normally gradually infused with Athanate Blood in a steady, controlled process which could take a year to complete. It was all dangerous. The infusion could kill. The transformation from human to Athanate could kill. Even the speed of the transformation itself could be deadly.

There had been no time to take it gradually with me. Master Song had infused me with a huge dose of his Blood in a desperate gamble that I would become Athanate enough, quickly enough, to heal myself.

It seemed the healing had worked, but there were still many dangers on the path.

Today was another step on that path: to show I was truly Athanate, and an acceptable member of House Song.

Today was the day I learned to take Blood.

Someone came and sat beside me.

I breathed in, reached out with my mind.

A man. Part of House Song, but not Athanate. No, this was one of the *katikia*.

An Athanate House consisted of Athanate and katikia, humans bound to the House. There were ten Athanate in House Song, and thirty-three katikia to provide the Blood that Athanate needed.

Athanate might exchange Blood with other Athanate for infusion, or pleasure, or to form ties between them, but to survive they needed—*I needed*—human Blood.

Needed. My jaw started to ache.

All Master Song's 'wives' and 'concubines' that had so upset Maman, were in truth katikia, as were the servants … and the young man who was sitting next to me.

My heart was racing and my voice hoarse and shaky. "Greetings, Shimin."

Shimin was a former sailor from the island of Hainan. He'd jumped ship in Saigon and had been lucky enough to find his way to Cholon, where he'd been taken in. He had no wish to become Athanate. He simply offered what he could—his Blood and service—in exchange for a home, food and drink, a much longer life, perfect health and protection.

And pleasure.

"Greetings, Gōngzhǔ."

Princess, he'd just called me. It was so surprising, it made me laugh. And quickly cover my mouth—that ache in my jaw was fangs ready to emerge. It was stupid, but I was embarrassed.

It wasn't just the thought of taking his Blood, or the pleasure involved with that.

Qingzhao had gently explained it to me. Athanate fed on Blood *and* emotions from their katikia. Those emotions formed a basis of what bound humans to the House. And to kindle and feed those emotions? The sensations of pleasure we shared from biting was a start, but as she'd delicately put it, *they share their Blood, we share our bodies.*

It wasn't that I was expected to leap into bed with Shimin right now — today was about Blood. But it was a knowledge that loomed large in my mind. And he was a most handsome young man.

Master Song murmured: "One thing at a time. Focus on Blood."

His presence flowed into my head. My ears filled with the slow pulse of my tutor's heart.

Calm.

I sensed Shimin stretching out his arm, until his wrist was just in front of me.

Even in the heat, I could sense the warmth of his body. Almost against my will, I lowered my face until my lips came into contact with his wrist.

"Breathe," Master Song said, and I forced my lungs to empty and refill.

I could smell Shimin's anticipation and that subtle scent that told me he was House Song, that told me his Blood was mine for the taking. I could feel his pulse on my lips, his Blood coursing just beneath his skin. Our hearts wanted to speed up, but Master Song pulled us back.

Calm.

That scent wrapped itself around me, drew me onwards.

Blood …

First, there were things I had to remember to do. Qingzhao had said …

Lick.

Qingzhao had told me my saliva would help make him feel only pleasure from my bite, and heal quickly afterwards.

I licked his wrist.

The taste overwhelmed me and fangs erupted from my jaw.

Shimin flinched, but I could not hold back. My fangs sank into his wrist.

I gasped.

It was one thing to have Master Song share his pleasure at biting me through our mental link, and quite another to feel my fangs sinking into Shimin's flesh.

Oh, yes!

I *pulled*. Shimin's Blood flowed into my fangs, down through Athanate channels into my chest, and the sensation exploded inside me.

We both groaned, sharing the pleasure.

The light seemed to dim. The world receded, and I *pulled* again greedily.

Mine. Mine. More.

I didn't want it to end. Couldn't stop. My whole world was the unbelievable sensation of feeding from Shimin's Blood.

But Master Song was there. Firm. Strong. Guiding. Calming. Holding me back.

Awareness flowed back into me.

I could have killed Shimin. I *would* have. The shock of how dangerous this was skittered through my body. My jaw shifted again. The fangs disappeared.

I lay panting as if I'd run all the way here from the Saigon docks. Half of me was bathed in a delirium of sensual joy, half in the cold trauma of how close I'd come to losing my mind and killing Shimin.

He unwrapped the blindfold from my head.

"It will get easier, Gōngzhǔ," he said, and kissed the palm of my hand.

He was still bleeding. I was supposed to lick the wound, stop the bleeding. I couldn't. I didn't dare. If I touched him again now, the fangs would come back out and I'd bite and *pull* and *pull* until there was nothing.

The Athanate of Master Song's House *never* killed katikia. To kill in mindless pleasure was to be declared rogue, and rogues were executed.

I had fed on Blood. I needed to keep feeding on Blood, but I had to learn to control myself, to find my way past this monstrous state they called crusis.

Qingzhao brought me a pillow, and they left me there in the shade of the tree to recover, all my attention focused inwards, aware of every pulse in my body, every touch of clothes, every kiss of air, every scent, every sound.

Aware and scared.

Chapter 49

It was half an hour before dawn. All the lamps were out. The sky had begun to pale and I was about to die again, painfully.

I wanted to live. I was surprised how powerfully that flame burned in my chest now, despite the utter peace I'd felt on the spirit lake. I didn't want to return and find what waited on the far shore. Not yet. But I couldn't forget it.

I stood utterly still, legs braced in the *Ma Bu*, the basic wide horse position, my chang gùn held motionless at the full stretch of my arm, my ears straining for the slightest warning.

Death stalked me silently.

Light rain fell, soft as a child's tears, pattering on the leaves of the trees around me, whispering over the roofs around the courtyard and sprinkling into the pools.

There! No more sound than a breath of wind, but my enemy approaches.

Wait. Wait. Wait ...

I spun and lashed out with the staff.

The shadows split, became a nightmare of movement and terrible speed that sucked the air from my lungs. I missed, dropped, rolled, sprang up, struck hard at empty air with the staff.

Her chang gùn stabbed me in the ribs. I coughed with pain.

"Dead," she hissed.

Ignore that. Focus. I whirled my staff to catch hers ... touched, slid off.

She rapped the side of my stomach.

"Dead."

My chang gùn bucked and leaped out of my nerveless fingers. Hers came at me like a snake strike, right at my eyes.

And stopped. If her blades had been out, I'd have had steel emerging from the back of my head.

"Dead," she said.

I muttered the rudest words I knew in Mandarin, and she smiled.

"Much better, though."

"Another hundred years and I'll be almost reasonable."

Qingzhao laughed and flicked my staff up into the air.

I snatched it, fell into the horse stance, and started fending off her probes, still amazed at the way my body responded.

Eight weeks.

It had taken just eight weeks. It felt like a lifetime. It felt like nothing.

I am Athanate. Time means something different now.

But not for Nhung.

"Concentrate," Qingzhao said.

Athanate. Meaning immortal. Our name for ourselves. Not Tò Dara. Not monsters.

The myths and legends got so little right. We Athanate walked in sunlight, looked in mirrors, ate garlic, prayed in churches and temples, slept in beds. We weren't dead and didn't live off the life force of humans, unless you counted Blood as the life force.

I was not a monster, but I was only truly Athanate if I survived the rest of the *crusis*, the time of trial every Athanate had to go through. If I didn't, Yi Song had simply extended my life for a few weeks.

Today was the day of another important crusis test: *xoietasi* in the Athanate language. A *vital* test, in the old sense of the word. *Vital*, meaning *of life*. Meaning if I passed, I lived.

This assault by Qingzhao with her staff was not part of that test. She was only keeping me distracted, although she had claimed it was just more essential training.

Training me was part of her duties as second-in-command of House Song. Her title was Diakon, and she wasn't Song's daughter.

"Over four hundred years too young for that." She had laughed when I asked.

As for him, he was about eight hundred years old.

Her staff rapped my knuckles in admonition for my attention wandering, but it was impossible to push all the other thoughts out.

Qingzhao's claim about training had validity. This exercise was not simply a distraction; it was an essential part of becoming Athanate. The

Blood I was now infused with repaid every physical effort many times over. I was stronger and quicker than I'd ever been before, and far beyond what I could have achieved as human. But if I were to stop exercising, for so little as a week, the Blood would consume me from the inside.

Everything about the Blood was a matter of balances. It had allowed me to recover from the blows to my head and heal myself. I wouldn't get ill again. I could hear and see and smell and taste and feel things in such detail, it was as if I'd lived my previous life wrapped in the softest cotton. But if I stopped infusing myself with fresh human Blood, I would die.

And today, there was a test to pass. A test to see if I would be allowed to live or not.

A gong sounded quietly from the innermost courtyard. Immediately, Qingzhao stood back and raised her chang gùn in a salute.

"It's time," she whispered. "I believe in you, Bian. Believe in yourself."

Chapter 50

Yi Song waited for me in his raised pavilion. We called it the Bloodstone Pavilion, because of the priceless cinnabar-tinted gemstones used to decorate it. In Chinese tradition, the bloodstone was said to deflect evil, better even than jade for that task.

And I supposed blood red was not a strange choice of color for a vampire.

I put my chang gùn and my shoes neatly by the bottom step, then ascended to walk barefoot across the lacquered wooden floor. I knelt and bowed in front of him, head touching the floor. Whatever I called him, he was no longer just my tutor; he was my Master. The Blood inside me knew. My whole body knew. Though the puncture wounds had all healed, I could still feel every place where his fangs had pierced my throat. They throbbed gently as I raised my eyes to meet his.

He motioned me to sit on his left. There were two cushions there. I folded myself down on the first one and crossed my legs. I put my hands on my thighs and willed them to stop trembling.

Opposite me, spanning the width of the pavilion, was a bloodstone mosaic screen depicting a phoenix rising in flight. Great good fortune, I hoped. Rebirth.

I was dead. I am alive.

I did not turn to look, but behind me, the matching bloodstone mosaic was a curling dragon that threatened to devour me.

If I could control myself to his satisfaction, I could remain alive. That was the heart of this test and the fundamental rule of Athanate law.

The Athanate loved and feared humanity. I needed to show I could understand and control those instincts before I was fully admitted to being Athanate.

The katikia of House Song willingly provided their Blood to us and were bound to the House. In return, the Athanate of the House bound themselves to the katikia. We would defend them. We would give them health, long life and pleasure. We would not kill them.

If any Athanate lost control and her need and pleasure combined to overwhelm her, as mine nearly had the first time I bit Shimin, she would kill the human providing her with Blood.

House Song would not tolerate this. I had to prove I could control myself. The alternative was to be declared a rogue, and killed.

But that was only part of the test.

Athanate also feared humanity. Not the katikia, *they* would not turn against us, but the mass of humanity beyond the House. Athanate history was passed down in instruction to new Athanate, and the history said that whenever Athanate were discovered by humanity, it ended with their deaths.

To prove I could walk this tightrope of living among humanity and fearing their discovery—this was the other part of the test I was to undergo today.

My Master, my lǎoshī, my gentle, kindly tutor, had been Athanate and leader of House Song for hundreds of years. His power and his senses were far beyond mine. He could hear my heart beating and the air flowing from my lungs. He could taste the fear and excitement in my breath. He would know.

If I failed this test, then my lǎoshī, my gentle, kindly tutor—he would kill me.

Bình tâm. Bình tâm. Keep calm. Keep calm.

I visualized the fear like a knot in my stomach, felt it unwind, become spirit mist and rise into my lungs, where I breathed it out. It disappeared in the warmth of the morning.

The phoenix will fly up from its ashes. I will rise. The dragon will not consume me.

He was watching me. He'd positioned me so that I had to look at the phoenix, knowing it would make me think about it and what it meant.

"The phoenix is not a symbol of the Athanate," he said. "Despite the legends of vampires, we do not have to die to become Athanate. And we are not locked in a cycle of growing old and being reborn."

He was easing me into the test, drawing me out, and I was grateful for it. But every answer still mattered and I spoke carefully.

"Yet we must all pass through crusis, which for any Athanate must feel like a death and rebirth, Lǎoshī. And much more so for me."

"Explain."

"It wasn't simply that I was dying when you bit me." I looked at the beautiful phoenix screen and let the memories and pain rise through my body and pass out with the air from my lungs, as if everything had happened to poor Ophélie, far away and long ago. Not to me.

"Even without the Fontaudins," I said, "I would not have survived as Ophélie. If it wasn't Bác Thảo, or Athanate enemies in House Zheng, or …" I waved a hand, "the Deuxième Bureau, or whoever has my sister, it would have been someone else. Even myself."

Myself. Like the bites on my neck, the scar I'd inflicted on my own arm was long healed, but I felt a gentle throb as I thought of it, remembered the small, insistent call, the lure of the release it promised.

And I breathed it all out, let it go. It was not me. It was not now.

"Qingzhao tells me you are very quick to learn the chang gùn," he said.

"She's kind. I'm clumsy compared to her, and I have only the first level of skill."

"The chang gùn is not your weapon, I think, but it's a good one to start with," he said thoughtfully. Then: "Your studies of our language and rules are also proceeding well."

I bowed my head to acknowledge the compliment. The Athanate language was difficult. As for the rules, I simply had to learn them. I'd mastered the basic ones. Without displaying full knowledge of what was at stake now, for instance, I would not have been here in this pavilion.

"Are we still monsters?"

My heart missed a beat, which I knew he would sense.

Even at the moment he'd saved my life, I'd thought of the Athanate as monsters. Waking up as one had spun me around. Even evil people do not regard themselves as monsters, and I'd learned enough in the last eight weeks to put my misconceptions to one side.

Yes, I needed human Blood to live, but I was no soulless demon.

"No."

He let my answer hang in the humid air. I felt a prickle of sweat and a tightening of apprehension.

Bình tâm.

Breathe it out.

"Then it seems the phoenix does hold a message for you. You say you would have died as Ophélie, that you needed this symbolic death and rebirth. When Qingzhao speaks of you, she calls you Bian. Yet you were once Ophélie Beauclerc, in body and soul. Tell me, are you content now?"

My heart stuttered.

"I am very pleased—to be alive, to have better health and senses and strength."

"And yet?"

I took my time, struggling to control my heart and breathing.

"I am not content," I said, and bowed my head low.

"Explain."

There was no point lying to my Master; he would know. If I were to die because of this, I was already as good as dead.

"I miss knowing what is happening outside." My eyes looked past the phoenix screen, to where there was a wall around the garden, and two walls more beyond it. On the far side of those walls were Cholon, Saigon and Khánh Hôi, Indochina and France, my birth family and my adoptive family, the whole of the rest of the world.

Part of the process of becoming an Athanate in House Song was to be emotionally isolated from that. The needs and rules of the Athanate had to be more powerful than any former ties.

I am reborn. I am no longer Ophélie.

Once Athanate, I couldn't go back to my old life. Even if I could hide the need for Blood from friends and family, how would I explain when I stopped aging?

The Athanate rules meant that Ophélie must appear to have died to the outside world. It was the harsh requirement of the most fundamental rule of the Athanate—to hide our existence from humanity.

I had to get used to that gradually, starting by not hearing any news from outside. Nothing in the last eight weeks. Any question I asked about Athanate rules, the way the House ran, or the changes to my body were answered. Nothing else.

Eight weeks hadn't made it easier. A thousand questions bubbled in my mind, yet asking any of them would give the impression that I hadn't absorbed the lesson: I was Athanate and my House was my world. I should be dead to the outside.

Song waited patiently.

Believe in yourself, Qingzhao had said. Well, this was me, and even if my life depended on it, I could not lie to my Master.

My heart rate picked up again. My mouth felt dry. A bead of sweat ran down inside my shirt.

"I do not feel content," I said. "To me, to be content would be to have no purpose left. To have achieved all I had to do. I do not feel that. I do not feel separated from the outside world. And I'm confused. If the desire that brought me back from the spirit lake, the desire to save Nhung, should now mean nothing to me, why bring me back at all? When you saved my life, you said I would become strong enough to rescue Nhung, but why would I rescue her if I didn't want to? And even if I somehow do it without caring, how am I supposed to rescue her without revealing I'm still alive?"

Perhaps I'd failed my test already. I breathed out slowly, trying to visualize my whole body relaxing. He hadn't killed me yet. I hoped that meant I hadn't failed, but I could feel the dragon coil behind me.

"In answer to your last question," he said eventually, "when you rescue your sister, you will be in the same position as any Athanate letting any human know about the Athanate world. You have two choices: cloud her memory of you rescuing her, or bring her into House Song, as human or Athanate."

I didn't know how to cloud memories yet, though I'd heard it described.

Another skill to learn. Another delay.

Or bring her into the Athanate world. What if she didn't want that?

He didn't let me complete that chain of thought.

"As swiftly as you have absorbed knowledge," he said, "you have not understood our doctrine of detachment."

I kept my eyes lowered.

Have I failed?

But he moved on. "It's time you heard some news of the outside world. For example, your friend Emmanuela has returned from her expedition along the Mekong. Unfortunately, she found that her father died in the jungles of Laos. A disease."

"I'm very sorry for her," I said. I was. There were many men who would be eager to comfort her, but I knew that wouldn't be what she wanted. She would want to talk. I could imagine it very clearly for some reason. A quiet room somewhere. Evening falling. No lamps lit. Her face in shadows. A rambling conversation of little scenes from her father's life, needing only a friend to listen. Such would be her grieving, and I could do nothing to help.

As before, Song gave me no time to think more about it.

"Lieutenant Governor Hubert's attempts to stamp his authority on the colony are failing badly. Even La Poste has printed negative comments about the way he's disrupted the local community."

That made me angry. The *arrogance* of the Quai d'Orsay in sending the man, and *his* arrogance in casting aside the very advisors he needed.

But there was nothing I could do. Not even the whole of House Song could force the French to change their course. In this, we had to be very Buddhist, and bend like the grass before the wind.

Song was waiting for me to comment. He would not let me sit there without speaking.

How would Papa have replied?

"It was a strange decision to appoint a career diplomat from Paris with no experience of the Far East to run the busiest colony in a new administrative region, and so far from any assistance," I said.

It was a good answer, but just thinking of Papa and the way he would speak made my eyes prickle.

It made it worse to know that Song was sensing what I felt and probing, probing. Testing me with words in exactly the way Qingzhao tested me with the chang gùn. Looking for weaknesses to attack.

"In fact, the Quai d'Orsay and Ministère de la Marine have become concerned enough to take action," Song said.

Something in the way he spoke alerted me.

Bình tâm. Bình tâm.

The early morning rain had stopped; the air I breathed in was moist and heavy, promising stifling humidity as the sun climbed. It would be uncomfortable at lunch, unbearable by mid-afternoon.

The actions of the Quai d'Orsay were so very far away and must remain meaningless to me.

"Monsieur Beauclerc was met in Marseille as the *Victorieuse* docked, and sent straight back on the next available naval ship."

My heart stopped. I felt as if I'd been punched again. I could not breathe.

One month. Maybe two. Papa and Maman would be here, stepping down onto the stones of the Quai de la Marine.

What had they heard? Would they expect me to be meeting them? Had they sent telegrams? Were they waiting for a reply?

My mouth worked soundlessly.

Ophélie is dead.

I could not meet them. I could not risk them even seeing me.

For the first time, I really felt the gulf that had opened between me and the world I'd known.

I bowed my head to hide the tears. *Stupid.* He knew I was crying.

"To take over as lieutenant governor?" I said. My voice wobbled and cracked in hope that there would be a little salve for his grief.

"No. To advise. And the greater part of his projects remain unapproved."

"He will be distressed," I managed to whisper.

The misery of it felt like a huge, cold stone in my chest. Papa and Maman waiting for a message from me that would never come, without even the distraction of his great plans for Indochina to ameliorate their grief. I could see them, exactly as I'd seen Emmanuela, sitting silently in the salon at Boulevard Bonnard, with evening creeping in at the windows and the lamps unlit.

"Naturally, there was no possibility that the politicians would ever concede that this situation is their fault. Officially, he has been sent back because claims have been made about the behavior of Yves Fontaudin, the man he left as executor of his estates here, and the rumors surrounding the sudden disappearance of his adopted daughter."

They knew. They would travel the whole six-week journey back with nothing but their fears, and arrive to find the worst of them true.

There was no hiding the tears now. The carefully constructed walls of isolation inside me broke.

And with that, it was time.

The true test began.

Chapter 51

"Shimin. Welcome."

He came in and bowed, first to Yi Song, then to me. I returned it automatically, and he came to sit beside me.

Of course it would be Shimin, the young man who'd provided my first human Blood.

I was trembling.

My eyes were drawn to his wrist, where there were small, nearly-healed scars. Some of those scars were from me. My jaw started to ache at the memory of it—that exquisite, soaring sensation of my fangs drawing Blood from his arteries.

Three days since I'd had Blood. It felt like a lifetime.

Master Song would know exactly what I was feeling and remembering.

Breathe. In and out. I am not a slave to my needs. I am not a rogue.

Even a rogue might control themselves in ideal circumstances, knowing the alternative was death. That's why Song was telling me about what was going on in Saigon. He was stirring up my emotions, watching to see if I could keep control even when I was angry or upset, and even if I'd fasted from Blood for three days.

If I were a good Athanate, I would feel isolated from these events in Saigon. Their effect on the House was minimal. The House should be everything to me.

"Monsieur Riossi appears extremely upset," Song said. "He has said he believes the Fontaudins have something to do with your disappearance. However, the inspectors of the Opium Regie are no longer searching for your sister."

I kept my eyes closed, and dipped my head to show I heard.

"Are you not angry with Riossi?" My lǎoshī would not let me get away with not answering. "You're strong now. You could visit the secret apartment he keeps in the town and kill him for the power he had over you when you were defenseless, and for his refusal to continue searching for your sister."

It was a shock to hear him speak like that.

Kill Riossi? Really?

I realized I could. Qingzhao's training had given me the knowledge to take advantage of being far quicker and stronger than Riossi would expect. I could kill him.

"This is not just talk," he prompted me. "I would not stop you from doing that. No one else would know. No suspicion would fall on us."

What did I feel? To my surprise, I didn't feel anger or hate toward Riossi. My tutor seemed angrier at him that I felt.

"No," I said slowly, grateful to have something that didn't affect me so deeply. "He's not a pleasant man. He would have … exploited me. He used his power to force me into a position where I had no choice but to be his whore. He's awful to his wife, and his daughter. But he didn't lie to me."

"That is so important? You don't hate him, even though he stopped the search for your sister?"

"No. I don't understand why, but no. I don't like him, but I don't hate him, and I couldn't kill him."

I felt a spark of confidence.

But then Song nodded, and Shimin stirred beside me.

I didn't dare look at him. I kept my eyes fixed on the phoenix that covered the opposite wall, but I couldn't see it clearly. There was no mosaic, no fabulous bird. All I saw was the color of Blood.

Shimin turned himself around and lay down across my lap, cradling himself in my arms.

Taking Blood from his wrist had allowed me a little sense of distance. That was no longer an option. I would need to take his Blood from his neck.

I kept very still. If I didn't look down I wouldn't see the way his neck was stretched so that the pulse in his throat was visible. I couldn't stop myself hearing it, loud as a drum. The memory of the taste of his Blood filled my mouth. The subtle scent that katikia have. The scent that says *I'm here. Take my Blood.*

"The Fontaudins responded to Riossi's claims by saying that you were in league with Jade and the other servants." Song continued to talk casually. Cruelly. "They say you stole from them. You attacked Monsieur Fontaudin and disappeared with his money and his wife's most valuable jewelry."

Fury fought with the blinding desire for Blood.

My breath stopped, my face twisted with hate, my heart thrashed. I wanted to crush their necks until …

Shimin gasped.

I forced my hand to release his arm. He'd have a ring of bruises around his bicep. I made my lungs start again. They felt somehow shallow.

My Master stood and spoke quietly: "Now, Bian."

I bowed my head obediently as he walked out into the courtyard. He was my Master.

Shimin moved again, settled. I could smell his fear and hear his heart racing. But he still lay there, with his neck exposed, knowing that I was not being guided by another Athanate.

That I might lose control and kill him.

The worst thing was that I found his fear exciting.

Emotion during feeding was all one thing for an Athanate. Fear worked as well as love and desire. Any strong emotion would do.

But the dragon bit its own tail; the Athanate *needed* that emotion, *fed* on it, *depended* on it … could lose themselves in it.

That was where rogues came from.

My heart was pumping; there was anger still boiling through my veins. Shimin's face blurred into the memory of Fontaudin's drunken lust, and my fangs almost exploded from my jaw, desperate to draw his Blood.

Fear!

Mine. His Blood is mine. He is mine.

Licking his neck. Feeling his pulse against my tongue. Inhaling the scent of fear. The aching need as my jaws stretch and I feel the heat of his skin against my fangs, the teasing resistance of his flesh.

His hand reached up and touched my hair gently.

"I believe in you, gōngzhǔ," he whispered, his heart thrashing in his chest.

Princess.

Slow. Slow. Slow.

The flesh parted. My fangs sank in and found his Blood.

Think.

Don't lose yourself in the sensation, Qingzhao had told me. *Think of what you're doing.*

Athanate do not drink Blood. The fangs are hollow. There are sensitive channels that form in the roof of the mouth to carry the Blood …

I groaned as I *pulled* and Blood flowed through my fangs and it burned with pleasure, burned every other thought or sensation out of my head.

Pull.

Shimin's fear was washed away in the storm of pleasure that crashed over both of us.

There was nothing else. Nothing but desire and pleasure.

Pull.

Three? It was important. Or four? Had I lost count?

Stop.

Something. Something far away. Something very important.

If only I could think more clearly.

Stop.

Shimin's hand was behind my head, pulling me down, urging me on. He wanted me to take more. It was alright if he wanted it, wasn't it? I was only doing what he wanted …

No. A test.

Stop.

With another groan, I lifted my head and my fangs slipped from Shimin's throat. Aching. Wanting. Needing.

No.

Qingzhao. Something more. What had she told me?

The katikia provide for our needs. We put their safety and pleasure ahead of our own desires. Their bodies are our treasures and their desires are sacred to us. We heal …

Oh, yes. Heal. I licked his neck, helping the wounds to seal and heal.

I'd scarred his neck badly. I had not been neat, or gentle. And I was a mess; I needed to blow my nose and my tears were leaking onto Shimin's face.

I had felt the stirring of the monster as I took his Blood. The unthinking need to *pull* and *pull*, and never be sated. I had stopped myself this time, but I only needed to fail once and I would fall into being rogue.

But his neck would heal and I had not tried to drain him today. A strange, muted elation replaced everything else in my head.

I am alive. The dragon will not consume me. I will rise like the phoenix.

Chapter 52

I staggered down the steps into the garden to find my Master, leaving Shimin to recover, sprawled asleep on the cushions.

Qingzhao and four other Athanate members of the House were waiting there, sitting on the ground beneath a shady Hoa Sua tree. They had gathered around a flat stone sculpture of the taijitu, the yin-yang symbol, with black and white spirals locked together within a circle.

They bowed to me. I returned the gesture.

Qingzhao smiled at me and I tried to respond, but it was an uncertain thing, my smile. The monster seemed to stir in the depths of my mind.

"Pluck a flower, please," my tutor said to me.

I reached into the limpid pond that divided the garden and took a lotus blossom, pale and uncanny in its perfect symmetry. I laid it in front of him and he gestured for me to join them around the taijitu.

"The sacred flower," he said. "Is it not beautiful? And is that scent not a gift of the gods themselves?"

He reached forward and laid the flower on the black and white sculpture we sat around.

"And yet, its scent and its beauty will pass, like all things in this world, even the Athanate. All human life is conceived in pleasure and born in suffering. Then Athanate pass through a rebirth when we are infused. We wake into chaos, into the dark side of the taijitu, into our time of crusis. We are *un*knowing and *un*known and *un*able, yet all the potential of the remainder of our Athanate lives is there, all the good we may do, merely waiting to emerge. Our crusis is a test of both suffering and pleasure. And yet we should keep in mind that suffering will pass.

Pleasure will pass. We must endure, and to do that, we must move to the center of the circle."

He waved a hand over the taijitu.

"The dark side is chaos: the unknown, rich with potential. That is where our raw power comes from. The light side is order: our culture, our sacred rituals. That is where all the raw power is channeled to useful work. For a person to be whole, in the timescales of the Athanate, there cannot be one without the other; in the heart of chaos, there must be the seed of order, just as in the heart of order, there must be the seed of chaos.

"Others see the world differently. The Athanate people are split by creeds.

"The Basilikos Athanate hold close to the chaos, and the power may engulf them. They transmute their own suffering into the suffering of their human Blood slaves, and take pleasure from it. That is not our way.

"The Panethus Athanate hold close to the order, and the power may leak away. They share their pleasure with their human partners, and accept the suffering that such partnership must bring at its close. That is not our way.

"Here, in quiet Cholon, in House Song, we seek to hold the center, in balance. We hold that chaos and order are only what we perceive, and that perception of them can only be true from the center."

He was silent for a minute, and then spoke directly to me.

"You have not yet understood our principle of detachment from the human world, as we practice it in this House. It is not a matter of isolation. In fact, it is almost the opposite. To isolate would be to lose all connection to the heart of chaos, to pick the one side of the taijitu. Secure in the order and ritual of the light side, you would look up one day and find that a hundred years had gone. Everyone you knew would be fading memories, and in your isolation, you would be forever the outsider, the pale, lamenting ghost that passes along the road.

"That is not our way. As soon as you are able, you must find and rescue your sister. It will be your decision to bring her here into the Athanate world, or blur her mind and leave her in the human one. An important exercise of your power, your responsibility, with all its attendant risks and limitations. This task will train your mind to be at the center, between chaos and order."

"And my adoptive parents?" I asked. I could not raise my eyes to look at him, and his answering words confirmed my fears.

"Too prominent, too visible, too dangerous." He sighed. "If one thousand things go in our favor, perhaps I will start again the plan I had to bring Monsieur and Madame Beauclerc into our secret."

Qingzhao spoke before I could ask any more.

"And the Fontaudins?" she said.

All the faces around the circle were blank, but my Athanate senses reached beyond and told me of great anger shared.

"Another exercise for Bian," my tutor said. "She must consider and decide what to do. As long as it does not damage us, the House will abide by that decision and I will aid in any way."

A gong sounded.

Yi Song bowed to us, and we bowed our heads to the ground.

When I came back up, he had gone.

The others left Qingzhao and me alone.

"Well done," she said, and held up a hand before I could respond. "I know you feel you haven't really passed. That you felt right on the edge, and at any moment the pleasure would defeat your control and make you rogue."

I felt my heart skip again, just as it had when my Master had tested me. Was the test still going on?

"We all feel like that," Qingzhao said, seeming to read my mind. "And every new day is a test. It's just part of being Athanate."

She had said before that while being Athanate was an incredible privilege, it also brought many burdens.

"What did he mean about a thousand things to go in our favor?" I asked.

"Yes, we owe you the truth now," she said slowly. She picked up the lotus blossom and inhaled its scent. "It's complex. What we had here in Annam was peace and the quiet pursuit of our own plans. We had this for so long, I think we forgot the rest of the Athanate world. Unfortunately, it has not forgotten us."

She took leaves from the tree that shaded us and began to arrange them on the ground.

"Here are Cochinchina, Annam, and Tonkin, stretching like a lazy dragon down the Indochina coast. Above, to the north, is the vastness of

China. Inland, to the west, are Laos and Cambodia. Beyond them, Siam and Burma here, all the way north to India and south, down the peninsula, to Malaya, here. On our little map, France rules the east, Britain rules the west, China the north. France and Britain contend over access to Siam and China."

She had made a map I was familiar with, naturally, from many discussions with Papa.

"So much for the human political geography," she said. "The Athanate map is different."

Her mouth set, she tore the lotus petals.

"Down from the Yunnan province of China to Laos and Cambodia—this is Basilikos territory."

Basilikos. I shivered. She'd used the tip of the petal like a dagger, pointing at us in Saigon.

"Zheng?" I asked. "He's Basilikos?"

"House Zheng is Basilikos," she said. "Zheng is from Kandal in Cambodia. He represents Basilikos and they want Saigon and all Cochinchina."

Kandal was not far from Saigon on her map. Zheng was the point of a spear.

"We are holding them back?" I asked. House Song was not a big House.

"In a manner of speaking. But Basilikos are not alone." She placed more torn pieces of lotus petal on her leaf map. "Here: Burma, Malaya and Siam—this is the territory of the British Athanate."

Whereas Basilikos were every bit the monsters I'd feared, the British Athanate were different. Their way sounded more like House Song—our cultures both honored and cherished the humans who provided for us. But the British Athanate spread mainly through the human British Empire, and I could not quite separate the two in my mind. Papa had always been adamant: the British were never to be trusted.

"And they want Saigon as well?"

"They do," she said. "What holds both Basilikos and the British Athanate back is the strongest of them all."

She placed a whole petal, untorn, above us on the map.

"The Empire of Heaven," I said, and she nodded.

I knew, as the name suggested, the Athanate Empire of Heaven originated within China. I also knew that House Song had been attacked by them before.

"The Empire holds Tonkin and Annam," Qingzhao went on. "They could defeat us whenever they wanted. However, we had a deal with them to stay independent and to act together to keep the British Athanate and Basilikos away."

"Had a deal? *Had?*"

She sighed. "The Empire of Heaven was interested in House Song's plan to form an association with the Governor of Cochinchina. Your father."

She raised her hand again to prevent me speaking. "Not that it was the only reason Song tutored you or that we befriended you. Rather, the other way around."

"So, the plan has failed? Papa is not governor. Our protection has gone?"

"The plan has been put back, and as our Master said, we must be lucky one thousand times to restart it. As for protection: so far, the Empire of Heaven has not spoken one way or the other." She was silent for a minute before finishing. "We'll work hard to be lucky."

I tried to get it all in order in my head, but there was so much. I would need time and many more answers to understand everything.

In the meantime, I had to assume responsibilities, as unprepared as I was.

"What can I do?" I asked.

Qingzhao smiled. "I told him you would say that." The smile disappeared. "I'm forced to accept your offer to help, even though you don't have the skills yet. We have many tasks and few hands, Bian. Nothing is safe."

One of the maids came in, carrying a black chang gùn. She handed it to Qingzhao with a bow and a smile to me, then took my chang gùn from where I'd left it at the steps to the pavilion and departed.

"Your practice staff will be kept with the others," Qingzhao said. "But it's time you had a real weapon."

It looked more like the chang gùn she'd carried when she saved my life in the alley. The surface was carved wood. It looked old.

She gripped the middle and twisted.

"This one has only one blade," she said. "Twist to release it. Then ..."

She made a strike to one side, the staff whipping through the air. When it stopped, there was a blade at the end.

"And then, twist again to lock."

She demonstrated, and prodded the trunk of the tree with the blade, before reversing the process and handing it to me.

"You'll need it," she said. "From tonight, you're part of the guard we set. We have invited all parties to a meeting under a Blood oath of truce, but I'm expecting an assassin, or even a dozen of them, before they even answer the invitation."

Chapter 53

It took them until the fourth night, and it was many assassins, all at once.

In the restless shallows of the fourth night, halfway between midnight and dawn, in the starless dark they come, quiet as moonshadow gliding across the rooftops, soft as a dream of velvet.

I had been hovering on the borders of sleep, thinking about who might attack us. Even the most desperate of local criminals would not be persuaded by any payment to attack Yi Song. They would have to come from far away. The costs would be unimaginable. Some of the others whispered about evil monasteries, hidden in the Hengduan Mountains of Yunnan, or the wilds of Manchuria, where boys were trained to be fanatical tools: fearless, unquestioning and skillful assassins.

How would it feel to be such a person? In the ragged tail of my half-dream, it was me looking down into the courtyard, steeling myself to attack, unconcerned that it might end in my death.

All sleep and dreams slipped away like a silk sheet. They were here.

I almost persuaded myself I could smell them. Quiet as they were, I could hear them. Even in their black clothing, I could see them. Had they been warned that we'd hear and see them? That'd we'd be alert and armed? Were they expecting to kill us in our beds?

To the men on the roof, this courtyard was unguarded, and only the sharpest eyes could tell I was not another statue.

Yi Song's house was sprawling, and the number of people to be protected was large. Qingzhao had gambled on which way the assassins would attack, leaving me alone here, and it seemed she'd gambled wrongly.

I might die, but the only way to be sure of dying was to let them kill me. And if I held them up for even a few minutes, that might mean the difference between life and death for the rest of the House.

Without moving, I gripped my chang gùn more tightly. The blade was already out and locked.

I imagined Qingzhao at my side, watching me as I struck them.

I would make her proud.

Moving as slowly as cold molasses, the first one lowered himself off the roof and dropped to the ground, alone. He crouched and went very still.

I imagined I could taste his excitement, leaking from the tightly wound silk that covered his body, but I was no centuries-old Athanate to have such developed senses.

They all waited, unmoving, to see if there was a reaction.

Qingzhao had been clear—*they'll come across the roof*, she'd said. *Get them down in the courtyard, hold them up and we'll finish them.*

But what if this was just one group of many? What of there was another at the other end of the house? We were spread out, with a group inside intending to rush to wherever the assassins tried to enter. But if they attacked from two sides, the group inside must split in two and only half come to my rescue. If they attacked from all sides, there would be no rescue.

The man on the ground rose to stand.

My chang gùn trembled and stilled.

He froze. Unless he was Athanate, surely he couldn't possibly see me or hear me, but he'd sensed something.

Qingzhao had said they wouldn't use Athanate. Not unless the Empire of Heaven had turned away from us.

Had we been betrayed?

But he wasn't Athanate and he couldn't see me—he moved again. A gesture to the others on the roof. One by one, they dropped like seeds from a tree of shadows.

Too many!

Near my foot was a taut wire. As the last assassin landed on the ground, I nudged the wire. A gong sounded from the other end of the courtyard. Once, to signal an attack. Twice, to signal more than one attacker. Three times, the last time for luck because there wasn't any signal for *help, too many.*

Some of them turned to face the direction the sound came from, but not all of them. That had been too much to hope for. It looked as if they had been trained to kill as a team, and to not be diverted by tricks.

In any event, there were too many for me to attack. I swallowed and moved as silently as I could into position between the two statues that guarded the door.

My slim advantages were that firstly, I'd practiced defending this position, and secondly, they could only come at me in ones and twos.

Alerted by my movement, heads swiveled around to look at where I was. There was a hissed instruction. One ran to check the room where the gong had sounded. The other four sprinted at me.

I struck the first one with the butt of the staff in his face. I couldn't stab him; the speed he was coming, my blade might have got stuck. I couldn't risk that. He blocked those behind him, which allowed me to spin the staff around and slash at the second, even as he collided with his colleague.

He staggered back, blood spurting, but didn't cry out.

The third gestured with one hand. There was a flicker of movement, and I felt the thump of something hitting my chest. I was wearing leather armor, but it cut through. I felt a sting, and a coldness blossomed out from that point.

Poison.

He raised his dao slowly above his head, waiting for the poison to take effect before he came to deliver the killing blow with its sharp edge.

I needed him to come at me now, before I weakened too much.

I staggered, lowering the staff slightly.

He leaped forward eagerly and I slashed upwards. He wore no protection of any kind. My blade opened up his belly as far as his ribs. His sword fell onto the floor.

But he didn't hesitate, or pull back. Covered in black silk, all I could see of his face was his eyes. Even in the darkness, they seemed to gleam. The poison inside slowed me down and weakened me, so my clumsiness allowed him to grasp the staff with his hands and deliberately pull it toward him, trapping the blade deeper and deeper in his body. His eyes were wide and triumphant. Finally, his bloodied hands reached out for me, and he hissed to his comrades, even as his widened eyes lost their focus.

It was over. I had my kris knife in the sheath behind me, but if I let go of the dead assassin to reach for it, they would swarm me, and so without a weapon, all I could do was hold the dead body in front of me. It might slow them down for another few seconds. Not many seconds at that—it was much more difficult to poison an Athanate than the assassin had realized, but whatever he'd used was making my muscles slacken and my head swim.

Something white floated down out of the sky and landed behind the assassins. My eyes had trouble focusing.

A flower? A huge flower, with streamers billowing?

I had a moment's respite as the surviving assassins turned to face the newcomer. The heaving quiet was rent by a sound like a serpent's hiss.

Her clothing had settled into place and the one nearest her had died before I recognized it was Qingzhao, dressed in her white áo dài.

The assassins left me alone to attack her.

Mistake.

Even if she was the greater threat by far, one of them should have kept attacking me. I dropped the dead man I'd been using as a shield and, staggering, picked up his dao. I thrust it into the nearest unprotected back.

The man gasped and tried to twist away, but the blade was too deep in his body. He struck weakly at me as he died.

By the time I looked up from that, there was only one left alive.

"Do you want to die tonight?" Qingzhao said. "We will spare you in return for information."

He said nothing and chose to die. He charged and her chang gùn's blade severed his neck in a blur.

One of the other Athanate, Li, was at my side to catch me as my legs buckled. She was followed by Wing, who picked up the metal disk that had cut my chest.

"The chakram's edges are poisoned," Wing said, and sniffed it. "Krait venom. I'll fetch the Master."

My lips were trembling; numbness crept over my face. The Athanate Blood that infused me fought against the poison, but there was something more needed to counter it.

I blinked and Yi Song was there, once again cradling me in his arms. My heart was racing in panic.

"I'm sorry, Lǎoshī," I managed to stutter. "I don't know what to do."

"I do," he replied. His fangs found my neck and I felt a great calmness spreading through my body, slowing everything down.

Li was peering anxiously over Song's shoulder.

I heard Qingzhao reassure her. "He is a Master of poisons, among many other things. She'll be fine. A day or two's rest."

As it happened, I didn't get even one day's rest.

Chapter 54

House Jian was the representative of the Empire of Heaven. She turned out to be a petite and beautiful woman, and she arrived in the mid-morning. By noon, the others had followed: House Zheng of the Basilikos creed, from Kandal in Cambodia; House Thorn of the British Athanate, living in Ayutthaya, the old capital of Siam.

I distrusted all three of them, not least because they had arrived so suddenly after the attack.

I had also been warned that there was one more to come. As is the way of these things, it was the one with the shortest distance to travel who would arrive last.

Yi Song welcomed the visiting Athanate to the airy Bloodstone pavilion.

The visitors came up the steps from the courtyard in a row of three, none of them demanding precedence. Behind them came the Diakons who had accompanied them.

Yi Song bowed, and they bowed back.

I could not have imagined a greater contrast between the guests.

House Jian looked like a painted doll standing in front of her Diakon. He was shaven-headed, big as a bear, deliberate in his movement, and his features marked him as a man of the Mongolian steppes. His eyes were narrowed and wary, but calm. They seemed to be focused on something a great distance away.

House Zheng's Diakon reminded me of the sketches I had seen of the Khmer statues that had been found in the ruins of abandoned cities, smothered by the liana vines of the Cambodian jungles. There was that exact blankness to his expression, that other-worldliness he shared with those statues, and a hint of cruelty he shared with his Master.

House Thorn's Diakon was a woman of Siam. He was tall and robust. She was sinewy, wore her long black hair tightly braided, kept her eyes hooded, and she walked as if every step was part of a dance to a music only she could hear.

As they all rose from their bows of greeting, Qingzhao gestured and the Athanate members of House Song filed into the pavilion from the other entrance. Everyone, including me.

We will show them we are not diminished, Song had said.

Most of us had been injured in the attack. There were missing fingers and broken bones, stitched cuts and bandages, bruises and strains. Others had been poisoned and no doubt felt like I did: sick and trembling. We would heal. Athanate fingers would regrow, scars would disappear, bones would set and the bruises were already fading.

There were no limps, no visible signs of pain.

We will not give them the satisfaction of knowing they have caused us pain, Qingzhao had instructed us. *We will not cower. We will offer no point of weakness.*

So we hid our pain and trembling, made our bows and sank to our knees behind Song. We did not look down. We did not look away.

A welcoming tea was being served even as we knelt, and there was polite conversation in the most formal of court Mandarin. House Jian and House Thorn declared they were delighted by the dragon and phoenix mosaics. They'd insisted on the opportunity of inspecting them. House Zheng remained seated on the floor, sullen and silent.

Completing her appreciation of the mosaics, House Jian turned to Song and frowned slightly. "Forgive me, House Song, I cannot escape noticing how many members of your House appear to have suffered recent injuries, however nobly borne."

There was absolute silence for a long moment.

"I am most pleased to see there were no fatalities," she continued. "But this must have been a considerable aggression. I had assumed no one would be so foolish as to attack you while we have an agreement of mutual interests and defense."

Yi Song smiled. A formal, polite smile.

"I agree. Very foolish," he replied. "It was a minor matter, in truth. A group of monks from a monastery you may have heard of: the Báisè De Shān in the Hengduan Mountains of Yunnan."

"The Shadow Warriors of the White Mountain!" House Thorn raised his eyebrows. "That is hardly some 'minor' matter."

They looked at Zheng. Everyone knew that the monastery was in Basilikos territory. His face remained immobile and he offered no comment.

It was as House Thorn had said. The Shadow Warriors were costly. A group of them, as large as had attacked us, would have cost a fortune. Unless, as Qingzhao had suggested earlier, their price had been part of some larger deal with Basilikos.

I'd been completely wrong in my assessment that Qingzhao had been mistaken about the direction of the attack. The monks who'd jumped into my courtyard had been the smaller group. More had tried to attack the other side of the buildings.

Where, unluckily for them, Song had been waiting.

The conversation ceased as Wing and Li escorted in the last person to arrive at the meeting.

With my senses enhanced by my Athanate Blood, I had smelled him as soon as the tiger demon entered the courtyard.

I turned my head.

He walked silently, his bare feet padding softly. He came alone. He carried his arrogance in the set of his shoulders, the hard and challenging stare, the refusal to return bows of greeting.

For the first time, I saw the tall man, lord of the gangs in Khánh Hôi, fierce as a tiger, cruel as death. Bác Thảo entered the Bloodstone Pavilion and I shivered.

Even within the safety of House Song, he scared me. I wanted to shrink, to hide behind the others.

"I don't drink tea," Bác Thảo said abruptly in Annamese when it was offered.

He stared at Yi Song and Qingzhao, but his threating look flowed off them like water spilt on a rock.

"I believe we all speak Annamese?" Jian asked, looking at Zheng.

He nodded.

"Of course," Thorn said. "And now we're all here ..."

Bác Thảo had shifted his glare to Wing and Li, now kneeling beside the rest of us. They stared back. His eyes moved on to the next. And the next.

No.

A weakness flooded my limbs. My mouth went dry.

Has the poison returned?

I felt the pulse in my throat racing and I knew it was not poison. To my shame, it was fear. I was terrified of the tiger demon.

I could barely hear Song speaking.

My world contracted and I lowered my gaze, knowing I could not meet Bác Thảo's eyes. I would shame my House by fainting, or running away.

Please. I need time to recover.

But there was no time. No one to heed my pleas.

I could sense his eyes moving, staring at the members of House Song one after another, becoming more and more angry that he could not force any one of them to look away.

Soon it would be my turn.

Qingzhao was kneeling in front of me, but she could not move to shield me. I could see her back, the graceful curve of her neck, the strength in her.

If I ran away, what could I say to her? How could I explain my cowardice?

I'd always feared tigers. I didn't know why. Stories from Minh's father when I'd lived in Ap Long? My birth mother's bedtime stories of hô con quỷ, who sit and watch you from the darkness? That awful tiger skin with its glassy eyes in the salon? My own foolishness in thinking that by naming them, that first night I'd been adopted, I'd called them to Saigon?

No!

I will put this aside. I am no longer a child.

I was a part of this House. I could not let them down, no matter how weak I was.

We will not cower. We will offer no point of weakness.

Beneath my own racing pulse, I felt a slower beat. I felt the supporting pulse of House Song, all around me. They understood. The believed in me.

I knew the moment when his eyes found me. I could feel the weight of his regard.

I will offer no point of weakness.

I raised my eyes and met his.

Fury. Unthinking, elemental anger. Waves of it, pounding down on me. Like standing against a crowd of panicked people. Like looking into the sun.

I quivered inside, but I did not flinch. I would not flinch.

"You have an interest in the child whore?" Zheng's voice sounded odd, as if he spoke from far away.

Chapter 55

"Do you?" Bác Thảo said. "It looks as if Song does."

And he laughed.

"A child in the bed warms your cold Athanate heart, does it?" he said to Master Song. "She bleeds one way or another."

Zheng joined him in laughter, slapping his knee.

I could feel the shock and anger from the rest of my House, and I finally understood what Qingzhao had been warning me about before this meeting; that it was no more than a continuation of the attack last night. She'd warned me of so many things my head had started to spin, but importantly, as the newest member of House Song, I might be the weakness they sought to exploit.

They were, and it was a well-chosen strategy.

Luckily, my own body betrayed me. If I could have risen, I would have, but I was too weak with anger. The effects of the changes in my Blood swamped me. I was so angry my muscles wouldn't work.

I wanted to kill them both, even though I had no weapon and they were powerful men. They'd kill me easily, but it was worse than that. They were here under Song's Blood oath that no harm would come to them here. Athanate did not break Blood oaths lightly. A Blood oath sank itself into your very being.

And if you ever have the strength to break an oath in desperation, Qingzhao had said, *be very sure you leave no witnesses. To break a Blood oath is to be declared rogue, with every Athanate obligated to kill you.*

My Master's Blood oath was my Blood oath.

Even with my chang gùn in my hands, I could not harm them. To do so would have been as much a betrayal as striking at my own Master. If I broke the oath he'd given, they would declare him a rogue. House Song would not survive.

Hidden from sight by Qingzhao kneeling in front of us, Li's hand came across the space between us and squeezed mine briefly.

Be strong. I believe in you.

I took a raw, painful breath, desperately seeking calmness against the rising fury in my mind.

House Jian and House Thorn, I saw, sat in stony silence. As did the Diakons, even Zheng's.

That helped a little, but Zheng himself wasn't finished.

"Did Beauclerc and Riossi not satisfy you, whore?" he said to me. "Not skilled enough, were they? Or simply not big enough?"

"That's the trouble, eh?" Bác Thảo said. "These whores get looser until only a horse will do."

Zheng found that hilarious. He pounded his hand on his knee and gasped in amusement.

My vision grew dark. I closed my eyes. If I looked at them, I would be overwhelmed with the desire to kill them, and the thought would become the agent of the deed.

Even in the blood-red darkness behind the shutters of my eyelids, I could sense their shadowy forms and I could feel their cruel barbs.

And then, as real as if I could touch her, I felt Maman kneel beside me and the darkness dissolved into the sharp-edged memories of another time, long ago, in my bedroom at Boulevard Bonnard.

I am ten, or eleven. Still struggling to find my place in this different culture.

I remembered it so clearly, the soft rustle of her dress, that scent of fruits and flowers I found so comforting.

I am not crying. I do not allow myself tears, but she knows.

What's happened? she asks.

They were rude again, I reply.

Sévigny? She doesn't really need to ask that.

I nod.

There will come a time, she says, and pauses for a moment, her voice catching. We shield our children, but there will come a time when we cannot. At that time, you will find you have become so very strong, my daughter. When Chantal Sévigny comes to her time of testing, and she will, do you think she will be as strong?

I opened my eyes again to reflected sunlight on the pavilion steps and the quiet ranks of House Song kneeling in the Bloodstone Pavilion.

These were crude insults from Zheng and Bác Thảo, cruder than I had ever heard aimed at me. I was vulnerable: weak from the poison; weak from the effects of the Athanate infusion in my Blood; weak from the emotional storms of crusis.

But I had been trained to endure insults by Chantal Sévigny, and these guffawing oafs with their blunt sexual slurs were nothing next to the stiletto of that viper's tongue.

I forced myself look at them directly and stay still.

I will be the death of both of you, I promised myself silently. *Some day, when I am not bound from harming you, I will kill you.* With a shock I felt my silent words sinking into me, cooling the temper of my Blood. *On my Blood: this is my Blood oath.*

Seeing in my eyes that he'd failed at the first attempt, Zheng tried again with a different approach.

"Why is she here?" he asked my Master.

"All Athanate in my House are here," Song responded. His voice was soft, without emotion, as if they were discussing the cost of rice.

"Athanate. Since when?" Zheng squinted at me. He'd met me on the docks, the day after the Harvest Ball, when he'd come looking for my tutor. He'd have known I wasn't Athanate then.

But he knew I was now. He knew I would still be in crusis. His insults had been intended to exploit that. This new attack was the same, but directly against Song himself.

Song had to realize it as well, but he answered, "Two months ago."

"Times must be hard when all you can find to infuse is a faithless child whore."

"She is none of the things you so ignorantly accuse her of," Song said, still speaking mildly. "She's not a child, she's not a whore and she's certainly not faithless."

And finally one of the others interrupted.

"For all your spies, you seem to be very badly informed about Saigon and House Song," Thorn said to Zheng. "Perhaps you're making assumptions based on the way things happen in the domains of Basilikos?"

There was a hiss of amused breath from Jian's Diakon, the big Mongolian, and a smile from the sinewy Siamese woman behind Thorn.

Nothing showed on the blank Khmer face of Zheng's Diakon.

Zheng spared a glance full of hate for House Thorn, but he concentrated on Song. "You can't deny she's young," he said. "The Agiagraphos is clear—to successfully become Athanate, the mind must be fully developed and settled in its nature."

Zheng had tried to show I was not successfully Athanate by making me respond to his insults. Having failed at that, he was trying to achieve the same end using the Agiagraphos, the book of rules governing Athanate life. The Agiagraphos was part philosophy, part rulebook. It was the sacred book of the Athanate. If Zheng persuaded the others that Song was breaking some rules in it, then the course of action was clear: all neighboring Athanate Houses must put aside any differences in creed or disputes of domain; they must combine to eradicate the errant House in their midst.

This attack I couldn't defend against. I could only watch.

"Strange days are upon us when Basilikos lecture others on the observance of Agiagraphos rules," Song said.

Zheng face reddened.

House Jian waved a languid hand. "Strange days indeed. No matter. She *is* undeniably young, House Song. She is, or was, also a prominent and recognizable member of the Saigon community. Crude insults aside, I'm interested in your reasoning for choosing this young woman as a suitable candidate to enlarge your House, given the original plan of an association with her father failed."

I could see Qingzhao's back stiffen as Jian spoke. She hadn't expected an attack from the Empire of Heaven. House Jian might not indulge in crude insults, but she was supporting the question of whether House Song had broken any of the Agiagraphos rules.

In my hurried talk with her earlier, Qingzhao had been clear who she thought the most potentially dangerous person at this meeting was: House Jian. The problem was, we couldn't be sure which side she was on, ours or theirs. Or neither.

That uncertainty made her next words chilling.

"The Emperor understood the need to advance an association with Monsieur Beauclerc, even though there would be extreme risk for the Athanate at the point where you revealed your true nature to him. The Emperor also understood the ploy of becoming tutor to the man's daughter, against the potential return when he became Governor

Beauclerc," she said. "Now, with all those returns apparently lost, you have still taken her into your House. *This* decision the Emperor does not understand. Does it mean you believe there is still hope for Beauclerc to become governor?"

She was offering a slim way out. Could my Master persuade her that my adoptive father had a chance to recover his position?

But Yi Song did not take the Empire's offered approach.

"The Emperor has misunderstood what you have termed a 'ploy'." Song's words, delivered without expression, might as well have been a slap across House Jian's face. Even her Diakon blinked. Zheng's mouth fell open.

"Please enlighten me, that I can inform him." Never had I heard such a politely worded request with such an undercurrent of threat.

"Gladly." Song sipped his tea. "Monsieur Beauclerc and his adopted daughter were one stratagem which became two. I don't need to explain again the advantage it would have been to have the Governor of Saigon as an ally." He looked at each of them for any disagreement. There was none. "Such an advantage deserved every effort, including tutoring his daughter. But it was quickly apparent to me that Ophélie was of great use by herself."

Bác Thảo snorted and smirked.

Song ignored him.

"Look at this new Athanate before you." He gestured to me. "You see an Annamese woman, dressed in the style of the Athanate of the Empire. One who speaks not only Mandarin and Annamese, but also French. She even speaks Trade and some Cantonese. In a matter of minutes she could change clothing and return here as a Frenchwoman, with all the knowledge of how that society works. She has lived, and can thrive, in every level of society here on the coast of Indochina, a talent that few of the rest of my House can boast. Few indeed, of any House."

He was exaggerating my ability, especially to appear as a Frenchwoman, but I wasn't going to argue.

House Jian paused thoughtfully before speaking.

"Admirable, and undoubtedly useful," she said. "Certainly good reasoning for her as a candidate. Nevertheless, the Emperor would not have approved of taking her into your House until she had faded from public view. Avoidance of the risk of the Athanate being discovered must remain the paramount concern of all of us."

"Ah." Song nodded, conceding the point with a slight downturn of his mouth. "The timing. Yes, that was most unfortunate. And quite unplanned. It was taken out of our hands."

He made a gesture to Wing, who walked across to an enamelled chest, opened it and took out a very large glass jar shrouded in a black silk cloth.

Wing placed it in front of Song and returned to his kneeling position behind him.

"Mam'selle Beauclerc was visiting Cholon when she was attacked by two Athanate intruders, intent on raping and kidnapping her. My Diakon believed, and I fully support her, that the kidnap attempt could only mean there was an intention to use her against me. She was therefore forced to intervene."

"From which House?" Jian's words were like ice.

"House Zheng."

"False allegations!" Zheng protested, almost coming to his feet. "No member of my house—"

Song removed the cloth covering the glass jar. Inside, floating in a murky liquid, were the heads of the two men who'd attacked me outside the brothel.

Chapter 56

"I recognize that fellow. The bigger one." House Thorn leaned forward to look closely. "He was a senior member of the Zheng delegation that came to talk to us when France took Laos from Siam a few years ago."

"I have no knowledge of what they were doing in Cholon," Zheng said. "No orders of mine. I sent them up to Phnom Penh."

Elder Athanate can taste the lies in words. I had no doubt that Jian could. Zheng must have planned for that possibility. Somehow, he must have given one order and arranged for someone else to override it.

House Jian stared at him for a full minute while the sweat stood out on his forehead, but she finally turned back to Song.

"You have not made your case, House Song. There is clearly a matter for further investigation and even reparations by House Zheng. And I understand why your Diakon needed to rescue Mam'selle Beauclerc, but not why that made it necessary to take the girl into your House. Her memories of the event could simply have been clouded."

"Observance of the Agiagraphos made it necessary, House Jian. My Diakon didn't kill both of these men. She killed the man that House Thorn recognizes. The other died from a blow struck by Mam'selle Beauclerc. She used a kris knife. Cut the arteries in his groin so badly, he bled out before he could stop it."

I tried to keep my face blank. I'd passed out after striking him. No one had mentioned what had actually happened that night at all. Perhaps they'd been worried that it might affect my crusis if they'd told me.

Across the room, House Thorn's Diakon smiled brightly at me and bowed her sleek head in acknowledgment. Even the Diakon of House Jian looked at me with his faraway gaze and nodded a fraction.

Song's voice continued dryly, as if he were lecturing me on the trade of the Saigon docks. "Since it was Qingzhao's duty, and Bian killed an Athanate in Qingzhao's defense, House Song became obligated to Bian. I'm sure the Emperor would agree that in accordance with the Agiagraphos, we were duty bound to treat her as part of the House from that point."

"You can't believe this!" Zheng protested. "A human girl killing a mature Athanate?"

Song smiled. "I've been told the goddess has blessed you, House Jian. She Who Hears the Cries of the World has gifted you the skill to sift the truth from falsehood. Hear my Diakon speak and know the truth."

"I am not Quan Yin—" Jian started to reply.

"Why am I here?" Bác Thảo interrupted suddenly. "What are we doing, talking about a child whore who's now part of an Athanate House? What's it to me? If you have Athanate problems, talk about them to each other."

"You're here because our meeting concerns all the paranormal community," Jian replied. "If we could find the Adepts hiding in this area, they'd be here too."

"A community?" he said insolently. "A happy village? Look at you, at each other's throats."

"Whereas the tiger shifters are at peace. At least since you killed every one that didn't bow down to you." House Thorn snorted. "The shapeshifters in Siam have talked of a war against you."

Bác Thảo was sneering a reply when House Jian cut across them both.

"That's the sort of stupidity which will get us all killed. This is not the sixteenth century. Human communities speak to each other. Their ships cross the oceans. Their telegraph wires connect continents and their telephone apparatus spreads through their cities. Humans are not isolated, fearful and ignorant. They control the cities with police. Their scientists study human blood to find tiny organisms that cause diseases. They count the numbers who die and try to discover the causes.

"What you might get away with in the upper reaches of the Mekong, House Zheng, or the Central Highlands, Bác Thảo, does not pass in Saigon.

"In this world, we cannot behave as we used to or even as we still do outside of populous areas. Saigon is full of armed troops. How quickly would they discover us if there was a war between shapeshifters? Or between Houses?"

"It's not my fault Saigon has troops on the streets," Bác Thảo snarled.

"But you're trying to take advantage of the discontent, and you're making it worse," Song said to him. "As for complaining we're talking about my newest Athanate, it was you and Zheng who started talking about her. Whatever your reason, House Zheng sees her as a point of weakness to attack me. Are you part of that attack? Have you made a deal with him against me? And against the Empire of Heaven?"

"No! Your arguments with each other are nothing to me," Bác Thảo said. "I don't care which Athanate are in Saigon, only that I will remain where I am in Khánh Hôi, and I will continue to collect the tribute of the humans."

"*Without* revealing your nature," Jian said, and he grunted a grudging acceptance. He wasn't stupid.

"The British Athanate have no interest in fighting for Saigon," Thorn said easily. "We'll accept the human borders. We'll remain on the Siamese side, or as agreed with House Song."

They all turned to House Zheng.

"Human borders mean nothing to us," he said. "Saigon is huge, especially when you include Khánh Hôi and Cholon. Why should we not share? Song in Cholon. Bác Thảo in Khánh Hôi. House Zheng in Saigon itself."

"I reside in Cholon," Song said, "but all Saigon and the country surrounding it is my Athanate domain. I will defend it."

"Saigon perhaps, but you're not strong enough to claim all of Cochinchina," Jian said. "It would seem you must reach a compromise. Perhaps your territory should reach as far as the Mekong. The remainder of Mỹ Tho province down to the Gulf of Siam might be shared between the British and Basilikos. The Empire of Heaven would agree to a border to the north. We seek settled borders, and secrecy for all paranormals, not more territory."

My Master was caught. Even I knew that House Song was not strong enough to hold all of Cochinchina. He would have to agree to some partition.

On the basis of their actions here, I had to favor the British to the south, whatever Papa had said about them. I hardly trusted Jian, but we couldn't dispute the Empire's control of Annam.

Which left Bác Thảo as our close neighbor in the city, and Basilikos not far enough away for me.

They argued it backwards and forwards.

"It seems we will not agree to a deal in one meeting," Jian said. "We should consider options and return to this discussion in a week."

More tea arrived. Bác Thảo looked like he wanted to leave, but Zheng and Thorn began discussing the land to the south of Saigon. It was clear to me Zheng was interested only in Saigon and the Mekong itself. But if the British Athanate came close to Saigon, and they had alliances with the tiger demons of Siam, then Bác Thảo would be threatened.

Caught up in listening to that conversation, I only became aware of House Jian's interest in me when she spoke.

"I am intrigued, House Song. I propose an exchange—a seal on our association if you like—a guarantee of our mutual interests. One of my House in Hanoi, a young man of that city. He's not so accomplished in languages, but his achievements with several traditional weapons would make him an excellent addition to your House, and it might remove someone who seems a cause for concern."

An exchange?

She was looking at me. My heart felt as if it were being squeezed. *No!*

Song shook his head. "I regret, although I'm happy that other Houses confirm their associations this way, it's not something I would contemplate." He looked thoughtful. "But perhaps you would be interested in the one surviving White Mountain monk instead. He knows nothing of the running of the monastery, but he's skilled in weapons and might be a candidate for your House or one of your sub-Houses."

I let out a quiet breath, and then Zheng's voice interrupted Jian's reply. "What's so valuable about the whore?" He put his hand up before Song could speak. "I know, you say she's not a whore, but she *is* the sister of a whore."

In the sultry afternoon, a chill entered the pavilion. I fixed my eyes on the rising phoenix, even as I felt Bác Thảo's yellow tiger eyes on me, slow and heavy with calculation.

"A whore of a sister she persuaded Riossi and the Opium Regie to try to find," Zheng went on, and he laughed. "We know what Monsieur Riossi's price was. So answer me this, when is a whore not a whore?"

I wasn't concerned about Zheng's insults anymore. But every fragment of knowledge got Bác Thảo closer to the truth, and Nhung was still out there, somewhere, defenseless against him. My Master had promised that I would be strong enough to look for Nhung, but I wasn't there yet. I couldn't win a race against the gang lord of Khánh Hôi to find her.

"You should ask our friend here to look for your sister," Zheng said, pointing at Bác Thảo. "I'm sure he'd agree to the same terms as Riossi. And after all, it's almost certain she's in some whorehouse in Khánh Hôi. Who better to find her?"

"Enough," House Thorn said. "I'm tired of hearing your coarse abuse, Zheng. The young woman has suffered tragedies. I sense she was well-born, and can't even guess what brought her family down so low that she and her sister ended up where they are. I find her efforts to save her sister at any expense noble."

I concentrated on the phoenix. *I will rise*, I chanted to myself. *I will rise.*

"You said 'every level of society in Indochina', House Song." Bác Thảo's voice was deep and sly. "I wonder how low that lowest level was, and how high the highest."

"Oh, the father was a mandarin, certainly," Zheng said. "No idea—"

"I know who you are now, *Bian Hwa Trang*," the lord of the gangs in Khánh Hôi said, his eyes gleaming with triumph. "And I will surely find your sister, now I know where to look."

Chapter 57

Wing and Li caught me and dragged me out of the pavilion before I could reach him. Zhengs's and Bác Thảo's laughter followed us.

My captors sat either side of me in the Autumn Courtyard in shocked silence. I did not struggle; the insanity of crusis rage had left me as quickly as it had come. But I had offered violence to a guest protected by my Master's Blood oath. My life was forfeit; that was the least of it. At worst, I had endangered the whole House.

I felt numb; it was as if I'd been struck in the head again. Jade must have been right, I was bad joss; I brought chaos and disaster with me. What else could it be but joss when even House Thorn's attempt to be kind to me was the very trigger that made Bác Thảo recognize me?

For myself, all that had happened was that I'd cheated death for a few weeks. My Master had saved my life in the house on Bonnard, and now he would take it back. The dark shore of the lake called me.

But Nhung would be left behind, helpless, and Bác Thảo would find her. She knew nothing except our parents had gone to Hué, but that wouldn't save her. He'd think she was refusing to tell him where our parents were, and he'd torture her until she died. Then Bác Thảo's spies would go to Hué. Maybe they'd find out more there. Maybe they'd follow the trail to the farm that Lanh said they now owned.

It was a bitter realization that there was nothing I could do for Nhung.

"Could I send a message?" I asked quietly, trying to keep my voice steady. "I would like a warning to go to Lanh, if he can be found. I will beg him to protect our parents. Please."

Wing hesitated, but Li spoke: "I swear, my sister, on my Blood, I will send that message. And I will beg the Master to attempt to rescue Nhung."

"Thank you."

My eyes stung and I bowed my head.

This was not their fault. I couldn't burden them with my sorrow.

There were noises from the main courtyard, guests leaving, and I felt a coldness spreading from my chest to my limbs.

Not long now.

It will be over very quickly.

I made a knot of my hair. My hands were trembling and Li had to help me. We pinned it up out of the way, leaving my neck bare for the blade. She didn't say anything. I whispered my thanks to her again.

"I'm sorry," Wing said, suddenly. "It wasn't your fault. No one would have been able to ignore that during crusis. I swear to help Li with your tasks."

I nodded, unable to speak. I would be content with that. I had done as much as I could to ensure the rest of my family would be safe.

I prayed silently to Quan Yin, the Goddess of Mercy, that I would take all my family's bad joss and have it die with me.

Song entered the courtyard, alone.

I understood. No one else should have to witness this.

Slung over his shoulder was the travel bag he used to disguise his zhan ma dao—the long, double-handed sword that he favored.

Wing and Li moved away to let me stand.

I took a step, bowed deeply to my Master and then sank down on my knees. I slipped my hands into my sleeves and gripped my forearms to hide the trembling.

I must be strong. I mustn't shame my family and my teachers. It will be over very quickly.

The ground beneath me had the first fallen blossoms from the Hoa Sua trees around the courtyard, like pale tears, caught in a dancing web of sunlight that shone through the leaves. The intense, sweet fragrance of the flowers filled the air. I could not have asked for a more beautiful, peaceful setting to die. Somewhere, Ophélie was weeping, but she had already died, really. I closed my eyes and tried to remember the faces of my families, and laughter, and happiness, in a sampan on the broad expanse of the Mother of Waters, and the joy with Maman and Papa in the house on Bonnard, but it was only Nhung I saw, and that curtain of hair as it fell across her face. All I was left with was that whisper: *whatever happens.*

It was enough. My mind grew still as the surface of the lake on which I would soon tread again. My body stopped shaking. It seemed I had one foot already poised above the clear waters, waiting only for the touch of the blade against my neck.

But the touch that came was to my arm.

"Up, Bian. Stand up."

He'd had to say it more than once. I blinked my eyes open in confusion. The world had been wide and dark. Now I was back in the small courtyard with the dappled sun playing over the ground.

The pressure of his hand raised me unsteadily to my feet.

Was this a trick of some kind? To think I was reprieved at the moment I died? An Athanate ritual? An old Chinese superstition?

"Come, Bian. You will not end your life here."

I was too dazed to understand what was happening. Wing and Li guided me through the house, which seemed in turmoil. My weapons, my sheathed kris knife and my chang gùn, were pressed into my hand. A straw hat placed on my head. Then we were outside, the four of us— Master Song, Li, Wing and me, walking down the high road to Saigon.

My chang gùn looked like an ordinary staff, and members of House Song often went out in public with theirs. The knife could not be carried openly without attracting attention, but I'd designed a strap with the sheath to keep it hidden beneath my tunic, and that's where it went. My hands moved of their own accord. My mind seemed to still linger by the silent lake.

When I finished tugging the tunic back into place, Song gave me a handful of longan fruits. I peeled them and savored the sweet flesh. I had never tasted any as good.

"What has happened, Master Song?" Wing asked eventually.

"Bian's sister, Nhung, is part of House Song," he replied.

I stopped and tried to speak. "But ..."

"We must keep moving," Song said.

I caught up, wishing to myself that everything would slow down for a while.

"Since your sister is part of House Song," he said to me, "then the threat against her, as implied by Bác Thảo, was a breaking of the truce under which his safety was assured."

"But ..." I repeated.

"Surely you recall requesting I accept her into the House. Of this, there must be no doubt. Nor that I granted it, despite her location not being known at present."

His hand rested on my shoulder. I felt the touch of his mind.

Had I asked? What had I said when we'd danced on the surface of the silent lake?

I remembered it was my oath to Nhung that had he had used to bring me back. Of course I would have requested that Nhung be part of House Song ... wouldn't I? How could it be otherwise?

No. I had not asked.

But I realized he'd told the other Athanate Houses that I had. He had to have used it to argue that I hadn't broken his oath, because the fault was on Bác Thảo's side. That was the only reason he could have for sparing me.

So was I even allowed to doubt his statement?

We walked in silence for some time.

My mind, so calm and clear awaiting my death, was now full of uncomfortable, jostling thoughts.

"You said House Jian can tell truth from falsehood," I said.

"I did," he replied. "As you saw, House Zheng certainly believes she can."

That was not the same as Song believing she could.

"Could you ..." I cleared my throat and tried again. "Would it be *possible* for you to tell House Jian a lie?"

"Not all claims for the powers of elder Athanate are reliable," he said, with a small smile. "But she did not say I was lying today."

So Song might be able to trick House Jian. A valuable skill.

"Do we still have the protection of an arrangement with the Empire?"

He laughed.

"Straight to the core of the problem; we've trained you well." He walked in silence for a while. "I cannot say. As I may deceive her, I would not underestimate her ability to deceive me. She might believe I was lying, but not want to alert me to that. She might fear for her own safety in calling me an oath-breaker in my own house."

Yes. As Qingzhao had said about breaking an oath—*leave no witnesses.*

"Then what of House Zheng and House Thorn? What do they believe?"

"Again, a good question. Should House Zheng think that Jian believes I lied, and therefore my oath was broken, he may well attack, trusting that Jian would not honor an oath with an oath breaker. He might even persuade House Thorn to attack with him, arguing he has to because of the Agiagraphos rules. That's why we are preparing for it. Maybe we'll find out tomorrow."

I understood that the activity back at the house was a preparation for war, and that all of us were carrying weapons, but not what we were doing walking away from the house.

But it was all one thing, larger than my understanding, as it happened.

Chapter 58

My thoughts spun in circles. Did House Jian believe my tutor had lied to save my life? If she did, would she allow Zheng to attack, or would she attack herself? The Empire had tolerated an independent House here in Saigon, but surely they would not tolerate Basilikos cutting off their progress down the coast of the South China Sea?

Or would we be attacked from two sides? Zheng and Jian?

"Yesterday morning, we spoke of the Fontaudins," Song said, interrupting my thoughts.

We had.

It had felt like another test when we did. Master Song had told me that the Fontaudins still maintained that I had stolen from them and run away. They'd rented out the house on Bonnard and lived on the Rue de Tombeaux without servants. As yet, no legal proceedings against them had started.

I didn't welcome this change of subject.

In truth, I would have preferred to remain in the Autumn courtyard at the house and let my mind return at its own pace from the peace I had found while waiting to die. Instead, I was now churning through the possibilities of an Athanate war, only to have the Fontaudins added to the mix.

My anger at them was like a smoldering bonfire; there were no flames visible, but I could not put out that glowing core. Perhaps I should have been angry at more people from my old life. Governor Hubert. Police Chief Meulnes. The manager at the Bank of Indochina. Riossi. Alain and Chantal Sévigny. 'Aunty' Kim.

I couldn't.

Somehow all the anger channeled through the Fontaudins. If they'd been decent and honest I would still be living in the house on Bonnard, expecting Maman and Papa back in the next month. Bác Thảo would be sitting in Khánh Hôi with no idea of what had happened to my family.

There were other things that might be happening to me now, of course, but I couldn't think clearly about them. Every time I heard the name Fontaudin I felt his sweaty, pudgy hands on me, the stink of absinthe on his breath. The shock when his wife took his side and blamed me that he was trying to rape me. The shock of the cane striking me on the head, and the strength fading from my limbs, the feeling of powerlessness.

I was not powerless now.

Song had encouraged me to imagine a revenge suitable for them, and when he'd asked me, yesterday, I'd been happy to be endlessly inventive—to demonstrate I could contemplate immense cruelty but not lose my Athanate control over it.

Now, I didn't want to think about it. What I'd said made me uncomfortable.

Why are we walking down the road that will take us past the house on Rue de Tombeaux?

"There is a drawback to the argument I made about you being part of my House since the night you were attacked outside the brothel."

This was more than uncomfortable, but I made myself respond. "What is that, Lǎoshī?"

"The Fontaudins' attack on you becomes, by Athanate law, an attack on the House. By that same law, it must be avenged. Since it was you they attacked, it should be you who takes that revenge. With my assistance."

I felt sick.

That got far worse when Shimin caught up with us, just as we started to pass under the gaze of the frowning arches of the old Khmer tombs. He was pushing a covered cart and I knew immediately what was beneath that covering. He must have been sent down to Cholon to buy them after the meeting had finished. I'd never visited those shops, but I'd heard about them.

I shuddered and my mind started running in frantic circles.

Why was I being so squeamish now?

It wasn't that the Fontaudins didn't deserve it. And I was being honored. Even Master Song was accompanying me, though of course the twisted revenge I'd described required him there.

But we were on the brink of war with at least one Athanate House. He shouldn't be here.

We came in sight of my parents' old house, and I was afraid I was going to vomit.

I should refuse. Could I refuse? Wasn't that an insult to the effort Master Song had put in?

How has this gone so wrong?

This wasn't what I'd envisaged yesterday.

My palms were sweating and my heart racing.

It wasn't fear. The Fontaudins could no longer do anything to make me afraid. It was them who should be afraid of the monster at the door.

The door wasn't locked. Not that locking it could have stopped us.

Song and I went in.

The Fontaudins were sitting in the salon. He'd stood up to find out who had come in. There was a drink beside his chair. Absinthe. She was also on her feet, gripping her cane.

Both of them gasped to see me enter.

Monsieur Fontaudin swore and made as if to strike my tutor, but Song simply grabbed his wrist and bit his arm. Fontaudin staggered back and fell onto the couch.

Madame Fontaudin swung the cane at me. After sparring with Qingzhao, it looked as slow as a leaf falling from a tree. I plucked the cane out of the air easily and broke it across my knee in one movement.

She froze, too shocked and terrified to resist when I offered her unresisting arm to Master Song.

He bit her and she collapsed.

Master of poisons, Qingzhao had called him.

With the Athanate Blood comes many potential skills. Any Athanate, even a new one such as me, has some ability to heal and harm with their bite. These skills needed to be studied and refined, and over time could become much more powerful and complex. Yi Song had studied for centuries and it was during a conversation with him about some of his capabilities that I had first begun to think of a use for one of his skills, for the Fontaudins.

Master Song could paralyze people, so that they remained completely aware of what was around them. The Fontaudins' bodies would keep them alive, they could see and hear me, they could feel what was happening to them, but they couldn't move. They couldn't even speak.

It'd seemed appropriate when I dreamed up my revenge—that they should suffer and that I should not have to listen to their lies. Or their pleas.

Song had performed his role. He gave me a nod and left without speaking.

Did he disapprove of what I was doing?

Why, then, allow it?

Fontaudin had stolen my family's money and tried to rape me. His wife would have succeeded in killing me if Master Song had not pulled me back from the brink.

They deserved this.

For a while, I was too distracted to think about anything other than preparing what I'd envisaged. I brought in the cages that Shimin had bought in Cholon and placed them in the center of the room. I dragged the Fontaudins to lie next to the cages.

Even with the covers still on, the cages rocked. A nerve-scraping chittering came from them.

I closed all the windows and doors to the room.

I could sense the fear coming off the Fontaudins in waves. Unable to move their heads, their eyes were wide and darting as they tried to see.

Athanate feed on emotions, just as they feed on Blood. Their fear was feeding me and it was so very sweet. And forbidden.

Basilikos fed on the fear of the humans who they forced to provide Blood. House Song did not feed on fear. We did everything to avoid it.

It's like acid, Yi Song had said to me. *It will eat you away from the inside. There will remain only the hunger for more.*

Yet it was so easy. So satisfying.

Shimin's fear that I would lose control hadn't been sweet like this. I didn't want to hurt Shimin. But I did want to hurt the Fontaudins.

Didn't I?

I'd said I wanted to torture them.

What does that make me?

Like House Zheng.

My stomach twisted and churned.

Yesterday, I had a speech prepared for an imaginary event, where I took my revenge. Today, it was real, and as they lay helpless before me, the words sounded as sick as I felt.

I took the covers off the cages.

"These are starving rats," I said. My voice sounded far away to my own ears. "It's very difficult to keep them, because when they're hungry, they'll eat anything, including each other. Each rat must be kept in its own cell and fed just enough to live. They're sold to people who make them fight each other for bets."

With the covers off, the rats were hurling themselves against the cages and squealing like demons. Shimin had bought a dozen.

The Fontaudins couldn't speak, but they were making noises like distressed animals.

"The rats are clever," I said. "They won't fight each other if they see there's enough food for all."

I lifted the wire grids at the front of the cages.

"Now I've taken the wire gates away, the rats are kept in the cages only by a mesh of grass cords. They will eat through those and come out looking for food."

I swallowed, trying not to vomit.

"You have about two minutes."

I ran from the room, slamming the door behind me, and out into the evening air.

Chapter 59

It was no good.

"I'm sorry, Lǎoshī," I gasped after a second bout of vomiting into the bushes outside the house. The others waited on the road, out of sight. Only Song patiently witnessed my humiliation.

"Is this not what you wanted?" he said.

I must have disappointed him. All his effort, but in the end, perhaps I lacked something—the confidence in my decisions, the strength to see them through. I knew my revenge was not what he would have wanted for the Fontaudins, but he'd said it was my choice. He'd helped and made it possible.

But I could hardly lie now.

"No." I pulled some clean leaves off the bushes and wiped my mouth. "I thought I did. I was wrong. I'm sorry."

"Why?" he asked, and stopped me as I started to explain how I felt I'd let him down and distracted him at exactly the wrong time. "No, Bian. Why is this revenge wrong?"

"I don't know," I said. "They're awful people. Evil. Maybe they deserve to die. If I'd killed them when they attacked me, I wouldn't care, like I don't care that I killed two of the White Mountain monks. But not this."

"Do you want to go back and kill them?" he asked.

I shook my head. I'd had enough of revenge. "I want to stop it," I said.

"Good. Then Wing will stay and help you." He held out my chang gùn. "Go in, quickly. Chase the rats away."

I burst into the house, threw open windows and doors, tried not to look at the horrific mess.

The rats were clever. I only had to kill two of them before the rest scuttled out and away.

The Fontaudins did not understand what was happening. They were still making noises, grunting with terror. They probably expected they would be the next victims of my staff's blade.

Their faces were streaming blood and tears. The rats had bitten cheeks and fingers and hands and legs. I made myself look. The flesh was torn, but the bleeding was slow. No arteries had been cut. They both still had their eyes and they would live.

I felt I was going to be ill again, but Wing came in at that point.

We dragged them onto the sofa. Screwing his face in distaste, Wing bit them on their arms, and made them unconscious.

"I sent a messenger to fetch a doctor from town," he said. "We have enough time for me to blur their memories. Take the cages and hide them away from the house."

I did that, and he was finished by the time I returned.

He had sprinkled absinthe on both of them. There were empty bottles lying on the floor and a pungent opium pipe on the table.

"They'll sleep now for hours," he said. "When they wake, they will remember the rats, like a horrendous dream. They may remember people being here, but it will all be confused."

"Won't it be suspicious? Both passed out at the same time, for instance. And someone might ask who sent the messenger."

Wing shrugged. "They'll blame it on the drink and the opium. They'll say a passer-by must have heard something and sent the messenger. It's not perfect, but the police don't have time and these aren't the kind of people to gain much sympathy."

We left.

Looking back from the first bend in the road, I could see the doctor's carriage already turning up the Rue de Tombeaux.

"We have to hurry," Wing said, urging me to a trot. "Master Song was worried."

"Why did he spend the time to bring me here then?" I asked.

Wing took a long time to answer.

"There are decisions he must make. There are ways to avoid a war. But he would rather a war than yield the principles of the House."

"So what happened with the Fontaudins was part of his decisions? My squeamishness is important?"

Another minute passed before Wing spoke again.

"It wasn't squeamish. Anyone might dream a horrible revenge. The Fontaudins might deserve it. To *enjoy* it would be too much like Basilikos."

This had been another test. Wing didn't need to explain any more.

Like the night falling swiftly around us, understanding fell into place in my mind.

If I'd enjoyed torturing the Fontaudins, I would not have returned alive to the house at Cholon. Song would have decided I'd failed the crusis and he would have executed me. Then he'd have used that action to repair any weakness in his association with House Jian.

But I'd passed the test.

Now, because of the principles he'd insisted House Song must live by, we prepared for a war against Basilikos, which we might survive, and perhaps against the Empire, which we wouldn't.

I swallowed painfully. It was a tremendous burden to be the cause of this.

Wing sensed my distress. "You mustn't think of it as your fault," he said. "You're just what triggered it at this time. It's a problem that was always coming."

I had to be content with that.

We were halfway back when we heard light, rapid footfalls in the darkness ahead. A child was running toward us from Cholon, as fast as his legs could carry him.

Seconds later, we saw Hamid, a note clutched in his hand, and I knew this wasn't good news.

Chapter 60

Hamid was so out of breath that he could barely speak. The message he carried was from Li, and written in haste.

Hurry.
Bác Thảo has started a riot in Khánh Hôi.
Police and army are being called out onto the streets in Saigon.
He's going to attack us in the confusion, with his tiger demons and his gangs.
House Zheng has begged sanctuary and been accepted.

The Agiagraphos was clear in its rules. Athanate would always help Athanate against other attacks. For House Song to refuse House Zheng sanctuary against the tiger demons would be as dangerous as I thought letting them in would be. The Empire of Heaven or the British Athanate could use it as an excuse to attack.

Every bad decision had a worse alternative. There was nothing we could do except to be there. We sprinted the rest of the way, and we were still late.

The noise of the crowd warned us at the outskirts of Cholon. Closer, we saw the glare of flames in the night. We burst into the square in front of Song's house to be met with a scene straight from the Christian hell.

The gangs of Khánh Hôi were here. Dozens of tattooed men swarmed around the main gate to the house. They carried blazing torches made from river rushes soaked in animal fats. Smoke and stench filled the square. Every man carried some kind of a club or a makeshift sword. People had already died—there was blood smeared on weapons and faces. They shouted and surged like savages, trying to overwhelm the defenders at the gate with their numbers, and trampling on their own fallen as they did.

The house was surrounded by tall walls. While the main concentration of Bác Thảo's gangs was at the gate, another was just setting a ladder in position on the wall. Whoever was defending the gate would be caught by an attack from two sides.

"The ladder," Wing shouted. "Leave the gate for now." He charged into the group of men with the blades of his chang gùn flashing.

I kept close, just out of the way of those blades and making sure no one got behind him. The gang with the ladder had expected everyone to be inside. They broke away in confusion. Wing killed four or five quickly while they were still getting in each other's way. One tried to come around him, ignoring me. I slashed his arm and chest open. His blood sprayed over the others and I saw the frenzy in their eyes begin to flicker as the shock took effect.

They retreated a few paces to regather their courage.

Immediately, Wing took a grip on the ladder and hurled it over the wall, out of their reach. That triggered them to renew their attack. We turned together to face them.

I didn't want to be pressed against the wall with Wing beside me and the swing of my staff restricted. I could use the kris knife in an emergency, but it wouldn't be effective against more than one person.

"Back to back," I said to Wing. "We have to attack."

He grunted and I could feel him ready himself. All House Song practiced fighting like this. Wing had done it for years. I had had eight weeks. I hoped the gang had none.

They were surprised when we refused to be trapped against the wall. That helped. They were too close to each other. That helped even more. One tripped and took another with him. I stabbed them both before they could regain their feet.

Short, sharp. Out and back. One and two. Qingzhao's chant in my memory kept me moving. *Don't let your blade become caught in a body. Turn and turn and back. Stab and stab. Left and right. Keep stabbing.*

It worked. Our chang gùn were longer than their clubs, more deadly than their swords. They couldn't get behind us; they couldn't get close. They retreated, stumbling over each other, getting in each other's way.

Wing pressed the attack. He let out a bloodcurdling scream and leaped forward. That gave him more room, and he whipped his chang gùn around in an arc, beheading the man in front of him.

It scared them, but it also distracted me. I thrust my blade too deeply into a man's chest. He coughed blood and started to fall, but my blade was caught in his ribs. His death was going to take my weapon. In desperation I kicked at the man's chest. I kicked harder than I knew I could. The dying man flew backwards into his companions, and suddenly they were all running.

Torches fell to the ground. Swords and clubs were abandoned.

Wing did not pause.

"The gate!" he said.

I picked up one of the burning torches and raced after him.

The gang at the gate didn't expect anyone to attack them from behind. I thrust the torch like a sword at two of them who tried to turn around. The burning animal fat splattered over their faces. I stabbed and stabbed, but by this time some of the men were so blood-crazed they didn't notice wounds in their backs. I slashed at the muscles of their thighs instead. I didn't care how maddened they'd become; if they couldn't walk, they couldn't fight.

Those that turned to see the danger behind tried to warn the others, and instead fell victim to blows from the front. What had been dozens of the gang's fighters at the gate quickly became a handful. Those that could, ran away. Others crawled, some limped.

Finally, all the attackers scattered and suddenly, I was next to Li and Shimin. They were splattered with blood and panting heavily.

"Shimin, stay here. Protect the gate. Get archers back on the roofs." Li turned to us. "Inside," she gasped. "The main courtyard. Quickly. The tiger demons leaped over the walls. Master Song is there with House Zheng."

Chapter 61

The courtyard surrounding the Bloodstone Pavilion had four entrances.

The tiger-demons had leaped over the walls and into the courtyard. The weakest human members of House Song had been barricaded into the Bloodstone Pavilion and it was this that the tiger attacked.

Groups of Athanate were forcing their way in at the gates. House Zheng himself attacked the west gate, Qingzhao was at the east, each with only a handful of Athanate.

With the addition of Li and Wing, we forced our way through the south gate and I saw that Master Song stood by the steps of the pavilion, a circle of death around him that measured the sweep of his great sword.

Athanate become stronger and quicker than humans. All Athanate must keep their bodies well exercised, otherwise something happens to the Blood; it turns on itself and kills its host. Athanate in House Song exercised by learning how to fight. Humans, even those trained like the Shadow Warriors of the White Mountain, were not our equals.

But the tiger demons were no longer human. They were as quick and strong as us.

In the flickering light of torches, they seemed like nightmares sprung to life. They ran and fought on two legs like humans, but their skin *rippled* between human flesh and rangy, striped muscles, and their heads were the snarling heads of tigers. For weapons they favored huge curved sabers, like the talwar of Indian warriors, but their hands could also become tiger paws and I saw Athanate with ripped, parallel wounds from claws.

Qingzhao broke through the east gate, but was halted inside, as we were. The battle hung in the balance. Dead bodies, ours and theirs, lay strewn over the ground.

We pushed the tiger demons back until they collided with the ones attacking Master Song.

Wing and Li were in front of me. I couldn't keep up with them. My grip was loosening on my staff and I had to keep wiping blood and sweat away from my eyes.

We redoubled our efforts. Li killed one more outright. Wing drove another backwards and Song's blade decapitated him. The tiger demons paired up to fight back to back, but they were outnumbered. Another fell to Li, another to Wing.

There was a roar that seemed to shake the ground.

A shape leaped off the nearest roof. A huge shadow.

Too big, too big, I cried silently to myself, trying not to die as a tiger demon slashed at me with his curved saber.

Bác Thảo landed right in the circle of death around Song. He landed softly, flowing seamlessly into an attack, curved talwar like lightning against the long reach of Song's zhan ma dao.

His entry into the fight heartened his tigers. I was driven back, unable to hold the line beside Li. She was forced to give a step, pulling the others back as well.

Song was not moved. However impressive Bác Thảo thought he was, however quick and agile, he could not advance. When he tried, he had to leap back with a screech of rage and blood flowing down his arm.

More screams came from the east gate. Qingzhao had broken through and she charged with the rest of her survivors, her chang gùn glittering wickedly. Three more tigers died in swift blows. I could see their eyes start to swivel, as if looking for a way out.

The tiger demons at the western gate suddenly pulled aside. House Zheng ran through. He had a pistol in his hand, and he fired it at Master Song.

It was a signal. All the Zheng Athanate and the tiger demons from the western gate attacked us in the center. Even ones that had 'died' jumped up and rushed forward.

I couldn't see much after that. Tiger demons surrounded us. Zheng's Athanate joined them. I was fighting back to back with Wing again, my failing arms strengthened for one last despairing defense.

Zheng fired his pistol again.

I heard Bác Thảo's roar again. In rage or triumph, I couldn't tell.

My chang gùn was beaten down by the combined blows of three opponents and one of Zheng's House raised his sword to kill me.

Li jumped forward and sliced all the way through the man's arm.

And at that moment she died, right in front of me, as another sword cut upwards and pierced her heart.

"Li!" I cried, and held her to me as if I could pull her back from death. She saved my life again, as blows meant for me struck her, and chakrams, sharp disks just like the monk assassins had used, came spinning out of the night and sliced into her skin.

One-handed, I tried to raise my chang gùn.

Must defend. Keep the staff up.

A heavy blow from a talwar cut the staff in two.

Li's body was torn from my grasp and thrown aside.

Wing tried to turn to help, but he was overwhelmed.

Zheng! Standing there. *Kill him. Kill him. I swore an oath.*

Hate boiled through me. I swung wildly at him with my broken staff. He ignored it and hit me, the back of his hand hard as a wooden board, snapping my head around. I fell.

The whole sky was wheeling above me and the battle was collapsing into a fierce maul. I could see Song's feet. He was moving slower. Chakrams littered the ground around him. I looked up. There was blood on his clothes. His Blood. He'd been shot by Zheng.

I coughed. It was wet with my own Blood. I tried to get up but my arms and legs were too weak.

Zheng picked my limp body up casually in one hand and bellowed "I have the whore."

Bác Thảo's eyes flickered across to me.

My hands fumbled, tried to grip. *My Blood all over. Everything's slippery. Concentrate. Pull.*

Bác Thảo's moment of inattention was almost fatal. Song's zhan ma dao flashed down and it would have split his head open had he not jerked back. As it was, it opened his flesh from collar bone to navel.

The kris knife finally came clear of the sheath hidden behind my back.

"On my Blood," I said to Zheng, and spat in his face. Then I buried the kris knife to the hilt in his chest.

He screamed and dropped me, clutching at the knife.

The South gate burst open.

Shimin! No! Too dangerous. Get back. Run.

He wasn't alone. The House Song katikia who'd been fighting the gangs followed behind, all carrying swords and torches. All of them were terrified. Every single one of them attacked the monstrous tiger demons.

From behind Song, those katikia who'd been put in the pavilion to stay safe boiled out. They were no match for Athanate or tiger, and they died, but still they came.

By some superhuman effort, Zheng managed to pull the knife from his chest. His heart's blood sprayed out. He tottered in a weak spiral and collapsed in front of his House.

Yes!

Qingzhao moved like a true demon from hell and killed three more of House Zheng in the time it took them to realize their betrayal had sealed their fate.

Bác Thảo's talwar had fallen from his hand. He clutched the gaping wound in his chest to hold it closed. With three strides and an enormous leap, he was on the roof. An arrow fired from the main gate struck his arm. He pulled it out, even as he leaped again and vanished into the night.

Four tiger demons escaped Qingzhao and were able to leap to the roofs. They followed Bác Thảo. The rest, along with all of House Zheng, died in a matter of seconds, on the steps of the entrance to the Bloodstone Pavilion, half of them clubbed to death by humans.

Chapter 62

I got to my knees with enormous effort and crawled toward Master Song.

To my eyes it seemed the whole world was swaying, but it was my tutor who was moving.

Qingzhao caught him as he fell.

He'd been hit by many of the poisoned chakrams, but the worst wound seemed to have come from Zheng's pistol, right in the middle of his chest. Qingzhao's hand pressed down, but the Blood continued to pulse out through her fingers.

Athanate, by nature, are masters of the art of healing wounds; otherwise our human donors would quickly die. Unless the bullet had destroyed a whole section of arteries or parts of his heart, Master Song should have been able to stop the bleeding. Yet he did not.

Qingzhao laid him down, frowning in confusion. "Master?"

He shook his head; a small, sorrowful movement.

"No!" She shouted out to others. "Xiu! Jie! Wing! Li! Help me."

Of all those she called, only Wing remained. He stumbled forward and knelt by Song.

If Master Song could not heal himself, others could do it for him, but he raised one hand, moving in obvious pain.

"No," he said hoarsely. "Stop. A trap. The poison …"

But he was the Master of Poisons. He'd bitten me and defeated the poison in the White Mountains' chakrams easily. I could not believe what I was hearing. Had his bullet wound weakened him? What trap?

"This is not a poison I have tasted," he gasped, his face contorting. "Fire in the veins. It attacks the Blood, the muscles, the organs. But it multiplies. My own Blood betrays me; it has become poison now. You must not …"

His whole body tensed and shuddered.

We held him. Wing tried to give him water. Most of it was spilled.

The remains of the House gathered around us. They saw. Their faces made a wall of fear and grief.

"Dark," Song muttered, and a lantern was placed by his head.

His body gave one final shake and relaxed. I felt a ray of hope, instantly dashed.

"It won't be long now," he whispered. "The pain is gone."

He coughed weakly. He was bleeding from his nose, his mouth, even his eyes. Wing washed them, but he could not see.

"Qingzhao?"

She was kneeling right beside him, bent over his face.

"Here, Yi."

"The House?"

"We survive."

"Good. Lead them well, Mistress of the House."

Her tears fell on his face.

His voice weakened more. "Bian? Is that you? I saw … Zheng. I sense you now, so close, but the veil of worlds is thin."

His hand was fumbling, searching. I took it, squeezed it between mine.

"Here, Lǎoshī. I'm alive. I'm right here."

"I'm so sorry, my daughter. I … Such plans. Greatness. So much to do … so little time. So little time."

He sighed and I felt the whole world shift, and drift away, like a dream in the morning, like a silk banner freed on the rising winds, like the rich, dark soil that bleeds into the unresting body of the Mother of Waters.

Chapter 63

Torches were held aloft; their flames crackled and danced. People were crying. Night breezes made sibilant laments in the leaves of the trees.

Then there was a movement, and it became a ripple spreading through the House.

Wing started it. He stepped back from Master Song, knelt and bowed to Qingzhao, his head to the ground.

"Mistress," he said.

I joined him in bowing, but could not speak.

My Master was gone. My Lǎoshī. The rock on which my Athanate being was founded. My third father, all of them gone from me, but the first to be taken beyond any mortal reach.

I could not speak.

All Athanate feel a need, like the compass needle seeks the northern star. Yi Song tutored me, he saved my life, he infused me and brought me into the Athanate world. I hadn't even exchanged Blood with the others yet.

The whole House now looked to Qingzhao.

She'd been in House Song for hundreds of years, many of those as Diakon. In the books that I'd been given to learn about the Athanate, it was explained that sometimes, a good Diakon cannot raise themselves to lead.

The survivors of House Song waited. In our grief, our Athanate senses reached out. I felt Wing's heartbeat as if it were my own, and Shimin's and all those around us. We were bound together as a House, as singular in our being as if we were one person.

Except Qingzhao.

I could sense only grief from her.

It seemed an age, but then she stood and gathered her powers like a cloak before her voice rang out, carrying to the shadowed corners of the courtyard.

"Our Master is dead and I am now Mistress of House Song," she said.

She had accepted the duty and the burden. We were still a House.

But there was a stir, a feeling of sudden panic, as if part of the building had caught fire. People turned to look to the unguarded southern gate.

"Do I welcome you as friends, or does death return to this House?" Qingzhao said, her head high.

I looked up.

Athanate. The British Athanate, with House Thorn's Diakon at the front.

She carried twin dao swords that gleamed evilly in the torchlight. Behind her were a dozen Athanate holding the long curved nagi, the Siamese pike-sword with the wide, black blade. Only a dozen, but more than we could possibly hope to defend against after our battle with Zheng and Bác Thảo.

Never trust the British, Papa had said.

But the Diakon knelt, and all behind her copied her actions.

"Friends," she said, placing her dao on the ground. "We came as soon as we heard, to fight alongside you. I am sorry we're late. With your permission, House Song, we'll stay and help. And grieve."

"Grieve?"

"To some here, perhaps he was simply your Master, but to those I say, know this: that Yi Song was honored through the peninsula of Indochina, peerless among Athanate, all the way up to the courts of the Empire of Heaven. We are all diminished by his loss."

"*Words.* Not so honored by the Empire that they stood by us in our need." Qingzhao voiced the bitterness we all felt.

The Siamese Diakon bowed her sleek head again. "Forgive me, but you're wrong."

"Explain."

"House Jian made an error of judgment only about the speed with which House Zheng would try and attack you." The Diakon's eyes looked across at where Zheng's body lay.

"She did not believe that the Basilikos Athanate would make common cause with the were-tigers. Nor that Zheng would apparently expect that Bác Thảo would honor it for longer than it took to kill Yi Song." She sighed. "House Jian's true goals were to bring House Song into the Empire, and to eliminate Basilikos from the Indochina peninsula. The Emperor himself approved her strategy and provided her the means. As we speak, House Jian and many hundreds of Athanate warriors are marching to attack every major Basilikos House in Laos and Cambodia. The Emperor himself has struck westwards into Yunnan. In a matter of weeks, there will be no surviving Basilikos House south or east of the Taklamakan Desert. Many new Houses will be founded, and all will be part of the Empire."

"You know this because House Jian told you?"

The Diakon nodded. "She does not want a war against the British Athanate, so she warned us. It also forced us to help them. My Master has called on every House in Siam to be at the frontiers to kill the fleeing Basilikos so they cannot turn into an invasion."

"Many will escape," Qingzhao said.

There simply weren't enough Athanate for the huge area she described. A million more would not have been enough.

"In ones and twos, or small groups," the Diakon conceded. "But we will find them all, eventually, if they try and stay."

Qingzhao bowed to the Diakon. A short bow; a House in her own domain to a visiting Diakon.

"We accept your offer of help, Diakon Thorn, with thanks. A new day is coming, and with it will come human eyes and ears and questions. The evidence of this battle must be erased or repaired. Before the dawn, the bodies of Basilikos and tiger demons must be taken far into the jungle and burned. For our own dead, we will have one day of mourning and one ceremony. We can afford no more."

Chapter 64

Others might have needed all morning to pack their belongings. I had almost nothing. Some changes of clothing. A few pieces of jewelry. Shoes. A brush. A peasant's straw hat. My kris knife and sheath. I made a small bundle of my possessions and sat looking at it in bleak despair.

Leaving Saigon would take away the temptation of seeing Papa and Maman, or the agony of knowing they were there and not being able to see them.

But Nhung would remain and Bác Thảo would find her.

Would Wing allow me to send a message to Lanh, to at least protect our parents?

He'd made an oath to help Li, not to send my message. Now that Li was dead, was Wing relieved of his oath?

Oaths were powerful.

I'd made a Blood oath to kill Bác Thảo as well as Zheng, but moving away, as my House commanded, relieved me of that oath unless I returned.

Or did it?

My stomach did not agree. The need to kill the tiger demon smoldered even more strongly than my hate of the Fontaudins had.

So strongly I might disobey Qingzhao?

Shimin's voice interrupted my thoughts, and I stood up guiltily, as if he could tell what I'd been thinking.

"House Song wants to see you," he said. "She's in the Bloodstone Pavilion."

There was a sinking feeling in my stomach.

What had given me away?

Nothing showed in her face when I entered the pavilion.

She was arranging Master Song's pun-tsai trees. The scent of larch and cypress was heavy and sweet in the heat of the day.

"We will be able to take none of these," she sighed. "And the new owners will not make the effort to keep them. Yi would be upset about that. More than the mosaics." She waved a hand indicating the priceless matching pair of dragon and phoenix, and then pinched a wayward leaf off one cypress. She crushed it between her fingers and inhaled the aroma.

"Come." She indicated the cushions in front of the dragon mosaic.

We sat, side by side, but she tapped my shoulder and turned me around.

I thought I understood. Only Yi Song had ever bitten me. He'd bound me to House Song, but now *she* was Mistress of House Song. I owed her my Blood as I owed her my loyalty. Every other Athanate in the House would have exchanged Blood with her many times. Of course she'd want to do this now.

I laid my head in her lap, and stretched, offering my neck.

It was a relief of sorts, to have things taken out of my hands. She'd bind me and my doubts would vanish. A few minutes of pleasure and I would be bound only to her. Not to oaths and tasks I couldn't complete anyway.

But she didn't bite. "You don't want to leave Saigon," she said.

My mouth went dry. "I'm a loyal member of the House, Mistress."

Mistress. She was House Song now, and just as my kind and gentle tutor had been prepared to kill me if I'd turned rogue or betrayed the House, so would she.

"I know." She sighed. "In another year, you would be a different person. We could have a different conversation. And you should know this: you will always be welcome in my House, Bian."

"I don't understand."

"You won't. Not for many years, I think. I'm not sure I fully understand, but this comes from what Yi Song said to me about you."

She stroked my hair.

"You are still in crusis. As an Athanate, you're all fresh growth. Like a young pun-tsai tree. Little pressures now will have effects that will not be seen for many years. The worst thing that can happen to you now is to be under a conflict between oaths you made to rescue your sister, and loyalty to a new Mistress. Especially one who will be distracted with the delicate politics of making a new home for her House, and not concentrating on her new Athanate."

"I wasn't Athanate when I made that oath to rescue my sister," I said. I shivered as I remembered the feel of the kris knife against my skin, the welling of the Blood in the night.

"I know. And yet Yi Song told me it counts the same."

Her eyes misted.

"I am not saying this well, and there are so many ways things may go wrong for you." She took a breath. "You will stay in Saigon, alone. The Emperor will send a House to claim the domain, and you must hide from them. Bác Thảo will heal and rebuild his pack of were-tigers, and you must hide from them. Your French father and mother will return, and you must hide from them. Saigon is full of people who might recognize Ophélie Beauclerc, and you must hide from them, too. You must obey the laws of the Athanate, and learn to hunt and feed without alerting humans. And while you are doing all that, it just may be that you can find and save your sister."

Part of me wanted to beg her to change her mind, but something deep and dark, something in my Blood, whispered *yes*.

Think of the practical aspects, Papa had said when I told him I was overwhelmed with something.

"All the Athanate laws?" I said. "Who will teach me the laws? Who will teach me to be Athanate?"

I knew that even the Agiagraphos did not contain all the rules. And much of what it took to be Athanate required another Athanate to explain. Healing, for instance. Blurring minds.

"You'll have to find your own way," she replied. "I cannot leave another with you. But I'll leave you a small library in the Yên Lặng Chùa."

The Pagoda of Silence—the smallest and strangest of Buddhist temples on the waterfront of Cholon.

She went on: "You can't stay there, but the monks will know who you are when you visit, and guide you to a room where you can study the books and keep things safely."

I had the feeling there was much more to the Pagoda of Silence that she was telling me. I suspected an old obligation due to Yi Song had been paid.

"Don't ask me about them," she said. "You'll learn what you will learn, but I cannot answer your questions truthfully. I've no wish to add to the harvest of lies that has brought you to this point."

A tear fell from her eye and she kissed where it landed on my forehead.

"This is even harder than I thought it would be," she said and hugged me. "I want to hold you to me. My heart tells me you belong to my House, that you are mine, and yet my head tells me Yi Song was wiser in these things than anyone else I have ever met."

She took a breath.

"So go. Go now with your possessions and disappear into Saigon. An envoy from House Jian has announced he will visit me and he will be here soon. He must not see you and I must not know where you go to hide. And remember, whenever it is you feel you have done all you can, find us and I will welcome you."

We got to our feet and I stepped back. I bowed deeply. Cast off or not, temporarily or not, she was my Mistress.

She walked me to the main gate. Wing brought my bundle of possessions and bowed, more deeply than I deserved.

He also brought a chang gùn, which he handed to Qingzhao.

"This chang gùn," she said, holding it out to me. "It was mine, many years ago. When I became Diakon, Yi Song gave me the one I have now, and I gave this one to Li. Now it's yours, my daughter. A gift from Li, and from House Song. May it find the hearts of your enemies and bring you the victory you deserve in the secret paths of Saigon."

I walked into Saigon, dressed in Annamese style, my straw hat covering my face from view. No one recognised me. I recognised no one. I didn't care.

Above, the clouds gathered. It might rain. Night would come. I would need to find somewhere to hide. Somewhere to stay. A base.

I was only what I carried with me.

My life had been stripped down to the barest essentials.

Air, food and water.

Shelter and clothing.

Blood.

Nothing remained to halt my pursuit of my two Blood oaths: to rescue my sister and to kill Bác Thảo.

Nothing happens but we do it ourselves, I thought as thunder rumbled.

I was right, and I was wrong.

AFTERWORD

If you enjoyed The Harvest of Lies, please write a brief review on Amazon or Goodreads. Series thrive on reviews. Thank you.

Bian's Tale is a companion series to the main Bite Back books and the following titles are planned:

> The Harvest of Lies
> The Words of the Dead
> The Rise of the River
> The Sword of the Son
> The Tears of the Leopard

At which point Bian's Tale will join the main Bite Back series. Bian is a major character in Bite Back, and reading those books should not detract from the Bian's Tale series. Bite Back follows the adventures of Amber Farrell, a former Special Operations sergeant living in modern Denver, Colorado (cover copy below).

All my books are marketed through Amazon:

https://www.amazon.com/Mark-Henwick/e/B008SBO5YK/

and include Science Fiction as well as Urban and Historic Fantasy.

If you want to be kept informed of the release of the rest of the Bian's Tale series, please email me at mark@athanate.com. You name and email will only be used to communicate my new book releases to you.

Cover copy for Bite Back book 1, Sleight of Hand:

"Vampires are the flickering illusions of Hollywood. They don't exist. We do. We are the Athanate."

For Amber Farrell, post-military life as a PI is tough: She's been hit by a truck. She's being sued by a client. Denver's crime boss just put out a contract on her. The sinister Athanate want her to come in for a friendly chat. And it's only Tuesday.

Enter Jennifer Kingslund: rich, gorgeous - a tough businesswoman who's known for getting what she wants in the boardroom *and* the bedroom. Someone's trying to sabotage her new resort and destroy her company - and she wants Amber to find out who.

The answers lead Amber into the paranormal community, right back to the Athanate - and a centuries-old war that could threaten not just Denver, but the nation that Amber swore to protect and serve.

And all sides want to claim her for their own...

https://www.amazon.com/dp/B008RJXPQM

"They represent some of the best the field has to offer."
Charles de Lint in the Magazine of Fantasy and Science Fiction

Printed in Great Britain
by Amazon